The Victims of Innocence

The Victims of Innocence

by

Chet Pleban

Gypsy Shadow Publishing

The Victims of Innocence
by
Chet Pleban

Gypsy Shadow Publishing, LLC.
Lockhart, TX
www.gypsyshadow.com

Library of Congress Control Number: 202

eBook ISBN: 978-1-61950-359-5
Print ISBN: 978-1-61950- 360-1

Published in the United States of America

First eBook Edition: March 20, 2020
First Print Edition: April 10, 2020

Dedication

To all who have been the innocent victims of injustice.

Prologue

Politics is a dirty business, made worse by social media. Whether seeking state, local or national office, a politician needs to hope for the best but prepare for the worst during the campaign. Dirty tricks, mudslinging and cheap shots are the norm these days. Every skeleton in the candidate's closet will be discovered and publicized, the candidate excoriated.

A powerbroker in the State of Missouri, Senator Winston Lee, is running for governor. His campaign is in full swing. Senator Lee has skeletons. The senator's estranged son Garner could reveal one of those skeletons.

"I've taken care of your little problem," Cassandra Lee said, immediately drawing her husband's attention. "Garner is living in London. He left town after the murder trial. He and his lawyer were going to launch an investigation to find out who really killed his girlfriend, but I poured cold water on that. He and Felbin won't be investigating anything," Cassandra said.

"How did you shut it down?"

"Don't worry about it, Winston. I took care of it, just like I take care of every mess you get yourself into."

"I *am* worried about it. If it comes out that I knocked up my son's girlfriend, we can kiss our chances of winning the election goodbye. What about Judge Cardwell? Can we trust her?"

"She has been in bed with us for several years."

"I'm aware of our history with her. It's not so much I don't trust her. I know if we go down, she goes with us. But she is so stupid and arrogant, I'm concerned she will say something which will bury all of us."

"I had a conversation with her. If the murder trial is resurrected, she will say her decision to set aside the guilty verdict in Garner's case was based upon her application of the law and had nothing to do with us. So, relax. Your screw ups won't see the light of day."

"I hope you're right."

While Lee was planning his strategy to become Missouri's next governor, Jonathan Felbin, Garner Lee's lawyer, was trying to figure out a way to unmask the killer. Unfortunately for Garner, the killer was also Felbin's client; he was ethically obligated to protect the killer's identity.

For Felbin, the Garner Lee murder case was a nightmare. When Senator Lee approached Felbin to represent his son Garner, who was being investigated for murdering his girlfriend, he thought it was a joke. But it was no joke. His son was in trouble and the senator and his wife, Cassandra, wanted Felbin. After meeting with Garner, Felbin accepted the case. But his new relationship with the senator quickly deteriorated when the case was mysteriously assigned to Judge Joan Cardwell. After he sensed Cardwell would be repaying a debt owed to the senator, Felbin tried to withdraw, but was unsuccessful.

Although his relationship with Garner's father continued to be strained, Felbin believed in his client. He knew Garner's father and the judge he purchased were corrupt, but believed his client was innocent. The jury disagreed. Cardwell's payback was complete when she set aside the verdict and dismissed the murder charge.

Felbin had never accepted defeat well. He and his investigator, Tony Carmine, decided they were going to find the killer. Their efforts came to a screeching halt. Garner Lee didn't kill his girlfriend. Felbin and Carmine knew who did, but they couldn't do anything about it. Meanwhile, their client would be relegated to living in a free world as a perceived killer. Felbin couldn't live with this outcome. It would haunt him for the rest of his professional life. He needed to do something. But what?

Then there was the matter of Judge Cardwell, a corrupt prosecutor who became a corrupt judge, thanks to a corrupt politician. The corrupt politician wanted to be the governor. The corrupt judge continued to administer justice as she defined it. Felbin knew he needed to do something about that as well. More frustration.

Chapter One

Trial lawyers, both civil and criminal, are a unique breed. Egocentric individuals whose lives are shaped by wins and losses. In this age of lawyer advertising, wins are publicized; losses are buried. After all, who would hire a loser? They market themselves as smart, no nonsense pit bulls, who would eat their young if it would benefit the client. They fear no one, and everyone fears them. Even their families are subordinate to the needs of their clients.

Criminal defense lawyers are different from civil trial lawyers. Civil trial lawyers fight about money, giving it and receiving it. Their criminal counterparts fight about freedom and life or death. Most civil cases are tried without public fanfare, making it easier to bury the losses. Criminal matters on the other hand generally attract the attention of reporters, both print and electronic. With attention comes criticism. Despite a constitution that presumes innocence unless guilt is proven beyond a reasonable doubt, criminal defense lawyers are not always embraced when an acquittal occurs. Most people are not inclined to wrap their arms around an alleged child molester who obtains his freedom based upon legal niceties.

Jonathan Felbin, known by all as simply *Felbin,* is a trial lawyer. His practice primarily centers on representing those accused of criminal behavior. But he is somewhat unique among members of the criminal bar because many of his clients are police officers. Those clients attract even more public attention than the average criminal defendant.

In addition to the obvious problems associated with the incarceration of police officers with career criminals, racial barriers can also impact the prosecution of law enforcement officers. When force is deemed necessary in altercations with minority suspects, allegations of discriminatory brutality often follow. Historically, the relationship between law enforcement in St. Louis and people of color is, at best,

strained. Improvement in the immediate future seems unlikely, making jury selection a challenge where the races of
the officer and the suspect are in conflict.

Then there is the matter of politics influencing criminal
prosecutions. Whether you are black or white, rich or poor,
educated or uneducated, male or female, fat or skinny,
tall or short, your life in some respect is shaped by politics
whether you like it or not. But politics and politicians have
no place in the criminal justice system.

Felbin was no stranger to politics and politicians cor-
rupting the criminal justice system. Recently, he'd had his
hands full with corrupt politicians, prosecutors and judges.
An elected prosecutor, Joan Cardwell, looking to curry favor
with an influential black politician, Winston Lee, prosecuted a white police officer, Bobby Decker, for murder amidst
protests of discriminatory brutality resulting in the death of
a black suspect. Then there was the payback. Now a judge,
Cardwell was assigned to the case of the politician's son,
who was charged with murder. Although a jury found the
defendant guilty, the Honorable Joan Cardwell found a legal technicality to set that verdict aside and free her bene-
factor's son. Felbin was the attorney for the defense in both
Decker and Lee's cases.

When Carmine walked into Felbin's corner office one
rainy afternoon, he saw him staring out the window deep in
thought. He knew what his boss was thinking.

"I just saw where Winston Lee's campaign for governor
is in full swing and he is doing well in the polls," Felbin
began. "If I hadn't screwed up, Garner would still be living
here, and his father would not be looking to be the next governor of Missouri. Unfortunately, we can't even investigate.
Any investigation would lead right back here to our office."

For once, Carmine resisted the temptation to respond
immediately. He had offered numerous suggestions in the
past which Felbin rejected because they violated the attorney-client privilege. Carmine didn't care about any privilege. He wanted justice for Garner.

Chapter Two

After most high-profile trials, Felbin would escape to the beach where he could put his professional troubles on hold, at least temporarily. The Garner Lee trial was no exception to his general routine. Now, almost a year after the Garner Lee trial, Winston Lee's campaign for governor resurrected old wounds. Felbin felt responsible for Garner's plight. He'd failed his client. He needed to escape. A change of scenery and a trip to the Florida beaches might provide some relief and give him time to figure out how to deal with some very unpleasant memories.

The flight from St. Louis to Daytona International airport was smooth and uneventful. Savoring a few drinks on his private plane helped him refocus. At the airport, he was met by his Florida driver, Brian Kober, and driven to the condo in Ormond Beach.

The sun was just beginning to set when he arrived at the eleventh-floor beachside condominium he shared with his girlfriend and confidant, Melinda Evans. After making himself a drink, he went out onto the deck. The view of both the Atlantic Ocean and the Gulf Intracoastal Waterway was spectacular. He could feel the warm salt air on his face while he watched the waves steadily roll onto the sandy beach. The sights and sounds of the ocean were an immediate respite from the world he'd just left. The only thing missing was Melinda. She would in the next day, delayed by a problem at one of her dental labs in Atlanta.

After a quick shower, Felbin headed to Houligan's, a sports bar, in Ormond Beach for some chicken wings, his favorite food and a specialty of the restaurant. He sat at the bar and entertained himself with several sporting events playing on multiple televisions. He really wasn't watching any of them. This was just part of the escape and his mental therapy. It would be a short evening. He was tired and had an early morning tee time with some friends.

LPGA International has two very challenging golf courses and is the home of the women who play golf professionally. At 7:40am, Felbin was on the tee at the Jones course
along with three of his friends, Bill Bell, Jim Kinsey, and
Brian's father, Roger Kober.

Kinsey makes the tee times and gets the group together
when Felbin is in town. He also plays by a different set of
golf rules. Actually, Jim has no golf rules. For example, in
Jim's world, putts are good if they are within the shadow of
the flag as it sits in the hole. Depending on the hour of the
day, shadows can extend fifty feet or more in length. Playing golf with Jim is always entertaining and certainly helps
Felbin forget his professional problems.

When Felbin arrived back at the condo, he was pleas-
antly surprised by Melinda. After a kiss and a hug, Melinda
said, "I finished early in Atlanta, but now I need to go out to
Denver for another problem." She owned several successful
dental labs throughout the country. She was a *hands-on*
owner and visited the various locations often to make sure
things were running smoothly. She had very little employee
turnover because she hired competent managers and technicians and paid them well.

"When do you have to be out there?" Felbin asked.

"I'm leaving in the morning. I got a voicemail while I
was in the air coming here. This work thing keeps getting
in the way of my social life."

"And mine," Felbin replied.

Felbin's friend, Jimmy Buffett, had opened a new
restaurant in Daytona Beach. Located on the beach, Land
Shark Bar and Grill has two bars: one inside and one on the
sand. The restaurant itself is roomy and in addition to an
outside wraparound porch, has windows that slide open,
giving even patrons who chose to dine inside a sense of
dining on the beach. With Jimmy, it's all about selling the
carefree lifestyle—flip-flops on the beach.

Ordinarily, Felbin avoided crowded restaurants. However, this restaurant was new, and he thought Melinda
would like it.

Surprisingly, they were able to get an outside table
quickly. Apparently, the vacationers hadn't discovered the
place yet. After they sat down, the first order of business
was to order a drink. Melinda, who claimed she didn't drink

before she met Felbin, usually wanted a drink menu. She was on a mission to sample everything she'd missed. While she explored the menu, Felbin decided on a Land Shark beer. After all, that was the name of the restaurant. Eventually, Melinda settled on a Blue Moon. She didn't care about the name of the restaurant. She was her own person.

While they waited for their drinks, they listened to the sound of the waves crashing onto the beach at high tide. They watched children building castles in the sand and enjoying the last bit of sunshine. There was no conversation. They knew each other well and were sometimes content to sit in silence just enjoying each other's company. Felbin knew Melinda needed a break as badly as he did. There was something about being together in Florida that made everything right.

When the drinks arrived, Felbin took a long drink of his cold beer and spoke. "When are we going to get rid of this work stuff, retire completely, spend more time in Florida, travel, go on some cruises, and just enjoy what's left of our lives?"

"That's one of the many things I like about you, Felbin, you get right to the point," Melinda said sarcastically.

Felbin ignored the comment. He had spoken about retirement before, but this time it was different. "I've had a lot of interesting things happen in my practice, but nothing like Garner Lee." He couldn't help himself. That case, along with the prosecution of police officer Bobby Decker, had shaped his mental health for the last several years. "I knew Cardwell was corrupt, but I didn't think the entire system was in the toilet." As with most conversations about Garner Lee and Bobby Decker, the names of Joan Cardwell and Winston Lee would eventually surface.

Before Felbin could finish his thoughts, the waiter came to the table to take the order. Felbin ordered a Philly cheese steak sandwich with fries. Melinda wanted a Chef Salad with blue cheese dressing. They both ordered another beer.

When the waiter left, Felbin changed the subject. "Did you get things straightened out in Atlanta?"

"Yes. I had to replace one of the managers up there who retired. We had a big retirement party. That was the good part. Trying to find someone of his quality to replace him was the tough part."

"And now you have to head out to Denver. That's what I'm talking about. We need to start enjoying life. And our jobs keep getting in the way. The stress will kill us both."

Melinda knew Felbin once again was reacting to the Garner Lee case. That case had taken a piece of his life he would never get back. She knew about the case since Felbin talked to her about most of his cases. But there was something else. Something Felbin was not telling her about Garner Lee. She knew Felbin felt bad about what happened to his client. He felt responsible. He knew his client was innocent, but he was doing nothing to find the real killer and clear Garner's name. That was not like Jonathan Felbin.

After the leisurely meal, they passed on dessert and additional drinks. Brian Kober needed to get Melinda to Orlando International airport, an hour and a half away, to catch an early flight to Denver. Felbin would spend some additional time on the beach and the golf course in Florida before returning to St. Louis.

After settling into his seat on his private plane and while awaiting his flight from Florida to St. Louis, Felbin stared out the window, looking at nothing in particular. The beach, golf with his friends, a short visit with Melinda, were only temporary distractions.

He knew political advertisements encouraging the election of his mortal enemy, Winston Lee, would be consuming the St. Louis airwaves upon his return. He would be unable to escape Lee's political pandering and the promises he had no intention of keeping. That was reality. If there was any justice in the world, somehow Garner Lee would be exonerated, Amy Deland's real killer identified, and Winston Lee defeated at the polls. But at the moment, all Felbin could do was hope and deal with his own guilt.

Chapter Three

Winston Lee already essentially ran the state of Missouri. If he didn't put his stamp of approval on it, it didn't happen. He was more powerful than the governor. Prior to his election as a Missouri State Representative where he served for 8 years, Lee was a lobbyist for the clients of McKenzie and Carter, the law firm where he was a partner. Forced to leave the House of Representatives because of term limits, he ran for and easily won a state senate seat. When term limits prohibited remaining in the senate, he decided to extend his political career by running for governor. But as a professional politician, he had no plans for his career to end there. Eventually, he'd set his sights on the United States Senate and certainly didn't rule out the White House. The only thing larger than his ambition was his ego.

Bill Shreiber, the current governor, was also term limited. It was widely believed Lee was the frontrunner to be his replacement. He had money, status, name recognition and support from many special interest groups. He was the first African American President Pro Tem of the Senate. He'd served in that position for the past 6 years and controlled all legislation. Clearly, the road to all political favors went through Winston Lee.

Lee's law firm, McKenzie and Carter, is one of the largest law firms in the state of Missouri. 173 lawyers occupy offices in St. Louis, Kansas City and Jefferson City as well as New York, Washington, D.C. and Los Angeles. The firm's client list is a who's who of corporate executives and people with money who were not shy about making political contributions either above or below the table. Winston Lee was the third-party beneficiary of their generosity.

Rubbing shoulders with people of wealth also had other advantages. These ne'er-do-wells had bought and paid for friends in powerful political positions both inside and outside Missouri. For every political dollar contributed, they expected a return on their investment. The clients of McKenzie and Carter wanted to see their lawyer become the next governor of the state of Missouri. "One can never have too many politicians in one's pocket," one of the partners once mused. Routinely, these contributors called in political favors seeking the endorsement and assistance of politicians throughout the country, from the United States Congress to the White House.

The beauty and personality of Lee's wife, Cassandra, also played a vital role in the campaign. She sometimes overshadowed the candidate, much to his displeasure. Her grandfather, Andrew Brook, was one of the founders of the McKenzie and Carter firm, a truly remarkable accomplishment at a time when there were few African Americans in the practice. Graduating at the top of his Harvard Law School class, he clerked for a Federal Appellate Court judge for a year, after which he joined a prestigious New York firm before returning to his home in St. Louis to start his law practice. His contacts at Harvard as well as in New York allowed him to partner with some of his colleagues to develop the firm of McKenzie and Carter.

Cassandra Lee did not rely on her family name to establish herself in the legal profession. A cum laude graduate of Yale Law School, Cassandra was a nationally recognized civil rights trial attorney. As an African American female, she understood racial disparity and discrimination. She talked about those issues, wrote about them and successfully pursued them through the judicial process. She was no friend of the police and the St. Louis Police Department in particular, having successfully sued both on several occasions.

While Winston was intelligent, Cassandra was the brainpower behind the campaign. She monitored what was said, how it was said and positions on all issues. She was a master manipulator of both people and issues. Occasionally, she would get push back from Kelvin Bellington, the campaign manager, on an issue usually involving financial disclosure statements and campaign contributions. As a skilled lawyer, Cassandra Lee would always interpret campaign laws in a manner favoring concealment over disclosure. At the end of the day, her position would control and Bellington would acquiesce. No one dared disagree with her, including her husband. Winston Lee understood his wife's money, family status and prestige had gotten him to his current position. Cassandra Lee created him and never let him forget it.

For Cassandra, it was all about the winning regardless of how you got there. For her, the governor's office was but a brief stop in the climb to power. Like her husband, she didn't rule out the White House and the title of *First Lady of the United States*. But her vision was like no other First Lady. She would not be planning dinner parties and conducting tours of the White House. Her husband would be answering to her as she would be running the country. Make no mistake. Cassandra Lee was not on some mythical journey to Oz. She had a goal that didn't end with her husband becoming the President of the United States. Where others had failed, she would succeed. She would follow her husband as the first female President, and no one would stop her.

Cassandra Lee also controlled the news media covering the campaign. For those she liked, she would provide access to the candidate and provide advance notice on significant issues. Those she didn't like would come in second in a two-person race.

Raymond Singer was Winston Lee's Republican opponent. The Attorney General for the state of Missouri for the past seven years, he was bright, and like most politicians, ambitious. But unlike many, he was ethical and honest, a straight shooter. He earned both his law and undergraduate degrees from St. Louis University, graduating first in his class in the law school. Rejecting lucrative offers from silk stocking law firms after law school, he joined the prosecutor's office in St. Louis County where he quickly advanced to felony prosecutions, including murder cases.

Singer had no prior political experience when he ran for the statewide office of Attorney General. His timing was right as the state was ready for a chief law enforcement officer who was not a politician. His predecessor, Craig Wilson, was a disaster. The office was for sale to the highest bidder. Singer easily defeated him and was elected to a second term. Now he was seeking to defeat another professional politician. That would be no easy task as Lee's war chest was at least four times larger. In addition to money, the powerful, both corporate and political, lined up behind Lee. Singer was clearly the underdog. But he believed, perhaps naïvely, that truth and honesty would carry the day.

Chapter Four

As with any election, a substantial amount of the daily news was devoted to the candidates and their activities. Today, Winston Lee captured a headline above the fold in the St. Louis daily newspaper. Darius Washington, an Academy Award winning actor, would be coming to St. Louis to campaign for Lee. McKenzie and Carter represented him through the Los Angeles office. No surprise for Washington to show up at some point during the campaign. Other celebrities were expected as well.

With a copy of the newspaper in hand, Tony Carmine, came charging into Jonathan Felbin's office like a bull chasing the red cape of the matador. Carmine, a retired St. Louis police officer, was Felbin's chief investigator. "Did you see this? This fuckin' piece of shit, Lee, is bringing Darius Washington in here to campaign for him," Carmine said in a voice loud enough for the entire office suite to hear as he threw the paper on Felbin's desk. Before Felbin had a chance to respond, Carmine continued. "What the fuck does Darius Washington know about Missouri politics? For that matter what does he know about Missouri? And what the fuck do I care what this guy knows about anything?"

Felbin, had just returned from Florida. His effort to leave his guilt on the beach having failed, he just stared at his investigator as he listened to his rant. Finally, when Carmine stopped talking—or rather yelling—Felbin said, "Feel better?"

"No, I don't feel better. I told you before and I'll tell you again, we need to torpedo this campaign and we also need to do something to put his fuckin' wife in the penitentiary for murder. That's what will make me feel better."

Felbin agreed with everything Carmine said. But the rules of professional conduct prevented him from righting the wrong for his former client, Garner Lee.

Carmine continued with his rant. "I can't get over it. I won't get over it. It consumes me every day. Winston Lee fucks his son's girlfriend, gets her pregnant, Cassandra Lee kills the girlfriend and they both stroll into the governor's mansion with no one the wiser. This is wrong on so many levels and I can't live with it."

"Well, you need to learn to live with it because there is nothing you can do about it. And you will make matters worse if you try." Felbin said pointing his finger at Carmine, hoping he got the message. Good advice, but ironic, coming from a guy who also hadn't learned how to deal with the issue.

Once again Carmine was not satisfied with the response. It was like he never heard a word Felbin said. "Listen, I talked to some friends in the department," Carmine continued.

Tony Carmine spent 25 years with the St. Louis Police Department. Felbin and Carmine had a long history dating back to the days when Carmine was a rookie with the department. With less than a year on, Carmine made a traffic stop that netted a cache of drugs found in the vehicle operated by Felbin's client. The cross examination at the suppression hearing began pleasant enough but didn't end that way. Carmine got a refresher course in the rules of search and seizure. While he lost the case, he gained a lesson he would never forget. He would go on to become a well-respected investigator who would be rewarded with prestigious assignments, such as the homicide division. Numerous future professional encounters over the years were not kind to Felbin, and Carmine enjoyed kicking the lawyer's ass. Eventually, the two became friends. When he retired, Felbin persuaded him to join his staff and work the other side of the street.

"You did what? Tell me Tony, that you didn't tell them anything our client told us." This was Felbin's greatest fear and the reason he needed to move Carmine off his crusade.

"Relax. I didn't use any names. I talked about a hypothetical case someone else had. But they said they would definitely pursue it."

"How hypothetical was this, Tony?"

"I just told them I had a buddy who worked for a law firm in Chicago. And he had a client who admitted to an unsolved murder and they wanted to leak it to the prosecutor and police. I told them my investigator friend couldn't say anything directly because of the attorney-client privilege. They said they would be interested in the case and would figure out some way to work around the privilege."

"First of all, those aren't exactly our facts. I explained to you the limited number of ways the attorney-client privilege wouldn't apply. Cassandra Lee confessed to us that she killed Amy Deland after she manipulated us into representing her. I screwed up, but the privilege still applies. We can't tell anyone, including Garner.

"Well, if we can't get her locked up, then why don't we torpedo the campaign? Can't we at least prevent them from becoming a powerful first family for the entire state?" Carmine pressed.

"No, No, No, Tony," Felbin said, irritation turning to anger. "We are not going to take any steps to get Cassandra Lee prosecuted, and we are not going to get involved in her husband's campaign for governor. And we are not going to talk about this again. Am I clear?"

"Yes," Carmine simply said.

But both Felbin and Carmine knew this would not be the last word on the topic. One of the things Felbin loved about his chief investigator—he was like a dog with a bone. Telling Tony Carmine he couldn't do something motivated him to try. It drove Felbin crazy.

Chapter Five

Felbin hadn't finished his first cup of coffee when the receptionist announced a phone call. Garner Lee was calling from London.

"Hopefully, you are just calling to see how I'm doing," Felbin began the conversation. He hadn't heard from his former client in quite a while and hoped he wasn't in trouble.

"I'm always concerned with your health, Felbin. You never know when I might need your services again," Garner said.

Putting that blunt reminder aside, Felbin asked, "But you don't need my services, do you?"

"Well, yes and no."

"Let's start with the *no* part," Felbin said after processing his former client's answer.

"I'm not in any kind of trouble and I don't need you to bail me out of jail."

"Well, that's good news since I didn't do very well the last time," Felbin added.

Ignoring the response, Garner said, "I am out of money and I need to come back to the United States. I can't get any real work here."

After the trial, Europe provided a place where Garner's past would not be following him. He could be anonymous. He was not the son of a politician who fixed a murder case. But now, Garner was figuring out Europe would not be a permanent fix. He couldn't stay out of the country forever. Sooner or later he would have to return to the United States.

"St. Louis?"

"I would prefer someplace else. But if that's the only place I can find work, I guess I'll have to take it."

Felbin wasn't sure whether his former client was thinking he would have an associate position available for him.

After all, he did have a law degree and license. And Felbin knew he wasn't a murderer.

But employment with Felbin's firm wouldn't work for a couple of reasons. First and foremost, as a member of the firm, his mother's file would be available to him. If Garner found the file and decided to go rogue and turn the information over to the police and prosecutor, both he and Felbin could be disbarred. But Garner might not care about his law license if he learned the truth about his mother.

The other problem would involve Garner's father. If Garner returned to St. Louis, he would get a daily dose of his father's effort to become the next governor. His father was the current front runner. Felbin was confident his former client would be motivated to do what he could to derail his father's front runner position. This effort would necessarily involve assisting his opponent to rekindle tales of his father's extracurricular activities with Amy. As much as he disliked Winston Lee and had no desire to see him as the next governor, Felbin didn't want his law firm involved in the political chaos.

"Do you have any particular place you would like to live? And do you have any idea what you would like to do?" Felbin asked. "I have friends in New York City and throughout that state. Friends in Boston. Some former college roommates and a bunch of friends in Philadelphia. A law school classmate in Denver and some others in Miami, Orlando and Daytona Beach Florida. These are mostly lawyers, but some are businesspeople, mostly corporate executives in the marketing field and some politicians. Take your pick. I would be happy to contact any or all for you."

This was a way Felbin could at least try to make up for his failures where this young man was concerned.

"Well, maybe New York or someplace warm like Florida. But, again, I have to go where I can get a job."

"Other than practicing law, are you trained for anything else?"

Garner didn't hesitate. He answered Felbin's question immediately. "I'm really not trained for anything. And you know my legal talents and experience or the lack thereof."

Garner was never much of a student, either in college or in law school. After spending some time playing in Europe and roaming the beaches in California, it was time to get serious. His mother refused to continue to finance his playboy lifestyle.

He'd thought law school would be a good idea. After all, it beat working for a living. Because his college grades were not good enough to get him in anywhere, he turned to his father for help. After a few phone calls, young Garner had attended law school at the University of Missouri. Ironically, he was the beneficiary of his father's political power and influence. Little did he know then how this power would severely damage him later in life.

"I know you don't have much legal experience," Felbin said, ignoring his knowledge of Garner's playboy past. "But inexperience doesn't automatically disqualify you from an entry level associate position."

"What about my murder conviction? I doubt many law firms will be rolling out the red carpet for a killer," Garner said facetiously.

"You weren't convicted of murder. You were acquitted," Felbin reminded his former criminal client. Actually, Garner hadn't really been acquitted. Rather, the slick legal maneuver Cardwell used was to grant Garner a new trial. But that new trial would never occur. The law does not allow prosecutors who engage in misconduct which results in a conviction to be rewarded with a redo. But rather than explain the legal complexities, Felbin believed it was easier just to say his client was acquitted.

"Felbin, you and I both know the case was fixed thanks to my father. No law firm in the world would view this prosecution as a legitimate acquittal."

"I don't know. I'll make some phone calls. But before I do, are you okay with practicing law?"

"Given my background, I can't afford to be selective. I'll take anything."

"I'll get back to you."

"Thanks, Felbin. I appreciate any help you can give me."

"We'll find you something and get you back on your feet. I promise," Felbin said as he ended the call.

Chapter Six

Tony Carmine walked into Felbin's office. "I heard we got a phone call from Garner," Carmine said.

"Just got off the phone with him," Felbin said.

After Felbin summarized the conversation, Carmine asked, "Why don't we hire him?"

"Think about what you just said, Tony. As a lawyer with this office, he would have access to his mother's file."

"So, what's your point?" Carmine asked knowing full well the point Felbin was making.

"You know, Tony, sometimes I think you say things just to aggravate me. You know exactly the point."

"He can see the file. Big fuckin' deal. What's the problem?" Carmine pressed.

After Felbin explained the many problems associated with hiring Garner Lee, Carmine asked, "Don't you think sooner or later he'll figure out what his mother did?"

"I don't know. But after having to tell him about his father, I don't want to have anything to do with the issues involving his mother."

"But I assume you are still on board with bringing this bitch to justice and putting her where she belongs—the penitentiary."

"Without a doubt, as long as we don't do anything that violates the privilege you are so fond of," Felbin said.

"I have an idea," Carmine said.

"Your ideas generally wind up causing problems for me."

Ignoring Felbin's comment, Carmine said, "Why don't we send a note to the bitch letting her know we are considering hiring Garner when he returns to St. Louis?"

"And other than screwing with her which I am sure you would like, what's the benefit to us?"

"It would certainly unnerve her for starters. And yes, I would enjoy fucking with her, particularly since she is in the middle of a campaign. But more importantly, it might cause her to make a mistake."

"You must have a short memory. This is the lady who told us she needed representation because she was concerned about criminal exposure and publicity in connection with the death of Amy and the circumstances of Garner's acquittal."

"I remember. And by that time, I believe we had excluded her husband as the killer because his DNA wasn't a match on the murder weapon."

"Right. We were speechless when she told us she killed Amy—after we agreed to represent her and the attorney-client privilege was in full force," Felbin recalled.

"I remember all of this. It's tough to forget a person who would come up with a scheme to derail the pursuit of a killer. It was criminal genius. But then again, she is a criminal."

"And this is the person you think will make a mistake? You're delusional, Tony."

"The way I see it, we now have a client we know killed Amy Deland. We also have another client who was accused of killing Amy Deland, found guilty by a jury and acquitted by a corrupt judge. We can't do anything about either one because of your bullshit lawyer rules. Rules, I might add, which half of the people in your profession don't pay any attention to anyway."

"That's pretty harsh," Felbin interrupted.

"Yes, but true. In any event, as I was saying, we have nothing now. I don't understand why we can't hire Garner. But if we lead his mother to believe we are going to hire him, she will eventually go nuts when she realizes he will get to see her file. She may then do something stupid. It's worth a try. We've got nothing to lose."

"Other than the enjoyment of screwing with her, I still haven't heard how this plan of yours gets her closer to a murder prosecution."

"I can't answer your question at this point because I don't know what she will do. But let me ask you this. Suppose she calls us and tells us we can't hire Garner because she doesn't want him to know about what she gave us? Is that protected by your fuckin' privilege?"

"The short answer is yes," Felbin said.

"Would the privilege apply to Garner if he did see the file since he wasn't here at the time she confessed?"

"Stop, please stop. We don't need any more discussion of this topic. Understood?"

"Understood," Carmine said.

But Felbin knew this was not the end as far as Carmine was concerned. Countless times before, Felbin said they were not discussing the situation. Consistently, like a child, Carmine would ignore the admonition and press the point, apparently believing he could wear Felbin down. While it might finally be the end of the conversation, it would not be the end of his investigator's resolve to put Cassandra Lee behind bars. This resolve would present a new problem for Felbin. It meant he would not find out what Carmine was up to until it was too late to do anything.

Chapter Seven

During his flight from London to New York City for interviews with law firms Felbin had arranged, Garner had time to reflect. First and foremost, he needed a job. Although he was thankful for the interviews Felbin arranged, he was not confident any firm would hire him after checking his background. And then there was the matter of his inexperience. The time he spent with McKenzie and Carter, the firm founded by his grandfather, was not exactly memorable. Since the firm had an office in Manhattan, he wondered whether that would be a benefit or a handicap. Given his relationship with his parents, there was no way to know whether his old firm would give him a favorable recommendation.

He sought the counsel of Felbin as to how he should handle the question of his checkered background. Felbin's advice was to be candid and straightforward. But what exactly did that mean and where should he draw the line? He would have to make that decision on the spot depending on the questions asked.

For Garner there really wasn't a good way to answer these inevitable questions. The first test would be with Goodman, Fine, and Goldstein, a prominent firm on Fifth Avenue in New York City, specializing in business litigation and representing Fortune 500 corporations around the world. They occupied ten floors in the heart of Manhattan to accommodate some 325 lawyers. The offices were plush and not dissimilar to those of McKenzie and Carter in St. Louis. As soon as he saw the layout, Garner knew the only reason he got an interview was because Felbin made a phone call.

After a short wait, Mark Goldstein, one of the named partners entered the reception area to greet Garner and show him the way to one of the many conference rooms for the interview. Garner was impressed. Usually, partners of his status don't wander into the waiting area to greet prospective employees.

With the initial introductions and pleasantries out of the way, Goldstein began the interview. "Jonathan Felbin gave me a call asking if we were hiring and said he had a candidate we might be interested in. How do you know Mr. Felbin?"

Wow. Right to the heart of the matter. What the hell did Felbin tell him? Surely, they had some conversation. Maybe this is a test to see how my answer will compare to his, Garner thought as he tried to decide how to answer the question. "He represented me," he finally said, hoping the next question would not be the most obvious one.

Goldstein looked confused. "He was your lawyer? And you know him because he represented you? What was the crime?"

Felbin clearly didn't have an in-depth conversation with this guy. Apparently, their friendship was good enough to get Garner an interview without explanation as to background and qualifications. Sooner or later this firm and every other place where he interviewed would learn about his checkered past. Deciding it would be better to be up front now rather than getting fired later, Garner explained he had been prosecuted for murdering his girlfriend and Felbin represented him. He offered no additional details.

"Murder," Garner replied.

Goldstein didn't immediately respond. He didn't have to. The look on his face made it abundantly clear he wasn't expecting his friend to send him a murder suspect. After an awkward silence, Goldstein finally said, "I assume Mr. Felbin did a good job and you were acquitted."

Now Garner had another decision to make. He knew the case was fixed thanks to his father. He could address the issue now or avoid it and simply agree with Goldstein's statement. Before any reputable firm hired him, he knew they would do a complete background check. This would involve a media search where the Cardwell fix would clearly be highlighted. Deciding some explanation now would be better than later, he began his self-serving explanation, carefully selecting his words.

"I was acquitted, and my lawyer did a great job," he began. Not completely true, but it would suffice for the moment. As Goldstein listened intently, Garner went on to explain that he loved Amy and didn't kill her. He was a victim of circumstances and some bad advice from his father. He was in the wrong place at the wrong time.

Goldstein didn't press for more specific details of Garner's rather general explanation but instead, asked, "What was the cause of death?"

"Blunt trauma. Someone hit her on the back of the head with a statue. The statue, which was determined to be the murder weapon, contained a DNA sample which was not mine."

"Whose DNA was it?"

"They were not able to match it to anyone. But the person who struck her was left-handed, or at least used the left hand to strike her. I'm right-handed."

Goldstein listened intently to Garner's explanation. His body language now suggested no signs of agreement or disagreement with what Garner was saying. After a moment and apparently believing Garner was finished with his explanation, Goldstein said, "Well at least the jury found your evidence persuasive and acquitted."

Decision time once again. While he could spin the reason he was charged, this was the second time an acquittal was mentioned. However, this time there was a reference to a jury verdict. Garner knew this issue was important to the person interviewing him and his firm. Technically, there was an acquittal. But the jury had nothing to do with it. Garner decided a full and honest disclosure was necessary. "Actually, the jury found me guilty."

Looking really perplexed now, Goldstein asked, "Then how were you acquitted? Did you get a new trial?"

"No. The judge determined there was prosecutorial misconduct and entered a judgment of acquittal." Not completely accurate as to the judge's motives and what actually occurred but good for this discussion, which was going nowhere.

With the look on his face, Garner knew Mark Goldstein was not persuaded his firm wouldn't be employing a murderer if they hired him. And Garner didn't blame him. He knew what he was up against and the only thing he could do was tell the truth. But the truth, even spun in his favor, wouldn't erase the *Scarlet Letter* he wore.

After a few additional questions about his experience, which Garner knew were a mere courtesy, the interview ended. Goldstein politely explained they had several additional candidates who needed to be interviewed and he would be in touch. Garner knew he would never hear from him again. That's how firms like this handled employment matters. They didn't waste time sending rejection letters.

Garner was interviewed by three other firms, thanks to Felbin. All were the same. The interview would be going well until the murder charge surfaced and Garner provided an explanation. The faces of all interviewers told the story. Politely and professionally each interview ended abruptly. All promising to let him know their decision. And each knowing it would never happen.

Garner contacted Felbin to let him know the interviews were concluded and he was not optimistic. When Felbin asked what happened, Garner said, "As expected, my past did me in."

"What did you tell them?" Felbin asked.

"The truth. I tried to spin it as best I could, but they can easily check the media coverage. It is what it is. Maybe I'm better off going back to London to see if I can find something there. It has to be better than coming to St. Louis."

Garner was feeling sorry for himself. There was no light at the end of the tunnel. He knew he had to learn how to live his life with the hand he had been dealt. He also knew it wouldn't be easy.

"Can you stay there for a couple more days?" When Garner indicated he could, Felbin said, "I have one other person I can contact. This is a place where your background may be a benefit. I should have thought of this earlier."

"I can't imagine my background helping but I'll wait to hear from you," Garner said, again thanking his former lawyer.

Chapter Eight

Cassandra Lee was in the midst of a very ugly name-calling campaign. She had abandoned her law practice to devote her entire attention to getting her husband elected as the next governor of the state of Missouri. But when she got word her son was returning to St. Louis and would be working for Felbin, the campaign took a back seat. She needed to address this issue immediately. She couldn't have her only son working for lawyers who knew she killed Amy Deland. She believed Garner would be pushed over the edge with no telling what he would do with the information, privilege or no privilege.

"Get off the phone," Cassandra demanded as she entered her husband's campaign office. When he finished his call, she said, "I just got some information. Garner is back in town and will be going to work for Felbin."

"How does that involve us?" Winston Lee asked.

Cassandra couldn't tell her husband the real reason she didn't want their son to go to work for Felbin's law firm. She had to make up something which would get his attention. "We haven't spoken to him since he was acquitted and left for Europe. Our relationship hasn't exactly been one which would rival Beaver Cleaver and his family. Felbin has never had a kind word for you, and I'm afraid putting them together could be a potential problem for the campaign."

"How so?" Winston asked.

"I believe they will feed off each other. Both hate us for different reasons. I'm concerned when Garner sees how well we are doing, he will do what he can to derail the campaign. And Felbin can help him with his many press contacts in this town."

"We have this election in the palm of our hands. According to the polls, we have a good lead. I doubt they can do anything to derail it. But, in any event, what is it you want me to do?"

"I think you need to call Felbin and object to him hiring Garner," Cassandra said, knowing full well her suggestion was ridiculous. But she was desperate, and this was the best she could do under the circumstances. The last thing she wanted was to have any conversation with her former lawyer.

"You've got to be kidding. He probably wouldn't take my call. Why should he, given our relationship? Plus, if he did take the call, what am I supposed to tell him? Don't hire my son because we are afraid the two of you may sabotage our campaign? If anything, I might be planting a seed he and Garner otherwise didn't have. I'll take my chances. There's nothing they can do to materially harm this campaign."

"Fine. Then I'll call him," Cassandra responded, anger in her voice.

"Let it go, Cassandra. I don't want you to contact Felbin or Garner. They will find some way to use your phone call against us."

"Fuck you, Winston. I'll do what I want. I don't want our son going to work for Felbin or having anything to do with him," Cassandra said as she left the office. There would be no further discussion, no argument.

The marriage of Winston and Cassandra Lee was one of convenience, particularly after Winston's fling with their son's girlfriend. She was always the dominant partner in the relationship. Winston needed her money and the backing of her family's law firm. She, in turn, wanted the power associated with the governor's office which she viewed as a path to national political recognition. Rarely would her husband refuse to honor her numerous demands. But his refusal to contact Felbin seemed to be one of the mountains on which he was content to die.

Believing there was little time to spare, Cassandra headed to her office to call Felbin. As she waited for his assistant to locate him, Cassandra was trying to figure out how she was going to approach this. She was not one to beat around the bush.

Before answering the call, Felbin summoned Carmine to his office to witness the conversation. After pushing the speaker phone button, Felbin said, "Hello, Ms. Lee. To what do I owe this honor?"

Skipping customary phone pleasantries, Cassandra began, "Are you on a speaker phone?"

"And it is also so very nice to hear your voice, Ms. Lee," Felbin said sarcastically avoiding the question.

"I asked you a question, Felbin. I also want to know if you are taping this since I'm not consenting to any tape recording."

"And I would note for the record I also asked you a question you failed to answer," Felbin replied.

Carmine was starting to enjoy this exchange. He knew Felbin's reference to the call being *on the record* would really piss her off because she would think it was a reference to a tape. Of course, he knew the call was not being recorded.

"If you hire my son, I will bring the wrath of God down on you. You will never practice law again, and it will be just the beginning of many problems for you."

"Wow. Sounds like a threat to me."

"It's a promise. I don't threaten. Do we understand each other, Felbin?"

"What I understand is I will hire anyone for this law practice I want, regardless of your threats. Do you have anything else you want to talk about?"

"Fuck you, Felbin," she said, terminating the call.

As Carmine got up from the chair in front of Felbin's desk, intending to quickly leave the office, Felbin said, "Sit down." Carmine knew exactly what was coming.

"I'm guessing I would be wasting my time asking you how she got the idea Garner was coming to work here," Felbin said.

"I don't know, boss. All I know for sure is you told me not to spread any fake news stories. But, as always, I stand ready to investigate. I'd like to start with calling that bitch and asking her where she got the information her son was coming to work here, if that's okay with you. I could also ask her if she would like a copy of the tape."

Felbin just shook his head and said, "Out," as he pointed to the door. He realized any additional conversation would truly be a waste of time.

Chapter Nine

After Carmine left his office, Felbin considered the phone call from Cassandra Lee. Clearly, she was concerned Garner would do something to publicly unmask her criminal behavior. Whether or not she was indicted, the disclosure her DNA was on the murder weapon would be the end of her glamorous and powerful world of privilege. Her money and power would not be able to eliminate the odor of death, it would follow her wherever she went. Carmine was right. The prospect of her kid finding out she was a killer shook her world because there was no predicting what he would do. The risk of losing his law license would not outweigh his appetite for the sweet taste of revenge.

As gratifying as it was to consider his former client's current mental anguish, there was nothing beyond the satisfaction of the moment. Cassandra would soon realize her son was not coming to work for Felbin, and her perfect world of privilege would be restored.

But what if he had no other opportunity and Garner had to return to St. Louis? Would Felbin consider hiring him then as a situation of last resort? Would it be fair to Garner? Would it be fair to Felbin and the people in his firm? As those thoughts swirled around his brain, Felbin began once again to feel the pain of guilty failure. The mistake of agreeing to represent Cassandra Lee would haunt him for the rest of his life. A single mistake would form the basis of an irrevocable bond between him and Garner Lee.

Felbin's mental pity party was interrupted by his assistant. "There is someone on line three I think you will want to talk to," she announced.

Without even asking who it was, Felbin pushed the button to connect the call. Talking to anyone was better than what was going through his head now.

"How are things in St. Louis?" the caller began, presuming Felbin knew who was calling.

He didn't need anyone to identify the caller. He immediately recognized the voice, particularly since he had just talked to him a few days earlier. And what a welcome call this was. It had to be some good news. Otherwise, there would be no reason to call, just as the others had not bothered to follow up.

When the interviews Felbin had arranged for Garner failed, he made one more call to a good friend in New York. Why he hadn't thought of this sooner he didn't know. It was a perfect fit.

In 1992, Barry Scheck and Peter Neufeld founded the Innocence Project in New York City. The Innocence Project was a not-for-profit organization committed to exonerating people who had been wrongfully convicted, primarily through DNA analysis. Their results were mind blowing. 362 people who were wrongfully convicted had been freed based upon DNA. Of this number, 20 spent time on death row. 99 percent of those freed had been males, with minority groups comprising 70 percent. Not only did the science free those wrongfully convicted but it also identified the true perpetrators. DNA was responsible for identifying some 150 people who were truly responsible for committing the crimes for which others had been convicted.

"Am I glad to hear from you. I haven't talked to you in a couple years and now we've talked twice in the last week," Felbin began. He and Barry Scheck had worked together on a couple of cases over the years. "I'm hoping you're calling with some good news. Lord knows, this kid needs some."

"I am. You're the second person to hear the good news. Garner was the first. We offered him a job and he accepted," Barry Scheck said.

"Great news. You won't be disappointed. Thanks."

"As you know, I've been involved in a lot of crazy cases. But I'm thinking his case tops any crazy case I've had. Unbelievable. And I'm guessing Garner didn't give me the full story."

"Tell me what he told you and I can fill in the blanks," Felbin told his friend.

Scheck summarized the explanation Garner provided which included the jury verdict.

"Did he tell you about his father?" Felbin interrupted.

"Yeah. He said this hot shot scum bag father not only was banging his girlfriend but knocked her up. Nice guy."

"Did he tell you about the DNA?"

"He said there was some DNA found on the murder weapon and it was not his or his father's. That's what persuaded me this guy was not good for this murder. He also said there was some evidence the person who struck the fatal blow was left-handed, and he's right-handed."

"Did he tell you how it ended after the jury found him guilty of murder?"

"After the jury returned the guilty verdict, the judge entered a judgment of acquittal based upon some sort of prosecutorial misconduct. Frankly, by this point, I really didn't care how the acquittal occurred because I knew he didn't kill anybody. I also knew you wouldn't send me someone you knew was a murderer, particularly given my line of work here."

"Well, the prosecutorial misconduct part is bullshit," Felbin said emphatically.

"The acquittal wasn't based on misconduct?" Barry asked, perplexed by Felbin's response.

"No, that's what the judge said." Felbin went on to explain the truth about how the acquittal occurred mentioning only that there was a connection between the trial judge and Garner's father.

"Wow. The case keeps getting better. You need to write a book about this one." Since Felbin hadn't mentioned the name of the judge, Scheck asked, "Who was the judge in Garner's case?"

"Cardwell."

"Joan Cardwell?" Barry asked.

Felbin hesitated before answering. "Yes. How did you know the name? Have you had some dealing with her?"

"Actually, I called you for two reasons. I wanted to tell you we hired Garner. But I also wanted to talk to you about Joan Cardwell."

Chapter Ten

Felbin knew the world was really a small place. Scheck lived in New York City and his office was in Manhattan. Joan Cardwell had lived her entire life in St. Louis. None of the St. Louis cases Felbin handled with Scheck involved Cardwell. Felbin had no idea why his friend wanted to talk about Cardwell. But whatever it was, it probably wouldn't be good for the *Honorable* Joan Cardwell. Barry was a good lawyer and dedicated to freeing those wrongfully convicted. Felbin could hardly contain his excitement while waiting for Scheck to tell him why he wanted to talk about Cardwell. But whatever it was, Scheck came to the right place. Felbin was in.

"We just got a new case in St. Louis. Before Garner arrived, I was going to call you. It's an old rape case. The guy, Larry Jenkins, was convicted of rape, sodomy and kidnapping. He's exhausted all his appeals and has been locked up for more than seventeen years. We've reviewed the trial transcripts, depositions and the discovery. The case is weak, and we think DNA can answer a lot of questions. We were going to send it your way and ask you to get involved with us."

"That's fine. I'll look forward to getting the documents," Felbin said.

"Since Garner's on board and he's from St. Louis and has a Missouri license to practice there, I thought I would assign him to the case as our liaison. You can show him the ropes."

Felbin hesitated, uncertain whether sending Garner back to St. Louis would be a good idea. But instead of going there, he asked, "Why did you want to talk to me about Cardwell? Is she involved in this?"

"She was the prosecutor."

"You're kidding." Felbin wondered where this was going. On the one hand, he really didn't need another issue with Cardwell. Good judgment told him to run from this one. However, whatever it was, he knew he couldn't resist. This lady was corrupt and Felbin wanted to play whatever role he could in identifying her corruption with the goal of removing her from the bench and perhaps from the practice of law.

"Our research so far indicates she was not a very good prosecutor. Although she didn't try many cases, her win/loss record was not very good."

"We like those prosecutors," Felbin added.

"We talked to the public defender's office in St. Louis. According to them, at the time of this case, she was thinking about a run for the elected position of circuit attorney and her opponent would be an experienced and successful prosecutor. She knew their records would be compared and she would come up short. She began to look for cases, easy ones, she could try and win. Apparently, someone thought the Jenkins case would be one of those, probably because of his lawyer. Jenkins was represented by a young public defender who had no trial experience. I'm guessing she thought he would be easy to take advantage of at trial."

"I thought you said the case was weak."

"It was a one on one without any physical or forensic evidence linking Jenkins to the crime. A *he said, she said* finger pointing contest. An attractive victim and a black defendant. The black guy usually comes out on the short end of the stick. Plus, Jenkins had an alibi, but it was never presented. Police laboratory technicians recovered human sperm and fluids from the victim's panties, a swatch from her sweater and the rear seat of her car but didn't perform any additional forensic tests. The lab reports were provided to the defense. Neither the prosecutor nor Jenkins' lawyer requested additional forensic testing such as saliva, blood type, secretor status or enzymes. As you well know, DNA can answer a lot of questions these days but wasn't available back then. Given the circumstances we've seen so far, DNA will free this guy," Scheck said.

"Given Garner's situation in St. Louis, do you think it's a good idea to send him here?"

"After he told me the story about his trial, I had the same hesitation about sending him into a snake pit. I just talked to him generally about returning to St. Louis on this

34

old rape case, given his own problems. He said he was fine with coming back there. Of course, as a new employee, I'm sure he would be fine with whatever we asked him to do. But I never mentioned the involvement of Cardwell. I'll talk to him about her involvement," Scheck said.

"Did he mention anything about his father's current political ambitions?"

"No. His father was some hot shot politician who apparently suggested he lie to the police and knocked up the kid's girlfriend."

"Well, in addition to fixing a criminal prosecution with a corrupt judge, his father is in the middle of a heated campaign for governor. And he is in the lead."

"No, he never mentioned anything about a governor's race. Frankly, since he has been in Europe, I'm not sure he knows the status of any campaign his father is running. What are your thoughts about his returning to St. Louis for this case?" Scheck asked Felbin.

"I have a concern about whether he will try to torpedo his father's campaign. I also have some concern about the additional publicity surrounding his case. When we file the Jenkins case, it will hit the news, and Garner's involvement will be a part of the story. He was emotionally fragile when he left for Europe and I don't know how opening this up will impact him. There's also the question of how all of this will impact the Jenkins case."

Scheck hadn't considered the issues Felbin was raising. "Obviously, I need to think about this a little more. But let me ask you about the publicity after Cardwell acquitted him. Was it favorable or unfavorable to her?" Scheck asked.

"Although there was no proof the case was fixed, it was pretty clear what happened. What she did and why she did it. The coverage was not kind and the commentary from all sources was brutal. But she survived and is still on the bench. Go figure."

"Was there any suggestion Garner was part of that fix?"

"No. My relationship and disdain for both Cardwell and Garner's father was well known. It was also clear to the media and everyone else Garner and I had nothing to do with her final decision about prosecutorial misconduct. He was innocent. Her decision might have kept him out of the penitentiary but didn't help him otherwise."

As Felbin was speaking, Scheck was trying to weigh the positives and negatives of Garner's involvement. Scheck had to do what was in the best interests of the client. "Since she was at least inferentially identified as corrupt, Garner's involvement might help Jenkins. If he were part of her decision to acquit him, he would not be returning to St. Louis to pursue her in an old rape case. That wouldn't make any sense. He would be doing what he could to support her. And presumably his father wouldn't do anything to help her since he's in the middle of a campaign and she would be toxic for him. But since he wasn't involved, Garner's presence might help focus attention on her corruption. Corrupt as a judge. Corrupt as a prosecutor. But we don't know how Garner will feel about all of this."

"I agree with your analysis about the Jenkins case. As far as Garner is concerned, you need to talk to him," Felbin said.

"I will, and he'll make the final decision. I'll call you and let you know what he decides. But we need to move on this case. If DNA is going to free this guy, we need to do it soon. He's been locked up too long."

"I'll wait to hear from you and look forward to getting a copy of the file."

When the conversation ended, Felbin began to wonder whether he should have explained his concerns about Garner's return to St. Louis in greater detail. The more he thought about it, the more he was thinking this wasn't a good idea. He had only spoken to Garner on the phone and was uncertain of his present state of mind. He knew Garner was depressed when he left St. Louis. With Cardwell back in the news, the murder prosecution would be revived, whether or not Garner represented Jenkins, since Felbin would be involved. But there would be added interest if Garner was representing someone victimized by the person who acquitted him of murder. Felbin hoped Garner would realize this when he decided whether to return to St. Louis. He also hoped revenge and retaliation would play no role in his decision.

Chapter Eleven

As promised, Scheck sent Felbin a copy of his file which contained the police report, trial transcripts and a very preliminary investigation into this cold case. According to the Innocence Project's file, Larry Jenkins had spent a good portion of his adult life in the penitentiary for rape. Actually, there had been two rapes. Or at least two times he'd been accused of rape. The first time he was arrested and charged, but the case was dismissed. The last time, the jury found him guilty and he had served seventeen years for the crimes of rape, sodomy and kidnapping.

One January evening more than seventeen years before, an African American man forced his way into the vehicle of a young white woman, Janet Costello, who was in a parking lot in the 3700 block of Lindell Boulevard in the City of St. Louis and raped her at knifepoint. At the time, Costello was a student at St. Louis University living in an apartment on North Taylor with her roommates, Cara Fowler and Virginia Paul. According to the police report of the incident, the attacker concealed his face with a scarf which came off during the attack. The victim described the assailant as a dark-skinned black male with thick lips, five-ten, about 185 pounds, clean shaven with a pudgy face and no identifying body marks.

The police report indicated the victim was shown fifteen mug shots including Jenkins, who was known to Ellen Rossi and Patrick Moore, the detectives handling the case. They knew Jenkins had previously been charged with rape, which is why his photograph was included in the spread. He also lived a few blocks from where the rape occurred. Jenkins was a light-skinned black, five-eight, 170 pounds with average size lips. Nonetheless, he was selected from the photo spread.

Within hours of the identification, Jenkins was arrested for rape. Joan Cardwell was an assistant circuit attorney at the time. In the city of St. Louis, the circuit attorney is elected and hires assistants to handle and try the cases. Decisions of whether to prosecute are made by the assistants based on information brought to them by St. Louis police officers. When Rossi and Moore brought the case to Cardwell, she issued a warrant for the arrest of Larry Jenkins for the rape of Janet Costello. Cardwell tried the case she issued, and a jury found Jenkins guilty of rape, sodomy and kidnapping after the victim positively identified him as her assailant. He was sentenced to life imprisonment plus an additional 30 years.

Jenkins was represented by a young public defender. Dean Williams had been out of law school for a little more than two years when he was assigned the case of State of Missouri versus Larry Jenkins. Although he had handled felony cases during his time at the Office of the Public Defender, he'd never tried one. His previous felony cases had resulted in negotiated pleas of guilty. But the case of Larry Jenkins would not be a plea. He had a prior arrest and was charged with rape, but it was dismissed. The state wanted him off the street and in the penitentiary. They believed he was also good for the rape which was dismissed. His picture was routinely placed in photo lineups where a rape was involved. But more importantly, Cardwell was about to toss her hat into the ring to become the elected prosecutor and needed a win. A win in a high-profile case would increase her stock when she ran.

The rape of Janet Costello occurred in the vicinity of St. Louis University campus. Her rape had been one of several in the area which had not been solved. The students at the university, along with their parents, were worried that a serial rapist was around the campus and would strike again. Their concerns were expressed in multiple print and electronic media accounts. The St. Louis Police Department was under mounting pressure to catch the person responsible.

The Public Defender's office in the city of St. Louis had some very fine lawyers. Most were young and working there to get trial experience. Unfortunately, these lawyers were overworked and underpaid. The Missouri legislature was not big on allocating funds to free rapists, murderers and the like. Annually, the office would publicly battle the legislature for more funds, and their pleas would routinely be ignored.

Eighty was the average caseload per public defender in the city. Because he was relatively new and inexperienced, Dean Williams only carried fifty on average. Investigators were also in short supply. The city had a total of three. These men and women did the best they could under the circumstances, but no one was surprised when things fell through the cracks. And the courts weren't about to set convictions aside because of public defenders being under-staffed and underfunded.

After Felbin reviewed the Larry Jenkins file Scheck had sent him, he asked Carmine to come into his office. They'd had little conversation since the last discussion about Garner following the phone call from Cassandra Lee. Felbin was still pissed Carmine somehow let her know Garner would be coming to work for them.

Without exchanging any preliminary pleasantries, Felbin told his investigator to have a seat when he entered the office. "We have a new case I'm confident you will be interested in. It needs some work. We have..." Felbin began. He was interrupted by Carmine.

"Listen. Before we get started with this new case, I just wanted to apologize for the Cassandra Lee incident. I know you think I got the word to her about Garner and you were pissed. And probably still are. I..."

Now it was Felbin's turn to interrupt. "Relax, Tony. We both know what you did and why you did it. You're the type of guy who would rather beg for forgiveness rather than ask for permission. I get it. I also know I'm not going to change you. We need to move on; otherwise you will spend the rest of your life apologizing to me. And, frankly, I'd rather listen to Cardwell lecture on judicial ethics."

"See, this is what I call progress," Carmine said.

Felbin just shook his head and then moved on to the real point of the meeting. "As I was saying, we have a new case which needs some investigation. Do you know where I can find a good investigator?"

Now it was Carmine's turn to shake his head, but he resisted the temptation to respond.

Felbin continued, "I got a phone call from Barry Scheck who sent another Innocence Project case here. This one is about an old rape. The guy's been locked up for over seventeen years. I read the file and confirmed Barry's thought. It was weak and a good candidate for DNA analysis. We may get some resistance from the prosecutor's office when we ask to test the evidence. I'll send a letter. In the meantime, we need to do some leg work and rework all the evidence including interviews of witnesses. There are some unanswered questions in the report. Here is a copy of the file Barry sent over," Felbin said as he handed Carmine the documents.

As Carmine began to look through the file, Felbin hesitated for a moment but then added, "There is something else you need to know. Actually, there are a couple other things you need to know."

"What?"

"First of all, the prosecutor involved in this case is Cardwell. The second thing..."

A loud scream of joy muffled Felbin's second disclosure. Carmine couldn't control his excitement. "Are you shittin' me? She prosecuted and convicted an innocent man who has been locked up for over seventeen years? Holy shit. Yes, there is a God."

"We don't know if he's innocent. The file I just gave you would suggest at the very least the case is weak."

"I'll bet my last dollar she pulled some illegal or unethical bullshit. It's in her DNA. But I guarantee I'll find it. And then maybe this time we can get her ass kicked off the bench and out of the profession for good," Carmine said, excitement still in his voice.

"There's also something else I need to tell you."

"Whatever it is, it can't be better than putting Cardwell in my cross hairs."

"I think it might be. Garner will be working with us on this case."

Carmine didn't react immediately. He was processing the information and didn't know what to make of it. Finally, he said, "What do you mean he will be working with us on this case? Did we hire him like I wanted?"

"No, we didn't hire him. But the Innocence Project did. They are sending him here to work on the case with us and be the liaison. At first, I wasn't sure this was a good idea and explained the problems with the murder prosecution, including the issues with Cardwell and his father. Eventually, we both decided to leave it up to Garner to decide whether he wanted to come here. I got a call a little while ago from Barry who said Garner decided to come."

"Holy shit. Can my life get any better? I get to fuck with Cardwell with the guy she fucked over. Wow. When do I start?"

"Immediately. If this guy is innocent, he shouldn't spend another minute locked up."

Chapter Twelve

Flight number 1262, nonstop from LaGuardia to St. Louis, was uneventful. Although Garner Lee was excited about starting his new job, particularly because it might involve a person wrongfully convicted, but he was also apprehensive about returning to his hometown. He read the Jenkins file during the two and a half hours he spent in the air. Even as an inexperienced lawyer, the more he read, the more he could see how weak the prosecution was. But as he read the trial transcript and in particular, Cardwell's direct examination of the victim, he knew he had to be objective in evaluating the case. This was about freeing an innocent man, not screwing an incompetent prosecutor, now a corrupt judge.

As the plane flew over the St. Louis skyline, Garner closed the Jenkins file. He could see the building that housed the criminal courts where a jury decided he'd murdered his girlfriend. Instantly, he flashed to Amy's apartment. He could see her lying on the floor, blood covering her head. She was dead. He knew it as soon as he opened the door and saw her lifeless body. The image was etched forever in his brain. But that wasn't the worst part. He didn't kill her and didn't know who did. It was what had kept him up almost every night he spent in Europe. He needed to find the killer and would not rest until he did.

After landing, the plane taxied to gate 58 on the A concourse, where the passengers on this full flight would deplane. He was in seat 58 B in the back. The Innocence Project was on a tight budget and didn't pay extra for prime seats. Garner would have to wait. He didn't mind. As he watched others in the seats in front of him gathering their belongings from the overhead rack, he began to wonder whether coming back to St. Louis was a good idea. Finally, his turn came. He made his way down the narrow isle toward the exit door, uncertain what the future would bring.

But he was certain of one thing. He could not allow the death of the woman he loved continue to live in his head.

Tony Carmine was waiting for him in the baggage claim area. As soon as Garner left the security area, Carmine spotted him. He rushed to welcome him home, a handshake giving way to a hug. While the murder case was pending, Carmine and Garner became more than client and investigator. They became friends. The friendship continued for a short time after Garner left for Europe. Then contact was lost. Garner was living in his own head and shutting out everything else.

"It's really good to see you, my friend," Carmine said.

"It's really good to see you too, Tony," Garner replied.

"We got you a suite at the Chase downtown. Do you want to grab some dinner and then I can take you to the hotel? Or would you rather go to the hotel first? We can also have dinner there. The Tenderloin Room is a great restaurant. Or we can hit one of the restaurants in the Central West End."

"Let's go to the hotel and I can drop my stuff off and wash up," Garner said. As an afterthought, he added, "The Chase? I didn't think the Innocent Project had that kind of a budget."

"It doesn't. This is on Felbin. He thinks you need to be comfortable during your stay, given what you went through the last time you were here."

Located in the heart of the Central West End of the City of St. Louis, the Chase Park Plaza Hotel has a celebrated history dating back to 1922. Elegance, luxurious amenities and location have attracted guests that included Frank Sinatra and President Jimmie Carter. The Central West End is an upscale community which is home to sidewalk cafes, antique shops, boutiques, and fine restaurants. Nearby Forest Park, the gem of St. Louis, is filled with lakes and attractions including the St. Louis Zoo, The St. Louis Art Museum, History Museum, Science Center and an outdoor amphitheater, The St. Louis Municipal Opera Theater (*The Muny*) with summer productions of both classic and contemporary Broadway hits.

The short ride from Lambert International Airport to the hotel was filled with small talk to renew an old friendship. Carmine had some other issues to discuss. But he wanted to wait until they were relaxing at a nice restaurant having dinner and a few drinks.

After Garner checked in, they decided to have dinner at the Tenderloin Room. Located inside the Chase Park Plaza, the ambience of the restaurant matched the elegance of the hotel. Dark oak, atmospheric lighting, linen tablecloths, white as a fresh winter snow and thick carpeting designed to stifle sound separated this restaurant from all other steakhouses. After ordering a couple of appetizers, carpaccio for Carmine, calamari for Garner and a 2014 Rombauer California Merlot for both, Carmine was ready to get down to business. He needed to have a conversation with Garner outside the presence of Felbin. Having dinner after meeting Garner at the airport presented an opportunity. But he also needed to make sure this conversation remained between just the two of them. He knew he would be in the unemployment line if Felbin ever found out.

"Have you kept up with the news of our fair city?" Carmine began.

"Actually, I haven't. Frankly, St. Louis and Cardwell were the last things I was interested in while I was in London. I spent a lot of time in the pub trying to get this place out of my head."

"I completely understand. But why did you come back here?"

"I asked myself the same question when the plane landed. As you know, after the trial, I ran, left town, instead of taking the good advice you guys gave me. I should have gotten some professional help. But I didn't. And the more I drank the worst it got. Then I ran out of money and had to come back to the states. Of course, I had no job and didn't know what I was going to do. Thanks to Felbin, I landed a spot with the Innocence Project. When this case came up and Barry asked me to come here, I knew sooner or later I had to face my demons. Plus, I really didn't want to tell the guy who just gave me a job I didn't want to take a case."

"How do you plan to face your demons?"

Before Garner could answer, the waiter arrived with the appetizers and wine. Carmine wondered how Garner would answer his question as the waiter uncorked the wine and poured a small amount in his glass. After a quick taste, the waiter received the approval to pour. A toast repeated Carmine's pleasure to see his friend again. Fine wine and good food temporarily replaced conversation, which was difficult for Garner Lee.

Finally, Garner answered his friend's question. But it was obvious he had no real game plan. "I need to take this a day at a time. I want to visit her grave and drive by her apartment, for starters."

"How do you think that will help?"

Garner considered the question for a moment before responding. Finally, he said "I really don't know. But it's just something I think I need to do. Maybe it'll help give me some closure."

"Have you had any contact with your parents?"

"I think you know the answer, Tony. I have no use for either one of them," Garner said, rekindled anger and frustration obvious in his voice.

"I assume you at least know your father's campaign is in full swing?"

"I obviously knew he was running for governor. But I have no idea about the progress of his campaign. I hope the son of a bitch gets his ass kicked."

"Funny you should say that." Carmine paused as the waiter approached. "I have some ideas about how an ass kicking can be accomplished."

Garner ordered the lamb chops, medium rare, and asparagus. For the investigator, a filet, medium and a baked potato with butter and sour cream. After the waiter poured more wine, the conversation continued.

"I'm listening," Garner said, obviously interested in anything designed to torpedo his father's effort to become Missouri's next governor.

After Garner learned of his father's involvement with Amy, he was determined to ruin not only his political career but also his marriage. First, he had a conversation with his mother. When she was more concerned about how this would impact her future political plans, Garner fled to Europe, depressed and disillusioned. He knew his father impregnated his girlfriend and had been a prime suspect in her murder. Nobody cared then. But now he was back with a renewed determination to do what should have been done before instead of running away.

"I have several ideas. But first you have to promise me this conversation is just between us. Felbin will not be on board with any effort to trash your old man. Deal?"

"Deal," Garner replied without hesitation.

"Your father is ahead in the polls currently." Carmine looked at Garner to see if there was any reaction. When he saw none, he continued. "I thought about a lot of ways to bring this bastard down, starting with the direct approach. I considered approaching him directly with a threat of releasing all of the details of his involvement with Amy unless he withdrew from the race."

"He would never withdraw. He'd figure if Trump, who has the morals of an alley cat, can get elected President of the United States after all the publicity about his philandering, people don't care about moral issues like this anymore. He would take his chances."

"And he may be right," Carmine said, shaking his head in agreement. "I think what we need to do first is let the media know you're in town. They'll find out soon enough anyway. Then we need to tell them you will be attending a big dollar fundraiser your father is having at the Ritz. Darius Washington will be there to campaign and raise money for him. The press will be all over it because he's bringing a celebrity to town. Instead of Darius Washington, I was thinking we can make you the headliner. Sound good?"

"Sounds great. I like it," Garner said, as the waiter appeared at their table and began to serve their dinners.

"I'll put together the details and let you know. Now let's enjoy this fine meal. We could also use another bottle of wine," Carmine said as he directed the waiter's attention to the empty bottle.

Chapter Thirteen

While Garner was meeting with Felbin early the next morning to plan the strategy for the Larry Jenkins DNA case, Karen Braxton was meeting with Judge Joan Cardwell. Braxton replaced Cardwell as the circuit attorney for the City of St. Louis when she went on the bench. She would hold the office for Cardwell's unexpired term. She would then have to run in order to keep the job.

Braxton had been the first assistant for the entire time Cardwell held this elected office. She came from a large firm and had no criminal law experience. For that matter, she had no trial experience of any kind. Among lawyers both inside and outside the circuit attorney's office, Karen Braxton was viewed as Joan Cardwell's lap dog. She was the person, along with Myra Long, the public relations director, who made Cardwell look good. If a case was successful and a notorious criminal was put away for a long time, Cardwell would take the bow. If a case went south, Braxton would take the fall. Neither enjoyed a reputation of competence.

Braxton had received Felbin's letter a few days prior requesting a DNA analysis. He said it was a rape case and wanted to compare any DNA on the victim's panties, a sweater or any other article of clothing with that of his client. She pulled the Larry Jenkins file. She was not with the office when the case was tried. Felbin's letter indicated he, along with Barry Scheck and the Innocence Project would be representing Jenkins. She knew the reputation of the Innocence Project and Scheck. And, of course, she knew Felbin.

The case looked straightforward. Not a lot of evidence but a clear, unequivocal identification of the defendant by the victim. There was no forensic evidence but those were the days when the benefits of DNA were unknown. Now, defense lawyers were demanding DNA comparisons in those cases where they deemed the evidence to be weak and convictions based almost entirely on victim identifications. The State of Missouri versus Larry Jenkins was one such case.

While the case looked straightforward, there was one wrinkle. Joan Cardwell was the prosecutor. Felbin and Cardwell together again after the Garner Lee trial would only be exciting to news outlets who were selling advertising time. It was nothing an interim circuit attorney would embrace. The Jenkins case wasn't going away, and Braxton knew it. She had to deal with the issue. Talking to her former boss was the first distasteful step.

Ordinarily, if Braxton wanted to speak to Cardwell, she would just show up at her office and close the door. This time was different. She called Mary McMurtry, Cardwell's long-time personal secretary and close friend, who was close to the mandatory retirement at age of seventy. She needed a private uninterrupted conversation at a time when Cardwell was in a good mood. McMurtry agreed to let her know when the time was right.

When Braxton arrived at Cardwell's chambers, Mary gave her a thumbs up. It was Friday and a good day. Cardwell was vacationing in Cancun the following week with a new boyfriend. She had been divorced for some five years, with two adult children who lived out of town. Since her divorce, she had been through several relationships, each ending badly. This time, Mary was optimistic the new relationship might last, at least longer than her usual two-week average. Relaxing on the white sandy beaches of Mexico could only help Cardwell's pathetic love life.

The conversation began pleasant enough, with Cardwell describing her new boyfriend and upcoming trip. Braxton knew things would change as soon as her real purpose for the visit was disclosed. It wouldn't be the challenge to a prior conviction which would set Cardwell into a tailspin. Rather, the involvement of Felbin in the wake of the Garner Lee case.

"I recently received a request to access some evidence for a DNA analysis in an old rape case of yours," Braxton began.

Cardwell hesitated and then asked, "What case?"

"Larry Jenkins," Braxton said.

When Braxton mentioned the name, Cardwell looked away. Obviously, she recognized the name but made no immediate response. Recognizing some discomfort, Braxton then added, "Do you recognize this case?"

"Vaguely," Cardwell responded tentatively.

Braxton sensed something was wrong. But she needed to press forward to let her former boss know everything. "I looked at the file and it looks like a pretty simple, straight-forward case. The victim made a positive unequivocal ID in a photo spread and at trial. The rape occurred around St. Louis University, and this guy lived in the neighborhood. Plus, he had a prior arrest for rape, but the case was dismissed. Ring any bells?"

Another pregnant pause and then finally, Cardwell said, "Not really. What are you planning to do?"

"I was planning to work out an arrangement where we can both do the DNA testing under conditions controlled by both sides."

"Why?" Cardwell asked.

"Because according to the police reports and the trial testimony, this was a strong victim with a positive identification. I don't think the DNA is going to contradict her. If it does and we have the wrong guy, I think we should know that as well. And if we have the wrong guy and recognize it, we can increase our stock with the black community around here. As you know, those folks think we have a different prosecutorial standard for them compared to white suspects."

This time Cardwell's response was immediate. "I disagree. You need to think about the victim and what this will do to her. She will have to relive this nightmare. This guy got a fair trial. A jury, not us, decided he was guilty. A judge sentenced him, not us. Then he went to the court of appeals complaining he wasn't guilty and lost there. How many times do we have to deal with this case and this guy? Nobody is ever guilty. Now, we have these defense lawyers running us all over the place with frivolous claims of innocence through DNA testing. Who represents this Jenkins guy?"

Now it was Braxton's turn to hesitate before answering. "Barry Scheck at the Innocence Project in New York and Felbin," she said in almost a whisper.

Cardwell erupted. "No fuckin' way. You are not turning anything over to that prick. He probably got involved in this case just to fuck me over for both the Lee and Decker cases. You know he will publicly crucify me."

"What am I supposed to do with the request?"

"Tell him to stick it up his ass," Cardwell replied in her most professional tone.

"I realize the problem with Felbin. But if we refuse to produce the evidence for a test, it will look like we have something to hide. We will be attracting more media attention than this is worth. It just seems to me the easiest course is to turn it over, coordinate the testing and be done with it, unless I'm missing something."

"They want this test because they know sometimes eyewitness identifications are wrong. This is a fishing expedition and needs to be stopped immediately," Cardwell said.

"Do you have any reason to doubt your victim? Was she wrong in her identification?" Braxton asked.

"I don't even recall the case but apparently the victim was strong and believable. I don't need any aggravation and bullshit while Felbin is doing his tests. Let's be clear on this. You are not going to turn over that evidence or agree to any testing. Are we clear?"

It was quite clear to Braxton. Although she believed this course would create more problems for everyone concerned, she had no choice. She was the current circuit attorney and technically would make the final decision. But she had to stand for election in the near future and needed the support of her former boss and her political allies.

Rather than put anything in writing which could wind up in the newspaper, she decided to call Felbin and give him the bad news. She would not be turning over any evidence or participating in any DNA testing in the case of State of Missouri versus Larry Jenkins.

Chapter Fourteen

Bagels, cream cheese, orange juice and hot coffee were brought into the large conference room of Felbin's office. Garner, Carmine and Felbin were meeting to plan the strategy for the Jenkins case. But before they talked about freeing Larry Jenkins, Garner had something to say.

"Before we begin, I just want to tell you how much I appreciate what you've done for me. Without your help, I don't know what I would be doing now. When I did the interviews with those New York firms, I wasn't sure what you told them about me. I quickly learned they didn't know anything about my checkered past. I had a decision to make when the questions began. I decided I wouldn't volunteer any information but would answer their questions truthfully. You should've seen the look on one guy's face when he asked how I knew you and I told him you were my lawyer. And the look didn't improve when I told him you represented me in a murder case."

"No shit," Carmine said. "I would've paid money to see that. I got no time for those silk stocking pricks."

While pouring a cup of coffee, Felbin said, "I didn't say anything because nobody asked how I knew you. I figured if they hired you and you did well, we could explain the background later if necessary."

"Well, maybe someday when we find Amy's real killer, there won't be anything to explain," Garner said.

Felbin and Carmine just looked at each other and didn't respond to the comment. Instead, Felbin changed the subject. "Have you had a chance to read the Jenkins file?"

"Yes, I studied it before I left New York and read it again during my flight here. I also talked to Barry about it at some length. I don't know much about criminal law, but the case looks weak to me."

"It looks weak to us, too. I gave the file to Tony after we got it and he has been doing some preliminary leg work. I'm assuming Braxton is not going to agree to let us do the testing given the involvement of Cardwell. What did you find out so far?" Felbin asked his investigator.

"Both Ellen Rossi and Patrick Moore, the detectives who worked the case, are no longer with the department. I haven't been able to find Moore, but I tracked Rossi down. She's living in the Florida Keys. The victim, Janet Costello, now Janet Snead, is married and living in Fenton. The judge who presided over the case is dead. I wanted to wait to contact people until after we had a chance to plan our strategy. I also don't think Braxton is going to cooperate and we need to move forward," Carmine said as he took a bite of bagel covered with about an inch of cream cheese.

"Once again, I've got no experience in this stuff, but I don't understand why Braxton wouldn't agree to let us test the evidence. Wouldn't she want to know if an innocent guy is in prison?"

Before Felbin could respond, Carmine said, "Wow, you are naïve and don't know shit about this business."

"This isn't about Braxton. It's about Cardwell. She took a lot of heat from the media in your case. She can't handle any more bad press if she prosecuted an innocent man. For her it's all about protecting the brand, which is herself," Felbin said.

"And she couldn't give a shit less about whether an innocent man has been locked up for half his life. Just as she didn't give a shit about prosecuting Bobby Decker, another innocent man. And then this fuckin' bitch killed him," Tony added.

No sooner did Felbin and his investigator finish excoriating Judge Cardwell than they were told Braxton was on the line. Felbin put her on the speaker phone so all could hear.

"Karen, how are you? I assume you are calling in response to my letter in the Larry Jenkins case. When can we pick up the clothing to do the DNA testing?" Felbin asked facetiously, knowing full well Braxton—or rather Cardwell—wasn't going to agree to anything.

"You're not getting anything," Braxton replied.

One of the few things Felbin liked about this circuit attorney. Although completely incompetent, she got right to the point. No bullshit. No idle chatter. "This is a weak prosecution and I think you have an innocent man who has been locked up for most of his adult life."

"I really don't care what you think, Mr. Felbin. Lawyers are always confident before the verdict. It's just afterwards when they share their doubts."

"DNA can prove me either right or wrong. And just think, Karen, if I'm wrong, you get to tell everyone I'm wrong. That should make you feel happy. But independently of this benefit, why would you not agree to a simple test?"

"A jury believed our victim and found your guy guilty of rape and I'm not going to put her through this again."

"There is nothing to put the victim through. You give us the clothes and we do the test. If you cooperate, there is no testimony needed from Ms. Snead. No reason to take her out of Fenton."

Felbin wanted to let Braxton know he had the victim's married name and address and would involve her, if necessary, to protect his client.

"Ms. Snead is still a victim of a rape, even if Jenkins didn't do it. I would think she would want the true perpetrator identified. I would also think you would want to prosecute the person responsible as well," he added.

"Notwithstanding your rhetoric, Mr. Felbin, as I said, we are not subjecting our victim to this."

"You're not subjecting your victim to a process of learning the truth about what happened or you're not subjecting Cardwell to a search for the truth for fear she convicted an innocent man? Everyone already knows she was just as incompetent and corrupt as the circuit attorney as she is as a judge."

"Mr. Felbin, this conversation is going nowhere and is over. Have a nice day," Braxton said.

"Before you hang up on me, I have something else you might be interested in. As I said in my letter, I'm working with the Innocence Project out of New York and Barry Scheck on this case. They have now assigned one of their young lawyers and sent him to St. Louis to assist us. You might recognize his name—Garner Lee. And you have a nice day as well, Karen."

As soon as Felbin hung up, Carmine said in a voice loud enough for Braxton to hear him twenty blocks away, "That was fuckin' sweet. Garner's on the case, bitch."

Felbin reacted with only a head shake as Garner was still trying to process the entire conversation.

"Did you plan to tell her about Garner?" Carmine asked.

"No, it just came out," Felbin said.

Although Garner had been forewarned, he was having trouble wrapping his arms around the idea a prosecutor would not be interested in the truth. At some level, he now understood why he had been prosecuted, given his denial about being in Amy's apartment. The science proved he was lying. But Jenkins was different. The science could establish his innocence.

"What do we do now?" Garner asked.

"We file suit and try to get a court order to do the test. In the meantime, Tony, you need to contact Rossi and Snead. I suspect we will eventually have a need for their testimony. I also think we need to try to track down Snead's roommates who are mentioned in the report. She might have had some conversations with them which would be useful to us. Thanks to Braxton and Cardwell, the victim will now be forced to relive a painful time in her life."

Chapter Fifteen

Carmine knew Ellen Rossi from his days with the St. Louis Metropolitan Police Department. They were friends. Although he was never her partner, he worked with her on a few cases and knew she had a reputation as an honest, hardworking detective. Rossi came from a large Sicilian family. Her father was a police officer, and relatives ran a popular Italian restaurant for thirty years in the city of St. Louis. Although her family was well known, she never used any political steam to get promoted, a necessity in this department, but rose quickly from a uniform patrol officer to detective based upon her investigative ability.

Rossi remembered the Jenkins case, which surprised Carmine. She agreed to discuss it with him if he wanted to visit her in Key West. He agreed, and she told him she would be available whenever his schedule permitted. She would look forward to the meeting and even promised to take him on a tour of the island.

In the meantime, Carmine needed to talk to the victim, Janet Costello-Snead. She was 40 and married, with two beautiful children. Her daughter was a senior and her son a sophomore in the high school where she taught English. Her husband, a former professional baseball player, was an executive with Anheuser Busch and they lived in Fenton, a suburb in St. Louis County. Her life was perfect. Carmine left several voicemail messages, but received no return call. They needed to knock on her door. Her perfect life was about to become complicated.

With school ending for her at 2:45, Snead usually arrived home around 3:15. Her children had after school sporting activities and didn't come home until dinner time. Garner and Carmine decided to pay her a visit before her husband got home. They didn't know what he knew about what had happened to her some nineteen years ago when she was twenty years old. Their purpose was to have a private conversation to see if she would consent to the DNA test.

Tony and Garner arrived at the Snead residence at 2:45 and waited across the street for Janet Snead to come home from school. At 3:10 on a beautiful, sunny, fall afternoon, the garage door opened and a red 320i BMW drove onto the driveway and into the garage. An attractive woman with long blond hair got out of the car. She wore grey slacks, a white starched blouse underneath a blue blazer and red flats. Janet Snead's driver's license photograph and description—5'10", 135 pounds—matched the person in the garage.

She was retrieving papers from the back seat of her car when Carmine called out her name, as he and Garner walked up the driveway. "Ms. Snead can we have a word with you?" She was startled and appeared to be frightened. In order to calm the situation, Carmine introduced himself and Garner. "I am an investigator with Jonathan Felbin's office. This is Garner Lee, a lawyer from New York. I left several voicemails for you. We would like to talk to you."

The introductions seemed to calm her. "What's this about? Why do you need to talk to me?"

"It's about a very private and sensitive matter which happened to you some nineteen years ago."

The blood drained from her face and her skin turned ashen. She looked as if she would faint. She knew exactly what they were talking about. An investigator and a black lawyer from New York could not be good for her. "My husband and my children don't know anything about this," she finally said.

"It is not our intention to say anything to them, which is the reason we are here now. We represent Larry Jenkins," Carmine said. With the sound of that name, a name she had not heard in many years, her body stiffened.

"He's still in jail, I hope."

"Yes, ma'am, he is," Carmine said.

"So, what do you want from me?"

"We would like to have your permission to do a DNA test on the clothing you were wearing the night of this incident."

"For what?" Snead asked perplexed by the request.

"We want to see if the DNA on your clothing matches Larry's."

"He brutally raped me. I thought he was going to kill me. He's an animal. His DNA will match," she said emphatically.

Garner observed her demeanor as the investigator continued choosing his words carefully. "I understand that you believe he's the one who did this to you. But sometimes our mind plays tricks during traumatic events. And we just want to be sure. When Larry's case was tried, we didn't have the science to absolutely answer these questions. Back then we had to rely primarily on the ability of victims to identify individuals during these traumatic events."

"I wasn't wrong when I identified him. I remember his face vividly as he was ripping my clothes off and then getting on top of me," she said, tears forming and her voice beginning to crack. She recalled her trial testimony and her identification of Larry Jenkins those many years ago. She was certain. She had to be.

"I understand. But this test will be conclusive."

"What happens if I don't agree?"

Carmine had anticipated this question. Even if this victim consented, Braxton didn't have to release the evidence for testing, and a suit would need to be filed. A public airing would be necessary to determine if enough evidence existed to persuade a court to order the test. Necessarily, it meant compelling the victim to testify. He decided to avoid the question. "If you consent, we just get the clothes from the prosecutor and do the test. You're not involved."

"And what happens if the DNA doesn't match?"

Carmine wasn't prepared for this question. Neither was Garner. "An investigation would be conducted."

"Which means this nightmare starts all over again and my husband and children are dragged into it. I won't consent, Mr. Carmine," Snead finally said.

Now Carmine needed to give her the really bad news. "Mrs. Snead, I need to tell you if you don't consent, we will have to file suit to ask the court to order the test. Unfortunately, your testimony will then be necessary."

"No, no, no. I can't go through this again." She began to cry uncontrollably. "Please leave."

On their way back to the office, Garner said, "She seemed pretty positive Larry was the guy."

"What I told her was the truth. Eyewitness identifications under traumatic circumstances are generally unreliable. I doubt she is an exception. The only way to be sure is through the DNA. I feel sorry for her, but if she's wrong, a great injustice has occurred. But we'll need to put this case aside for the moment," Carmine said, changing the subject. "We need to attend your father's gala fundraiser tomorrow evening at the Ritz. Maybe you can shake hands with Darius Washington and tell him what you think of the campaign."

Chapter Sixteen

The next day, a civil rights suit was filed in the Circuit Court for the City of St. Louis seeking injunctive relief to compel the circuit attorney to surrender the evidence necessary to do DNA testing. The suit attracted minimal media attention. Apparently, Garner Lee's name on the pleading was missed. Through phone calls to every reporter covering Winston Lee's campaign, Carmine made sure Garner's presence at the Darius Washington big fundraiser would not be missed.

The main ballroom of the Ritz in downtown Clayton, a city within St. Louis County, was packed by the time Garner and Carmine arrived. They decided to hang back until the speeches began. This strategy would give them the most bang for their buck.

Everyone who was anyone in business or Democratic party politics was there. Each looking to be seen and anxious to hitch their wagon to what they perceived to be a winner and reap the eventual spoils. This was one of the many things Garner Lee hated about politics. People giving money to politicians who lie, to them to get elected and then look to recoup their investment after the election. Garner had witnessed this show his entire life. He couldn't think of a single politician who always told the truth. Tell them what they want to hear, get elected and then do what you want afterward. The standard playbook of every politician.

As Garner waited for the moment to make his grand entrance, his thoughts turned to Amy. Since the trial, he'd had plenty of time to reflect on the behavior of her and his father. Who did he blame the most? How could two people he loved be so callous and cruel? Maybe it was his fault. He searched his memory for answers. Was it a repayment or revenge? These questions and others lingered without answers. They haunted him as much as the entire case haunted Felbin.

But now was the time to get his revenge. He wondered how it would feel afterwards. His father had betrayed his only son. Obviously, that meant nothing to him. The only thing he really cared about was his precious career. And now Garner was going to do what he could to damage his father's career and prevent him from becoming the next governor of the State of Missouri. He would be doing everyone a favor. Someone like his father who was morally bankrupt could not be trusted to be the guardian of Missouri's children.

When Darius Washington began to speak, Garner entered the room from the rear. He was wearing a dark blue business suit, white shirt and a pink tie. The *Raymond Singer for Governor* campaign button he wore proudly on his lapel was attracting some attention and quiet commentary as he slowly made his way through the crowd toward the stage.

As people recognized him along the way, the comments grew louder, finally attracting the attention of the reporters. The television cameras, which had been focused on the celebrity on stage were now pointed at Garner, who was nearing the front as Darius Washington introduced the candidate. After soaking in the adoration for what seemed like an eternity to Garner, Winston Lee began to speak.

As the candidate was waxing eloquent about what he was going to do for Missouri with the actor by his side, Garner was now standing in front of the stage and staring at his father, knives buried deep in his eyes. Finally, he couldn't take it anymore and yelled, "Why don't you tell them what you did for me, your son? Why don't you tell them how you had sex with my girlfriend, the white woman you hated? And don't forget to mention the most important thing. You got her pregnant."

Winston Lee had been heckled before. But never by his son announcing to a room full of supporters his moral indiscretions. When the yelling began, Lee didn't recognize the voice. But it didn't take him long to see the source. He froze. His son was trying to humiliate him and disrupt his campaign.

When their eyes met, Garner said, "Hello, father. Glad to see me? Tell me, what did it feel like when you were having sex with Amy, the woman I loved? Were you thinking about me when you were doing it? How many times did you have sex before she became pregnant? Did you pick out a name for my half brother or sister? Oh wait. No time to discuss names because she was murdered. Right, my dear father?"

Lee was speechless. He didn't know what to do. But his head of security did. All eyes were focused on Garner as two very large muscular men dressed in blue blazers each grabbed one arm and escorted him out of the ballroom. Garner offered no resistance as the three walked to the door in the back of the room. Three television news crews and about fifteen reporters from around the state followed.

As Garner was being escorted out of the room, the candidate needed to decide. He could ignore the incident and pretend it never happened. Or he could comment. Either way, the damage had already been done. Darius Washington, still on the stage, looked confused at first and then concerned. He heard some suggestion his candidate killed someone to cover up a pregnancy, but he didn't completely understand what was going on. Winston Lee knew exactly what his son was doing.

In the few seconds he had to make his decision, Lee became angry with what his son had done. Even though it's never a good idea to make decisions in the heat of the moment, he couldn't ignore what just happened. He wanted to retaliate, even though Garner was no longer in the room.

"You just met my son. Given the button on his lapel, he apparently favors a different political party and candidate." The *Kool-Aid* drinking audience reacted with laughter. "Many of you may remember him when he was indicted for killing his girlfriend but was acquitted on a technicality." This time the audience didn't laugh. Before he returned to lauding his own greatness, he said, "Please forgive the rude interruption, as you can see my estranged son is intent on hurting me and bringing me down. But we are not going to let that happen. Are we?" His question was answered with resounding applause.

Cassandra Lee, who was standing next to Washington, showed no emotion. But like her husband, she was shocked and angry. What her son had done was inexcusable, at least in her world.

61

Outside the hotel, Garner Lee was telling a different story to the reporters as his father's security team and Tony Carmine looked on. He explained he had been living in London and was now living in New York. "Technically, by title only, he is my father. I haven't spoken to him since I found out he impregnated my girlfriend. Imagine finding out you might have a new little brother or sister whose mother you dated and loved."

"Was it your intent in coming here today to embarrass him and damage his campaign for governor?" one of the reporters asked.

"Since I returned to St. Louis, I found out he was out there selling himself to the unsuspecting people of Missouri. I know the real Winston Lee and I wanted to share it with those people in that room. If these disclosures embarrass him or damage his campaign, so be it. People need the whole picture to make an informed decision," Garner said.

"Do you plan to attend additional fundraisers or become actively involved in the campaign of his opponent whose button you're wearing?" another reporter asked.

"I'm here to represent a client who was wrongfully convicted many years ago. I'm working for the Innocence Project in New York, along with Jonathan Felbin, and we filed a lawsuit to do some DNA testing on this old rape case. I will speak about the person who claims to be my father when the situation warrants."

These political reporters weren't interested in Garner's legal case. They wanted to know about any future scuds he planned to drop into his father's campaign. These folks live for good drama in a mud-slinging political campaign. "Why don't you think he would he be a good governor? After all, he has a lot of political experience and knows his way around the state capital," one of them said.

"You're kidding! Did you not understand what I just said? My father was sleeping with my girlfriend. Having sexual intercourse with her, a woman my age and half of his. And he got her pregnant. Then she was murdered. If she hadn't been killed, she would have given birth to person who would have been my half brother or sister. Do you really think a person like him is good for Missouri or any other state?"

"This country elected a president who has the morals of an alley cat," someone commented. Garner ignored the comment.

"Do you believe your father murdered your girlfriend?"

"I think all of you need to go back inside now before he finishes delivering his bullshit and ask him the very same question you're asking me," Garner said as he headed for the parking lot with Carmine. They had to catch a flight to Key West to talk to Ellen Rossi.

During the short ride to the airport, Garner reflected on what he had done. On one level it felt good; but revenge always does. On another, all he really gained was sweet revenge since he couldn't turn the clock back. Amy was dead and she was unfaithful to him with his father. Those facts would never change, no matter what was done or said.

Carmine sat silently trying to figure out what he was going to say to Felbin who surely would see the coverage and blame him for failing to keep a tight leash on Garner. Or worse, encouraging him to do what he'd just done.

Chapter Seventeen

As he was finishing his speech, Senator Lee was looking for an escape route to avoid the throng of reporters awaiting him at the bottom of the stage stairs. There was no escape. There was also Darius Washington. He couldn't very well ask him to sneak off the stage and out of the hotel. As he descended the stairs followed by his wife and Washington, the questions began. "Your son said you impregnated his girlfriend? Is this true," one yelled. "He suggested you murdered her. Did you?" another asked.

The candidate had another decision to make. He could walk quickly toward the exit and ignore the questions, or he could respond along the way. He decided to err on the side of responding. "I didn't kill anyone."

"Then why would your son suggest you did?"

"He was the one who was charged with that murder by the prosecutor," Lee said as he continued to walk toward the exit with a very confused actor and an angry wife by his side.

"Did you get your son's girlfriend pregnant?"

Lee ignored the question.

"Does your wife know you were involved with your son's girlfriend and got her pregnant?"

Another question ignored.

The same question was directed to Cassandra Lee. She also ignored it and kept walking in search of the exit.

"Did your son suggest you killed this girl who apparently was half your age because you got her pregnant?" Now the reporters were baiting Lee, hoping he would give them some response.

With the last question, the candidate stopped, looked directly at one of television cameras and said, "Look, for the last time, I didn't kill anyone. As I said before, my son was charged with the murder of his girlfriend. He went to trial and a jury found him guilty. But eventually he was acquitted of murder based upon a legal technicality. There was never a finding by any judicial body or anyone else as to his actual innocence. So, you need to ask him whether he killed his girlfriend. I have nothing else to say."

Darius Washington listened to what his candidate was saying, uncertain what he was hearing. As he wondered whether he was supporting the wrong candidate, the reporters turned their attention to him. "Mr. Washington, did you know anything about Senator Lee's background and his involvement with his son's girlfriend before you decided to support him?"

"I know both Senator Lee and his wife, Cassandra. They are both good and decent people and I know the senator is what is best not only for Missouri but the country," the actor said.

"You didn't answer my question, sir. Did you know he was involved with his son's girlfriend and got her pregnant?"

"What he does or doesn't do in his personal life is his business. Obviously, the relationship with his son is strained. But as far as I'm concerned, his personal family issues have nothing to do with his ability to govern this state," Washington said as he entered a waiting limousine along with the candidate, his wife, and Kelvin Bellington, his campaign manager.

"What the hell was all this about? Murder, a pregnant girlfriend?" Washington asked. He needed some answers.

"Like I told them," Lee said pointing in the direction of the reporters, "my son's girlfriend turned up dead. He was charged with her murder and found guilty by a jury. He was later acquitted because of some legal technicality."

"What kind of technicality gets a murderer off the hook?" Washington pressed.

Lee knew exactly how and why the guilty verdict was set aside. But he wasn't going to share any information with Washington. He needed the support of Darius Washington. More importantly, he needed the financial support of Washington's Hollywood friends. He needed to make it sound like Garner was guilty, but an error by the prosecutor allowed him to go free. "The trial judge believed the prosecutor said something during the trial which was so bad the jury's verdict had to be set aside. And because of that misconduct, not only was the verdict set aside but an acquittal was entered. Because of the judge's decision, my son can never be tried for this murder again. This is exactly the reason I said there was never any finding my son was actually innocent."

"Wow," was all Washington could say as he tried to wrap his arms around the nuances of the criminal justice system. After a short pause, he said, "I gotta say this whole story sounds unbelievable to me. But I'm not a lawyer or a judge, thank God. In any event, were you involved with this girl and did you get her pregnant?"

Cassandra said nothing and showed no emotion. She wondered how her husband was going to handle the question.

Lee expected the question. He knew, given the reporters' questions, Washington was not going back to LA without some answers. The uncertainty was whether the truth about the pregnancy would ever be made public. He knew Felbin had a DNA test which proved he didn't kill Amy Deland. But he also had a test which proved he was the father of her child. Obviously, Garner also knew about the test, which is why he made the comments Washington heard earlier. If he told the truth, he ran the risk of not only potentially drying up his west coast funding but also of publicizing his admission. On the other hand, his denial could be refuted by the paternity test in the hands of Felbin, his mortal enemy, and his own son.

While looking out the window, Lee said, "I'm not the father of this lady's child. I had nothing to do with my son's girlfriend." After a short pause, he looked at the actor and added, "Obviously, if my son didn't knock her up, someone else did. My wife and I always felt she was a tramp who was using our son for his money and status."

The decision was made. This is how Senator Lee was going to play it. Denial. He would take his chances.

But Washington didn't let it go. "Why would your son make those allegations if they weren't true?" he pressed, apparently not completely buying Lee's denial.

"From the start, Cassandra and I didn't like this girl. As I said, we thought she was a tramp who was using our son to climb a social ladder. While we couldn't prevent him from seeing her, we could make our position known. Cassandra would get into it with her at social events. He didn't like our position and many arguments resulted. I suspect his accusations directed at me are really a thinly disguised effort to get back at his mother."

Darius Washington had agreed to come to St. Louis for the fundraiser because of his relationship with Cassandra Lee. The two had worked together on several civil rights projects and become friends. He really didn't know the senator or anything about his politics. The two had met only a couple times.

Finally, Cassandra spoke. "This whole thing, Darius, has been very traumatic for all of us. As a parent, you certainly hope your son is not a murderer. But the evidence didn't look good for him." The Lees needed west coast support, particularly for their future national campaign. She was not going to risk it even if it meant suggesting that her only child was a murderer. "Garner was in his girlfriend's apartment when she was killed and lied to the police about it. His fingerprint in her blood was found on the inside doorknob. This is how the police knew he was there. Some idiot judge who didn't know the law acquitted him because of a comment made by a prosecutor. The ruling was totally inappropriate and legally incorrect; but it is what it is."

"You mean the judge shouldn't have acquitted him?" Washington asked.

"Correct. And we were blamed for her erroneous decision because the media suggested Winston and I were responsible for the ruling, as if we bribed a judge. Eventually, we got it straightened out and everyone understood we had nothing to do with any pregnancy or his acquittal." As the limo approached the St. Louis suburban city of Chesterfield where Washington's Bombardier Learjet 70 was waiting for him at a private airport, Cassandra needed to be sure his support would continue. She said, "I apologize for the behavior of my son. His childish act was embarrassing and inexcusable. I certainly hope his bad behavior doesn't impact our relationship and your support of Winston."

"You never know what your kids are going to do," Darius Washington said as he got out of the limo.

On their way out of the airport, Kelvin Bellington said, "What the fuck was Garner doing tonight?"

"He was trying to sabotage the campaign and get back at me," the senator said.

"What do you mean get back at you? Get back at you for what?" Kelvin asked.

"For fucking and knocking up his girlfriend," the candidate replied.

Kelvin looked stunned. He obviously hadn't known. "So, what you told Darius was total bullshit and a lie?"

"Totally false. But we are going to continue to deny because this will come up again since the media has it," Senator Lee directed. "It will be my denial against his speculation." Obviously, his campaign manager didn't know anything about the DNA paternity test, and Lee was not about to educate him.

"What else is he going to do? Can we expect to see him at other fundraisers and campaign stops?" Kelvin asked.

"I have no idea. But I suppose we have to prepare to see him at every stop from now on."

"What do you mean prepare? How do we prepare for these future attacks?"

"You'll figure it out, Kelvin. You always do," Lee said as he dialed a phone number to return a call from an important financial supporter.

Chapter Eighteen

Carmine and Garner got out of town before the coverage of Garner's visit to his father's fundraiser hit. They both knew they would have some explaining to do. Postponing the inevitable might allow some of Felbin's anger to subside. In any event, they would deal with the backlash later after they interviewed Ellen Rossi, who had played a key role in the investigation which put Larry Jenkins behind bars for a long time.

Key West is both an island and the southernmost city in the contiguous United States located in the Florida Straits. Cayo Hueso is the original Spanish name for the island. Bone Island, the English translation, is 4 miles long and 1 mile wide, with a total land mass of 4.2 square miles. A tropical island, scenic with a fascinating history and charm, laid back, friendly and free spirited, it provided visitors with the opportunity to escape the stress of daily life and enjoy one continuous Happy Hour.

Along the route to Casa Marina, a Waldorf Astoria Resort on the southern edge of the island, Tony Carmine admired some of the features of this unique part of the country. This was his first visit. He hadn't had time to do any research.

Along the way, Garner, who also had never been to Key West, asked the cab driver to talk about some places to visit and things to see. The driver, Carlos Manuel, who was born and raised there and claimed to be a distant relative of Fernando Moreno, the island's mayor in 1852, was happy to comply. At age 70, he fashioned himself as the chief historian for the island. During the day, he also drove the Conch Tour Train, delighting his passengers with the legends and lore of this tropical paradise. Some fact, some fiction. He began with his hometown's most famous residents and visitors: Ernest Hemingway, Tennessee Williams and Harry Truman, among other United States Presidents.

Pauline and Ernest Hemingway lived at 907 Whitehead Street from 1931 when his wife's rich uncle gave it to them as a wedding gift. He lived there continuously from 1931 until 1939, when he and Pauline divorced. Although he owned the home until his death in 1961, he visited only occasionally. While in Key West, Carlos explained, Hemingway wrote *For Whom the Bell Tolls, A Farewell to Arms, Death in the Afternoon, The Snows of Kilimanjaro,* and *The Short Happy Life of Francis Macomber.* "Here is somethin' you probably didn't know," Carlos told Garner, who was listening intently. "Hemingway wrote a part of *A Farewell to Arms* while living above the showroom of a Key West Ford dealership. He was waitin' for the delivery of a Model A Roadster his wife's rich uncle bought for him," Carlos explained, although he really didn't know if the story was true. But it made for a good story.

Because the ride to the hotel from the airport wasn't very long, Carlos had to give Garner the abridged version of his verbal tour of the island. "We don't have no time for me to tell you 'bout all those four to five toed cats livin' at the Hemingway house even now. You'll have to take the Conch Train Tour to get them kinds of details," Carlos teased.

Next on the list was another author, Tennessee Williams. It was not until 1949 Williams bought a house in Key West and claimed it as his permanent residence until his death in 1983. Before 1949, he was a regular visitor and wrote the first draft of *A Streetcar Named Desire* while staying in the La Concha Hotel, which is still in business. "Even though Hemingway and Williams lived here at the same time, they met only once at Hemingway's home in Cuba," Carlos said, with little concern for the accuracy of this statement.

Because they were at the door of the hotel, the stories about the presidents had to be reduced to simply listing those who visited. Harry Truman, Franklin D. Roosevelt, Dwight D. Eisenhower, John F. Kennedy and Jimmy Carter who visited the most both before and after they left office.

Carmine paid Carlos and was in the lobby of the hotel before the lecture ended. Garner was thrilled with the history lesson, thanked Carlos, gave him an extra tip and followed Carmine into the hotel.

When the duo reached their oceanfront two-bedroom loft suite with balcony, they were more concerned about a voicemail than their luxury accommodations. While on the flight, Felbin called Carmine. The message was simple and terse: "Call me immediately," with emphasis on the word immediately. Both Garner and Tony didn't need a house to fall on them to figure out why Felbin was calling. Typical of Carmine, the return call could wait. He was tired and didn't need the aggravation. Plus, time would not only allow the anger to subside, but it would also give him time to craft a story. More importantly, he needed to call Ellen and arrange a meeting time in the morning. If he didn't have a job, he could always cancel the meeting.

Chapter Nineteen

Ellen Rossi had always known the day would come when someone would inquire about the Larry Jenkins case. She just didn't think it would take so long. She remembered Janet Costello and the rapes occurring in the area of St. Louis University at the time. There was a lot of publicity and concern about the attacks and the safety of the students. Pressure was mounting to catch this rapist.

She also remembered Joan Cardwell as an ambitious assistant prosecutor. Prior to the Jenkins case, Rossi, as a uniformed officer, had a few cases with Cardwell but not enough to form an opinion as to her ability. But she was aware of Cardwell's reputation. She was more of a politician than a prosecutor. Her conviction rate was not very high, probably because her courtroom presence was weak. At the time Janet Costello was raped, it was widely believed Cardwell was looking to become the elected circuit attorney for the City of St. Louis. A high-profile case like the prosecution of an individual who was raping coeds around St. Louis University would enhance her reputation and win her some endorsements when the time came. But she had to win the case first. A loss would be devastating and surely spell defeat at the polls.

Ellen was assigned to the sex crimes unit about the same time as the rapes were occurring around the University. She had been with the department for five years as a patrol officer. The Costello rape investigation was her first assignment as a detective.

Ellen came from a law enforcement family. Her father, now retired, was a St. Louis police officer who spent a twenty-year career in uniform and on the street. He had no interest in a plain clothes assignment. His relatives owned a popular restaurant in the city and were well known. But he didn't try to use their influence to rise above the rank of patrolman. Her uncle was on the St. Louis County police department. He, too, was now retired and spent most of his time in uniform, other than a short time attached to DEA. Her mother was a grade schoolteacher while her brother worked for LinkedIn and lived in New York City.

Ellen was raised in the traditions of the Catholic Church and her parents were deeply religious. They attended mass every Sunday, received communion and went to confession regularly. Her father was a deacon in their parish church and her mother volunteered for many church functions. When Ellen moved out of her family home, she continued with the traditions established by her parents.

Ellen's parents also believed in education and hard work. After receiving a degree in criminal justice from the University of Missouri at the St. Louis campus, Ellen decided to follow in her father's footsteps and applied to the St. Louis Police Department. Her 3.9 college grade point average, together with her father's position with the department, made her an attractive candidate. She graduated first in her academy class and was assigned to a patrol vehicle in the city's south side.

After working the streets in uniform for five years, she was transferred to the sex crimes unit. There she was paired with Patrick Moore, a seasoned detective. Moore had been with the department for ten years, the last eight in sex crimes. He spent an unusually short time in uniform, on the street in a patrol car. He was well respected not only by the detectives in his unit but also by the command staff. He had been a sergeant for the past two years and was on his way up the ladder. Patrick Moore would serve as Ellen Rossi's trainer, mentor and most importantly her friend. She had a lot to learn and realized almost from the first day Patrick would be a good teacher.

He had some limited involvement with the pending rape cases at the university which were being worked by other detectives. When the Costello rape occurred and the other cases had no solid leads, the commander of the unit decided to assign Moore. Because the unit was shorthanded, Ellen, the newcomer, was assigned to assist.

Ellen Rossi remembered the case of Janet Costello very well. Even as a young detective, she had her concerns about the guilt of Larry Jenkins. The case lingered in her memory until she left the department. Now, for the first time, a former colleague and a lawyer representing the man who had been locked up for all those years would be asking her questions. Several issues occurred during the investigation of Larry Jenkins, causing Ellen some concern. As a young detective, she shared those concerns with no one. Instead, she rationalized and did anything else designed to ease her conscience and justify her silence. Now the question was whether she would share her concerns with the people trying to free what could be an innocent man when she met with them in a few hours.

Chapter Twenty

Ellen arranged to meet Garner and Carmine in a little coffee shop, the Cuban Coffee Queen, close to her house. Dressed in shorts and a T-shirt, the island uniform, she arrived first and ordered a cup of black coffee, a Cuban bagel made with cream cheese—pressed Cuban bread topped with honey and a special bagel mix. She grabbed a paper while she waited. She read the paper every morning, particularly to catch up on any criminal activity which had occurred overnight. Her passion was criminal law. Even as a retiree, Ellen did some part time investigative work for a local defense attorney.

She hadn't gotten very far with either her bagel or the paper when Carmine and Garner arrived. Carmine was greeted with a big hug from his old friend. She extended her hand to Garner after Carmine introduced Garner as a lawyer with the Innocence Project in New York representing Larry Jenkins.

"The coffee here is great. Cuban and strong. I would also recommend the Cuban breakfast burrito. And if you're adventuresome, you can kick it up with some jalapenos," Ellen said with a smile.

"I realize that we were close to Cuba here, but didn't know Cubans were here opening restaurants," Carmine said, also smiling.

"If you are a strong swimmer, you could probably swim to Cuba from here," Ellen said facetiously. "You are 93 miles from Cuba. The marker buoy out there," she said pointing to the ocean, "says 90 miles but it's actually 93. The island is the farthest point and only a mile separates the Gulf of Mexico from the Atlantic Ocean. But unlike the Atlantic up north, we have no waves here because of the coral reefs. Those reefs extend for seven miles and captured many unsuspecting navigators in the old days."

Garner Lee was a student of history and recalled reading articles about the ships hitting the reefs and the townspeople hurrying to rescue the people on board. The first to the wreckage were also rewarded with the lion's share of the cargo when it was divided among the town's people.

Ellen confirmed Garner's recollection of the history of the island and continued with additional fun facts. "US Highway 1 ends here and is marked with a sign which reads 0. That sign disappears about seven times a year, mostly during spring break," she said, an obvious reference to college kids vacationing on the island.

"How long have you lived here?" Garner asked.

"I have lived here long enough to be known as a *freshwater conch.*"

Both Carmine and Garner were confused by her answer to such a simple question. "What the hell is that?" Carmine asked.

"If you are born here, you are a *conch.* But if you have lived here for more than seven years, you are known as a freshwater conch."

"I have been to a lot of places both here in the United States and Europe, but never here. This place is unique from what little we've seen of it so far," Garner said.

"If you have time later, you should take a tour of the island. You can ride the Conch Tour Train and the driver will give you a whole bunch of fun facts about this place. You can also get a drink at Jimmy Buffet's place. The original Margaritaville is here on Duval Street. He wrote a bunch of songs about the island. You can also watch the sunset, a sight you will see nowhere else. In fact, those are so important to the natives they require the cruise ships to be out of here by 5:30 because they would block the sunset from the pier where they're docked. But for now, what can I do for you on the Larry Jenkins case?"

"We believe an innocent man was convicted of rape," Garner began.

"Disheartening," she said after a long pause, her voice lacking any emotion. "What makes you think he's innocent?"

"We think the case is weak. The identification is bad, for starters. The victim described her attacker as a dark skinned black, five feet ten, 185 pounds, clean shaven with a pudgy face and large lips. Larry had light skinned, weighed about 60 pounds less and had unimpressive lips," Garner said.

"Lots of vics can be off a bit with the identification, particularly when they are looking at a gun or knife in a dark car at night. And if I recall, this guy had a knife. If I also remember correctly, the victim picked him out of a photo spread. And I think we showed her quite a few pictures."

"But, to your point, if it was dark and the victim, Janet Costello-Snead, had a knife in her face, how reliable could her identification be?" Carmine asked. "Plus, Jenkins had an alibi."

"I'm sure all of that came up at the trial and Mr. Jenkins lost."

Carmine began to think this was a wasted trip and his old friend, a former police officer, wasn't going to help them. "Ellen, let me ask you this. I read the police report, which is kinda lacking on specific details about this crime. Is there anything you guys saw or found which is not included in the report?"

After another long pause, Ellen said, "Nothing I can think of at the moment."

"How did Cardwell get involved in this?" Carmine asked.

"There were several rapes around St. Louis University at the time and no suspects. The folks at the university were getting nervous thinking this was a serial rapist and demanding answers. When the Costello rape occurred, Patrick Moore was assigned to do the investigation. Pat was good and the commander of the sex crimes unit. He was getting heat from the chief who decided the head of the unit needed to investigate the latest rape. I was new to the unit and assigned to assist him. By the time we got in, the circuit attorney had already appointed Cardwell to oversee the rape cases."

"So, you were working with Cardwell from the start of the Jenkins case and she made the call to prosecute him? And you got along with her okay?" Garner asked.

"Yes, to all of your questions."

"Did you and Moore have any disagreements with Cardwell? Did she refuse to let you do something? Or did she tell you to do something you didn't want to do?" Carmine pressed.

After another long pause, Ellen again said, "Nothing I can think of at the moment," leaving herself a little wiggle room.

This was the second time she gave the same calculated response. It was not only what she said but how she said it, which troubled Carmine. *At the moment* was an escape route in case she was boxed in later. The hesitation, the uncertainty in her voice, the equivocation, and her demeanor generally. This was not the confident Ellen Rossi he knew and respected. But clearly, they were not going to get anything helpful from her, at least not now.

After thanking her for her time, Garner and Carmine headed back to the hotel. They needed to get a flight back to St. Louis and Carmine needed to return Felbin's call. Hopefully, Felbin's anger had begun to subside.

Chapter Twenty-One

Although convenient, Key West International Airport had a limited number of flights. The alternative was to take a shuttle to Miami or Fort Lauderdale. Either way, the earliest flight they could get would be in the morning unless they wanted to fly stand by. But Tony wasn't anxious to get back home, given the conversation he'd just had with Felbin. To say his boss was upset would have been an understatement. Carmine had witnessed Felbin's anger in the past. He had seen him peel the flesh off adverse trial witnesses. And from time to time, he had been the target of Felbin's displeasure. But this tongue lashing went to the top of the list.

Notwithstanding his denials, Felbin blamed Carmine for the fundraiser he and Garner blew up. He suggested his investigator was responsible for returning the case of State of Missouri versus Garner Lee to the headlines. Garner's confrontation with his father was covered by all media outlets and was now fertile ammunition for radio talk shows.

"Where the hell were you when he was accusing his father of knocking up his girlfriend and killing her?" Felbin demanded.

When Carmine didn't answer, Felbin said, "And you knew what he was going to do once you two got to the political rally. You knew Darius Washington was going to be there. It was well publicized. And my guess is you told Garner about the event and encouraged him to show up. You might have even scripted what he would say to the thousands of people in attendance."

Carmine continued to listen. There was no future in responding. It would just make matters worse, if that was possible.

"And now you have dragged the firm back into the middle of the Lee murder case, along with Garner and his mother, both former clients of ours. And if it isn't enough for you, our current client, Larry Jenkins, may also suffer some backlash because of your stupidity..."

As Felbin continued his rant, Carmine began to wonder where he would find another job, particularly as much as he liked the one he was about to lose. He was so engrossed in those thoughts he didn't even hear Felbin abruptly end the conversation before he could relate the conversation he had with Ellen Rossi.

Since they couldn't get a flight out until the morning, Garner suggested they tour Key West starting with a ride on the Conch Tour Train Ellen had recommended. But Carmine wasn't in the mood for sightseeing. Garner could go alone, and they would catch up later for dinner. Some bar stool had Carmine's name on it while he contemplated his future employment options.

Tony Carmine walked down Duval Street looking for Jimmy Buffett's Margaritaville, as he replayed his conversation with Ellen. Although they were never partnered, he'd worked cases with her and observed her work ethic. The person he knew was confident in her ability and a straight shooter. She was vocal when breaking down a crime scene and developing an investigative theory. Her integrity was important to her and above reproach. But now her hesitation, the long pauses when responding to Carmine's questions were out of character. In particular, her hesitation when he asked whether there was anything she and Moore found which was not included in the report. But Carmine excused Ellen's conduct as breathing too much Key West salt air as he entered the restaurant.

When he arrived at Buffett's place, he moved directly to the bar while observing the décor. The restaurant was quaint with Jimmy Buffett memorabilia dotting the walls. The bar was long and narrow with fifteen backless stools by his estimation. Given the hour of the day, he had no trouble finding a stool. The lunch crowd had not yet arrived. Apparently, the food was pretty good. Probably cheeseburgers, Jimmy's signature song, were the biggest seller. But he was not there for the food or to admire the décor. The bartender, a well-endowed, dark haired woman in her mid-twenties of Cuban or Spanish descent, wasted no time getting to his spot at the end of the bar. Since he was at Margaritaville, he ordered a margarita. When she put his drink on the bar, he noticed photographs of Buffett at various stages of his career embedded in the top of the entire bar.

As he drank the first of what he planned to be several beverages, his thoughts turned to Felbin and his future with the office. He knew Felbin was right. He was responsible for what happened at Senator Lee's fundraiser. He was the one who told Garner about his father's campaign event and encouraged him to attend. Although he hadn't known exactly what Garner was going to do, he knew it would be a public scourging the likes of which the good senator had never experienced before. And it was everything Tony Carmine hoped for. He enjoyed it. He enjoyed watching Garner extract his pound of flesh particularly in a forum where his father was the most vulnerable. Now the question was whether it was worth losing his job.

Aside from the celebration playing in his head, Carmine knew he screwed up when it came to Larry Jenkins. The little embarrassing show Garner put on would attract more attention to his previous murder case than the effort to get a DNA test. And the public spin would probably be negative. The headline Carmine envisioned in his head read, *Former Accused Murderer Now Seeking to Free Convicted Rapist.* When this headline hit, Carmine would be in the unemployment line—not without just cause. Just as his pity party was getting started, Carmine's phone rang. It was Ellen Rossi and she needed to meet him alone. He told her he was at Buffett's place and she was welcome to join him there. She agreed.

Chapter Twenty-Two

Carmine knew Ellen was not requesting a meeting to renew an old friendship. He hoped her unusual behavior earlier in the day would soon be answered in a way which would benefit Larry Jenkins. It might then get him out of some of the hot water he was in with Felbin. His curiosity would soon be satisfied as he saw Ellen walking in. He waited for her at the bar and moved to a table in the corner of the restaurant at her suggestion.

When they arrived at the table, he said, "I didn't expect to see you again so soon."

"And I didn't expect to see you again either," Ellen said.

"I assume you're not here to talk about old times."

"I'm here to talk about your client, Larry Jenkins," she said, this time without hesitation, but with stress in her voice.

She waited for Carmine to say something. But when he didn't, she continued. "I wasn't completely forthcoming with you when we talked before."

Again, no response or a reaction from Carmine.

"The police report Moore prepared wasn't complete," she continued.

"How incomplete was it?" Carmine asked.

"It left out an essential detail. I believe this detail contributed to shaping the outcome of the case."

"You mean this exclusion contributed to the guilty verdict?"

There was another hesitation. But Carmine knew this time it was not a matter of measuring her words to conceal the truth. This time she was going to tell the truth and felt guilty, ashamed and embarrassed about what she was going to confess. Carmine was sure his friend had never had a conversation like the one she was about to have with anyone else.

"Janet Costello was not as certain in her identification of Jenkins as the police report made her out to be."

"What do you mean? What specifically did you leave out?" Carmine asked.

"I didn't leave anything out. I didn't prepare the report. Moore did," she said defensively.

A distinction without a difference, since she and Moore were partners, Carmine thought, but didn't press the point. He needed whatever information she was willing to give him. "What specifically did Moore leave out of the police report?" he asked generally.

"As you already know, Janet looked at fifteen suspects in the photo spread. This fact was included in the report."

"Before you didn't know how many mug shots she was shown," Carmine said, this time interrupting her.

"I knew exactly how many we showed her. I just didn't bother to tell you because I wasn't planning to help you with this case when you arrived."

"What caused you to change your mind?"

"Partially you, but mostly my conscience. I have been living with this case for nearly twenty years now. When I saw you, I was reminded of how my life used to be before this case. I always considered myself an honest hard-working cop. Sure, I cut some corners like everybody else. Have there been times I've told less than the whole truth? Sure. Like all other cops. But never have I done anything to harm anyone intentionally. Suspect or victim. Then came Larry Jenkins."

Although Carmine had no idea what was to come, he understood her pain. She was correct. Cops did cut corners. Some even committed perjury under the theory of the mere *shit bum* rule. If the guy wasn't good for the crime with which he was charged, he was certainly good for one he got away with. But most cut corners on nonessential items, as they defined the term. Before this case, Carmine believed Ellen Rossi would never intentionally harm anyone. His opinion of her might soon change.

"When we showed her the fifteen photos, she looked at them for a long time. Although I wasn't timing her, I would say she spent a good fifteen to twenty minutes. Finally, she pulled three out and set them aside. None of the three had dark skin or exceptionally large lips. She carefully studied each again for an extended period, probably another ten to fifteen minutes. While she looked at them, she kept saying, 'I'm not sure, I'm not sure, they all look alike.' She would look at one, shake her head, go to the next and shake her head again. She did the same thing for all three photos. Finally, she said, 'I'll go with this one'. Not exactly a ringing endorsement."

Carmine listened, both confused and amazed at what he was hearing. "What did you or your partner say when she was telling you all black people look alike and she couldn't say who raped her?" he asked.

"I didn't take it as a racial slur."

"Whatever. What did you say to her?" Carmine asked, anger and frustration punctuating his words.

"We told her she needed to be sure."

"That's it? You didn't tell her she needed to be absolutely certain? And if she wasn't certain, she should say so? Depending on the photo she selected, a man's life could be ruined?" Carmine asked incredulously.

"Oh, please Tony, spare me your self-righteous, condescending tone. When did you ever hammer a rape victim like that? It's easy for you now to criticize with the twenty-twenty hindsight of your DNA. But unfortunately, we didn't have the benefit of the science back then. Look, I don't feel good about this whole thing, and I don't need you to make it worse. I asked you to meet me because I want to help. I want to finally make this right and I don't need your bullshit in the process."

"I'm sorry, Ellen," Carmine began—not a phrase which flowed effortlessly from his lips. "I don't mean to put this all on your shoulders. But a man has spent a substantial portion of his life locked up for a crime he didn't commit. I guess I'm seeing things a little differently since I'm now working the defense side of the fence. In any event, we want and need your help. I appreciate your talking to me without the bullshit. Was it your decision or Moore's to leave the critical piece of information out of the police report?"

"Neither one of us," Rossi said.

"What do you mean? You were the only two involved in this. Correct?"

"No. There was one other person who was not only involved but was calling the shots."

"And who would that be?" Carmine asked, a confused look on his face.

"The prosecutor."

"Cardwell? The *Honorable* Joan Cardwell? We are aware she tried the case, but what did she have to do with the police report? Did she want more evidence before she would issue the rape charge?"

In the city of St. Louis, the investigating officer contacts a prosecutor, seeking the issuance of criminal charges. The police report is provided, along with any other relevant evidence the officer has gathered. If the prosecutor is satisfied with the evidence, a warrant is issued. Occasionally, a prosecutor will request the applying officer to obtain additional evidence and come back. In the event the prosecutor is not satisfied the evidence supports the issuance of any criminal charge, the warrant application will either be refused or taken under advisement.

"The original report included the victim's equivocation. Moore wrote it exactly as it happened, complete with the statement, 'I'm not sure, I'm not sure, they all look alike,' including references to the victim's head shakes and uncertainty. Frankly, we thought we had a refusal. Not only was she uncertain on the photo spread, but the guy she picked contradicted her original description. When we took the case to Cardwell, she told us to take out all the uncertainty, water down the conflicts in the description and bring her a report with certainty as to the identification."

"What did you two do when she told you to change the report?"

"We argued with her. We told her she wasn't going to make the case. The victim would not hold up during cross examination. Plus, we pointed out the conflicts would come out, whether we highlighted them in the report. She didn't care. The rapes in this area around the university were high-profile and there was pressure to get a conviction. She told us she would handle it. I think she was hoping if she issued the charge, there would be a plea because this was the second time he was accused of rape. His prior rape was the reason we put his picture in the spread."

"But the prior rape charge was dismissed. There was no conviction," Carmine pointed out.

"We knew that. But I think Cardwell believed she could offer him a deal he couldn't refuse and justify it by saving the victim from the embarrassment of testifying at a public trial. She would then be the hero. Case solved. But when Jenkins declined to take any plea bargain, she was forced to try the case. And you know what happened then. In my opinion, Cardwell didn't win it. The inexperienced lawyer representing Jenkins lost it. And here we are with you and me having a *true confessions* conversation."

Carmine didn't respond immediately. He was trying to fully comprehend what his friend was telling him. He knew Cardwell was a corrupt judge. He learned that lesson when she presided over Garner Lee's murder trial. He also knew she was corrupt as the elected circuit attorney when she prosecuted Bobby Decker to curry political favor. But now he was learning something new. Her corruption began early in her career and well before she ascended to the bench and to her role as the elected prosecutor. Certainly, prosecutors have the right as well as the duty to require police officers to find more evidence if necessary, to prove the essential elements of a crime. But they don't have the right to demand that police officers fabricate the contents of a police report.

Carmine didn't want to beat her over the head with what she had done. He needed her to come to St. Louis and testify. Larry Jenkins' freedom depended on it. But he had to have an answer to one more question. Struggling to frame his question to avoid an accusatory tone, he finally said, "You were a great police officer. What I don't understand is why you followed Cardwell's demands."

"Tony, that's a question I have been asking myself for many years and I don't have a good answer. I didn't know then what I know now about Cardwell. But I did know at the time she was more of a politician than a prosecutor. She was not the best and the brightest prosecutor in their office and more Ls than Ws. The rumor was Cardwell had her sights set on running for circuit attorney and this case was important enough to help her get there.

"Rather than getting in a fight with her particularly if she became the head of the office, we thought, given what we knew about the case, at the end of the day she would either get a plea or have to try it. If he pled, it would mean he was good for the rape. If she had to try the case, she would lose and be embarrassed by an acquittal and perhaps abandon the idea of becoming the circuit attorney. That's the best I can do for you now as I look at my behavior in the rearview mirror."

Carmine listened to the explanation but said nothing. Neither looked at the other. Instead, they pretended to look at the memorabilia on the walls which defined the musical career of Jimmy Buffett. Finally, Ellen spoke. "All I can say to Mr. Jenkins and to you is *I'm sorry.* I violated my oath as a police officer and caused great harm to an innocent man. I need to make it right."

"Would you be willing to come to St. Louis and testify in our effort to get DNA testing?"

Immediately, Ellen agreed.

Although Ellen's testimony would help, there was no guarantee the court would order DNA testing.

"I appreciate your willingness to help. I'm sure you understand even if you put the truth out there about what Cardwell did, we still have no guarantees we will win, particularly since we would be taking on a sitting judge. I want you to understand that."

"I am aware of the risks. But I'm doing this as much for me as I am for Larry Jenkins. Perhaps even more for me than him."

Carmine watched her as she spoke. She seemed calm, her face expressionless. He had seen the look thousands of times during his career, the eyes and faces of those who have confessed. The burden had been lifted from the shoulders of Ellen Rossi.

Chapter Twenty-Three

When Carmine returned to the hotel, he decided to call Felbin. The conversation did not begin very well. "Tony, I really don't have any time to talk about the fiasco with Garner and his father," Felbin said.

"I'm not calling about that. There is nothing I can do about that right now. But I am calling to give you some good news about the Jenkins case." Starting the conversation with the phrase *good news,* Carmine figured would at least prevent Felbin from hanging up like he did before. Felbin listened as Carmine explained what Ellen had told him.

When Felbin did not immediately respond, Carmine thought he'd lost the connection. But finally, Felbin said, "Son of a bitch. Here we go again. Another round with Cardwell. We knew she was involved and had a political interest in the outcome. We didn't know she was in the business of redrafting police reports. Of course, given our experiences with her, I suppose we should have suspected something untoward was going to pop up. I suppose my first question is whether you have any reason to believe Rossi is not telling the truth."

Relieved that he still had a job, at least for the moment, Carmine said, "There is no doubt in my mind she's telling the truth. She has absolutely nothing to gain and everything to lose by telling this story now. When I asked if she would be willing to testify, she agreed without hesitation. She also said she understood the risks involved."

Felbin understood Rossi had nothing to gain by admitting to misconduct which resulted in the wrongful conviction and incarceration of an innocent man. But was this development a positive or a negative for Larry Jenkins? Injecting misconduct by a sitting judge might change the focus and the end game for the defense. Jenkins' DNA suit was assigned to Judge Mark Nealon. Although he enjoyed a reputation of fairness and impartiality, the question concerning Felbin was whether he could maintain his objectivity when the career of a colleague might be in jeopardy. Nealon's relationship with Cardwell was an unknown, but they were both members of the same exclusive club.

Felbin decided to contact Barry Scheck for his input. After explaining what Ellen Rossi told Carmine, Felbin said, "I'm trying to figure out whether we want to use her, since Cardwell is currently a sitting judge. Additionally, her conduct in connection with the Garner Lee case was the subject of a lot of media criticism. Not sure whether this helps or hurts."

"If I remember correctly, you told me Cardwell found a reason to set aside a guilty jury verdict and acquit him. Something to do with prosecutorial misconduct. But was there a lot of media criticism of her?"

"Yes. There were several articles, editorials and letters to the editor for several days. I think the reporters and other people saw it for what it was: a payback."

"Did those articles suggest the jury got it wrong and Cardwell was just righting a wrong? Or was she viewed as setting a guilty man free as a favor to a politician? If we use Rossi, I assume we will open an old wound for her and perhaps for us," Scheck noted.

"I suppose it was fifty/fifty on that aspect of the coverage. As I told you before, there was no suggestion Garner and I had anything to do with Cardwell's decision. And yes, we will resurrect the issue if we have Rossi testify about what Cardwell did." After a short pause, Felbin added, "Barry, there is something else you need to know. What I was concerned might happen, has happened. Garner's return to St. Louis was not without some fanfare and I'm afraid he and Tony caused it."

The comment caught Scheck's attention. He knew Tony Carmine. They had worked together on other cases and he had great respect for him as an investigator. "What exactly do you mean?"

After Felbin explained the incident with the Darius Washington fundraiser, he discussed the news coverage. "The coverage was not kind to Winston Lee. The article in the *St. Louis Post Dispatch* was brutal. The spin they put on it was directed at Winston impregnating Garner's girlfriend. Although they didn't specifically say it, they implied

Winston killed her to cover it up because he was planning to run for governor. Obviously, knocking up your kid's girlfriend is not a career enhancer. I'm anxious to see how this moral misstep is going to impact the governor's race. I'm pretty sure the press is not done with this issue as long as Winston Lee stays in the race."

"We knew Garner's involvement in the Jenkins case would ultimately resurrect the murder case. Maybe what he and your investigator did was helpful because it put the murder on his father's shoulders and off his. Like we talked about before, if he was guilty, why would he come back to St. Louis for any reason? But at the end of the day, does it really matter to the Jenkins case one way or another what the press does with Garner and Cardwell?" Scheck asked.

"My concern is whether the murder case and Caldwell's involvement will overshadow Jenkins. And if it happens, will it impact the way Judge Nealon looks at the case? Of course, I'm quite confident Nealon figured something was up when Cardwell set aside the guilty verdict. As you know, those rulings don't happen very often. A murderer goes free because of something a prosecutor did. Usually, these judges are protecting the prosecutors. Plus, the coverage, both before and after the trial, suggested Cardwell was in the pocket of Garner's father. But the unknown is Nealon's relationship with Cardwell. If I had to guess, I would think Cardwell is not his type."

"I don't know Judge Nealon and have no idea how he would react. In my experience, most judges don't like to criticize other judges, particularly when the case is high-profile. But I'm going to have to rely on you to make the call on Nealon. However, in the meantime, I think we need to see how this plays out."

"I agree. I'll talk further with both Garner and Tony Carmine when they get back from Florida and I'll get back to you," Felbin said, ending his conversation with Scheck.

Chapter Twenty-Four

John Peterson was Ray Singer's campaign manager. When Singer decided to run for the office of Attorney General more than eight years before, he'd wanted someone he could trust to run his campaign. But most of all, he wanted someone with high moral and ethical standards. He understood and witnessed first-hand political corruption. The incumbent, Craig Wilson, was a back-room politician who made it a practice of selling the Attorney General's Office to the highest bidder. If you had money and were willing to contribute to Wilson's cause, whether legally or illegally, you became a member of the club. Singer spent his career as a prosecutor and had little regard for politicians generally, but no tolerance for the chief law enforcement officer for the State of Missouri, who was corrupt. Although inexperienced and lacking in funds, he put his faith in John Peterson, a newcomer to the world of politics at the time and the good judge of the people of Missouri. In the end, Singer, with the help of Peterson, defeated his incumbent opponent and went on to win a second term.

Now Singer was in a race to defeat what he considered to be another corrupt politician. But he faced a challenge. The candidate's son publicly accused his father of impregnating and, by inference at least, murdering the woman he loved. Singer was aware of the case. He also knew the outcome of the case and the suggestion of political favors. More corruption, if true. But now the question for Singer was what to do with this latest serious accusation. It is one thing to suggest Lee impregnated his son's girlfriend, but quite another to suggest he murdered her to cover up the pregnancy and protect his political career.

The campaign staff gathered at Singer headquarters in Jefferson City. The campaign rented an office on High Street a few blocks from the Supreme Court building where the Attorney General's office is located. Peterson called the meeting with key staffers to address the fiasco of the Darius Washington fundraiser. How could they use the son's accusations to benefit their campaign? He decided to have the meeting without Singer.

Peterson's office had an adjoining conference room. He sat at the head of the conference room table, flanked on the left by Lori Stamp, who was directing the campaign out of St. Louis; Calbert Phillips, directing the Kansas City side of the state; to his right. Mark Hollingsworth, who was responsible for the central portion of the state, and who was running late.

Peterson began the discussion. "We need to decide how we want to handle Lee's son's tirade during the recent fundraiser with Darius Washington. Lori, you were there. Tell us what you saw and heard."

"At first, I don't think anyone knew what was happening. I was watching Lee when his son began to speak. Or I should say yell. He was telling everyone his father was having sex with his girlfriend. I would estimate the crowd to be about a thousand. He then accused the senator of impregnating his girlfriend. But it didn't stop there. The kid pressed, asking how many times he had sex and whether he thought about him—Garner—while he was having sex with his girlfriend. It was brutal. Lee remained expressionless as the attack escalated. I then looked at Darius Washington. At first, he looked as confused as everyone else. But then his face had the look of 'Oh shit. Get me the hell out of here.'"

Mark Hollingsworth entered the room and heard Lori's comment about Darius Washington. Hollingsworth was an experienced fundraiser who had national contacts. "My sources in California tell me Darius is done with Lee. The funding, at least from Darius and his rich celebrity friends, is over. He didn't buy Lee's denial at least as far as the pregnancy was concerned. Apparently, he was on the fence about whether the kid or his father killed the girlfriend," he said.

"Is it worth reaching out to your sources to see if we can talk to Darius to see if we can either swing him over to our side or at least kick in some money to our effort?" Peterson asked.

"From all I hear, this guy is a pretty straight shooter with no bullshit. But apparently, he agreed to appear at the fundraiser because of his connection with Lee's wife. I'm told they worked together on some cases and became friends. So, if that's the case, I doubt he would switch teams," Hollingsworth said.

"All right, we can check him off the list. But we need to decide what we want to do with what his kid is alleging. Obviously, this is serious stuff."

Lori was the first to respond. "After I left the fundraiser, I decided to look into the prosecution of his son by the circuit attorney's office in St. Louis. As you know, he was charged with murdering his girlfriend and a jury found him guilty. I did some checking and talking to people who were involved with the case. The consensus is the guilty verdict was set aside on some ridiculous technicality because the trial judge owed the kid's father for putting her on the bench. She is apparently as corrupt as the senator. These folks say it's a close call, but they don't believe the kid was good for the murder."

"But then the senator becomes the prime suspect. What evidence do we have he killed the girlfriend?" Phillips asked directing his question to Lori.

"We don't have a smoking gun, if that's what you're asking. And we can't get a copy of the transcript because it got sealed after Judge Cardwell dismissed the case against his kid. So..."

Phillips interrupted her, anxious to understand at least some of the particulars of the dismissal. He was from Kansas City. "Can you walk me through the case, since obviously it didn't get any attention in KC?"

Lori complied, with as many details as she could remember from the media coverage since she didn't attend the trial. "As you know, Garner Lee, the son, was accused of murdering his girlfriend and lying about it when the police questioned him. A jury found him guilty, and the defense filed a motion for a new trial. The judge granted the new trial because she said the prosecutor did something to prejudice the defendant's rights. She then indicated there would be no new trial because of prosecutorial misconduct and then dismissed the murder charge. I am not a lawyer and really don't understand this, but apparently because of this misconduct, Garner Lee was a free man and could never be prosecuted for this crime again. This is my understanding in a nutshell."

"Doesn't sound to me like an innocent man was freed," Phillips said.

Peterson, who was a lawyer, didn't think it necessary to explain Cardwell's legal gymnastics. At one level, it mattered whether Garner Lee was a murderer. But *Winston* Lee was their opponent, not Garner. "We're not going to retry the murder case during this campaign," Peterson began. "Obviously, it would be nice if we could prove Senator Lee was a murderer. But we can't. The issue for us is whether we can irrefutably establish he fathered a child with his son's girlfriend. That seems like it might be an easier task although I'm not convinced we can get there either. Any suggestions?"

Lori recalled at some point during the trial Garner admitted under oath knowing he was not the father of the child. "When I heard that, I wondered how he would know definitively he was not the father. My guess was his lawyers did a DNA test," she said.

"Makes sense," Phillips injected. "Do you think we can get the lab report from his lawyers? Or do you think Garner would give us a sample?"

"Given his hostility toward his father, I'm guessing Garner would gladly give us a DNA sample. But it won't do us any good unless we have something to compare it to. I have some contacts at the Felbin firm and maybe I can talk them into giving us a copy of their lab report, assuming they have one," Lori said.

Mark Hollingsworth sat, silently listening to the discussion. Of the members of the campaign staff, he was the most experienced and the most aggressive campaigner. At times, Peterson had to rein him in. "That's all well and good. But in the meantime, I think we need to act on the kid's diatribe before it becomes stale news. As it now stands, Garner Lee publicly accused his father of knocking up his girlfriend. His father denied it. I say we put out a press release suggesting the good senator voluntarily take a paternity test to clear up the issue and we will arrange and pay for it. In the meantime, we can try to get whatever documents are out there to definitively prove he is the daddy."

Peterson considered the suggestion, uncertain whether their candidate would approve of the strategy. Ray Singer was not a fan of mudslinging politics. His game plan was to focus on his own record and avoid the finger pointing. But these were different times. The country had elected a president many suggested was a philanderer who paid women for sexual silence, apparently fearing those disclosures could impact his election. And now the country was paying the price.

Peterson wondered whether there would have been a different result if the electorate had a complete picture of Donald Trump's womanizing, philandering and other corrupt behavior before they cast their ballots to make him the Forty-fifth President of the United States. While the country made a mistake, Peterson decided Missouri was not going to follow the same path of destruction. Winston Lee might be a philanderer like Trump. But he might also be a killer who might, like Trump, take care of problems which had the potential to impact his election.

Peterson made a decision. He would put out a press release challenging Lee to take a paternity test and offering to pay for it. Uncertain of Singer's reaction, he decided the risk benefit was the chance of incurring Singer's wrath.

Chapter Twenty-Five

The parties appeared as ordered in the courtroom of the Honorable Mark Nealon for a status conference. At the age of sixty-eight, Judge Nealon was nearing the mandatory retirement age of seventy. He was an experienced, no nonsense trial judge who had been on the bench for fourteen years. Prior to his appointment, he had a private trial practice and then served as the General Counsel to the St. Louis Metropolitan Police Department for eleven years. During the time he spent with the department, he provided legal advice and representation on the Board of Police Commissioners. He also defended the department in civil rights claims as well as civil lawsuits brought by labor organizations, civil rights groups and others. Felbin knew Judge Nealon well, having tried numerous cases both with him and against him when he was representing the police department. Joan Cardwell was also well acquainted with Judge Nealon; he presided over many criminal cases when Cardwell was the elected prosecutor for the City of St. Louis.

At precisely 9:30, the judge entered the courtroom and the bailiff opened court for the day. Judge Nealon had little tolerance for lawyers and litigants who were late. None of these were. He believed everyone's time was valuable and expected the same respect in return.

A status conference is a gathering of the lawyers to discuss scheduling, the anticipated length of the trial, as well as discovery matters and other preliminary issues. This is a nonjury matter to be decided by the judge alone. Bench trials can be conducted with less formality because the schedules of jurors don't have to be respected and coordinated. But this case involved a man who had been in the penitentiary for the past seventeen years. And he could be innocent.

The petitioner, Larry Jenkins, was represented by Jonathan Felbin and Garner Lee, while Karen Braxton—the

Circuit Attorney herself—appeared on behalf of the state. Felbin wondered what was going on. Braxton hadn't tried a case or appeared in court since replacing Cardwell as the elected prosecutor for the City of St. Louis. But this wasn't just any case. This one involved all the prime-time players—Cardwell, Garner Lee, Barry Scheck, Felbin and perhaps an innocent man. If this went south, it would spell political disaster for Braxton, as well as her mentor, the judge she continuously protected.

While the initial filing of the petition attracted little attention, that changed after Garner Lee's performance at his father's fundraiser. Now, although this was a simple status conference, the room was filled with reporters who had more interest in Garner than Jenkins.

Judge Nealon was the first to speak. "I read the pleading. The petitioner, Mr. Jenkins, is seeking to have the state produce some evidence from his rape case so he can do some DNA testing. Is that correct, Mr. Felbin?"

"That is correct, Your Honor," Felbin said.

"Seems simple enough. Are you contesting this request, Ms. Braxton?" the judge asked.

"We are, Judge," Braxton said simply, anticipating Nealon wasn't going to let the inquiry end there.

"Do you think you could enlighten me as to why you would be fighting this? Their request, at least on its face, seems reasonable to me."

Before Braxton responded, Felbin leaned over to his co-counsel and whispered, "I think he is pissed because he thought this was going to be a one and done deal. And now he has a contested case with media packing the place."

"The victim has objected," another short answer.

"Why has the victim objected? Did you have anything to do with encouraging her to object?"

"This matter was very traumatic for her and she has since moved on. She has a family now and doesn't want to relive it. She also doesn't want to face the defendant again. And although I didn't encourage her to resist this, I do agree with her. We get a lot of DNA requests when all else fails and all the appeals are exhausted. We can't have all these rapists demanding DNA re-dos. This guy had his jury trial and he exhausted all his appeals years ago. Now some liberal special interest group with an agenda is filing these cases here and all over the country."

The judge looked at Felbin, who was on his feet at the counsel table. "The Innocence Project is involved in this and other cases throughout the country. Their successes highlight the need for DNA testing." Felbin recited some of the numbers both for the benefit of the judge as well as the reporters in attendance. "To date, 362 people who were wrongfully convicted were freed, based upon DNA testing. Of that number, some 150 who were responsible for the crimes were later identified. 20 of the 362 were on death row. The various states were going to put these innocent people to death and would have, had it not been for DNA. Unlike eyewitness testimony, the DNA doesn't lie and doesn't make mistakes. The Innocence Project is hardly some left wing special interest group, or whatever she called it."

"I'm familiar with the Innocence Project and Mr. Scheck's work. However, I do agree generally with the prosecutor. We can't DNA test every rape case. What makes yours different?" Nealon asked Felbin.

"Several things. This is a one on one. *He said, she said.* The victim's description of the perpetrator doesn't match Jenkins. The victim was attacked in her car at night with a knife to her throat. Statistically, identifications under those circumstances are unreliable. 70% of the DNA exonerations were based upon eyewitness misidentification. And 41% of the 70% involved cross racial misidentification. Here the victim is white and the defendant black. You can verify these statistics through the Innocence Project. They keep the numbers. In addition, the public defender handling the case was young, inexperienced and overwhelmed. Jenkins had an alibi the jury never heard. DNA is a science. It doesn't rely on descriptions provided by victims who are worried about dying."

One other piece of evidence which made the Jenkins case different from other rape cases where DNA testing was sought. Trial lawyers are always looking for the *smoking gun,* the poison in the opponent's case capable of giving them the upper hand. The smoking gun in the Jenkins case was Ellen Rossi. Once vital information like this was found, trial lawyers had to decide when to play the card. Felbin decided he would wait for the hearing to play his card. He didn't want to give the prosecutor any time to prepare for Rossi's testimony.

Without giving Braxton the opportunity to respond to Felbin's argument, Nealon said, "I'm going to set this matter for an evidentiary hearing. We can sort it out then. I'm going to..."

Braxton interrupted. "Your Honor, I would ask you to consider the victim's position and the emotional damage which certainly can occur if she is forced to relive this matter."

"Ms. Braxton, I understand your position and the victim's. But I also appreciate the position of the other side. An innocent man may be in the penitentiary. As I mentioned, I am familiar with the Innocence Project and the number of people who have been exonerated through the science of DNA. I would certainly hope you might find a way to accommodate the wishes of Mr. Jenkins while minimizing any inconvenience to the victim. In the meantime, I will schedule this matter for an evidentiary hearing as expeditiously as possible," Judge Nealon said and then adjourned the status conference.

As they were leaving the courtroom, Felbin decided to try again to persuade Braxton to surrender the evidence for DNA comparison. "Karen, listen," he began, "I'm not interested in damaging this victim. I would like to work this out in a way which will protect the victim while at the same time providing some DNA closure to this case. We can even have the police department lab do the analysis."

"As far as I'm concerned, this case is closed. Your client had his trial and appeals, and we are done," Braxton said emphatically as she walked out the door without stopping to continue the conversation.

"So, where do we go from here?" Garner asked.

"Looks like we're having a public hearing which may not end well for some people," Felbin said.

Chapter Twenty-Six

The Singer press release was simple but explosive. Singer would meet the press at his headquarters in Jefferson City to address issues relating to Senator Winston Lee's fitness to be the governor of the state of Missouri, considering his son's allegations of murder and sexual misconduct. Not surprisingly, the word spread like a wildfire in a forest which hadn't seen rain in a year. It also didn't escape the notice of Singer himself.

Ray Singer was on the phone with his campaign manager as soon as he saw the television coverage announcing the time and location of the conference. "John, Fox 2 just said we are having a press conference in Jefferson City tomorrow to talk about murder and sexual misconduct allegations relating to my opponent. Would you mind telling me what they are talking about?"

"The press release was a little over the top. It went out before I had a chance to look at it and I'm sorry. As you know, Lee's son, Garner, said his father impregnated his girlfriend. And inferentially at least, suggested his father murdered her to protect his reputation and prevent it from getting in the way of his efforts to become the next governor. The staff and I met and decided it would be a good idea to clear up this accusation one way or the other. And the way we are planning to do it is by offering to pay for a paternity test," Peterson said.

"You're going to ask Senator Lee to take a paternity test?" Singer asked, uncertain what he had just heard.

"Yes."

"Other than his son's accusation, what evidence do you have which connects Lee to this woman's pregnancy or her murder?" Singer asked in a less than friendly tone.

"None."

"Well here is the bigger question, John. Why wasn't I consulted before you put out this inflammatory press notice?"

There was really no good answer to the question, and both Singer and his campaign manager knew that.

Before Peterson could respond, Singer decided to answer his own question. "You didn't ask me about this because you knew how I would react. And you decided to take a chance and put it out, knowing full well I couldn't do anything after it was released. This is nothing more than sleazy, gotcha' politics. We have never done this before, and I don't plan to start now."

Singer was upset, and Peterson knew it. But he had to try at least to offer some type of explanation. "This is how I looked at it. The issue was out there and whether or not we offered a paternity test, the issue was damaging to Lee. So, consistent with our philosophy of avoiding mudslinging, I thought I would offer him a way to respond to his son's very serious allegations."

Singer did not respond immediately. Finally, he said, "You're kidding, right? You want me to believe you were looking for what was best for Winston Lee? Trying to help him clear his name and reputation? Incredible. I would have to be the village idiot to believe your ridiculous justification. You were better off without any attempt to explain this."

"If this is true, Lee is unfit not only to be the governor of this state but to hold any public office. This country has a president who has the morals of an alley cat. He was heard on the Access Hollywood national television show bragging about kissing and groping women without their consent. His exact words were that he *grabbed them by the pussy*. And if that's not enough, there is now evidence he had sex with some porn actress and a Playboy bunny his lawyer paid off to keep them quiet during the campaign. Despite those, as well as other issues of corruption, Donald J. Trump was elected President of the United States. But here is the worst part. That guy carried the state of Missouri. Frankly, I don't want to repeat the embarrassment with this gubernatorial election."

"I hear what you're saying, and I certainly agree. The problem is we don't have any evidence to support the allegations made by his son. And I doubt he will agree to take the test. I'm sure his refusal will be okay with you because it makes him look guilty. So, all it will do is..."

"If he's not the father, I don't know why he wouldn't take the test," Peterson said.

"Because he might have had sex with this lady without protection and doesn't want to take a chance on the results of a paternity test. His response will include something to the effect he and his son don't get along for whatever reason and this outrageous allegation is the payback. I'm confident he will also say it was his son who was charged with murdering his girlfriend and got off on a legal technicality. There was never any innocent finding. This is the son's way of shifting the blame to help his own reputation, particularly since he is back in St. Louis and apparently practicing law these days. Without any evidence to back up our request, it will be characterized as the political stunt it is. In any event, the allegation is out there, and Lee can do whatever he wants to correct it. I don't want to be a part of this. Please cancel the press conference. But I will make a deal with you. If you get any evidence to support the accusations, I will reconsider."

"Yes, sir," was all Peterson could say.

While Singer and Peterson were having their conversation, Winston Lee's wife and Kelvin Bellington, campaign manager, were huddled in Lee's Jefferson City campaign office for a hastily called meeting. The subject: Singer's press conference. One of Singer's campaign staffers had leaked the true purpose of the conference to one of the television stations. In turn, the station contacted Bellington for a comment on whether Lee would take a paternity test Singer would request at his press conference. The topic of conversation for this meeting was how best to handle the request they knew was coming. No time to waste. An immediate reply was necessary, and Senator Lee was in California trying to answer questions from Darius Washington's money people about Garner's allegations.

"What do we do now?" Bellington asked, knowing Lee couldn't take the test because after the Darius Washington fiasco, his candidate admitted he was the father of the dead girl's child.

Cassandra Lee just looked at Bellington as though she was uncertain why he called the meeting. "What do you mean, what do we do now? We deny, like we said before. You know we can't take the test."

"I understand we deny paternity or any involvement with this girl. But how do we respond when Singer demands a paternity test? What are we going to say?" Bellington asked.

Cassandra had a suggestion. "What if we agree to take the test? Where are they going to get the DNA markers for the slut and her bastard child which would be necessary to do a paternity test?"

"I have no idea," Bellington said.

Kelvin Bellington had limited contact with Lee's wife. Their relationship was not the best. He didn't trust her and didn't like her. Nothing specific, but he felt she always had a hidden agenda. Clearly, she wanted to be the first lady of Missouri. He also knew her ambition didn't end there. Kelvin had worked for a lot of candidates and was usually on the winning side. His victories were the result of hard work and ethical campaigns. But after the fundraiser with Darius Washington, he began to wonder whether he was on the right side of this election. His candidate admitted a sexual relationship with a young woman, his son's girlfriend, no less. His wife knew about it, but apparently didn't care. Then there was the question of who murdered the young pregnant woman.

When Kelvin heard his boss admit he was the father in the presence of his wife, he hadn't known what to think. He wondered how a wife could listen to her husband admit he was the father of his son's girlfriend and stay married to him. Then there was the matter of the murder. How could she be sure her husband didn't kill the young woman? But Hillary Clinton didn't give Bill the boot after the Monica Lewinsky affair became a matter of public record and even an impeachment. Politics created marriages of convenience, and the Lees were no exception was the only conclusion to be drawn.

Cassandra Lee would answer her own question. "I think they would have to go to the circuit attorney to get the sample to compare. And we can control her. Braxton is not going to be handing out pieces of evidence to do any paternity testing, particularly if she knows what's good for her. I think we can say we are willing to take the test. Or at least, we have no problems taking the test if Singer wants to arrange it. He will then hit a brick wall when he tries to get the DNA markers to compare."

Once again Cassandra Lee was suggesting a misleading and dishonest approach to a serious issue, one which benefited her husband and her. Bellington was getting used to these suggestions. But this one could backfire. "Are we certain the circuit attorney would be the only source of whatever item is needed to do the test?" Kelvin asked.

"The medical examiner would have the DNA for both victims from Deland's autopsy. He would be the only other place. And we control this source as well," Cassandra said.

"I think it's too risky, and we really haven't thought it through to make sure we covered all the bases. Plus, it's just wrong. We know he is the father. He told us he was," Kelvin said.

"I don't give a shit what he said. We are in this to win, not come in second in a two-person race," Cassandra said. She had made her decision and didn't need any more time to think about it. She was willing to take the chance because her son's allegations were hurting the campaign. "I don't think it's risky at all," she emphatically told Kelvin. "We need to put this story to bed and this is the way we are going to do it. Prepare a press release. I want it to say Garner Lee was working for the Singer campaign when he made his malicious allegations. In the unlikely event Ray Singer would like to arrange and pay for a paternity test, Senator Lee will take it. I want this out before Singer's press conference."

"How do you know your son was working for the Singer campaign?"

"I don't. Just put it in the release."

"Shouldn't we check with the senator before we go down this road?"

"Dear God, no. He is out in California trying to get our financial supporters back in line, thanks to the damage our kid did. Now, please just go and do what I just said."

Chapter Twenty-Seven

John Peterson was on the phone with Singer when an aide came into his office and interrupted his conversation to alert him to an important developing issue. "The news media has been calling wondering whether we were going to arrange for a paternity test for Winston Lee," Peterson told Singer.

"What are you talking about? I thought we were going to cancel the press conference," Singer said.

"We were in the process when the calls came in from the reporters. They were asking if we were going to set up a paternity test for Lee. I asked one of the reporters where this was coming from. She said it came from the Lee campaign. Apparently, someone from our side leaked information about the paternity test and our willingness to arrange and pay for it. Believing this was going to be requested at our press conference, they got out in front of it and struck first," Peterson said.

The very thing Singer was trying to avoid now became an even greater problem. With the phone in hand, Singer was shaking his head, trying to figure out what to do next. He was upset with his campaign manager before, but now he was angry. "I want you to cancel that press conference immediately. Then we need to figure out how we are going to fix this mess. It would also be nice if we could identify the source of the leak on our side."

"Every campaign has leaks. You're not going to stop those. But as far as the paternity test is concerned, since he is volunteering to take it, why don't we accommodate him and pay for it?"

"One of the problems with is we get tagged for starting this after I promised we wouldn't take this campaign into the mud like every other politician."

Peterson disagreed. "You didn't start this. His son did. Our plan was just to follow through on what was started.

But now if we back away and don't follow through with what the press believes we were proposing, it makes us look worse. Like this really was a political dirty trick and Lee called our bluff. It also exonerates him regardless of whether he is the father of the child. So, I say we just proceed with what he volunteered for. We tell the press we will arrange and pay for the test."

Singer thought about the proposal. He didn't like it, but really didn't have much of a choice. Reluctantly, he had to agree. "I don't like it. But go ahead and notify the media. We will make the arrangements and pay for him to take a paternity test," he instructed his campaign manager.

The reporters wasted no time. Within minutes of the notification, the story was on the internet and in text messages. Later, the television, radio and print outlets would cover it.

Singer was on a dead-end street, a road to nowhere. Cassandra Lee knew it. She played the scenario in her mind. Her husband would look good because he volunteered to prove his innocence with a paternity test. If they couldn't get the markers for the test, it wouldn't be Senator Lee's fault. Singer couldn't get it done. Or didn't want to get it done. Guilty people don't volunteer to take paternity tests. He was now an innocent and injured party defamed by a malicious allegation fabricated by his opponent. The only wrinkle was a counter argument suggesting her husband could do the test on his own. But if Singer couldn't get Deland's DNA markers, neither could her husband. The campaign's response to any argument—guilty people don't volunteer to take tests which prove their guilt. She couldn't wait to give her husband the good news when he called her after he finished his meetings in California.

When the call came, the conversation didn't go as Cassandra had planned. "You did what? Are you fuckin' kidding me? This is a joke, right?" the candidate said when his wife described her brilliant campaign plan.

Surprised by her husband's reaction, Cassandra said, "No, I'm not kidding. What the fuck is your problem, Winston?"

"My problem? What the fuck is *my problem?* I'll tell you what my problem is. Felbin has my DNA. He took a fork and a glass after I had lunch with him and sent it to a lab to do a fuckin' paternity test. And guess what? The test proved I was the father."

"I'm aware of everything you just said." The truth of the matter was Cassandra had overlooked the lab report in her haste to take the air out of Singer's press conference. Her ego would not allow her to admit the mistake, particularly to her husband. "But they don't have the DNA markers from Deland and the child to do the test now."

"Well they did have them. How the hell else do you think Felbin got it tested?" the senator said.

"Having some report from a lab your enemies hand-picked claiming you are the father of the child and doing a live test through an independent lab are two different things. Plus, we don't even know if Felbin has a report. We never saw one. But even if he does, we can discredit him and Garner and still remain ready to have an objective lab do the test. Without the markers, it can't be done. I'm not worried. And I think this was the best play to counter what Garner did."

"You're not worried, but I am. You fucked up, admit it."

Winston Lee was screaming at his wife so loudly, Kelvin, who was not on the call but was in the room, could hear it. This was not the first time he'd witnessed exchanges like this between the two. If Felbin released the confirmatory test, the Lee campaign would have big problems, despite what Cassandra was saying. The wild card was Felbin. Kelvin knew there was no love lost between Felbin and Lee. And now he knew why. But he wondered whether a loss for Lee would be a win for Missouri. Now all Kelvin could do was sit and wait and hope if the lab report came out it would be at a time the Singer camp could not benefit. In the meantime, he was not motivated to do anything to prepare for this potential disaster. In fact, he considered submitting his resignation. This was not the type of campaign he was used to running.

"Stop yelling at me. I'm not your fucking lap dog. And while you're at it, if you hadn't fucked that whore, we wouldn't be involved in this mess. You're nothing but a piece of shit, and I should have divorced you a long time ago," Cassandra replied, not concerned about who was listening to her side of the conversation.

"Divorce me? That's a joke. You didn't give a shit about what I was doing or who I was fucking because all you cared about was climbing the political ladder. We both know you had your sights set beyond becoming first lady of Missouri. I was only a means to your end game. Right, Madam President?" Winston said facetiously.

"Go fuck yourself, Winston," she said as she hung up and looked at Kelvin. "What do we do now?"

"I have no idea. I suppose we sit and wait to see what Felbin does."

Although unwilling to admit it, Cassandra also knew the paternity test was a smoking gun which could bring down the campaign. She was also concerned about the additional potential problems which could result from revisiting the murder of Amy Deland.

Chapter Twenty-Eight

Not surprisingly, it didn't take long for Tony Carmine to be on the phone with Garner Lee. "Not sure if you saw the latest," he began.

Garner had no idea what he was talking about.

"The Singer campaign apparently offered to pay for a paternity test for your father to determine whether he is the father of Amy's child. And he agreed to take the test."

"But we know he is the father and so does he. We have the results of the test we conducted. Why would he agree to take this test? This can't help his campaign."

"I'm guessing he thinks Singer won't be able to get the DNA markers for Amy and the fetus to do the test. And without those, there can't be a test. He'll then claim he wanted a test to clear his name, which is the reason he volunteered to take it. He will then hope he can put this issue to bed."

"Son of a bitch," was all Garner could say.

Carmine was on a mission. He hated Winston Lee for what he'd done to his son. But he hated Cassandra Lee even more. She killed Amy Deland and remained silent while her son was accused of the murder. Then she used a legal technicality to prevent a search for the real killer. Carmine was determined not only to bring down the campaign but more importantly to put Cassandra Lee in the penitentiary where she belonged. Of course, he also knew he could not involve Felbin in any plan to accomplish either objective.

"Listen Garner, I have an idea. But I need your promise. This is another one of those conversations which is totally off the record. We are not having this conversation. Agreed?"

Garner wasn't sure what Carmine was going to say. But he had an idea it involved taking down his father's campaign which couldn't involve Felbin. For anything involving his father, he was all in. "Agreed," he said.

"Okay, here's the deal. You were our client. We represented you in the murder case. You'll remember the time Felbin invited your father to lunch. After he left, Felbin took some items like a fork, napkin and some things your father used during the lunch to get his DNA. His DNA was then used for comparison to the DNA markers for Amy and the fetus we got in discovery during the criminal case."

Garner listen intently, not sure where this was going.

"So, this is what I want you to do. Go to Felbin and ask him to see the file. As the client, you have the right to see your own file. But the problem is going to be we don't have a report on the paternity test. We didn't want it because we knew if we got it, we would have to turn it over to the prosecutor. At the time, we weren't sure of how the prosecutor would use the information. However, I know the guy who ran the test has the data and his conclusions are in a file. He's Felbin's buddy. You don't need a report. You just need his file."

"What if Felbin refuses to give me the file or get the data from the lab guy?"

Carmine was amazed at how little Garner knew about the practice of law. "He can't refuse. You're the client and are entitled to your file. He won't refuse. But he'll figure out why you want it and will try to talk you out of doing anything with it. He'll be worried about Larry Jenkins' case and whether this will hurt the effort to get the victim's DNA. He may also say he needs to talk to Scheck. If that happens, you need to tell him your request for the file is as a client. Then it will become an attorney client communication and he can't say anything to Scheck."

"What do we do when we get the lab results?"

"We give it to Singer and let him release it. Then we sit back and enjoy the show."

When Carmine finished his conversation with Garner, he went into Felbin's office. Felbin was on the phone talking to Barry Scheck. They were planning the strategy for the hearing, which was a week away. The judge had promised an expedited hearing date and he delivered. "Glad you're here. I'm talking to Barry," Felbin said to Carmine as he entered the office. "Barry, Tony just came in. I'm going to put you on speaker, so we can all talk."

Decisions needed to be made regarding Ellen Rossi and whether they put her on the witness stand. The other issue was how to handle the victim, Janet Costello-Snead, who wanted no part of any of this. She'd made her position perfectly clear to Garner and Carmine when they talked to her. And Braxton made the mental health of the victim the centerpiece of her argument in opposition to Felbin's request.

"Tony, the question is whether we put Rossi on the stand. Since you met with her in Florida, tell us about the meeting and your thoughts about her," Felbin said.

"When Garner and I first talked to her, she gave us nothing. She took the position the ID of the victim was credible, and Jenkins had his day in court. Just another guilty guy trying to get out of prison. She claimed she could think of nothing unusual about the way the case was handled by anyone.

"But then later, she called me, asking me to meet her alone. Now the story was different. This time she claimed the victim's ID was extremely tentative. She looked at fifteen photographs for an extended period of time. While looking at them, according to Rossi, the victim kept saying 'I don't know. They all look alike.' Finally, Costello said, 'I'll go with this one' and selected the picture of Larry Jenkins.

"Rossi and her partner put all of the equivocation in the report. Actually, her partner prepared the report. When they took it to the circuit attorney's office, they thought it would be a refusal. But when they got there, they were directed to Cardwell, who told them to rewrite the report and take the uncertainty out. They argued with her. Unfortunately, in the end, they did what they were told, and thereafter kept their mouths shut."

"So, she lied to you when you first met with her?" Scheck asked.

"She did. But then she called me and wanted to meet."

"Why the sudden change of heart? Did she think we had something which could expose her misconduct and make matters worse for her?" Felbin asked.

"We didn't suggest we were holding something back which could hurt her. I just think she has lived with this for a long time and saw it as an opportunity to do the right thing. A little guilt mitigation. I believe she is now finally telling the truth."

"Do you believe Rossi because she is tossing your nemesis, Cardwell, under the bus?" Scheck wanted to know. Felbin had told him Carmine had no respect for Cardwell and would do anything to screw her given what she did to both Garner and Bobby Decker, the city police officer she also accused of murder.

"I can't say I'm sorry she is painting a target on Cardwell's forehead. But I believe she is sincere. I think she has been living with what she did to this guy for a long time. After she told me what she had done, it was like someone stuck a pin in a balloon and let all the air out."

"I think we need to get her to St. Louis for the hearing at least. She is not going to do us any good if she is in Florida. I suppose whether we use her will depend on what we do with the victim. We have the burden of proof. I'm not convinced we have enough to meet our burden if we don't put her on," Scheck suggested.

"We have several inconsistencies in the victim's description. For example, the height, the weight, the skin color, the lips. We also have the alibi defense counsel never used. Of course, the prosecutor will say the inconsistencies in the description were covered during the trial and the alibi issue was addressed in the filings for post-conviction relief based upon the ineffective assistance of defense counsel. And Jenkins lost on all counts. While we're persuaded DNA will free Jenkins, I'm not sure Nealon will be as convinced. And if that's our case, we are left with the victim and Rossi," Felbin said.

"I think you're right. If we put the victim on and break her, we won't need Rossi. Obviously, having the victim recant will be preferable to a cop admitting she obstructed justice. Tony, what do you think our chances are with the victim?" Scheck asked.

"I don't know. She really didn't want to talk to us. Maybe it's because she didn't want to relive this traumatic event. Or maybe it's because she knew she lied on the witness stand," Carmine said.

"We need to put the victim on first, as distasteful as it might be. If we break her, there is no need for Rossi and maybe no need to involve Cardwell. But if we don't put her on, Rossi won't be able to testify to any conversation she had with her. It would be hearsay," Felbin said.

Although the Jenkins hearing would be decided by a judge, not a jury, Felbin knew Nealon would apply the rules of evidence. Some judges relax the rules a little when a jury is not present. But not Nealon. For him, the rules were the rules and the facts were the facts wherever they led.

The hearsay rule is misunderstood and misapplied by trial lawyers and judges alike. Technically, the rule is simply defined as an out of court statement offered to prove the truth of the matter asserted. But the hearsay rule is filled with numerous exceptions. If only Rossi testified, Felbin could not ask her what Janet Costello told her. That would be hearsay and inadmissible. However, if Costello testified first, Felbin could ask her if she made a particular statement to Rossi. If she denied making the statement, Felbin would then be free to call Rossi and ask her if Costello made the statement. That's hearsay, but it's an exception to the rule because Rossi would be testifying as to a prior inconsistent statement made by Costello. The net effect is to challenge the credibility of the person who refuses to own the statement.

"Rossi will be critical. She establishes Costello's equivocation. The statement 'they all look alike' highlights her uncertainty and suggests a racial bias since all fifteen of the photos were black males," Felbin added.

"What about Cardwell? If we are going to have Rossi testify about what Cardwell told her and her partner to do with the police report, we will need to put her on the stand as well," Scheck said.

"I agree," Felbin said.

"Sounds like we made a decision. Costello, Rossi and Cardwell will be testifying. Shall I get subpoenas out to them?" Carmine asked.

"Yes. And then we need to wait for the explosion. We'll keep you posted, Barry."

Chapter Twenty-Nine

Carmine wasted no time preparing the subpoenas. He then contacted Rossi to let her know she would be called as a witness for Larry Jenkins. Her response was as he expected. She was anxious to resolve this case and get the monkey off her back. But she was not thrilled about coming to St. Louis and publicly admitting to what would be viewed by some as obstruction of justice. And an obstruction which perhaps put an innocent man in the penitentiary for a very long time.

"I will be there," was all Rossi could say.

Carmine could feel Rossi's pain. He knew the reporting on this would not be kind to her. She was a police officer, sworn to uphold the law and ensure justice was done. Here she failed. But no one is perfect, including police officers. During his career, he made many mistakes. But one in particular stood out. While assigned to a drug task force, one month he had made some twenty-two arrests. Most were pleas but one defendant decided to take his chances with a jury. Because of dilatory defense motions and tactics, the case didn't come to trial for over a year. The prosecutor failed to prep him for his testimony and as a result, he went on the witness stand cold.

During any criminal trial, the arresting officer is asked to identify the person he arrested. This case was no exception. Looking at the defense table, Detective Carmine noticed what he presumed was the defendant's lawyer sitting in the first chair with a note pad and papers in front of him. Two males were seated next to him. Each with nothing in front of them and both were wearing dark suits, white shirts and ties, one red and one blue. Both were in their early thirties with short dark brown hair, long sideburns and clean shaven. Carmine had looked at a police report and the mug shot of the defendant prior to testifying. At the time of his arrest, the defendant had long dark brown hair and a beard. These two guys looked nothing like the guy he arrested. Usually, the identification was no big deal. The defendant was the guy, looking scared to death and sitting next to the lawyer. But now he had two to choose from and he couldn't very well say he had no idea which one was the defendant. He had a fifty-fifty shot. He picked the wrong one and the defendant was eventually acquitted.

"I'll send you a plane ticket. And we will want you here a couple days before the hearing so we can do the prep. Thanks, Ellen. We appreciate your help," Carmine said.

After finishing his conversation with Rossi, he was off to serve Cardwell at the courthouse. This could be the highlight of his year, perhaps even his career.

When he arrived in Cardwell's courtroom, he was met by the bailiff who wanted to know his purpose in seeing the judge. Rather than stating his true purpose, he simply indicated he had something he needed to deliver to her.

After a few minutes the bailiff returned, delivering a message from the judge. Whatever it was, Carmine could leave it with the bailiff. When the bailiff refused to tell the judge the delivery had to be made directly to her, Carmine left.

The judge's chambers were situated directly adjacent to the courtroom. However, judges could leave their offices through a door leading directly to a bank of elevators without going through the courtroom. While the judges had a private elevator, it was situated in a hallway containing five public elevators. Sooner or later, Cardwell would have to leave her office and use the private elevator. Carmine would wait for her in the hallway.

He didn't have to wait very long. At about 2:15, Cardwell appeared in the hallway heading for the private elevator. She was leaving for the day.

"Done for the day, Judge?" Carmine asked.

Startled by the question, Cardwell looked at Felbin's investigator and chose to ignore him as she pushed the button to summon the elevator.

"I have a little present for you, *Your Honor*," Carmine said sarcastically as he handed Judge Cardwell the subpoena. "Hope you enjoy the rest of your day off, *Your Honor*." As he walked away, Carmine whispered, "You piece of shit."

"I heard that," Cardwell said, referring to Carmine's comment as she examined the subpoena.

Instead, of going home as she had planned, Cardwell headed for the circuit attorney's office.

"What the fuck is this?" Cardwell demanded as she threw the subpoena on Braxton's desk.

Karen Braxton picked up the document from her desk and saw it was a subpoena in the Larry Jenkins case. "It's a subpoena in the Jenkins case," she said, stating the obvious.

"I know it's a subpoena for the Jenkins case. I can read. Why am I being subpoenaed?"

Braxton wondered the same thing. Given Felbin's relationship with Cardwell and particularly now that Garner Lee was also involved in the case, it could be simply their effort to aggravate her. On the other hand, they could know something Braxton didn't which would mean Cardwell was withholding some important information. She decided to press the concealment issue.

"I don't know, Joan. Perhaps *you* can tell me why you have been subpoenaed."

"How the hell would I know? This case goes back twenty years or more, or whatever it is. It's an ancient case. And it was just another rapist I put where he belonged. What I remember is the victim was sure of her identification and the jury believed her. I would have thought you would be on top of this case and would know why a sitting judge is being dragged into it over some DNA bullshit."

Braxton decided to confront the issue directly. With Cardwell, this approach was always risky. "Is there anything about this case that you are not telling me? I don't like surprises, Joan."

"Didn't you hear what I just said? This case is ancient history. I'm guessing this is Felbin's way of fuckin' with me."

"Maybe. Or they may have something they believe will help them get the DNA test they're looking for and perhaps even more. What do you want me to do?"

Cardwell didn't respond immediately. Her initial inclination was to file a motion to quash the subpoena. But there were risks. Felbin could be bluffing and the filing of a motion would put the issue before the public. It would look like she had something to hide by trying to avoid testifying in a case she prosecuted. And Nealon could deny the motion, which would reinforce the suggestion she had something to hide. On the other hand, if he sustained the motion, it would look like all the judges stuck together regardless of whether an innocent man was in the penitentiary. Cardwell was in a bad spot, and she knew it.

"We probably need to file a motion to quash if for no other reason than to flush out whether they intend to call me as a witness and, if so, for what purpose. But I don't want to do it right away. I want to see how this plays out, for the moment at least. In the meantime, you need to call Felbin and see if he will tell you why I got the subpoena. I doubt he will explain. But maybe he will say something we can use to quash it. In the meantime, I want to know everything that's going on in this case. Are we clear?"

Like all good political lap dogs, Braxton agreed.

Chapter Thirty

Although she knew it would be a waste of time, she had to call Felbin to satisfy Cardwell. She organized her thoughts while she waited for him to pick up the phone.

Felbin was in his office with Carmine, who had just returned from serving the subpoena on Cardwell. He had an ear-to-ear smile, and Felbin knew why. Few things pleased Carmine more than getting under Cardwell's skin. And it didn't get any better than serving her a subpoena to testify in a high-profile case where a man's freedom was at stake. Just as Carmine began to explain his encounter with Cardwell, his excitement was interrupted by Felbin's assistant. Braxton was on the phone. And Felbin knew why she was calling.

After putting her on the speaker so Carmine could hear, Felbin began, "So, you decided to do the right thing and give me what I need to do the DNA test and free an innocent man."

"Dream on, Felbin," she replied.

"Well there can only be one other reason for this call. Your mentor was just served with a subpoena."

Braxton knew Felbin was talking about Cardwell. She decided to ignore the reference. It would only detract from her effort to find out the reason for the subpoena. "Perhaps you can explain why you subpoenaed a sitting judge for a case this old?"

"Because she wasn't a sitting judge when Larry Jenkins found his new home behind bars. In fact, she put him there."

Those responses triggered the beginning of the back and forth lawyer games. In the end, neither would give up any information which wasn't known before the conversation began.

"I am aware she was the prosecutor. She prosecuted many cases while she was in this office. Do you really expect her to remember anything which could possibly assist you in this matter?"

"Why don't you ask her what she remembers? Surely, she remembers something."

"I did ask her, and she doesn't remember the case."

"That's surprising. This was a high-profile case. And she tried it at a time she was auditioning to become the circuit attorney. Given her miserable conviction rate while she was an assistant, she needed a conviction, and this case was going to launch her campaign to become the next elected prosecutor. Even she should remember this setting," Felbin said as Carmine gave him a thumbs up sign.

"All I can go by is what she tells me. And she told me she doesn't recall the case at all," Braxton said, knowing she was stretching the truth.

"Well then I suppose we will have to refresh her recollection when we put her on the stand."

"Refresh her recollection with what?" Braxton asked, attempting to have him show at least some of his hand.

"The facts," Felbin replied.

"Stop playing games, Felbin. If you have something, tell me. Maybe what you tell me will convince me to agree to your test."

"Games? You've got to be kidding. You and I both know even if I laid out my entire hand, you wouldn't agree to the test. And it has nothing to do with your victim and everything to do with Cardwell. You've got your marching orders. I know *her* game. I suggest you ask Cardwell to tell you the truth about this case. Of course, given her track record, I don't think she is likely to be forthcoming with you or anyone else. I guess you'll just have to wait until the hearing to see my hole card. You *will* be impressed. Have a nice day, Karen."

When the conversation ended, Braxton had some concerns. As expected, Felbin gave her nothing of any substance. Just a lot of smoke and bluster. This was what lawyers did and Felbin did it as well as anyone. Braxton had a feeling there would be fire under the smoke. The problem was she didn't know what it was, and Cardwell was either unwilling or unable to help. Added to her concern was Cardwell's recent recollection. Initially when Braxton talked to her, she had no recollection of this case. But now she remembered the certainty of the victim's identification. Braxton didn't know whether the recollection was actual, or Cardwell was just repeating something Braxton had said during their earlier conversation. Time would answer the question. In the meantime, a motion to quash the subpoena needed to be prepared and filed with Judge Nealon.

Chapter Thirty-One

When appearing before Judge Nealon, Felbin liked to be in the courtroom and ready to go at least fifteen minutes before the call of the docket and the appearance of the judge on the bench. The prosecutor's motion to quash Cardwell's subpoena was scheduled for 9:30 am. Felbin, along with Garner and Tony, were seated at the counsel table at 9:15 am. Braxton had not yet arrived.

The reporters began to wander in around 9:25 am. Felbin had alerted them to the hearing. It's not every day a sitting circuit judge is subpoenaed to testify in a case involving the prosecution of what may be an innocent man.

Felbin was not surprised when he received the motion to quash. Neither Cardwell nor Braxton knew what was coming. In most cases, the lawyers were required to share a witness list prior to trial. But not a requirement here. This was a case seeking injunctive relief and the production of evidence used in Jenkins' trial, which the judge would decide. Since no witness list was required, the prosecution was unaware of the potential appearance of Ellen Rossi and probably would not be prepared to challenge her testimony when she did appear.

Filing the motion to quash was not without its risks. Cardwell had something to hide was the spin Felbin would put on it. Certainly, if she was convinced Jenkins was guilty, she would welcome the opportunity to testify. The judge could reinforce Felbin's position if he denied the motion to quash and guaranteed her appearance at the hearing.

At precisely 9:30 am, the court was opened for the day by the bailiff after Judge Nealon took the bench. Braxton was nowhere to be found.

After viewing Felbin at the counsel table, the judge asked, "Is Ms. Braxton representing the state in this matter? I see she signed the motion to quash."

"As far as I know, she is, Judge," Felbin replied.

"Let the record reflect Ms. Braxton is not present to represent the state. Mr. Felbin and Mr. Lee are present to represent the petitioner, Mr. Jenkins. We are here today to take up the state's motion to quash a subpoena issued to Judge Cardwell. Is that correct, Mr. Felbin?"

"Correct. We are appearing today pursuant to the state's notice indicating they will be taking up their motion this morning at 9:30."

"In view of the fact that the state is not represented here today, do you have anything to say, Mr. Felbin?"

"I do, Your Honor. Since the state has defaulted on its motion to quash the subpoena issued to Joan Cardwell, a material witness for Mr. Jenkins, I ask you to deny the motion and enforce the subpoena."

"I agree. The state's motion to quash the subpoena issued to Joan Cardwell will be denied," the judge ruled.

Just as Judge Nealon finished his ruling, Karen Braxton was opening the court room door. As soon as Nealon saw her, he said, "Ms. Braxton, this court does not send invitations to the circuit attorney's office to appear here, particularly to argue motions you filed. I'm sure you have a good reason why you're late."

"No excuse, Your Honor," was Braxton's casual response as she took her seat at the counsel table.

Her response was going to be a problem. Felbin had seen this judge reprimand lawyers who were late. The severity of the verbal reprimand was in proportion to the sincerity of the apology. Braxton forgot the apology part. Not a good start.

"Am I correct in assuming you know how to tell time, Ms. Braxton?"

"Yes, sir."

"Since you can tell time and have no excuse, I assume you intended to keep all of us waiting. And intended to disrespect this court and your opposing counsel."

"No, sir.

"Do you understand what this case is about? The serious nature of these allegations?"

"I do understand the issues here, judge. I also understand our position. The victim made a positive identification and the jury believed her. And as I explained to you

122

before, we are resisting this because it is traumatic for the victim to relive this nightmare."

"The court still hasn't heard an explanation of why you were late today," Nealon said.

"Again, Your Honor, I have no excuse and I do apologize to the court and counsel for the petitioner."

"Because this is not the first time this has happened with you specifically, Ms. Braxton, I'm considering a $500 sanction. I will make a final decision at the conclusion of this case. You can be assured this sanction will in no way influence the way this case is decided."

"I can assure the court this will not happen again. May I now be heard on my motion to quash the subpoena served on Judge Cardwell?" she asked in an attempt to move Nealon off the tardiness issue on which he was fixated.

"Your motion was ruled before you arrived, Ms. Braxton. It was denied," Judge Nealon said.

Braxton looked confused at first. But after the full impact of what the judge had just said settled in, she was angry. She was going to have to explain to Cardwell the motion was denied by Nealon because she was late. Cardwell would need to appear and be cross examined by Felbin. Unable to contain her anger, she said, "Are you kidding? You overruled my motion because I was a couple minutes late?"

Felbin, Garner and Tony sat back to watch the show. There was nothing they needed to add.

"I would be careful with your tone, Ms. Braxton. You're already on thin ice."

After taking a deep breath to control her emotions, Braxton said, "I'm sorry, Your Honor. But as you are aware, judges in this circuit have dockets which would choke a horse. To take Judge Cardwell away from her docket to sit here waiting to testify about a case that occurred many years ago and about which she has no recollection is a disservice to her and the entire circuit."

Felbin turned to Garner and whispered, "That's her argument? Is she serious?"

"I am confident Mr. Felbin will not require Judge Cardwell to sit here for the duration of the hearing and will contact her just before her testimony is needed. I have ruled, Ms. Braxton. We are adjourned," Nealon said and then left the bench.

Braxton just sat at the counsel table wondering how she was going to break the news to Cardwell. Regardless of how she was going to explain this, she needed to do it now before Cardwell read it in the paper or heard it on television.

It was a short walk to Cardwell's chambers, but Braxton was in no hurry. She knew whatever she said would not be well received. She would be verbally assaulted, which was Cardwell's style.

When Braxton entered the chambers, as usual, Cardwell's door was open, and she was on the phone. Mary McMurtry, Cardwell's secretary, was at her desk outside the judge's chambers. McMurtry had Cardwell's secretary for many years when she was the circuit attorney and stayed with her when she became a judge. Braxton knew her well, having worked with her during her time in the prosecutor's office. "How is the mood today?" Braxton asked.

"Not good. She has been in one of those moods ever since you told her about the Jenkins case. She was pushed to the edge when she found out Felbin and now Garner Lee were representing Jenkins. But the subpoena put her over the edge," McMurtry said.

"Great, and now I have more bad news for her. Nealon is making her come to the hearing and testify."

"Oh no. Good luck." When Cardwell's phone call ended, McMurtry said, "She's off her line, you can go in. I think I'll go find a cup of coffee somewhere far away from here."

Cardwell knew Braxton had met with Judge Nealon, and wasted no time getting to the point. "Did Nealon quash the subpoena?"

"No, he didn't," Braxton said softly.

"Are you fuckin' kidding me? What was the basis of his decision? What did he say? I always suspected he didn't like me, even when I was circuit attorney," Cardwell shouted. She was in a free fall rage.

Braxton had a decision to make. She could either tell her the truth or lie. But there was one little problem if she lied—the press coverage. So, she opted for the truth, but with a little sugar coating. "I had some other pressing issues in my office and was a few minutes late for court. When I arrived, I learned he had already denied the motion to quash your subpoena. I argued with him, but it was apparent to me at least, he had made up his mind on this well before today's hearing. He was determined to make you appear."

Braxton studied Cardwell's reaction. At least for the moment, Cardwell was considering what Braxton had said. Considering her options without immediately lashing out at the messenger. To make sure this new reaction continued, Braxton added, "I think I tend to agree with you. Nealon doesn't like you or me."

After a few more minutes of uncomfortable silence, Cardwell finally said, "You fucked up big time and now I'm going to have to pay for your screw up. I'm not sure why you're handling this as opposed to one of your assistants who knows what to do in the courtroom. You need to figure out how to turn this mess you created around. Your future will depend on it. Now, get the hell out of here."

Once again, Braxton was verbally abused. She understood Cardwell could damage her future political aspirations. But she wondered whether the cost of constantly satisfying Cardwell was too high.

Chapter Thirty-Two

Braxton filed a motion asking Judge Nealon to reconsider his prior ruling on Cardwell's subpoena. The judge scheduled the motion to be heard on the same day as Jenkins' DNA hearing.

At precisely 9:30 am, as always, the bailiff called the court to order and Judge Mark Nealon appeared. The courtroom had few spectators other than print and electronic reporters. Aside from his lawyers, no one was there representing the interests of Larry Jenkins. After more than seventeen years in the penitentiary, Jenkins' friends had long since abandoned him. His parents had died while he was in prison. He had three brothers, two older, one younger and an older sister. His younger brother had been murdered in a drive by shooting in his neighborhood as he was walking his dog. One of his older brothers died of natural causes and the whereabouts of the other was unknown. His sister was ill and spent her time in and out of the hospital. Larry Jenkins was alone. He had no family left who cared about him, and his only friends after seventeen years were those he met in prison and who were also doing time.

Unlike the last hearing, this time all the parties were in their places. In fact, Braxton was ten minutes early. Judge Nealon directed Felbin to call his first witness.

Felbin, Scheck, Garner and Carmine had met several times to map out the strategy for the hearing after the state's motion to quash Cardwell's subpoena was denied. They decided to call Cardwell as their first witness. Their reasons were simple. They needed to ask Cardwell whether she directed the detectives handling the Jenkins investigation to eliminate certain critical details from the police report. They knew she would lie. They would then be allowed to call Detective Ellen Rossi to rebut Cardwell's prior sworn testimony.

"The petitioner will call Judge Joan Cardwell," Felbin announced.

With that announcement, Braxton was on her feet. "Judge, we have a motion for reconsideration pending on Judge Cardwell."

The announcement piqued the interests of the reporters in the audience. They had previously written about Judge Nealon's decision. An editorial followed suggesting Cardwell had something to hide by her refusal to cooperate in a search for the truth about Jenkins' involvement in a rape.

"I'm aware of your motion, Ms. Braxton. Please explain why I should reconsider my prior ruling," Judge Nealon said.

"Thank you. Judge Cardwell is currently a sitting judge with a full docket. Requiring her to appear here presents a great inconvenience to her and the parties on her voluminous docket. Second, I do not believe a party can subpoena a sitting judge."

Braxton's argument was made with little enthusiasm. Given her last conversation with Cardwell, part of her welcomed the opportunity to witness Felbin take her apart on the stand. Poetic justice would be served, since Cardwell was the reason Braxton was fighting Jenkins' DNA request in the first place. Like Judge Nealon, Braxton believed the request was reasonable and would have agreed to it. But, once again, Cardwell's threats shaped Braxton's course of conduct.

"Do you have any legal authority to support your statement that a sitting judge cannot be subject to a subpoena?" Nealon asked.

"I do not," Braxton said.

As Felbin began to rise, the judge motioned for him to sit down. He was prepared to rule and didn't need to hear from Felbin. "Is Judge Cardwell standing by and in her chambers now?"

When Braxton indicated she was, Nealon said, "Then please ask her if she can join us at this time. Your motion for reconsideration is denied. And Mr. Felbin, I'm sure you will recognize Judge Cardwell's busy schedule and be brief."

Although only a short walk away, Cardwell took her time getting to Nealon's courtroom. Nealon was not pleased.

He could have called a recess, but instead had everyone wait in their places for her arrival. It was clear to Nealon the delay was a sign of her dissatisfaction with his ruling. When she finally arrived, he said nothing and simply pointed to the witness stand, clearly a sign of his dissatisfaction.

After the oath was administered, Judge Nealon looked at Felbin and said, "You may examine this witness."

After establishing her identity and current occupation for the record, Felbin got right to the point. "When you were with the circuit attorney's office, you prosecuted Larry Jenkins, is that correct?"

"I believe so," Cardwell said.

Felbin expected equivocation, but he was going to set the tone of this examination from the outset. "You believe so. Are you telling this court you did not prosecute Larry Jenkins for rape?"

"I just told you, Mr. Felbin, I believe I did. It was a long time ago."

"In an effort to refresh the recollection of this witness, I have marked as exhibit A, the circuit court file in the matter of State of Missouri versus Larry Jenkins, Cause Number 00762. I ask the court to take judicial notice of the file."

"The court will take judicial notice of its own file," Judge Nealon said.

Turning to the witness, Felbin said, "I'm handing you exhibit A and asking if this file refreshes your recollection that, without any doubt, you were the one who prosecuted Larry Jenkins for rape?"

"My name is listed as the prosecutor on the court file," Cardwell said.

Before Felbin was able to ask his next question, Judge Nealon, who was clearly frustrated, said, "Judge Cardwell, are you saying someone other than you handled this case?"

Before answering, Cardwell stared at Judge Nealon. She was clearly agitated by his question. Finally, she said, "No."

"Judge Cardwell, this will go a lot faster and you will be able to get back to your docket, if you will provide direct answers to direct questions," Judge Nealon added, motioning for Felbin to continue with his examination.

Felbin hesitated before asking his next question. He was waiting for an explosion. But Cardwell didn't respond or react to the bait.

"Since you were the only prosecutor on the case, do you now recall dealing with Detectives Patrick Moore and Ellen Rossi?"

"Yes."

"And they investigated the rape of Janet Costello and brought their investigation to you for your review, correct?"

"Yes."

Cardwell was now responding with yes or no answers.

"And after police officers complete their investigation, the decision as to whether to prosecute rests sole with the assistant circuit attorney. Correct?"

"Yes."

"And in the case of Larry Jenkins, you alone as an assistant circuit attorney at the time, made the decision to prosecute Larry Jenkins. Correct?"

"Yes."

"I'm going to show you what I have marked as Exhibit B and ask you whether you recognize this as the police report prepared by Detectives Moore and Rossi regarding the rape of Janet Costello?"

"Yes."

"Did you have a meeting with these detectives to discuss the rape of Janet Costello?"

"Yes."

"When you met with them, did they bring a police report they had prepared?"

"Of course they did," Cardwell responded sarcastically.

"When the detectives brought their report to you, did you direct them to remove anything from that report?"

"No."

"Did you direct them to amend any part of their report?"

"No."

"During your time as a prosecutor, did you ever direct a police officer to remove or amend a report of a criminal investigation?"

"No."

"I want to direct your attention to the police report regarding Larry Jenkins again. According to this report, Janet Costello was firm in her belief and identification of Larry Jenkins as the person responsible for raping her. Correct?"

"Yes."

Felbin wanted to ask her very narrowly tailored questions to continue to elicit yes and no responses. "Is this the report that was originally provided to you by the detectives?"

"Yes."

"Isn't it true the original report contained equivocation and uncertainty by Ms. Costello in connection with her identification of Larry Jenkins as the person who raped her?"

"No."

"Isn't it true the original report reflected Ms. Costello's uncertainty with her identification? When Ms. Costello looked at the photographs of potential suspects, shook her head and responded with 'I don't know, I don't know, they all look alike', finally saying, 'I'll go with this one' which was Larry Jenkins?"

"No."

"And isn't it also true, the original report contained Ms. Costello's description of the suspect as having dark skin and large lips, which contradicted the physical description of Larry Jenkins?"

"No."

"And isn't it true you directed the detectives to remove the equivocation in Ms. Costello's identification and eliminate her description of the suspect?"

"Absolutely not. You are way out of line, Felbin, and I resent your suggestions and implications," Cardwell said, clearly angry and expanding her previous yes and no responses.

"Did the detectives argue with you when you told them to change their report and suggest you wouldn't make the case even if the report was changed?"

"I just told you I didn't tell anyone to change a report. And I did, in fact, make the case. Your client was convicted by twelve neutral, fair and objective people. And then the court of appeals affirmed the conviction."

"I have no further questions for this witness," Felbin told the court.

On his way back to the counsel table, he looked at Braxton. She had her head down, looking at some notes she had made. Felbin figured she had no idea where he was going with this line of questions.

As Braxton reviewed her notes, she was trying to decide whether to ask Cardwell any questions. She had no idea what Felbin had. But she was certain Cardwell had not been completely candid with her.

Against her better judgment, Braxton decided she better ask Cardwell a few questions. Otherwise, it may look like she is agreeing with Felbin's suggestion of misconduct through his accusatory questions. But she would keep it short.

"Judge Cardwell, when you were a prosecutor, did you refuse to prosecute cases brought to you by St. Louis police officers?" Braxton began.

"Of course, many times."

"And were there also times when you would ask the officers to do additional investigating and bring you more evidence before you would agree to prosecute the case?"

"Yes."

"And in each of those instances when you asked for an additional investigation, did you ever direct the police officers to change a police report?"

"Absolutely not," Cardwell responded while looking directly at Felbin.

"And if additional evidence could not be found, what would happen to the case?"

"I would refuse it."

"Now turning to the case of Larry Jenkins. You were shown a police report, Exhibit B, which I will hand you again. Is this the report the detectives brought to you when you met with them?"

"Yes."

"Did you make any changes on this report?"

"As a prosecutor, we don't make changes on police reports. So, the answer is no."

"Did you direct these detectives to add or subtract *anything?*" Braxton asked, dramatically emphasizing the word *anything* while raising both hands above her head.

"Absolutely not."

Braxton spent a short time looking through her notes before announcing she had no additional questions.

But Felbin had a few more. "And you are absolutely certain you didn't order any changes in the original police report because that would be improper. Correct?" Felbin asked substituting the word *order* for *direct*.

"And you are certain you didn't order any changes because as a prosecutor, you *never* ordered a police officer to change a report. Correct?" Felbin asked, emphasizing the word never.

Felbin didn't need to ask Cardwell any more questions. Rossi was now set up to refute Cardwell's sworn testimony. The wild card would be the victim. Could Janet Costello hold her own with aggressive cross examination? The parties would not have to wait very long to find out. Janet Costello-Snead would be Felbin's next witness.

Chapter Thirty-Three

As Felbin was nearing the completion of his examination of Cardwell, he went to the counsel table and told Carmine to go to the witness room and get Janet Costello-Snead. The plan was to make sure Cardwell and Snead passed each other in the courtroom as Cardwell was leaving and Snead was entering.

Felbin was uncertain how much time, if any, Braxton spent preparing the next witness for her testimony. He was certain Cardwell had not been completely candid with Braxton in explaining her role in the alterations to the police report. Braxton knew the victim performed well enough to convince a jury that Jenkins had raped her. Based on her trial testimony and because Cardwell was not candid, Felbin concluded Braxton spent very little time preparing Snead for this hearing. If he was correct, he would have a huge advantage. He would just have to be careful he didn't elicit any sympathy through his cross examination. After all, regardless of whether Larry Jenkins was guilty of rape, this lady was still a victim.

When Janet Snead entered the courtroom, her facial expression and tentative gait told Felbin she would rather be jumping out a plane without a parachute than coming to court to testify. When she passed Cardwell, there was an added look of concern. Felbin didn't know what to make of it. Cardwell, however, gave no indication she even knew who Snead was. Neither spoke.

Felbin had expected Braxton to lodge some frivolous objection to prevent him from calling this witness. When Braxton didn't make any noise, the witness was sworn and took the stand. Felbin was now ready to begin his examination. But he had to be careful. While he was firmly convinced she'd lied when she identified Larry Jenkins as the person who raped her, he reminded himself she was still a victim. And sometimes victims of crime are honestly mistaken. Given what Ellen Rossi had told them, Felbin didn't believe this was some honest mistake. He believed Snead was coached. And her coach was Joan Cardwell.

Felbin left his seat at the counsel table, walked to the podium and began with simple background information, education, occupation, length of employment, age. He intentionally avoided any questions relating to her family and residence. Victims of crime were never anxious to disclose personal family information for obvious reasons. But eventually both knew the tough questions would be coming.

"Ms. Snead, you have previously identified Larry Jenkins as the person who raped you. Am I correct?" Felbin asked.

"Yes."

"Do you see Larry Jenkins in the courtroom today?"

The witness looked around the room like she was trying to find a grade school classmate she hadn't seen in years. Apparently, she had not expected the question and had not been briefed on where the defendant would be seated. Finally, she said, "I believe it is the person over there," pointing to an individual seated at the counsel table.

Snead had consistently claimed she was raped by a black man. But two black men were seated at the counsel table. Jenkins was seated next to Garner Lee and both were wearing jackets and ties. Felbin wanted Jenkins to appear in business rather than jail attire.

"Ms. Snead, there are three people sitting at the table where you pointed. Please describe what the individual you are identifying is wearing. And please take your time."

After another hesitation, she said, "I believe it is the black man wearing a blue blazer, white shirt and red stripped tie."

Although she selected his client, twice she equivocated by using the phrase *I believe.* He needed to pursue this. But he knew if he simply asked her if she was certain she would say yes. He had to come at her a different way. He needed an open-ended question. One which would force a narrative response.

Felbin moved away from the podium to a place where he blocked Snead's view of his client. He then said, "Ms. Snead, please describe the physical appearance of the person who raped you to include height, weight as well as any unique or unusual characteristics."

Another hesitation. This time longer than the others. "Sir, it has been a long time and it was dark and..."

Felbin didn't give her a chance to complete her answer. "Are you saying you didn't get a good look at the person who did this to you either because it was dark, or you were understandably scared or both?"

This time her response was quick and firm. "No sir. I got a very good look at him. He was wearing some type of a mask to hide his face, but it came off. He raped me," she said pointing at Larry Jenkins. "Your client raped me and now I have to relive this."

This wasn't where Felbin wanted to go, but he needed to press on. "Ms. Snead, all I am asking you to do is describe the person who raped you. Can you do that?"

"He was a black man. After these many years, I can't be specific at this time with respect to height, weight and the other things you want me to tell you."

"Understandable. Let me see if I can help you. Do you recall talking to two detectives, Ellen Rossi and Patrick Moore?"

"Yes."

"And do you recall telling these detectives the person who raped you had dark skin and large lips?"

"I don't remember. It was a long time ago and tried to put this horrific ordeal out of my mind after it happened."

After Felbin moved back to the podium, allowing the witness to have an unobstructed view of Jenkins, he said, "Does the individual you identified previously look like he has dark skin and large lips?"

"No," the witness admitted.

"Did the detectives show you some photographs and ask you if the person who raped you was among those photos?"

"Yes."

"And when you looked at the photos, did you tell the detectives, 'I don't know, I don't know, they all look alike'?"

"I might have. I was very upset at the time they were showing me those pictures."

"Then did you select the photo of Larry Jenkins and tell the detectives, 'I'll go with this one'?"

"Same answer, sir. I was upset at the time. I don't re-call the specific words I used then or now."

"I realize this was a traumatic experience, Ms. Snead..."

"It was extremely traumatic. Worse than you can ever imagine," the witness injected.

"I can certainly appreciate what you are saying, Ms. Snead. But when you selected the photo of Larry Jenkins were you guessing he was the one who raped you?"

"I was certain."

"Thank you, Ms. Snead." He had no additional questions for this witness.

Janet Snead did a decent job of walking the fine line. She injected the issue of emotion into her identification. Most, if not all, victims of this violent crime are emotional at some level. Janet Snead was no exception. But in the end, she testified with certainty as to her identification of Felbin's client as the person who raped her. At this moment, she was a credible witness. But Felbin was not done.

With no questions from the prosecutor, Felbin told Judge Nealon there was a possibility he might need to re-call the witness and asked that she not be excused. Over the prosecutor's objections, the court directed Ms. Snead to remain in the courthouse subject to recall.

Chapter Thirty-Four

Ellen Rossi had been waiting in the room designated for defense witnesses. She was pacing nervously around the room as she waited for her turn to testify. She had testified in criminal cases many times. And she had made her share of mistakes. But never before did she have to confess acts of misconduct. Never did she knowingly participate in a scheme to convict what might have been an innocent man. She didn't feel good about what she had done. But she had to set the record straight, come clean and admit everything. Although it wouldn't excuse her conduct, in the end the DNA would positively tell whether she was responsible for putting an innocent man in the penitentiary for a long time.

It wasn't a very long walk from the door of the courtroom to the witness stand. But it seemed like miles to Ellen Rossi. The reporters seated in the front row didn't do anything to calm her nerves. She acknowledged Judge Nealon with a nod as she walked past the bench. He didn't respond. Rossi had appeared in his court many times when she was a city police officer. She believed he respected her. But now she wondered if he would feel the same after he heard her testimony.

"Do you solemnly swear the testimony you are about to give will be the truth, the whole truth and nothing but the truth, so help you God?' the bailiff asked after asking her to raise her right hand.

The truth of the matter was she screwed up and now she needed to take her lumps. But in a couple hours, she would be on her way to the airport and back to Key West to begin the process of putting this matter behind her. At least down there, she would not have the constant daily reminders of what she had done.

She responded with a resounding "I do."

For the first time in this case, she would finally be telling the whole truth.

Recognizing the witness was nervous, Felbin began
with some background and soft ball questions to calm her
down. Her resumé was impressive. She was first in her
class at the police academy and spent only five years in
uniform before her transfer to sex crimes. There she received a variety of awards and commendations which Felbin reviewed with her. She had an extraordinary ability to
calm traumatized rape victims, which was recognized by
the white shirts running the department and put her on a
fast track for promotions. She was a lieutenant when she
retired and in charge of the sex crimes division.

She and Sergeant Patrick Moore were assigned to investigate the rape of Janet Costello. She was new to the
unit, and Moore, who was now deceased, had been her
mentor. Several rapes had occurred in the area of St. Louis
University, and there was no suspect. The university and
the students, along with their parents, were concerned
about a serial rapist who would continue to attack coeds.
The department and the circuit attorney were under pressure to make an arrest and convict the person responsible.

"Did you and Detective Sergeant Moore interview the
victim of one of those rapes, Janet Costello, now Snead?"
Felbin asked as he was now getting to the heart of the matter.

"We did," Rossi said.

"And did she give you a description of her assailant?"

"Yes. She said he was a black male with dark skin,
thick lips, pudgy face, clean shaven, about five feet ten
inches tall and weighed about 185 pounds."

"So, her assailant was not wearing any type of mask?"

"I believe initially he was. But it came off during the
attack."

"What about tattoos, scars or any identifying marks?"

"She didn't say he had any identifying marks."

"Did you show Ms. Costello any photographs of potential suspects?" Ordinarily, if Felbin was trying this case to
a jury, he would lay a foundation for the photo spread. But
Judge Nealon knew what a photo spread was and didn't
need Felbin to waste time laying a foundation.

"Yes."

"How many photos did you show her?"

"Fifteen."

"At the time you showed Ms. Costello the photographs, did you actually have a suspect?"

"No."

"Then how did you decide which photographs to show her?"

"We knew several rapes had occurred in the area. We were not investigating those other cases, but we talked to the detectives who were and compared notes on suspect descriptions. We then went to our file and selected photographs of those individuals we knew had some type of history of rape or sexual assault. Since Larry Jenkins had previously been arrested and charged with rape in St. Louis, we included his picture," Rossi said.

"This really wasn't technically a photo lineup because you didn't have a suspect, am I correct?"

"Yes. I suppose we could have had her look at the mug shot book. But we decided to save some time and reduce the field since there was a lot of heat to get this thing solved and an arrest made."

"Please tell Judge Nealon what happened when you showed Ms. Costello these photographs."

"She looked at all fifteen of them for a long time. A good fifteen or twenty minutes. Then she pulled out three and set them aside. She studied these for another ten to fifteen minutes. She would look at one, put it down, pick up another one all the while shaking her head and saying, 'I'm not sure. I'm not sure. They all look alike.' Finally, she said, 'I'll go with this one.'"

"And the one she said she was going to go with, whose picture did she select?"

"Larry Jenkins."

"When you showed her these fifteen photographs, what did you say to her?"

"I didn't say anything. But Detective Moore told her to take her time and let us know if there was anyone who looked familiar to her."

Felbin led her through the preparation and content of the police report by Moore, which included the manner in which the victim selected Jenkins' photograph. Not only did Moore detail Costello's hesitation but also included verbatim the statements she made during the process. Rossi then went on to describe the journey of the original report.

Once completed, it was taken to the circuit attorney's office. Once there the matter was assigned to an assistant circuit attorney for a review of the completed report and a determination of whether Jenkins would be prosecuted for raping Janet Costello. Joan Cardwell was the prosecutor who would make the decision.

"When you took the report to the prosecutor, you knew the identification was tentative at best. So, why didn't you just continue to investigate and take the case to the prosecutor after you had more evidence?" Felbin asked.

"Because of the heat on the case. The chief and the circuit attorney needed a suspect, an arrest and a conviction. And since she did make an identification, we didn't want to be criticized later if we didn't have the prosecutors look at it and decide what they wanted to do. Frankly, Mr. Felbin, the way the report was written, we thought we had a refusal," Rossi said.

"But that's not what happened, is it?"

"No. Joan Cardwell told us to rewrite the report and leave out all the details of the tentative identification. She then charged Mr. Jenkins with raping Janet Costello." Rossi identified exhibit B as the amended report which excluded the details of the victim's tentative investigation.

"Did you know whether Larry Jenkins had an alibi for the time Janet Costello was raped?"

"I don't know."

"Did you ever investigate whether he had an alibi?"

"No, because your client was not talking to us after we arrested him."

"Did you make any effort to talk to him before you arrested him?" Felbin pressed.

"We did not. Like I told you, we thought we had a refusal when we took it to the circuit attorney's office."

"But when you didn't get a refusal, why didn't you continue to investigate and find out if, for example, he had an alibi?"

"Because we knew Joan Cardwell was going to go forward with this prosecution regardless of what we brought to her," Rossi said, a response helpful to Jenkins, but not to her or her partner.

"I have one final question, Detective Rossi." Felbin had a copy of the trial transcript. He knew neither Rossi nor her partner testified. Usually, one or more of the investigating police officers would be called by the prosecution. Knowing Judge Nealon would not read the trial transcript, Felbin asked, "Did Assistant Circuit Attorney, Joan Cardwell, call you as a witness during the trial?"

"She did not put me on the stand," Rossi said. She then added, "She didn't have my partner testify either."

As soon as Felbin announced he had no additional questions, Braxton was on her feet. She didn't like the way this hearing was going. "Do I understand you are telling this court you falsified a police report?"

"If that's how you want to categorize it, then yes, I did," Rossi said looking directly at Braxton.

"And despite the fact the chief was putting pressure on you to make an arrest, you say it was Judge Cardwell who made you change the report?"

"That's exactly what I'm saying here under oath."

"And you said you didn't testify during Mr. Jenkins' trial?"

"Yes."

"Either for the prosecution or the defense?"

"Correct."

"But you do know the victim testified at the trial and she said Larry Jenkins raped her."

"I wasn't at the trial. However, I assume she would have testified and apparently the jury believed her."

"As you sit here today, do you believe Larry Jenkins didn't rape Janet Costello?"

"I don't know one way or the other."

"After you arrested Mr. Jenkins, was there another rape in the area of Saint Louis University?"

"No."

"And you now claim this initial report you and Moore prepared contained all of the details regarding Ms. Costello's identification including the specific words she used when making her identification?"

"Yes."

"But all we have now is your word and Judge Cardwell's denial," Braxton said as she looked at Felbin while walking back to her chair at the counsel table.

"My word and this police report," Rossi said as she pulled a document out of her purse.

Braxton who had not reached her chair, stopped and quickly turned to look at the witness. The look of immediate panic on her face told the story.

Felbin leaned over to Carmine, asking whether he knew anything about this. Carmine shook his head looking as confused as everyone else in the room.

Judge Nealon had no idea what was happening.

Braxton approached the witness asking to see the papers she was holding in her hand. After reading them and handing them to Felbin, she told the judge she had never seen the document before this moment. Felbin scanned the papers he was just handed. They appeared to be pages of the original police report. He also acknowledged he had not previously seen them.

Braxton started to complain about Felbin sandbagging her, but the judge cut her off. "Ms. Braxton, Mr. Felbin said he has not seen this report before today. I take him at his word. Also, was any discovery exchanged between the parties before today?"

When both Braxton and Felbin said no, the judge instructed them to move on, asking, "Do either of you have any additional questions for the witness?"

In response, Felbin had the report marked as exhibit C and showed it to the witness. After identifying it for the record as the original report, she was asked why she kept it for so many years. "Because I never felt good about what I had done to Mr. Jenkins. Although I thought the identification was weak, I didn't really know for sure whether he raped Ms. Costello. And I thought or at least hoped, if he was innocent this report might come in handy someday to prove it."

As the witness was finishing her statement, Felbin looked at the judge. A look of concern was on his face. "How do we know you didn't prepare this document recently?" Felbin asked.

"Because the computer time-stamped the report when it was printed. You can see the marking in the upper right. I believe if you compare this date to the date the charges were issued, you will see the printing date on this document occurs before the charge of rape is issued."

Felbin moved for the admission into evidence of all exhibits and announced he had no further questions.

Braxton had only one question. When Rossi denied providing a copy of the original report to Felbin prior to today, she was excused.

Before the court took a short recess, Felbin announced he wanted to recall Joan Cardwell. Braxton objected. The judge said, "I think recalling her would be a good idea under the circumstances, Ms. Braxton. Please ask her if she can be here in fifteen minutes."

Chapter Thirty-Five

As soon as the judge left the bench, Braxton went to bring Cardwell the *good* news about her return to the witness stand and the reporters gathered around Felbin asking to see both reports. While the reporters read the documents and made notes, Felbin asked Carmine if Rossi ever told him she had the original report. "She never said a word. I had no idea," Carmine said.

Felbin then looked at Garner Lee and asked the same question and received the same answer. Garner then asked, "Do you think her pulling out the copy of the original report helps us or hurts us?"

Felbin thought about the question. It was a good one. Rossi clearly admitted to acts of misconduct which certainly would have violated the rules of the police department, if not the criminal statutes. But she was no longer a police officer, so the internal rules didn't apply. And the statute of limitations for any criminal offense had long since expired. Under the circumstances, Rossi had nothing to lose except her reputation as a good, honest police officer.

Clearly, by coming forward, Ellen Rossi wanted to set the record straight. But several questions remained. Did Cardwell see the original report? Or did Moore and Rossi decide to change it and put the case on Jenkins because of the pressure to arrest someone for at least the Costello rape? If Cardwell prosecuted the case and lost it, she would take the heat as long as no additional rapes occurred in the same area. Regardless of what Cardwell knew when she issued the rape charge, Ellen Rossi played a substantial role in putting what might be an innocent man in the penitentiary for a very long time.

"I'm not sure," Felbin said in response to Garner's question.

Cardwell was on the phone when Braxton arrived in her chambers. "What kind of a mood is she in?" Braxton asked Mary McMurtry, Cardwell's secretary.

"Not the best day. After she testified, she came back and slammed the door and hasn't opened it since. What's going on with the case which would upset her? From what I read in the paper, this is a guy she prosecuted, and he was convicted. Now he wants to do a DNA test. Doesn't sound very complicated to me," the secretary said.

"It's not." But Braxton knew the police report Rossi produced was going to be a problem. From the time she first told Cardwell about the DNA request, she was concerned she wasn't getting the whole story. "Did the judge ever say anything to you about Larry Jenkins or anything about his prosecution?"

"She never mentioned it. But she has certainly been in a mood ever since you came here and told her about the case. Not sure why," McMurtry said with a look of confusion. "Is the hearing over?"

"Not exactly. Unfortunately, I'm here to tell her she needs to come back. Felbin wants to put her back on the witness stand."

McMurtry's look of confusion turned to a look of fear—like someone had just pointed a loaded weapon at her and was ready to pull the trigger. McMurtry had been Cardwell's secretary for a long time. Mood swings were nothing unusual. Her boss was always demanding and very difficult to please.

There were times when McMurtry questioned why she would remain with such a person. She came seriously close to quitting on two occasions. Once was when Cardwell was the elected circuit attorney and she was prosecuting Bobby Decker. The other was when she presided over the trial of Garner Lee, accused of murdering his girlfriend. In both cases, McMurtry had known the political connection between Cardwell and Senator Winston Lee and his wife. Not only would she overhear telephone conversations Cardwell was having with various people, but sometimes her boss would just want to talk, get McMurtry's perspective, confide in her or just get something off her chest. During those private conversations, Cardwell was usually pretty candid.

145

She trusted McMurtry. She was not only her secretary but also considered her a friend.

McMurtry would be retiring shortly. "Maybe I'll start my retirement today," McMurtry said after Braxton told her the reason for the visit. "Looks like she's off the phone. You can go ahead in. But I might knock first if I were you."

Once Braxton was inside her office, Cardwell asked, "Is the hearing over?"

"Actually, it's not. Judge Nealon told me to come and get you. Felbin wants to put you back on the witness stand," Braxton said.

"What the fuck?" Cardwell screamed loud enough to be heard throughout the courthouse. McMurtry closed the judge's door. Always the loyal secretary protecting her boss from embarrassment. "Why does he want me back on the stand?"

Braxton didn't know exactly what Felbin was going to ask her. But before she could let her know what Rossi was saying, Cardwell erupted again, "Tell Felbin and Nealon to get fucked. I'm not coming."

"Settle down, Joan. I don't know what your relationship is with Nealon. But he has got a room full of reporters up there. If you thumb your nose at him, Felbin will no doubt ask him to lock you up and he'll do it."

Cardwell didn't respond immediately. She was considering her options. Finally, she said, "Tell him you can't find me, and I'll leave for the rest of the day. I don't have anything else on my docket."

"I'm not going to lie to Judge Nealon. That won't end well for either of us. Plus, there is no jury and he will just reschedule it at a time you *are* available. We will just be delaying the inevitable. Frankly, Joan, I just don't understand why you are behaving like this. From the outset, you have resisted me on this. I wanted to just allow the DNA request since you said it was a good prosecution and conviction. What is your problem?"

"My problem? What's my problem?" Cardwell asked rhetorically.

Challenging her on any issue was never a good thing for anyone. But Braxton heard what Rossi said and had to ask the question. She needed to know who was telling the truth.

"My problem is Felbin and his sidekick who likes to murder women, are harassing me over some DNA bullshit and you are letting them do it. That's my problem."

"Hold on, Joan. First, you were the one who acquitted Garner Lee by throwing my prosecutor under the bus. And we all know why you did that. Second, Rossi just testified you told her to change the report and remove the victim's uncertainty as to the identification."

"Bullshit. Total bullshit. I didn't tell anyone to change any report."

"Rossi produced the original report, Joan."

Unfazed by Braxton's statement, Cardwell said, "Then she just prepared it. This report is as phony as she is."

"And after all these years, why would she take the time to prepare a phony police report about an old rape case? She has nothing to gain and everything to lose. And if, as you say, this is a good case and Jenkins is good for the rape, why would Rossi claim the victim wasn't sure? It makes no sense."

"How the fuck am I supposed to know why these cops do anything? All I know is I never saw any police report where this victim wasn't sure Jenkins raped her."

Just then the chamber's door opened and McMurtry told her boss Judge Nealon's bailiff had called to say the judge was waiting for everyone and was anxious to get on with the hearing.

Chapter Thirty-Six

Cardwell stared at Felbin as she walked past the counsel table on her way to the witness stand. Turning to Nealon, she said, "I don't appreciate being called back here a second time."

Judge Nealon didn't respond immediately. He didn't need to. His facial expression told the story. His left eyebrow rose, his face began to turn red and his jaw became rigid. The entire courtroom knew he was not pleased with the comment and waited in anticipation of his response. But all he said was, "Sit down," as he pointed to the witness stand.

"You understand you are still under oath," Felbin began.

"Of course, I understand. I'm a judge in this circuit and I know the rules, Felbin. I also know the only reason I'm back here is so you can harass me and I..."

She didn't finish her statement before Nealon interrupted her. This time he had something to say. "Hold on. Let's get something straight. First, you are not here as a judge. You are here as a witness in this courtroom where *I* am the judge. Second, you will answer all proper questions posed by either party. Third, the lawyers will be respectful to you and, in turn, you will respond respectfully to their questions. Finally, we don't need any editorial commentary. Just answer the questions and you will get out of here sooner. Do I make myself clear?"

Garner sat at the counsel table, not sure what he was witnessing. He had never seen one judge dress down another one. Neither had Felbin.

As she listened to Nealon address his colleague, Braxton was concerned. Her case, along with her credibility might be going south. Although Nealon was a fair judge, she worried he would order the DNA test for no other reason than to embarrass Cardwell. No real harm in ordering the test, which was what she thought from the beginning. If the DNA matches, Jenkins goes back to prison. If it doesn't, she and Cardwell may have some explaining to do.

When Cardwell didn't immediately respond to Nealon's question, he repeated in a louder voice, "Do I make myself clear?"

While looking away from Judge Nealon and at an empty jury box, Cardwell said, "Yes."

Resisting the temptation to ask another question which would set her off again, Felbin simply asked her whether she had ever seen the report Rossi brought with her to the hearing.

"I have never seen this document before."

"Did the lawyers who represented Mr. Jenkins at his trial take Ms. Costello's deposition?"

"No."

"Did you meet with the victim, Ms. Costello, to prepare her for her trial testimony?"

"I met with her one time shortly after I issued the case, and it was brief." Cardwell's testimony had been limited to one word or short responses to Felbin's questions. For this question, she felt the need to expand her answer. "I told her how the case would proceed and what was going to happen at the trial if the defendant did not plead guilty. What defense attorneys like you would try to do to her. I did not rehearse her testimony like you defense lawyers do. There was no need. She lived the horror of the rape and knew what happened."

Felbin knew Cardwell was lazy when she was an assistant circuit attorney. She cut a lot of deals rather than doing the work to prepare and try the case. Her statement that she didn't prepare the victim, the most important witness in a rape trial, was not surprising. But if Rossi was to be believed, someone had to prepare Costello. "Did anyone to your knowledge prepare Ms. Costello for her trial testimony?" Felbin asked.

"No."

"Did you call either Detective Rossi or her partner, Patrick Moore, as a witness to testify in the state's case during the Jenkins trial?"

"No."

"Why not?"

"Because I didn't need either one of them. All I needed was the victim. If a problem developed with her, I would have called one or both of the officers. But it wasn't necessary because the victim did a great job."

Felbin had no more questions. He didn't need any more questions. He laid the foundation with Cardwell. She said she didn't prepare Costello for her testimony. Now he needed to recall the victim to see if she would agree with Cardwell's testimony.

As Felbin began to ask the questions, Braxton began to understand where he was going. When Janet Costello-Snead, finished testifying, Felbin said he might be recalling her. Braxton now knew why. What she didn't know was what this victim would say when Felbin put her back on the stand. Fearing Cardwell could only make the matter worse, she decided to pass on asking her any additional questions.

As soon as Braxton said she had no questions of Cardwell, Felbin announced his desire to recall the victim. He wanted Cardwell to hear his announcement and see her reaction. She didn't disappoint. As she was leaving the witness stand, Cardwell looked at Judge Nealon, then at Felbin and while shaking her head mumbled, "More harassment of a rape victim." While passing the counsel table, she looked at Braxton, and in a voice louder than her first comment, said, "Object" as she hurried to the door. The judge ignored the comment and directed Felbin to recall the witness. Braxton lodged no objection.

Chapter Thirty-Seven

When Janet Snead re-entered the courtroom, once again she looked like a deer caught in the headlights. Felbin began by reminding her she was still under oath. He then apologized for having to put her back on the witness stand to ask additional questions. Regardless of whether her identification of Jenkins was correct or incorrect, she was a victim and had to be treated accordingly. The last thing Felbin needed was to beat up a rape victim with the media watching the show. On the other hand, Felbin needed answers. Someone was lying, and he had to identify the liar. He also needed to determine what role, if any, Janet Snead played in convicting what he believed was an innocent man.

"Ms. Snead, you testified in the Larry Jenkins' jury trial, correct?"

"Yes."

"Earlier you told us you were not clear on the exact circumstances surrounding your identification of Larry Jenkins as the person who raped you given your emotional state. Do you recall your testimony?"

"Yes," Snead said, unclear of why she was being asked about the testimony she had already given.

"But then when I asked you if you were guessing when you selected Larry's photograph and identified him as the person who raped you, you indicated you were certain. Do you recall that testimony?"

"I was certain. I don't know what someone else told you, but I was certain when I picked out his picture the police showed me."

Felbin told Snead about the testimony the court heard from another witness which contradicted what she had said in her earlier testimony. "Detective Rossi was clear. You were not certain Larry Jenkins was the one who raped you when you selected his photograph. As a matter of fact, she produced a copy of a police report she and her partner had prepared in connection with this case." Felbin handed the witness a copy of the original report Rossi brought to the hearing and asked her to read it.

Snead accepted the document and tentatively began to read it. Felbin waited. He was in no hurry. He knew the longer it took her to read the report the greater the pressure. She would have to explain the discrepancy between her certainty and the equivocation and uncertainty reported by Rossi and her partner. Finally, after what seemed to be an eternity, Felbin asked, "Have you finished reading the police report?"

"Yes," Snead said as she looked up from the document.

"As you can see, the detectives had a different perspective as to your identification of Larry Jenkins."

"They're wrong."

"Or could it be you are wrong?" Felbin asked firmly, sensing the need for a more aggressive approach with this witness. "And could it be you are incorrectly recollecting the exchange with the detectives, given your admitted emotional state?"

"No."

"How much time did you take looking at the pictures the detectives showed you before you selected Mr. Jenkins?"

"I don't know. I wasn't timing it."

Moving to another issue, Felbin said, "Did you have any meetings with Joan Cardwell, the prosecutor, prior to the trial?"

"Yes."

"How many meetings did you have with her?"

"Several."

"How many is several?"

"I don't know."

"More than fifteen?" Felbin thought he would start with a high number and work his way backwards.

"No."

"More than ten?"

Usually by this time the opposing lawyer is up and objecting, suggesting the witness had already testified he didn't know the number. But Braxton sat silently at the counsel table, making no objection or attempt to interrupt

Felbin's cadence. Sitting silently was not one of Braxton's strong suits.

"No."

"Somewhere between five and ten?"

"I would say maybe five or less."

"Did you meet with her alone?"

"One of the meetings there was another person who attended."

"Do you know who that was?"

"It was a black female. I got the sense she was some kind of an assistant to Ms. Cardwell."

"Do you remember her name?"

"It was an unusual first name. Kizzy. I remember it because she said she was named after character in the book *Roots*. I don't recall her last name."

"Kizzy Lewis?"

"Yes, I believe that was the name."

"What was her role?"

"We had several rehearsals. And then at either our last meeting or second to last one her assistant was there. At this one, Ms. Cardwell would ask questions first and then Kizzy would ask questions. Her questions were more aggressive and harder. It was like she was mad at me."

Felbin asked Judge Nealon for a moment to speak with his investigator. Felbin knew what the witness just described was a practice session of direct and cross examination to prepare Snead for her trial testimony. Cardwell did the direct while Lewis did the cross. This would directly contradict Cardwell's sworn testimony on several levels. Felbin knew Kizzy Lewis was no longer with the circuit attorney's office and wanted Carmine to locate and interview her.

After thanking the judge for the brief interruption, Felbin continued questioning the witness. "When you finished your meeting with Kizzy Lewis, did you meet again alone with Joan Cardwell?"

"Yes. I met one more time with Ms. Cardwell."

"Ms. Snead, during the question and answer session, did Kizzy ask you questions about how certain you were when you selected the photograph of Larry Jenkins as the person who raped you?"

The witness didn't immediately respond. She just looked first at Felbin and then around the room like she was searching for someone to answer the question for her. Finally, she said, "I don't remember."

"And during these sessions, did Cardwell tell you how to answer the question relating to how certain you were with respect to your identification of Larry Jenkins?"

"There was some discussion," Snead said.

"Did you ever tell Cardwell that you were not sure Larry Jenkins raped you?"

Once again, she didn't respond and instead, looked at the audience for answers. When it became obvious the witness was unwilling to answer the question, Felbin asked, "You testified under oath at Mr. Jenkins' trial. Did Cardwell tell you to say he was the one who raped you?'

Again, Snead didn't respond. Sooner or later, Felbin would need to ask the judge to order the witness to answer the questions. But Felbin wanted to ask one more question before he turned to the judge for help. "While a student at St. Louis University, your roommates at the time of the rape were Cara Fowler and Virginia Paul," Felbin began. He knew the witness would not answer the question. But he didn't care. It was more important to make a statement. Send a message to the witness. "In fact, Ms. Snead, contrary to your sworn testimony here today, isn't it true you told your roommates you were not sure the guy whose photograph you selected was the one who raped you?"

Braxton was on her feet. "Judge, we need a recess."

Felbin agreed, but he needed to make one more point in the presence of the witness. "I want to make my position with respect to this witness perfectly clear," Felbin said as he pointed to Janet Snead who was still seated on the witness stand. "I believe perjury has occurred during this hearing. And the only way this perjury can be corrected is for the witness to come back into this courtroom during these proceedings and tell the truth."

Judge Nealon did not agree or disagree with Felbin's comment. Instead, after granting the prosecutor's request for a recess, he said, "Ms. Braxton, I assume you will have a conversation with Ms. Snead and explain the applicable law to her."

After Braxton agreed, she left the courtroom with the witness. The reporters left to file their stories on this breaking news.

Chapter Thirty-Eight

As Braxton was in her office speaking with her victim, Felbin and Garner Lee were in the court holdover talking to their client.

Larry Jenkins was not formally educated. He never finished high school and through the years didn't enjoy a lot of full-time employment. Prior to his arrest, he was working for a large St. Louis produce company doing miscellaneous jobs as a day laborer. He was never married. His parents had passed away. Of his four siblings, only the location of his sister was known, and she was ill. His father was also an unskilled laborer and his mother worked as a maid in a hotel in the city of St. Louis, making beds and cleaning toilets. Neither finished high school. They did the best they could to provide food, clothing and a clean home for the family. The children were forced to leave school and work to contribute to the support of the family. Larry's family was by no means wealthy. In fact, they were poor. But they had each other and loved each other. They suffered the same indignities experienced by other poor African American families. But other than Larry, no one else in the family had been convicted of a crime.

Larry Jenkins didn't completely understand what just happened in the courtroom. "So, Miss Costello lied? She said I raped her, but she didn't know if I really did? And now she won't answer your questions? What does all this mean? Is she going to jail for lying?"

"Well, we know she lied, but her lies are only part of the story. Detective Rossi was clear when she described Costello's uncertainty in selecting your picture. Cardwell said she never prepared Costello to testify at your trial. If we believe Costello, she had several meetings with Cardwell and another prosecutor. This victim would have no reason to lie about those meetings. She had no idea Cardwell emphatically said there were no meetings.

"The question now is why Cardwell would have to prepare Costello so many times if Costello was certain you
raped her. And why would Cardwell have to lie about it? I
suspect the answer is Costello was not certain, and Cardwell had to coach her about what to say. She had to convince a jury you were the guy and there could be no hint of
doubt in her testimony.

"They also had to be sure the first police report didn't
surface. Your lawyer never saw a copy of it. This is the
reason Rossi and her partner weren't called as witnesses
during your trial. Cardwell couldn't risk the detectives testifying they prepared a different report at Cardwell's direction.

"Now we come down to the threshold question. Will
Costello return to the courtroom after her conversation with
Braxton and tell the truth about her uncertainty in identifying you as a rapist? If she doesn't, Braxton can prosecute her for perjury. If she does testify honestly during this
hearing, there can be no prosecution for perjury," Felbin
explained.

"But she already lied. She testified at my trial I raped
her, which was a lie. Why can't she be put in jail for what
she said there?" Jenkins asked.

"That's a good question, given what you have been
through thanks to her. Unfortunately, too much time has
passed, and the statute of limitation would prevent her
from being prosecuted now."

Garner Lee listened carefully to Felbin's comments. Although he was a lawyer, he had little experience in cases
such as this or really any other type case. "What is your
guess as to what she is going to do?" he asked referring to
Costello.

"I really don't know. But I do know she's scared," Felbin said.

"Maybe the better question is what do you think Braxton will do if Costello doesn't purge herself of the perjury?"
Lee asked.

"Prosecutors don't charge very many people with perjury, particularly given the number of people who lie on the
witness stand. The penitentiary would probably be overflowing if they did."

The discussion was interrupted by the bailiff who told them the witness and the prosecutor were back and the judge was ready to proceed with the hearing.

"Here we go. In a few minutes we will know which road this victim selected," Felbin said as he and Garner left the holding cell.

Chapter Thirty-Nine

When Felbin entered the courtroom, he saw Janet Snead seated on the bench behind the prosecutor's table inside the bar. Her eyes were fixed on the floor and her breathing was labored. There was little question she was scared.

Braxton sat at the counsel table tapping a pen on a legal pad. When Felbin entered the room, she looked at him but then quickly looked away when their eyes met. This case was rapidly becoming a political nightmare even if the DNA was a match and Jenkins was not the innocent man his lawyers were portraying. There was Cardwell and Rossi to deal with, not to mention the victim. At this point, while Braxton didn't know who, she knew someone had to be lying.

Felbin considered approaching her to see if there was anything they needed to discuss before the judge returned to the bench and the hearing began again. Ultimately, he decided this was her problem and if she had anything to talk about, she would approach him. He had given her the opportunity to do this the easy way and agree to the test without court intervention. She'd declined, claiming it would be upsetting to her victim. Felbin wondered how upsetting the current situation was to Braxton, her victim and whoever else opposed the test. He suspected Cardwell was probably pulling the strings on Braxton, her puppet. Regardless, Felbin felt like he was in a good position. And it might even be a better spot than had Braxton agreed to the test. Funny how things work out.

The reporters scrambled to get to their seats so they wouldn't miss a minute of the show. The electronic media spent the recess setting the tease.

"We are at the courthouse and the Jenkins hearing is in a recess so the rape victim can talk to the prosecutor about

whether she perjured herself. The victim claimed Larry Jenkins raped her. But now she refused to answer Jonathan Felbin's questions about the details of her identification of Jenkins. Felbin suggested she committed perjury when she identified his client as the rapist, and she needs to tell the truth or be charged with perjury. The judge directed Karen Braxton, the circuit attorney, to meet with her and explain the law relating to perjury. We'll bring you more details as they become available to us."

After Judge Nealon directed the witness to return to the stand, he told Felbin to resume his examination. Felbin rose slowly from his chair, buttoned his suit coat and looked directly at the witness. The entire courtroom waited in anticipation, wondering how both Felbin and Snead were going to handle the situation. Felbin moved away from the counsel table and walked slowly toward the witness stand and stopped some ten feet from the witness. There he stood for what probably seemed like an eternity to the witness. Finally, he said, "Ms. Snead, let's get right to the heart of the matter." Pausing briefly, he continued, "I want to know whether you were certain Larry Jenkins was the one who raped you when you met with the detectives and selected his photograph."

Without any hesitation, the witness looked at Felbin and said, "I was not certain Larry Jenkins was the one who raped me when I picked out his picture."

"Earlier today you testified you were certain Larry Jenkins was the one who raped you when you selected his photograph. Are you standing by your earlier testimony?"

"No, sir, I am not standing by my earlier testimony."

"Then let me ask the question again at the risk of repetition," Felbin said. No objection from either the judge or prosecutor. The issue was too important for a variety of reasons. There could be no confusion with either the question or the answer. "As you sit here today, right now, were you certain Larry Jenkins was the one who raped you when you selected his photograph?"

"No, I was not."

"Let me see if I can summarize what you just said. When the detectives showed you photographs, you selected Larry Jenkins as the one who raped you. But then you were not certain he was the one. And today, you previously said you were certain Larry Jenkins raped you. But now you have recanted your previous testimony. You are now saying you are not certain Larry Jenkins, the man seated over there, raped you," Felbin said pointing to his client. "Did I summarize your sworn testimony here today correctly?

"Yes."

"When you selected the photograph of Larry Jenkins, according to Detective Rossi, you said and I'll quote 'I'm not sure, I'm not sure. They all look alike. I'll go with this one'. Did you say that?"

"I can't tell you those were my exact words, but certainly they are close if not exact. Mr. Felbin, the point is I was not sure Mr. Jenkins was the man who raped me at the time I met with the detectives."

"If you were not sure, why did you pick Larry's picture?"

"I have obviously never been through anything like this before. I was scared. I was embarrassed. I was young and had been violated. Frankly, I thought the detectives knew who raped me and his picture was in the stack they showed me. I did all I could to tell them I wasn't sure. And if I picked out the wrong guy, I thought they would tell me. When they didn't say anything, I just figured I got the right guy."

"You testified during the trial you were certain Larry was the one who rape you. When did you become certain?"

"I was not certain when I testified at the trial," Snead said.

"Your trial testimony was also false?"

"I was not certain he was the one when I testified." The witness couldn't bring herself to specifically admit she gave false testimony. She had to sugar coat it, just in case the person she selected had been incarcerated as an innocent man. It was her way of dealing with the horror of it all. She had dealt with the rape. Now, she might have to learn to live with herself and deal with what she might have done to this man if it turned out he didn't rape her.

Larry Jenkins just stared at the witness. Her trial testimony had put him in the penitentiary for the past seventeen years. He couldn't believe what he was now hearing. She was admitting she lied when she told the jury she was certain he had raped her. He recalled the exact moment during the trial when she looked him in the eye, pointed directly at him and said 'Him. He is the monster who brutally raped me.' He would never forget those words. They'd rattled around in his brain every day since.

"Ms. Snead, I'm trying to wrap my head around your trial testimony and how it happened. Can you help me, and this court, understand how it was you testified the way you did at the trial, despite your uncertainty over the person who raped you?"

"When I first met with the prosecutor, she said I was critical to the case. My identification of Mr. Jenkins was the most important part. I told her then what I told the detectives when I selected Mr. Jenkins' picture. She told me I picked out the right guy and they had other evidence. I couldn't be tentative when I would be asked during the trial to identify him as the guy who raped me. We rehearsed how I would respond to this critical question during the trial. I guess the meetings were to make sure I didn't mess up the case. We needed to have several meetings because apparently, I wasn't strong enough to satisfy her. She told me to use the word 'monster' when I pointed him out during the trial which I did."

"When you say 'she', you are referring to the prosecutor, Joan Cardwell?"

"Yes."

"And you believed what she was telling you about this other evidence in addition to your identification?"

"Yes. I didn't know. I didn't want to put an innocent man in jail. I didn't think..." She couldn't complete her sentence. Tears started to fill her eyes and she began to cry. The court reporter who was seated next to the witness stand handed her a box of tissues. It was hard for Felbin to feel sorry for a person who perjured herself and put what he believed was an innocent man in the penitentiary for seventeen years.

After the witness regained her composure, Felbin said, "Have you finished your answer?"

"Yes, sir," Snead said.

When Felbin had no additional questions, the witness looked at Larry Jenkins and said, "I'm sorry. I know my apology doesn't make up for what happened to you, but I just have to say it."

Larry Jenkins didn't react to Snead's statement. He didn't know what he was feeling. This woman's lies put him in prison. And those lies continued seventeen years later and most recently during this hearing. Her lies would have continued, had she not been challenged with the suggestion she had engaged in a criminal act worthy of criminal prosecution. Larry Jenkins shed tears, many tears, during the seventeen years he was locked up. His entire family, mother, father brother and sisters, all shed tears when the jury announced the guilty verdict and they witnessed him being led from the courtroom in handcuffs. And then there was the embarrassment. Their son and brother was a rapist. No apology could repair the damage done to Larry and his family.

Braxton had a few questions for the witness. "Ms. Snead, are you saying you are sure Larry Jenkins didn't rape you?"

"No."

"If I understand your testimony correctly, you are telling this court you are unable to currently identify the person who raped you. Am I correct?"

"Yes."

"And with respect to whatever other evidence existed regarding Larry Jenkins, you are not aware of those particulars. Correct?"

"That's right. I don't know."

"You indicated Kizzy Lewis was present for a preparation session. Did she ever suggest you say something which was not true?"

"No. She would just ask me really hard questions. If Ms. Cardwell didn't like my answer, she would change it and Kizzy would ask the question again."

"Ms. Snead, you admitted to having lied during this hearing and during Mr. Jenkins' jury trial. How do we know you are telling the truth now?"

The question was fair. While considering her answer, Snead looked first at Jenkins, then Felbin and back to Braxton. "I suppose at this point in time, you don't. All I can say is I knew what I said at the trial was not true. I was not certain this man raped me," Snead said, pointing to Jenkins. "I made many mistakes in dealing with my situation. My biggest was going along with what I knew was wrong. I can give you excuses and rationalize why I did what I did. I was traumatized. I wanted it over with. I wanted someone to pay for what happened to me and I believed what anyone told me if it would make that happen as quickly as possible. But in the end, I knew what I did was wrong. I put it behind me. I moved on with my life and didn't consider the consequences to anyone else."

Braxton was not going to let her off the hook that easily. The stakes were too high. Snead's recantation, if believed, not only called into question the guilt of Jenkins, but it also involved potential criminal activity of a sitting judge. "Well, that's all well and good, Ms. Snead. But the point is you came into this hearing and told the same story you told during the trial. You were certain this man raped you," the prosecutor said, as she was now pointing at Jenkins. "Then you changed your story after I explained the law of perjury to you. Correct?"

"Yes."

"And when you changed your story, you knew detective Rossi testified here contrary to your testimony. You were even shown a report Rossi claimed the detectives prepared which contradicted your testimony. You then decided to conform your testimony to Detective Rossi's and a police report she brought from Florida, in order to avoid a perjury charge. True?"

"I had never seen the police report before. In fact, I never saw any police report. When I met with Ms. Cardwell, I told her about my uncertainty and what I told the detectives. Apparently, from what I'm hearing here, she already knew about their report and what I had said. Yet she told me I couldn't be tentative. And they had other evidence. The police report I saw here didn't have any information about other evidence. In fact, it sounded like I was the only witness and I wasn't sure. It was then I decided to do the right thing and tell the whole truth."

Braxton knew Felbin had suggested Snead told her roommates of her uncertainty in identifying Jenkins. She decided to stay away from this line of inquiry believing any such conversation, if true, would lend credibility to the truthfulness of what Snead was now saying.

Janet Snead made her position perfectly clear. She was untruthful for the reasons she used to rationalize her bad

164

behavior. She wasn't going to deviate. Believing additional questions would only do more harm than good, Braxton told the court she had nothing else for this witness.

But Felbin had one more. He knew why Braxton stayed away from the roommate conversation. Since this apparently was true confessions day at the courthouse for this witness, he decided to take a chance with the question Braxton avoided. Given the admissions Snead already made, it couldn't hurt. "Ms. Snead, prior to the recess, I asked you about a conversation you had with your college roommates. Let me revisit that. Did you tell your college roommates you were not sure the person whose photograph you selected was the one who raped you?

"Yes, I did."

After Felbin said he had no additional questions, the court asked the lawyers if the witness could be excused. When both agreed, the judge asked Felbin if he had any additional evidence. He said he might have one additional witness who would not be available until the morning. Judge Nealon then looked at Braxton, who thought she might have one witness. With those announcements, the hearing was adjourned for the day and would reconvene at 9:30 in the morning.

Chapter Forty

As the courtroom was clearing, Felbin approached Braxton. The prosecutor was on the horns of a dilemma. From the outset, she had resisted Felbin's effort to do a DNA test claiming it would be traumatic for the victim. Braxton was right. It was certainly traumatic for the victim, but not in a way she anticipated. There was no good way out. If she agreed to the DNA test, the media would suggest she caved because she believed Snead was finally telling the truth and Cardwell was lying. If she continued to resist and the court ordered the test, it would suggest the court believed Snead over Cardwell, which might be worse. Either way, the circuit attorney was in the middle regardless of whether a DNA test was ordered. Evidence of potential criminal behavior was now in the public domain, would occupy headlines above the fold and could not be ignored.

Felbin wanted to know whether the Jenkins case could be worked out with the prosecutor by an agreement to do a DNA test. Although he was comfortable with the evidence he presented, and confident the judge would rule favorably to his position, nothing was for sure. Felbin was not going to be satisfied with just a DNA test. He wanted more. He firmly believed his client did not rape Janet Snead and a DNA test would scientifically exonerate him. He was equally confident Snead was finally telling the truth. But both Snead and Cardwell committed perjury during the DNA hearing and the prosecutor suborned Snead's perjury during Jenkins' jury trial.

"Given what you heard here today, are you in a position to consent to a DNA test?" Felbin asked.

"I heard a lot of things today. I'm not sure what to believe," Braxton said—the consummate trial lawyer, never acknowledge the weakness in your case or defeat.

"Karen, I understand you are in a tight spot," Felbin began. He wanted to stay away from any reference to Braxton's refusal to consent to the test. He figured it would only aggravate her and do nothing to facilitate a settlement discussion. "You have multiple people lying, along with a variety of other criminal activity which would make Donald Trump proud. But I think the best evidence is Snead. She is finally telling the truth. She admitted telling her roommates she was not sure of her identification. Her uncertainty at this point corroborates what Rossi said and what the detectives wrote in the first police report. The uncertainty in Snead's identification results in an uncertain consequence. A man has spent seventeen years in prison. Given the testimony we heard here today, regardless of the party we represent, as professionals and defenders of this judicial system, we have the responsibility to make sure the system got it right. The DNA test will tell us one way or the other."

"Look Felbin, you say I'm in a tight spot and you're correct. We can certainly agree on one thing—lies were told in this case. And one liar may be a sitting judge," Braxton said. She wanted to have a candid conversation with Felbin to explain her discussions with Cardwell and her initial inclination to agree to the DNA test. But she knew she couldn't, particularly since she might be compelled to initiate a perjury and obstruction investigation against several individuals. "The Jenkins case has become considerably more complex."

"No doubt, this case has gotten more complex. But beyond the question of whether perjury and obstruction of justice charges lie, we still have a guy who has been locked up for seventeen years and is innocent."

"I don't know he is innocent. If I accept the recent testimony of the victim, she doesn't know one way or the other whether he is guilty or innocent. She simply is unable to say. Her inability to say he is the guy doesn't mean he isn't good for this rape. Then there is the whole question of whether she was lying during the jury trial or now. Remember, after all these years, she came into this hearing and stood fast on her identification. It was only after you threatened and intimidated her that she changed her story. Then she hitched her wagon to Rossi. You then threw in the conversations she had with her roommates. And while your cross was obviously effective, I don't know which version to believe," Braxton said.

"Well, let me see if I can help you. I never spoke to her roommates. I had no idea what they would have said. When I asked her the question, I took a shot in the dark. But when she admitted it, I knew then she was telling the truth about everything," Felbin said.

"By the time you were done with her she probably would have admitted to shooting Abraham Lincoln. Your little trick doesn't do anything to instill confidence she is telling the truth now."

"All the more reason for the DNA test. Karen, we both need to be sure, one way or the other."

"When all else fails, the appeals are exhausted, the ineffective assistance of counsel claims are denied, request a DNA test. Do you know how many requests like this we get from those doing long stretches in the joint, particularly in rape cases? They have nothing to lose."

"I understand. Scheck gets some three thousand requests to file for DNA tests per year. Before I took this case and agreed to assist Barry, I did some checking on the statistics. I gave the court some of those stats as you heard. As of now, 362 people, mostly minority males, who were convicted of serious crimes, many of them rapes, have been exonerated through DNA testing. But here is the thing which should be of the most interest to you. Of the 362 exonerations, in 44% of those cases, the person responsible for the crime was identified. Here, no one even looked for the person responsible thanks to Cardwell, who was more interested in becoming the elected prosecutor than finding out who raped Janet Costello."

"I don't have any evidence Cardwell did whatever she did to get herself elected to any office."

"You may not have any evidence of Cardwell's political motives at the time, but you know both Rossi and the victim, herself, say the identification was flawed. This should be enough to cause you to agree to a DNA test."

"I'll think about it," Braxton said.

"Thanks. But Karen, let me ask you a question you may or may not feel comfortable answering. Did you want to contest the DNA test? Was it your idea?" Felbin inquired. "Or did you object because it was what Cardwell told you to do? I'm asking because given the way this case is going, her effort to prevent a test is significant. Of course, I can always ask the court if I can put her back on the stand. And Judge Nealon has been quite generous with his rulings regarding his colleague. I'm thinking she may not be his colleague for very long after this case ends."

"I do understand and appreciate your position. And I hope you understand my position when I tell you I have some thinking and checking to do. I also need to have a conversation or two."

Felbin knew where she was going for one of those conversations. He just wished he could be a fly on the wall when this was occurring. "Okay. I guess you have until tomorrow morning to make some decisions."

Karen Braxton was dependent on Joan Cardwell for political support. She was able to deliver money and endorsements when it came time for Braxton to run for the position of circuit attorney. But this was before the Jenkins hearing. And before the anticipated news coverage which would not be kind to Cardwell or anyone else, other than Jenkins. He would be portrayed as an innocent man who had spent the last seventeen years in prison for a crime he didn't commit, thanks to a corrupt prosecutor who was now a judge. If Braxton didn't do anything about it, she would be tossed headfirst into the cesspool of corruption. Then she wouldn't have to worry about support for any election.

Braxton needed to decide whether to have a conversation with Cardwell now or allow her to get an update on the hearing from media accounts. The several other conversations she had with Cardwell hadn't gone very well. There was no reason to believe this one would be any different. Braxton wasn't sure whether Larry Jenkins raped Janet Snead. But she was certain, based upon what she heard at the hearing, the prosecution of Jenkins was unusual. It obviously had some issues. Unfortunately, Cardwell had not been candid during their previous discussions, and Braxton was blindsided by the evidence presented. Taking everything into consideration, Braxton knew Rossi and Snead were telling the truth and Cardwell was not. The decision was easy. She would let Cardwell get her update from the media.

Chapter Forty-One

The local television statements covered the Jenkins hearing as the lead story. The focus was on the recantation of the rape victim and the involvement of Cardwell. Because television has only about four minutes on average to devote to the story, the online *Post Dispatch* story was substantially more detailed. The story not only quoted the actual testimony of Rossi and Snead, but it also resurrected the prosecution of police officer Bobby Decker and Garner Lee. The article covered the career of Cardwell as an assistant circuit attorney, the elected circuit attorney, and as a circuit court judge. The coverage was not flattering.

The article quoted several unnamed sources who suggested Cardwell was seriously considering a run for the position of circuit attorney at the time of the arrest of Larry Jenkins. According to the sources, her win/loss record as an assistant circuit attorney would be subject to criticism by an anticipated formidable challenger. She had more losses than wins on the limited cases she'd tried. Because this rape was a high-profile case and one of several in the area of St. Louis University, a conviction or even a plea would enhance her candidacy. She convicted Larry Jenkins, used his conviction to bolster her candidacy and was elected the chief law enforcement officer for the City of St. Louis. Now the prosecution and conviction of Larry Jenkins was being seriously challenged.

According to the article, Larry Jenkins launched the career of Joan Cardwell. While holding elected office, she was able to curry favor with politicians who would be useful to her in realizing her future goal of becoming a member of the judiciary. Several retired police officers were interviewed. Each was quoted as saying the murder prosecution of Bobby Decker was a politically motivated effort to gain support for her judicial candidacy. And it worked, thanks to the backing of political power broker, Senator Winston Lee.

As with all political favors, the article noted, there comes a payback. In the career of Judge Joan Cardwell, the payment was demanded sooner rather than later. According to a former prosecutor in the circuit attorney's office who wished to remain anonymous, the acquittal of Garner Lee, the son of Senator Winston Lee, was an installment payment on a political debt.

Felbin and Garner Lee were in Felbin's office watching the television coverage and unwinding with after work cocktails—a gin and tonic for Felbin and a beer for Garner—when Tony Carmine came in. He had been tracking down Kizzy Lewis. He located and talked to her. Unfortunately, he didn't get any information. "She refused to answer any questions about the Jenkins case," Carmine said as he grabbed a beer from the bar. "It was clear to me, based upon how she acted when I mentioned the name, she recalled the case."

"Did she claim she didn't remember it?" Felbin asked.

"No. She said she wasn't going to answer any questions about it. No half-assed excuses. Just flat out, I'm not answering any questions about Jenkins."

"Where did you find her?"

"She is in a small office downtown with a couple other lawyers. I think it's a general practice. She wasn't much on conversation. I guess she was pissed because I caught her in the parking garage. The receptionist at her office told me she was too busy to see me without an appointment. So, I ambushed her ass in the garage."

"Did you lay a subpoena on her?"

"You bet. Then she started to use language even I never heard before," Carmine said with a smile.

Assuming Lewis wouldn't file a motion to quash the subpoena, Felbin needed to decide whether to put her on the witness stand. Ordinarily, trial lawyers aren't inclined to call a witness when they have no idea what the testimony will be. Never ask a question unless you know the answer. Witness trolling can be a dangerous game. But in this case, Felbin might be willing to take the chance. It doesn't happen very often where a rape victim recants at a DNA hearing and throws a prosecutor, now a judge, under the bus in the process. "Given her refusal to cooperate, do we put her on the stand blindly?" Felbin asked Garner and Tony.

Garner was the first to respond. "As you both know, I don't have any experience in cases like this. But as an observer who has watched the reaction of this judge as the evidence was coming in, I think we have a winner. I think he will order the DNA test."

"I agree," Carmine added.

"Judge Nealon is a fair guy, and I think we'll get the test. But I'm looking beyond just a test which I'm convinced will free Larry. I'm looking at finally getting rid of Cardwell, either through a criminal conviction and incarceration, or removal from the bench and the practice of law—or both. If this is our end game, it might be worth taking the chance to call Lewis as long as it doesn't hurt Larry. What's the downside?" Felbin asked.

This time Carmine, the one who'd met with the witness, was the first to answer the question. "What if she says she never participated in the preparation of Snead for her trial testimony? The unknown is whether she would be loyal to Cardwell and lie to protect her. Of course, I'm assuming Snead is telling the truth about the involvement of Lewis."

"But how will she know where we are going with her testimony to be able to protect Cardwell?" Garner asked.

As he was asking the question, Felbin was pulling up the online story in the *Post Dispatch*. "This is how she is going to connect the dots," Felbin responded as he directed the attention of both Tony and Garner to his computer screen.

When they finished reading the article, Carmine said, "Holy shit. I think I need another beer." As he headed for the bar again, he turned to Garner and asked if he could get him another one. Garner nodded.

While Garner applauded the excoriation of Cardwell, he was unhappy with the reference to his case. The article made it sound like he was guilty, and he got out from under a murder conviction, not because he was innocent, but because Cardwell owed his father for putting her on the bench.

Felbin saw Garner's reaction as he read the article. He could feel Garner's pain. He knew the truth of who murdered Amy Deland but could do nothing about it. Felbin decided to avoid a conversation about Garner's case and stick with the issue at hand. "Kizzy Lewis is named in the article as having helped prepare Snead, who has now confessed to perjury," Felbin said. The article suggested Lewis might have conspired with Cardwell to suborn perjury, and it was difficult to ignore if you were reading the piece as a neutral third party. "Certainly, after she reads this, she will have an incentive to lie to protect herself."

"But then how would Snead even know the name Kizzy Lewis?" Garner asked, also opting to avoid a discussion about the reference to his case in the article. "She isn't exactly hanging around the prosecutor's office. And Kizzy is not exactly your everyday name. Of course, she could admit she helped prepare Snead, but contend Snead was firm in her identification of our client, which would make Snead a liar."

"Or she could tell the truth: admit Snead was not firm in her ID and she and Cardwell worked to firm her up," Carmine said as he took another swig of his Budweiser.

Referring to Carmine's scenario, Felbin said, "You're saying you think Lewis might admit she helped suborn perjury, even though the statute of limitations has run. And after all these years, she has now found religion and wants to cleanse her soul? How many beers have you had?"

"Apparently not enough," Carmine said, referring to the beers. "But I say, let's take a chance. Even if Lewis contradicts Snead, I'd put my money on Snead's testimony, particularly after you are finished kicking her ass all over downtown St. Louis during your cross."

"If I have any standing to vote, I would like to do whatever we can to contribute to the downfall of Cardwell as long as our client is not adversely impacted," Garner weighed in. "As you can imagine, this is obviously a personal issue with me. Maybe, just maybe, something might shake loose and the truth about my whole case might come out. I dare to dream. But if there is any justice, sooner or later, I have to be exonerated."

Once again, there was nothing Felbin could say.

Chapter Forty-Two

The bailiff opened court for the day at precisely 9:30 am. The parties were all in place when the judge entered the courtroom. Both sides were ready to proceed. Karen Braxton considered Felbin's request for an agreement on a DNA test. In the end, she decided to allow the case to play out and let the judge make the decision. Judge Nealon directed Felbin to call his next witness.

When Kizzy Lewis entered the courtroom, Braxton looked surprised to see her. Felbin thought Lewis would contact her former colleague to let her know she had been subpoenaed and get some guidance. This development gave Felbin at least some hope he had made the correct decision in putting this witness on the stand without any idea what she would say.

Kizzy Lewis had been an assistant circuit attorney for the City of St. Louis for eight years and was now in a general private practice. During her time with the prosecutor's office, she said she tried approximately forty felony jury trials to conclusion. It was her practice to personally interview crime victims and prepare them to testify in court. Occasionally, depending on the case, she would ask one of the other assistants to help with the preparation by doing the cross on the witness. She couldn't think of a single time she put a witness on the stand without any preparation. It was standard procedure while she was there to prepare all witnesses for their trial testimony.

"When you were with the prosecutor's office, were you familiar with Joan Cardwell?" Felbin asked after establishing the particulars of her professional background.

"I was. She was an assistant prosecutor at the same time I was there," Lewis said.

The witness didn't limit her responses to one word. More encouragement for Felbin she would tell the truth. It was time to find out. "Were you familiar with the prosecution of Larry Jenkins for rape more than seventeen years ago?"

"I am."

"How are you familiar with his case?"

"Joan Cardwell was the prosecutor who was assigned the case," Lewis began. "The defendant refused a plea deal, and the case needed to be tried. Joan asked if I would assist her in preparing the victim, Janet Costello, for trial. My job was to play the role of the defense attorney and do the mock cross examination."

So far, so good for Felbin. "Can you estimate how many times you met with the victim?"

"I met with her only one time."

"When you did the cross examination, please assess for this court the certainty with which the victim identified Larry Jenkins as the person who raped her."

"When Joan was doing the mock direct examination, Ms. Costello was certain the photograph she selected of the several the police showed her, was the man who raped her. But then on cross, the certainty broke down."

"Did Cardwell respond to the victim's uncertainty?"

"Yes," Lewis said. Felbin waited to ask the next question giving the witness a chance to continue her response. After a short delay, Lewis added, "She scolded her, telling her she had to be firm and positive in her testimony and say the defendant was the one who raped her."

"What did you say at this point?"

"I didn't say anything."

Lewis was a prosecutor experienced with turning a rape victim inside out with her mock cross examination in an office setting, as preparation for the pressure in a courtroom during a trial. At some point, Felbin believed Lewis would have had a conversation with Cardwell about the ability of this victim to identify the individual who raped her. He needed to press her to get the conversation on the record. The testimony of this witness corroborated both Rossi and Snead. But he needed more to put the final nail in Cardwell's coffin.

"Why didn't you say anything to Cardwell when she made her comment?" Felbin continued.

"Because witnesses get excited when they are being pressured through cross examination. I sensed she was just nervous and confused because she wasn't used to this. It was a whole new world for her," Lewis said.

True, but this wasn't the response Felbin was looking for. He needed more. "Did her certainty with respect to her identification of the defendant get any better as your questioning continued?"

"No. As a matter of fact, at one point when I kept pressing her, she became frustrated and said something to the effect, 'I don't know. They all look alike.'"

This was exactly what Snead told the detectives. It would be hard for Cardwell to credibly rebut this evidence. But Felbin still wanted the conversation he believed was inevitable between this experienced prosecutor and Cardwell. "Did you say something to Cardwell at this point?" he asked.

"I did," Lewis said. "I told her the victim was not going to hold up during cross at trial. I also questioned whether the victim knew who raped her. I knew this was a high-profile case due to the rapes in the area of the university. Frankly, I suggested she rethink pursing the case against this defendant."

Bases loaded, two outs, bottom of the ninth, game tied, the home team needed one more hit to win the game. Felbin was confident he was going to get his base hit. "What did she say?" he asked.

Without any objection from Braxton, Lewis answered the question. "She told me she had confidence in her victim, and she had the right guy. She was positive in her identification when the detectives showed her the photo spread and she picked the defendant. I knew what she was saying was true because I read the police report before I did my mock cross. I figured she knew her case better than I did, and she could always use the detectives if the victim stumbled at trial. So, I just left it alone and moved on to my own cases."

Felbin had one more question. "Before you came in here this morning, had you seen any news coverage about this case?"

"No. Actually, I have been preparing for a complex, lengthy trial for the last several weeks, leaving little time for anything else, including watching the news."

"What was your relationship with Judge Cardwell when you were in the circuit attorney's office?" Braxton began her questioning.

"I really didn't have any relationship with her other than she and I were both prosecutors in the same office and knew each other," Lewis said.

"Were you able to form an opinion about her reputation as a prosecutor during the period of time you worked in the same office?" Braxton felt comfortable asking this question. Both Lewis and Cardwell were members of the same club. But when Lewis hesitated before responding, she thought the question might have been a mistake.

"Um, let's just say she had some issues," Lewis said hesitatingly.

Braxton didn't ask for an explanation. It wouldn't be good. Instead, she moved onto the next question. "When you attended the session to prepare the victim for her trial testimony, you actually heard the victim say unequivocally the defendant raped her, is that correct?"

"I did during the mock direct examination Joan was doing."

"Do you know whether Judge Cardwell had any other prep sessions with her after yours?"

"I do not."

"And do you know how the victim testified at the jury trial?"

"I do not."

"But you do know the jury convicted the defendant."

"Yes."

"And do you know the rapes in the area of St. Louis University stopped after this defendant was convicted?" Braxton asked as she pointed to Larry Jenkins.

"I believe I do recall there were no additional rapes reported in the area."

After these many years, Kizzy Lewis clearly recalled this case and her interaction with both this victim and Cardwell. There was a reason she remembered the case, and Braxton decided not to press the envelope. She figured given the evidence, Nealon was going to grant the defendant's motion to do the DNA test. Felbin didn't need Lewis to make his case. He put her on the stand only to try to gift wrap Cardwell for either criminal prosecution or disbarment. Because the criminal part of the issue would fall into her lap, Braxton decided she was not going to help Felbin in this effort.

Felbin was not going to end his pursuit. He was interested in the reputation issue Braxton raised with this witness but failed to develop. Clearly, Lewis had an opinion which probably wouldn't be flattering to Cardwell. Felbin wanted her opinion on the record. "Ms. Lewis, in response to the prosecutor's question about Joan Cardwell's reputation while in the circuit attorney's office, you mentioned she had some issues. What were those issues?"

Both the witness and Felbin waited for Braxton's objection the question. It never came. "Joan had some issues, like I said. She did not enjoy a good reputation among the other prosecutors in the office. And this case, the Larry Jenkins case, didn't do anything to help her reputation. The rapes in..."

"How so?" Felbin interrupted, anxious to hear the connection to his client.

Continuing, Lewis said, "The rapes in the area of St. Louis University were high-profile. Joan was considering a run for circuit attorney, or at least this was the rumor at the time. She didn't try many cases and her win/loss record was not very good. She would work out sweetheart deals rather than try a case. Her potential opponent in a race for circuit attorney was a skilled trial lawyer. Joan lobbied to be involved in those university rape cases. Let me just say the people in the office were concerned. We felt these very serious rape cases were not in good hands with Joan. I think there was also some animosity, given what many believed was a political motive for her involvement. These rapes were not the cases where people needed to be playing politics."

"But she won. The jury found Larry Jenkins guilty," Felbin pointed out, anxious to hear her response in light of her testimony regarding Cardwell's political motive.

"Maybe not," was all Lewis said.

Felbin was impressed with the ability of the witness to recall details of a case this old. Vague responses were conspicuously absent. She was not at all evasive. Something about this case was important to Lewis and Felbin decided to see if he could find out what it was. The rule of never asking a question where you don't know the answer was abandoned from the beginning with this witness. "Ms. Lewis, I am impressed with your ability to recall details of a case this old," Felbin began. "I'm wondering whether there is something unique about this case which caused it to remain in your memory for so long."

"Frankly, Mr. Felbin, after my mock cross examination of the victim, I was concerned we might have the wrong guy. But I did nothing about it. I excused my opinion, probably because the rapes stopped after Mr. Jenkins was arrested. Of course, as a prosecutor, I knew there could have been a lot of reasons why they stopped which would have nothing to do with Mr. Jenkins. And then he was convicted. Since I didn't see the trial, I kinda buried my concerns and moved on. But now here we are. And right now, I'm not feeling very good about myself."

Felbin had no other questions and no additional evidence.

Braxton likewise had no additional questions of this witness and no evidence the state wished to present.

Both sides having rested, Judge Nealon announced he would take the case under advisement and have a written decision in a few days. After adjourning the hearing, the court wanted to see all counsel in his chambers.

Judge Nealon wasted no time getting to the point once the lawyers arrived in his chambers. "I heard a lot of disturbing things over the last two days," he began. "Ms. Braxton, you are the chief law enforcement officer for this city, and I don't intend to tell you how to do your job. But I also have some obligations apart from deciding this case based upon what I heard in there," Nealon said, pointing to the courtroom. "I intend to take no immediate action and instead will wait for a reasonable period to see what develops. In the meantime, you will have my decision on the defendant's DNA request in a few days." And with those comments, the judge excused the lawyers.

Felbin just looked at Karen Braxton as they left the chambers. Neither spoke. But the judge's message was clear. Both criminal as well as ethical issues needed to be reviewed. While he had no jurisdiction over the criminal, Judge Nealon could pursue an ethics complaint with the judicial commission. He would wait to see what the circuit attorney would do. Felbin would also wait to see what both Braxton and Nealon would do. At the moment, he was feeling pretty good about everything.

Chapter Forty-Three

The gubernatorial campaigns of Senator Lee and Ray Singer were heating up, considering the news coverage involving Larry Jenkins. With the issue of whether Winston Lee impregnated his son's girlfriend still unresolved, the press shifted its interest to the relationship between Lee and Cardwell. After the confrontation with his son in the presence of Darius Washington, Lee held no press conferences. Instead, he did private fundraisers to raise money and spread his message. A day after the Jenkins hearing concluded, Lee was holding a fundraiser in a hotel in downtown St. Louis. News coverage of the hearing now included a summary of the testimony of Kizzy Lewis and her suggestion Cardwell sought the prosecution of Jenkins for her own personal political gain.

Somehow reporters, both print and electronic from St. Louis, got word of Lee's fundraiser and attended. He tried to ignore them at first as he worked the room. They persisted and asked about the paternity test. All he would say was he had agreed to take the test and was just waiting for the Singer camp to tell him where and when. He was feeling comfortable with his response until the focus shifted.

"What is your relationship with Judge Joan Cardwell?" a reporter with a St. Louis television station asked with the camera rolling.

Lee was stuck. Surrounded by reporters, he couldn't run or ignore the question. The reporter would run footage of him trying to escape. Given the coverage Cardwell recently received in the Jenkins case, it would look like he had something to hide. "I have no relationship with Joan Cardwell."

"Did you have anything to do with Judge Cardwell's appointment to the bench?"

"No."

"How do you respond to the suggestion you used your influence to put Judge Cardwell on the bench as a payback for her prosecuting Robert Decker, the police officer, for the murder of a young black man he was trying to arrest?" a *Post Dispatch* newspaper reporter asked. Whether Lee liked it or not, this was an impromptu news conference and the St. Louis reporters were going to take full advantage.

The Decker case was old news. But the members of the fourth estate were trying to connect the dots between Cardwell and the man running for governor. They tried unsuccessfully after the Decker verdict and again after the trial of Garner Lee over which Cardwell presided. The Jenkins case reignited interest in Cardwell and her path to the bench.

"How did it happen Judge Cardwell presided over your son's murder case?" another reporter asked.

"I have no idea," Lee said, looking for an exit.

"You're saying this was just mere coincidence and had nothing to do with any payback?"

These were the same questions and issues raised at the time of the trial. "We have already been through all of this when my son was charged. I told you then and I will tell you again, I was not involved in Garner's case, either before the case began, during the case or after the case ended," Lee said emphatically. "I would hope we could move on from this topic."

"We have information that you supported her candidacy when she ran for circuit attorney. You endorsed her. How well did you know her then?"

"I didn't know her at all and don't recall endorsing her," Lee said, carefully choosing his words. "But if you say I did, it was probably because we were from the same party."

"Do you support the Nonpartisan Court Plan Missouri uses to select some trial and all appellate judges?" another reporter asked.

Lee looked confused by the question, but eventually said, "I support the plan." Finally locating an exit, Lee pushed through the reporters and was gone.

While Lee was holding his fundraiser in downtown St. Louis, Singer was making his pitch for money and motivating his supporters a few miles away in a hotel in the St. Louis suburb of Clayton. But unlike Lee, Singer made no effort to escape those pesky reporters looking for breaking news. After some policy questions, the focus turned to the issue of paternity. "Mr. Singer, you called for Senator Lee to take a paternity test to determine whether he impregnated his son's girlfriend. Senator Lee has agreed to take the test, but the test has not occurred. Why not? What's the hold up?"

Singer was expecting the question. He was uncomfortable with the entire issue and was opposed to raising it from the beginning. But the issue was out there, and he had to respond. "In order to do a paternity test, we need two DNA samples," Singer said. "One from my opponent and the other from the fetus. We have one sample, but not the other. My opponent is aware of this. We know the circuit attorney has the sample from the fetus, as does Garner Lee's defense team. We have reached out to both asking for a sample so we could do the test. Neither has responded to our request. We also have reason to believe both the prosecutor and the defense ran the paternity test and have the results. But again, we have received no response. As soon as we get the sample, we can do the test. Or if we get the results of the test the lawyers ran, we will make those available to you."

"Do you think your opponent agreed to take the test because he knew you would not be able to get any comparison samples?"

Singer knew this was exactly the reason Lee quickly agreed to take the test. But he really didn't want to go down this road. Certainly, if Lee had a role in the murder of Amy Deland, it was fair game for an inquiry. Fixing the criminal case through Cardwell as a payback for her appointment to the bench, was fair game. But Singer didn't feel comfortable creating a political issue related to a personal matter involving marital indiscretion. This was something Lee and his wife needed to work out. In this age of politics at a local, state or national level, he knew politicians got down in the mud and nothing was out of bounds. He didn't want to play this game and didn't think he had to. He wanted to win on his own merits and believed he could. "I don't know. You would have to ask him," he said, expressing some displeasure with the question.

The questions then turned to the issue of judicial appointments and whether he had any information confirming

Senator Lee was responsible for the appointment of Joan Cardwell to the bench. When he denied knowing anything about it, a reporter asked him to explain his position on political influence in connection with judicial appointments.

Although Singer had never been a judge, he was a lawyer and the Attorney General for the state of Missouri. He was quite familiar with the politics surrounding judicial appointments. For the larger cities of St. Louis County: St. Louis, Kansas City and Springfield, the Nonpartisan Court Plan was adopted for the appointment of circuit or trial court judges due to the heavy influence of political machines in those densely populated areas. Each of the counties within those judicial circuits had its own judicial commission. A judicial commission consisted of the chief appellate judge of the circuit district, two lawyers elected by the Bar and two citizens appointed by the governor. The commission reviewed and interviewed the applicants and sent three names to the governor, who picked one of the three. Trial judges in the outlying areas of the state were elected. All appellate judges were selected through the Nonpartisan plan. He was aware no system was perfect and immune from political influence.

"I am aware judges in this state get judicial appointments through political influence under the Nonpartisan Court Plan," Singer said. "Judicial candidates pay large sums of money to political campaigns in order to have these elected officials use their influence to endorse their candidacy. Here's how it works: putting aside for the moment the politics involved in selecting the members of the commission, I want to talk about the role of the governor in this process. When the names of the three candidates are sent to the governor, the politicians, heavy hitters and campaign contributors—along with everyone else who has an interest in buying a piece of a judge line up at the starting gate outside the governor's office. The race for the roses begins with the payout looming large in multiple respects. The result—an incompetent judiciary. We don't get the cream of the crop. Instead, we get the best of the worst and maybe not even that. If we are truly lucky, some may fall within the normal range of awful. Sometimes I get the impression some of these judges acquire universal knowledge by divine inspiration. Oh yes, occasionally, we get the best and brightest. But it's only because they had the money to buy a politician who had significant influence.

"Now let's talk about the judicial commission. As I said, the Missouri Bar has an election to seat two lawyers on the commission. Like politicians, the lawyer candidates for the commission spend large sums of money to get themselves elected. Why do they do that? I think the answer is obvious. When you become part of a short list to put someone on the bench, it can't hurt you or your clients in the long run. And then there are the gubernatorial appointments to the commission. This gives the governor two bites of the apple. You would be naïve to conclude the governor makes his appointments to the commission from a telephone book, an enemies list or from the opposition party. You would be equally gullible to believe campaign contributions didn't influence the selection. And finally, we have the chief judge of the appellate court presiding over the commission. Of course, this person would have been appointed to the position through the same Nonpartisan plan. I don't think I need to say anything else about this individual."

The print reporters were taking notes while the radio and television people had their cameras and tape recorders going, each seeking to be precise with any statements they would attribute to the candidate. Most of the St. Louis, Kansas City and Springfield reporters were familiar with the Nonpartisan Court Plan. They had reported on the positives and the negatives of the Plan before. The only interest for the outstate reporters whose judges were elected by the people in a general election was how this candidate intended to improve the selection of judges for the entire state. These reporters were aware of the problems and controversies which develop through the ballot process from which their judges are selected.

"Now that we have discussed the problem, let's talk about the solution," Singer continued. Before he became the attorney general, Singer was a prosecutor, a trial lawyer who was used to convincing juries—twelve strangers—his position was the correct one. He used that skill and experience to convey his positions precisely on various issues during the campaign. The selection of judges without political influence was a high priority. "Whatever the solution, I know it will not be without some form of politics. But I want to make sure the political influence is minimized.

"Here is what I propose. First, I want the Nonpartisan Court Plan to apply to the entire state for all trial courts. It already applies to the selection of appellate judges. Second, I want to change the composition of the commission. I propose the number of lawyers be increased from two to three and the number of citizens from two to not less than six, depending on the number of counties in the judicial circuit. Third, all would be elected. The Missouri Bar would conduct the election for the lawyers. The citizen members would be elected in the counties where they are running within the circuit. The number of commissioners would vary. Fourth, the appellate representative would be eliminated. Fifth, the name of each judicial candidate sent to the governor would have to be approved by a two-thirds majority of the commissioners. Sixth, as governor, I wouldn't accept any recommendations or lobbying efforts on behalf of any candidate.

"And one final point," Singer said. He was on a roll. Clearly, the issue of political influence invading the judiciary was important to him. "As I said, the current system does not allow us to either identify or appoint the best applicants. Right now, we use no objective universal criteria to screen these applicants. Instead, the commissioners ask a couple of perfunctory questions during their interviews. At the end of the current process, the governor has no idea of the candidates' qualifications, because they have not been objectively vetted and tested. Their judicial knowledge and temperament are just two examples of the unknowns. Certainly, the governor can review their self-serving statements on the lengthy applicant form. This form doesn't tell the complete story. As governor, I would encourage the commission, in conjunction with the Missouri Bar, to develop objective criteria to include oral and written testing to vet applicants. All of this would go a long way to putting the best and the brightest on the bench to preside over and decide issues critical to all of us."

Chapter Forty-Four

The morning news and the newspaper showed the request of Larry Jenkins for a DNA test. But the real story was about Joan Cardwell and her role not only in the Jenkins case, but her political rise to fame. The *Post Dispatch* newspaper article contained not only more detail about the case than the TV news, but also incorporated the issue of judicial appointments.

John Pertzborn, one of the morning anchors on Channel 2, the Fox affiliate in St. Louis, read the teleprompter—*Judge Joan Cardwell seems to be in the middle of the Jenkins case. Larry Jenkins was convicted of rape and has spent the last seventeen years in prison. He is seeking a DNA test to prove his innocence. Chris brings us up to date. What's going on?*

Chris Regnier, a reporter with the station, was standing in front of the courthouse where the Larry Jenkins hearing was being held.

Good morning, John. Joan Cardwell was the one who prosecuted Larry Jenkins. And now her actions are being questioned by not only a police detective who investigated the case, but also by one of Cardwell's colleagues, another prosecutor in the circuit attorney's office at the time, and the victim herself.

According to Ellen Rossi, the detective on the case, the victim was not certain in her identification of Jenkins as the one who raped her. But when she presented the case to Cardwell, she made the officer change the police report she and her partner had made to reflect a positive identification of Jenkins by the victim. Cardwell denied the allegation she forced anyone to change the report and testified the victim was sure Jenkins was the one who raped her. But both the victim herself as well as Kizzy Lewis, another prosecutor who was also involved in the case, contradicted Cardwell's testimony. Lewis said when she helped Cardwell prepare the victim for trial, she wasn't sure Jenkins raped her. The testimony of Lewis was eventually confirmed by the victim herself under cross examination by the defense attorney. Judge Nealon took the case under advisement and a decision on whether Larry Jenkins gets his DNA test is expected in a few days. Chris Regnier reporting. Back to you in the studio, John.

Like the Fox report, the first half of the *Post* article covered the same basic information about the Jenkins hearing. But the second half focused on Cardwell, beginning with her election as the circuit attorney and progressing to her judicial appointment. The article revisited the Decker case and Felbin's criticism of the prosecution of Robert Decker for the death of an African American young man he was trying to arrest. According to Felbin, the prosecution was designed to curry favor with Senator Winston Lee to secure his support for Cardwell's appointment to the bench. Her eventual judicial appointment became controversial again when she was appointed to preside over the murder prosecution of Lee's son for the death of his girlfriend. Eventually, Cardwell dismissed that case due to what she referred to as prosecutorial misconduct.

In connection with the Lee murder trial, the article also referenced Singer's challenge for Lee to take a paternity test to determine whether he impregnated his son's girlfriend. Lee denied a relationship with the woman who was murdered and expressed a willingness to take the test. Unfortunately, according to Singer, he cannot obtain the necessary comparison DNA from the fetus to do the test.

Cardwell's handling of the Jenkins case, her election as the Circuit Attorney and her appointment to the bench gave rise to the issue of political influence in judicial appointments and became a subject for discussion with the gubernatorial candidates. Each of the candidates expressed an opinion on the Nonpartisan Court Plan. But each refused to comment on the testimony and whether Judge Cardwell perjured herself or obstructed justice in prosecuting Jenkins years ago. Singer took the position the issue was one for the prosecutor and the court. Lee took a similar position. But he added that prosecutions for perjury are rare and difficult to prove and made even more difficult when a sitting judge is the target. He went so far as to imply this type of prosecution, given the disruption it would cause to the state and community, might not be worth the effort.

John Peterson, Singer's campaign manager, was quick to respond to Lee's suggestion, calling it outrageous and itself an effort to obstruct justice as no one is above the law, including the person he put on the bench. Peterson was quoted as saying, "Senator Lee is part of the problem and not the solution. He represents all that is wrong with judicial appointments in this state and all that is wrong with political influence at any level. This cancer growing on our judiciary needs to be cured."

Felbin didn't see the morning television coverage. He was in his office having a cup of black coffee and reading the newspaper when Garner Lee arrived. He was at the part of the article dealing with Garner's murder trial. Garner had watched the Fox coverage and read the online version of the *Post* article in his hotel room. He was not feeling very good, and Felbin could see it in his face. He knew sooner or later the murder case was going to surface again, particularly after the evidence at the Jenkins hearing surfaced. As expected, the coverage excoriated both Senator Lee and Cardwell, suggesting her history of corruption began when she was an assistant prosecutor and extended to the dismissal of Garner's murder case. The article painted a picture of a murderer who got away with it thanks to a family political connection.

Neither Garner nor Felbin mentioned the article immediately. But after Garner poured himself a cup of coffee and they speculated about when Nealon would decide the DNA issue, Garner said, "I can't continue to relive my case." Felbin knew exactly what he was talking about. "I have to find a way to prove my innocence."

Felbin knew proof of Garner's innocence was never going to happen. Once again, he didn't know how to respond to the man, once a client and now a colleague.

While Felbin was thinking of something to say, Tony Carmine came bouncing into the office. He wasted no time commenting on the article. In his unique style, Tony said, "Holy shit. Did you see the *Post* article this morning? Cardwell got it stuck up her ass once again. And it will be even worse when Nealon grants our motion and Larry is proven innocent. That bitch."

Garner listened and waited for him to finish before pointing out the obvious. "I was also mentioned in the article and not in a positive way." Tony just looked at him, finally realizing what he had done. But he, too, knew he could do nothing to help. At least nothing on the record or with Felbin's knowledge. But Carmine was innovative. His mother taught him at a very young age there is no such word as *can't* in the English language. Like Felbin, he could see the pain on Garner's face.

An uncomfortable silence enveloped the room for a few minutes which seemed like an eternity. Garner stood at one of the several windows in Felbin's spacious corner office, his back to the others, staring at the arch and Old Cathedral below. Carmine and Felbin looked at each other, wondering what to say. They knew the truth about the murder of Amy Deland. Finally, Garner broke the silence. "I need answers," he said as he turned away from the window to face them. "I need to find out who killed Amy." This wasn't anything new. Felbin and Carmine had heard it before. "But I can't seem to get them. I have to do the next best thing."

"And what is the next best thing, Garner?" Felbin asked.

"We know my father didn't strike the fatal blow which killed Amy. We have his DNA which didn't match the DNA on the murder weapon. What we don't know is whether he had it done. But we do know for certain he is the father of the child someone killed when they murdered Amy. I know he's the father because of the paternity test we had done after my trial," Garner said looking directly at Felbin. "According to what I read, he denied he is the father and to prove something he knows is false, he has agreed to take the paternity test offered by Singer. His agreement rings hollow because he figures Singer can't get the DNA from Amy and the fetus to do the comparison. His lie is safe, and he moves on to become the next governor of this state. I can't allow this to happen. While I can't prove I didn't kill Amy, I can prove he is the father of her child."

Felbin looked at Carmine. Although they both knew what Garner was talking about, Felbin asked, "What are you saying?"

"I'm saying I want to go public with the lab report we have. I want the public to know what my father, the honorable *Senator Lee,* did. I want to identify him for the liar he is."

Carmine was on board. He wanted everything released, including the DNA which proved Cassandra Lee murdered Amy Deland. It was Felbin who had an objection. Something about ethics Carmine didn't understand. Or perhaps he did understand but didn't care.

"I can certainly appreciate what you want to do," Felbin said. He enumerated several problems. The first; a concern the disclosure would impact the Jenkins case, given the involvement of both Garner and Felbin. The second; Felbin's friend, who did the paternity test as a favor. He didn't prepare a report because Felbin didn't want anything he would have to turn over to the prosecution. The third; a concern the paternity issue would be spun to serve as Garner's motive to murder Amy if his father was not responsible.

But even with those concerns, Garner wasn't backing off. "I can appreciate the issues which could develop. But I hope you can appreciate what I have to do, particularly because I continue to carry the weight of this murder on my shoulders."

"Will it make you feel better to prove he is the father of this child, since you already put it out there when you and Tony ambushed him at his fundraiser? And will you feel better in the long run after you did this—because there will be no turning back."

Garner hadn't considered how he would feel in the future. But for the moment, he wasn't worried about the future. He would never again have a relationship with his father. He wanted revenge. The recent news coverage rekindled his interest in a payback for what his father had done. "I don't want to do anything which might interfere with the Jenkins case. I certainly appreciate people who have unjustly been accused of a crime. But Felbin, all I'm asking for is part of my file to do with as I please. You don't have to be a part of whatever I do. But as a compromise, how about if we do this? I would agree not to go public with the information until after the judge decides the Jenkins case."

Considering the *Post* article, Felbin didn't want to prolong this discussion. "Let's agree to revisit the issue after Judge Nealon rules."

Chapter Forty-Five

It didn't take long for Judge Nealon to issue his order and findings of fact. When Felbin received a copy of the opinion, he, along with Garner and Carmine, rushed to the city jail to give Larry the news. Each had his own copy of the decision and they brought one for Larry. As they waited for the jailers to bring him into the attorney conference room, they read and reread Judge Nealon's words. When they heard steel doors opening, they looked up to see their client, dressed in an orange jumpsuit, white socks and flip flops, walk through the doors. Because it was an attorney visit, no handcuffs were necessary. When Larry saw the three of them, they were not smiling, and he became concerned. He figured they were there to let him know the judge decided his case.

After some preliminary greetings, they sat down. Carmine was the first to speak. "We kicked their fuckin' asses," he said as Felbin handed his client a copy of the decision. Carmine always had a way with words.

His eyes filled with tears when he heard those words and Larry began to cry. "I waited a long time for this day and finally, I will be getting out," he said.

As expected, the court sustained the motion for a DNA test and ordered the circuit attorney's office to arrange for the police department's laboratory to do a DNA test. If the defendant objected to the police department laboratory, he could arrange for a certified laboratory of his choice to do his own test on the evidentiary items to be provided by the prosecutor's office. While the order allowing the test was not a surprise, what the judge wrote in his opinion about Cardwell surprisingly grabbed the headlines.

The court summarized the testimony of Joan Cardwell, the prosecutor; Janet Costello-Snead, the rape victim; Ellen Rossi, the detective who was assigned the case; and Kizzy Lewis, a prosecutor and associate of Cardwell. The summary tracked the relevant statements each made at the hearing. It was straightforward. But the testimony conflicted in multiple respects. It was up to the court to decide credibility—who was telling the truth and who was not.

Larry moved his finger slowly across each word of each sentence in the judge's opinion. In addition to savoring the moment, he wanted to make sure he completely understood what the judge was saying. "Having summarized the testimony of each of the witnesses, the burden of determining credibility now falls upon the court," Judge Nealon wrote. "Initially, the court recognizes the clear conflict between the testimony of Cardwell and Rossi. According to Rossi, Cardwell directed her and her partner to change their police report to reflect certainty in the victim's identification of Jenkins as the person who raped her. Cardwell denies this. The determination of this issue is critical to a fair and just resolution of the issues in this case. Ordinarily, this would be a *he said, she said* situation. However, in this case, there is a tie breaker—Janet Costello-Snead."

Larry clearly recalled the testimony of the victim both during the jury trial as well as the two times she testified during the DNA hearing. He was more than casually curious as to which version the court would choose to believe. The court also recognized the inherent problems with the victim's various statements. "Snead testified twice during the hearing," the judge began. "Initially, she corroborated Cardwell's position as to the certainty of her identification. Had she maintained her testimony in this regard, the court might have been inclined to deny the petitioner's request for a DNA test. However, after some veiled suggestion of perjured testimony and a recess, the witness returned to the witness stand and recanted her prior testimony. Not only did she rebut Cardwell's testimony, but she also admitted her prior testimony regarding the identification of Jenkins as the rapist was false."

When he reached this part of the court's opinion, he stopped. Removing his finger from the document and staring at one of the conference room walls, he relived the day when Costello pointed at him and told the jury he raped her. His mind then raced to the current hearing when it happened again. Twice she accused him of raping her. But the false testimony of this victim came as no surprise to

194

Larry Jenkins. He knew she lied. He didn't rape her. And now, finally after these many years, the court also recognized her for what she is—a liar. Satisfied with this recognition, he continued to read the court's opinion.

"The admission of false testimony regarding the petitioner here as the perpetrator of the crime of rape, should be enough in any case to grant the request for DNA testing. However, in this case the court would be remiss if it didn't address the circumstances surrounding the victim's recantation which occurred after petitioner's counsel suggested the possibility of a perjury prosecution. Counsel represented to this court that the testimony of this witness would conflict with statements she made to her roommates close in time to when this crime occurred regarding the identification of the perpetrator. Regardless of the legal viability of a perjury prosecution, this court must be satisfied this witness did not change her testimony based upon a fear of a future prosecution. The resolution of this issue turns on the testimony of Kizzy Lewis, a prosecutor in the same office as Joan Cardwell. While the court didn't have the benefit of the testimony of the victim's roommates, it did have the benefit of Ms. Lewis. At the suggestion of Cardwell, Ms. Lewis assisted in the preparation of the victim for her trial testimony. The court finds the statements made by the victim to Ms. Lewis during her trial preparation were consistent with her recanted testimony here. In sum, other than based upon a suggestion by Cardwell, Janet Costello-Snead was never certain that Larry Jenkins raped her. According to this victim, her testimony was shaped by Joan Cardwell who led her to believe other evidence confirmed petitioner was the one who raped her and told her she needed to be certain in her identification in order to obtain a conviction."

Everyone was pleased with Judge Nealson's decision to grant the request for a DNA test. His written opinion was well reasoned. But Felbin, Garner, Tony, and Larry, each for their own personal reasons, read and reread the concluding paragraph of the court's decision.

"Having granted petitioner's request for a DNA test, the need for additional commentary would ordinarily be unnecessary and serve no worthwhile purpose. However, this is not an ordinary case. The evidence this court heard is concerning in several material respects. Specifically, the concern centers on the testimony of Joan Cardwell. This court takes no pleasure in evaluating the credibility of a sitting circuit judge. Nonetheless, no matter how unpleasant, the interests of justice demand nothing less. The testimony of Joan Cardwell was unworthy of belief in all material respects. In fact, based upon the totality of the evidence, the court concludes the testimony of Joan Cardwell was false and intentionally designed to mislead. Prosecutors are clothed with tremendous power not because they represent an ordinary party to a controversy but because they represent the sovereign. Rather than winning and losing, their duty is to see that justice is done. These individuals are servants of the law whose oath requires them to govern impartially while insuring that guilt shall not escape or innocence suffer. As a prosecutor, Joan Cardwell violated her oath of office regardless of the outcome of the DNA testing in this case."

A circuit court judge threw another circuit judge under the bus, calling her a liar. Felbin couldn't believe what he was reading. Nealon didn't specifically say she perjured herself or suborned perjury or that she should be prosecuted for those crimes. Although it isn't a quantum leap to come to that conclusion based upon what he did say, Felbin figured Judge Nealon left the question of a formal perjury prosecution for Braxton to decide.

The focus of the news coverage was Cardwell. After the evidence was presented in Judge Nealon's courtroom, few, if any, believed Jenkins would not get his DNA test. The surprise was what the judge wrote about a colleague. The *Post* article quoted several practicing lawyers and a law professor. Both Felbin and Braxton declined to comment. Each couldn't recall a time when one trial judge excoriated another in a written opinion. However, they noted the unique aspects of the Jenkins case. This wasn't an ordinary case where a judge misapplied the law or failed to allow the jury to hear some evidence which was prejudicial to one of the parties. This was a case where a prosecutor obtained a conviction with known false testimony. It just happened the prosecutor was now a sitting trial judge.

A *Post* editorial didn't wait for the results of the DNA test before suggesting the removal of Judge Joan Cardwell.

Joan Cardwell has been the subject of previous editorial comment by this newspaper, the editors began. *A political decision to prosecute a police officer for murder, followed by the dismissal of a murder charge for the son of her political mentor, raised serious questions about her fitness for office. But now we learn she suborned perjury to obtain a conviction of what might be an innocent man. Again, political gain was the motive; this time to become the Circuit Attorney for the City of St. Louis. While the statute of limitations has expired on the subornation of perjury, it has not expired on her recent testimony in a DNA hearing held to determine whether the man she prosecuted and convicted with perjured testimony should be freed. Her recent behavior makes the matter even worse. Once again, we witness Joan Cardwell lying to protect herself and her position at the expense of another. This behavior from anyone is unacceptable. But it is even more egregious when a sitting judge, the gate keeper for the integrity of an entire judicial system, does it. She has violated public trust and her oath of office. Karen Braxton must decide whether to prosecute her for perjury regarding her recent testimony. In the meantime, action must be taken by the Commission on Retirement, Removal and Discipline of Judges, an independent state agency, as well as her fellow judges to immediately remove her from the bench. Given her past practices, it is unlikely she will do the right thing and resign.*

Chapter Forty-Six

While Felbin and company celebrated their victory, their opponents were trying to figure out how to do damage control. Karen Braxton was in a closed-door meeting with Holly Hermann, her first assistant, and Myra Long, the public relations director. Two issues were on the table—how to handle the publicity and what to do with Cardwell. The first was an easier fix than the second.

Long suggested a simple press release indicating the office would comply with the court order and immediately make the necessary arrangement for the police department laboratory to do the test. Felbin declined the court's invitation to do his own independent testing and agreed to the department's lab. Long recommended against a live press conference. Questions would center on Cardwell and whether she would be prosecuted for perjury. Braxton was not prepared to deal with this issue. At least not yet.

Charging a sitting judge with perjury is unprecedented for good reason. It is not without consequences, both legal and political. Myra Long focused on the political. Cardwell had friends, wealthy friends, and friends who were active in politics. Seeking citywide office can be expensive and Braxton would need financial help if she wanted to continue as the circuit attorney. An indictment of Cardwell would close many important doors, Long argued.

Holly Hermann focused on the legal issues. Perjury prosecutions were difficult to prove, which was why you didn't see many. The statute requires an intent to deceive through false testimony on a fact material to the inquiry. This situation occurred many years before and memories fade, which would present a decent defense for Cardwell. Neither Braxton nor Long offered any counterpoints. It was obvious no one in the room was terribly anxious to charge Cardwell with perjury, just as no one had been anxious to charge Garner Lee with murder.

The decision was made to do the press release regarding compliance to the test proposed by Long. The issue of what to do with Cardwell was tabled.

Felbin agreed to allow the St. Louis Police Department laboratory to do the DNA test as long as everyone agreed to expedite the process. Felbin had numerous cases involving the department's lab. He believed the people who worked there had integrity and knew what they were doing. He was also confident DNA would free his client. Felbin also knew if his DNA was found on the victim's garments, Larry Jenkins would spend the rest of his life in prison. The perjury Cardwell suborned, and the false police report wouldn't matter. The end would justify the means for the public. Jenkins wasn't worried. He knew he didn't rape anyone, and the science would confirm what he had been saying for all these years. He would finally smell the sweet scent of freedom.

Although the discussion about Cardwell had been tabled, Braxton knew if DNA exonerated Larry Jenkins, there would be a public clamor to indict Cardwell. Given what she heard at the hearing, Braxton was pretty sure the DNA of the man convicted of raping Janet Costello would not be found on her clothing.

Then there was another decision to be made. How would a lying victim be handled? And what about the cop who went along with the submission of a false report? Although Rossi was retired and Patrick Moore, her partner who authored the report was dead, the police department would be criticized. The chief law enforcement officer for the City of St. Louis would be expected to comment on all of it. Braxton knew she had to prepare for the worst and hope for the best. In the end, she hoped the system worked. If Jenkins didn't rape anyone, he should be freed. But she needed to be prepared to defend herself from accusations she was responsible for a wrongful conviction, even though she had nothing to do with the prosecution of Larry Jenkins. She hadn't even heard the name Larry Jenkins until it had landed on her desk a short time before.

Chapter Forty-Seven

As promised, the St. Louis Police Department expedited the DNA analysis and the results were in. Don Heaman, the laboratory director, asked Braxton and Felbin to meet him at the lab. He knew this was a matter with a lot of media interest, and he wanted to disclose the results of the test to both sides at the same time.

Braxton arrived first and asked Heaman to tell her the result. He declined. When Felbin arrived, he took both to a conference room. He was holding a document which they believed were the DNA results.

"First of all, I realize the public interest in this case was fueled, I'm sure, by the media coverage. I want to thank both of you for having the confidence in our lab to do this test," Heaman began. Not only was he the director of the lab, but he was also its biggest cheerleader. He never missed an opportunity to face the television camera and promote his lab or, as some would say, himself. "We expedited the test pursuant to your request but, of course, did not compromise accuracy."

"Oh, for the love of God, Don," Felbin interrupted, "get on with it. It's just the three of us here and no cameras. What the hell is the result of your test? Is the DNA of Larry Jenkins present or is it not?" Although Felbin believed the police department lab was one of the finest in the country, he would occasionally spar with Heaman, who sought the spotlight by providing editorial commentary detrimental to Felbin's clients. Laboratory directors needed to report the science and leave the rest to the judges and lawyers to sort out. He didn't want Heaman in the middle of this, beyond reporting the test results.

"I'm getting to that but..."

"Well get to it, Don. No *buts*. I don't have all day to listen to your PR bullshit."

"Okay, but in this case, you may like my PR bullshit."
Vintage Heaman—always needing the last word. "The DNA
of Larry Jenkins is not on any of the clothing samples we
tested. Happy, Felbin?"

Felbin resisted the temptation to continue this unpro-
ductive exchange with Heaman. Instead, he just thanked
him for the analysis and asked for a copy of the report.

Outside the conference room, Felbin wanted to talk to
Braxton to see what her position would be on the next step.
The result of the test came as no surprise to Felbin, and he
hoped it was not a surprise to the prosecutor. He planned
to present the test results to the court, request the court
to set aside the conviction and seek the immediate release
of his client. He was interested in how cooperative Braxton would be. This case was clear. No DNA, and the victim
not only recanted her identification, but admitted to lying
during the jury trial. A no brainer for any prosecutor. But
he had learned over the years, things obvious to the defense
might not be so crystal clear to the prosecution.

Felbin presented his plan to Braxton and waited for her
response.

The result was the result. Braxton figured Felbin anticipated an exculpatory DNA test. He consented to the police
department doing the test because he knew she would not
be in a position to contest the result from her own lab. However, she could force him to put Heaman on the stand to
testify to the result. The inevitable would only be prolonged
unnecessarily. More importantly, it would subject her to
additional criticism. She was prolonging the incarceration
of an innocent man, which would probably earn her a spot
on the editorial page of the newspaper.

On the other hand, there was the matter of Joan Cardwell and Janet Snead. She could take the position the conviction should stand, even though no DNA was found. If
Nealon set aside the conviction, she could appeal. Another
waste of time which would all but guarantee her need to
find employment outside the world of politics, and perhaps
even outside the city of St. Louis. There really wasn't any
choice. She would stipulate to the DNA findings and not
oppose the release. In fact, she would embrace both as a

just result, while reminding everyone she had no role in this case at the outset.

Give the adversary publicity, Braxton thought. It was rather odd she hadn't heard from Cardwell. She was probably trying to do some damage control with her fellow judges. Ordinarily, Cardwell would be in Braxton's office or on the phone screaming at her. Never one to engage in any introspection, Cardwell would be quick to play the blame game. Braxton was a favorite target. With her position on the release of Jenkins, Braxton was confident she would hear from her former colleague. And it would not be a pleasant conversation.

Felbin and company were back at the jail to meet with their client and give him the good news. Although he knew his DNA would not be on the victim's clothing, he became emotional once again. "I can't believe this nightmare is finally over. It is over, isn't it?" he asked, looking at Felbin who nodded. "When will they let me out?" Larry was now excited.

"Well, first, we need to present the DNA test results to the court and after those are accepted, we move to set aside the conviction and for your release. We contacted the court and Judge Nealon's clerk told us to come in at 9 tomorrow morning. You will be transferred to the penitentiary in Jefferson City, where they will process you out. We will monitor the situation and make sure they don't drag their feet."

Larry was grateful for everything everyone had done for him. Before they left the jail, he hugged Felbin, Garner and Tony, tears again filling his eyes while thanking them, along with Barry Scheck and the Innocence Project.

Chapter Forty-Eight

At precisely nine o'clock, Judge Nealon took the bench. The parties were in their respective positions at the counsel tables and the reporters were primed and ready for the news. Incredibly, the DNA test results had not been leaked. For the second time in many years, Larry Jenkins was dressed in casual civilian clothes, which Carmine had brought to the jail for him. His attire gave people in the audience a hint of what was to come. This time instead of a jacket and tie, he wore a red golf shirt and tan pants accentuated by a tan needlepoint belt with multicolored stars Melinda had made for him, and brown loafers. Among her many talents, in her spare time, which wasn't much, Melinda made needlepoint belts. Felbin had twelve with different designs from the names of famous golf courses to polo ponies and frogs. Larry sat between Felbin and Garner. As the reporters noted, Larry was smiling as he was brought into the courtroom by the deputies—another hint of what was to come.

When the judge asked the lawyers if there was an announcement, Felbin rose and slowly approached the podium. "Your Honor, we have the results of the DNA test conducted by the St. Louis Police Department laboratory," he began. "We also have a stipulation as to those results." Felbin then marked as an exhibit a copy of the lab report Heaman had prepared and given to him. "The report from the laboratory, which I have marked as an exhibit and now offer in evidence, states the DNA found on the rape victim's clothing in this case, does not belong to Larry Jenkins. I repeat, does not belong to Larry Jenkins."

"That evidence will be received. Please give me a moment to review the report," Judge Nealon said. After a few minutes, Nealon said, "For the record, I have read the report and it clearly concludes the DNA found on the clothing of the victim is not that of the defendant, Larry Jenkins."

The judge then looked at Felbin and asked, "Is there a motion, Mr. Felbin?"

"There is, Your Honor. At this time the defendant moves to set aside and hold for naught the rape conviction and order the defendant discharged."

"Any objection, Ms. Braxton?" Nealon asked.

"No, Your Honor."

"The conviction of Larry Jenkins for the rape, sodomy and kidnapping of Janet Costello-Sneed will be set aside and held for naught. Mr. Jenkins is ordered discharged and released forthwith. So, ordered."

"Your Honor," Felbin said, "there is one other motion we have. We move at this time for the expungement of the conviction and criminal record of Mr. Jenkins to include his arrest for this offense."

"As much as I would like to sustain your request, Mr. Felbin, as you know, it is beyond the jurisdiction of this court and would require the filing of a separate motion. The law enforcement agencies have the right to weigh in on your request. The expungement isn't automatic by statute, although it ought to be in this case. And I am confident the circuit attorney will cooperate with you in this endeavor."

Felbin knew he had to file a separate expungement motion. But he wanted to make a point for the reporters in attendance. Although Larry Jenkins' conviction would be set aside and he would be released, his fight wasn't over in multiple ways. In fact, it might just be starting.

Rather than simply recessing the proceedings, Judge Nealon felt the need to say something. He was charged with the responsibility of dispensing justice. Sometimes justice is denied. Sometimes it is delayed. Certainly, in the case of Larry Jenkins, justice was delayed. While Judge Nealon did not participate in this delay, he felt the need to apologize because he was at least part of a system which failed this man.

"Mr. Jenkins, I would be remiss if I sent you on your way without saying something," the judge began. "The criminal justice system failed you. The courts failed you. Prosecutors failed you. The police failed you. And your defense lawyers failed you. The extent to which each participated is for others to decide. All I can say is I'm truly sorry all of us failed you. But at least we *finally* got it right, which I know is little consolation for all you have endured. While I can't give back the last seventeen years of your life, I can give you your freedom and the remainder of your life. Is there anything you would like to say, sir?"

Larry Jenkins stood, looked around a courtroom filled with media and other interested onlookers. All strangers to Larry Jenkins. He had no family. Overwhelmed by the emotion of the moment, slowly he began to speak. "Nothing other than I am grateful to my lawyers for all they have done. They believed in me. Since the time this nightmare began, I have said I didn't rape this lady. Finally, someone listened, and Judge, I'm grateful to you for being that person."

Judge Nealon acknowledged the comments. Then he turned to Karen Braxton. "Ms. Braxton, I trust you will finally check the DNA found on the victim's clothing with the data base to see if you can finally identify the person actually responsible for the commission of this crime."

"We will, Your Honor."

"Ms. Braxton, can you give Mr. Jenkins any reason why you didn't do that comparison at the time he first filed his request for a DNA analysis?" Judge Nealon asked.

Karen Braxton was not ready for the question. She hesitated before responding, trying to choose her words carefully. "None other than I was told the jury got it right when it returned a guilty verdict. Obviously, not the case. I would also add something else. Like you, I was not a party to this seventeen years ago."

Nealon didn't like her choice of words. "I fully realize you were not involved seventeen years ago. But like me, you are a party to it now. And I trust your office will do whatever is necessary to compile all the facts which caused the prosecution and conviction of this innocent man. The jury didn't get it wrong here, Ms. Braxton. It played the hand it was dealt by your office."

"You can be sure, my office will do all it can to get to the bottom of this," Braxton told the court. She then turned to Jenkins and said, "I, too, am sorry about this, Mr. Jenkins. It's an embarrassment for all of us and cannot be tolerated. Although I had no involvement in your prosecution, I also want to apologize on behalf of all the current men and women in the circuit attorney's office. We deeply regret what happened to you."

Totally amazed at what they were hearing, both Judge Nealon and Felbin listened to the apology. They couldn't believe it. This was the woman who refused to agree to the DNA test, a simple procedure which would categorically have decided whether Larry Jenkins did the rape. Instead, she forced him to jump through additional hoops after spending so many years locked up. And now she was telling the man she tried to keep in prison she was sorry. Felbin and everyone else in the courtroom knew what she was doing. She had to put some distance between herself and Cardwell. But the real test of her sincerity would come if she decided to prosecute Cardwell, a thought echoed by the judge, at least inferentially.

"Your apology will mean more to this gentleman," Nealon said pointing to Jenkins, "when you bring the people responsible for this travesty to justice."

And with those final words, the case of State of Missouri verses Larry Jenkins was over, and the court was in recess.

Chapter Forty-Nine

Larry Jenkins had to process out through Crossroads Correctional Facility, a maximum-security penitentiary about fifty miles north of Kansas City, where he'd spent a good portion of his life. The processing took about a week. Felbin complained about the delay, but to no avail. These government institutions don't care. They do what they want, when they want. When the day finally came, he, Garner and Carmine were waiting for Larry outside the walls. The reporters were present to cover the event.

Dressed in the clothes he'd worn to court and carrying a manila folder containing his legal papers, his only possessions, he walked slowly through the steel door—the door which separated freedom from incarceration. Once through, he stopped to look around, smell the air, and gaze up at the clouds on this sunny day. He had been in this institution for most of his incarceration. Other than walking in the yard within the walls for exercise, the only time he was able to view the outside world was from the window of a van while chained to his seat on the way to St. Louis for his DNA hearing. But now he was free. He could go wherever he wanted and do whatever he wanted. He couldn't believe it was actually happening. It was surreal.

The enjoyment of his first few moments of freedom was interrupted by reporters. With cameras rolling and microphones in his face, the reporters wanted to know what he was feeling, what he was thinking. Another new experience. No one was ever interested in his thoughts on anything. Somewhat intimidated by the attention, he struggled to answer the questions. "I... I'm happy to be out. I never thought it would happen. I thought I would spend the rest of my life here."

"What are your plans now?" one reporter asked.

"I don't know. I really have no plans."

"Given the testimony at your hearing, will you be planning to sue anyone?"

Felbin had been listening to the questions and his client's answers. But for this question, he didn't give Larry a chance to respond. "We will be exploring our options," Felbin said. "As you know from the hearing, several people are responsible for this travesty. I hope the circuit attorney will also be exploring her options. Throughout this, she has been part of the problem, rather than the solution. She could have agreed to the test. But instead, she prolonged Larry's incarceration by making him prove an entitlement to a DNA test. And now she is apologizing to him. Too little, too late."

After thanking the reporters for their past coverage of the case and encouraging them to keep the pressure on Braxton, he, Garner and Carmine guided their client through the crowd toward a waiting vehicle for the long trip to St. Louis. But this time would be different. This time he would not be chained to his seat and could stop for a restroom break without the presence of prison guards clearing the restroom before he could enter.

Felbin wanted to talk publicly about filing a lawsuit. But first, he needed to talk to Larry about his future plans. When he left the penitentiary, he received a handshake from the warden, who sincerely wished him well. Larry was a model prisoner and the warden liked him. In addition, he was given one hundred dollars in cash for a bus ticket to St. Louis and some food. The money, along with his legal papers, were Larry's sole possessions. When prisoners are paroled, they are sent to a halfway house where they receive food, lodging, and assistance in finding employment. Because he was not paroled and not under the jurisdiction of the state, he received none of those benefits, minimal as they are. He was on his own, left to fend for himself.

Felbin wanted to know if he had any plans after they got back to St. Louis. "I have no idea what I'm going to do," Larry explained. "My head has been spinning."

"I realize this is overwhelming, Larry. But you need some type of a plan starting with where you will live. Is there anyone you could stay with until you get settled?"

"I have no family left. As far as friends go, being put in prison for rape doesn't help you keep friends. Since I have no money to pay rent, I was going to see if I could find someplace where a cheap room was available to rent. All I need is a bed. I was hoping I could stay there while I find a job and then I could pay the rent. I thought I'd give them the hundred dollars I got from the prison as a down payment. I have no credit or credit card. I also don't have the car I'll need to look for a job."

Garner understood what Larry was saying. He could feel his pain. Both did not commit the crimes with which they were charged. When their cases concluded, they were without family and friends. No place to go; no one to turn to. And in Garner's case, the woman he loved was dead. But at least Garner had some money when he was released and was able to escape to Europe, at least until his funds ran out. Although it wasn't much, he thought he could offer Larry something at least temporarily to help him. "Larry, I have a hotel room you can use," he said. "I'll be staying for a little while longer before I go back to New York and you can stay with me. I also rented a car we can use to help you find a job. I'm guessing you don't have a driver's license, and I can drive you wherever you want to go. I'll check with Barry to make sure it's okay. But I'm sure it will be."

Another first for Larry Jenkins. Someone offering him a place to stay and to help him look for a job to get back on his feet. It was a good feeling and he was grateful for any help.

With the issue of housing temporarily resolved, Felbin turned to the issue of a civil rights lawsuit against those who took his client's life away. The potential defendants included Cardwell, Rossi, the Board of Police Commissioners for the St. Louis Police Department, and Snead. Each of these individuals combined to deprive Larry of due process and a fair trial, the right not to be arrested without a sufficient showing of probable cause, the right not to be accused and tried on the basis of evidence fraudulently procured and intentionally or recklessly fabricated. This was at least the theory of the case.

"Do we have a chance to win?" Larry asked. "Seems like when you fight the government, you lose."

"There could be some problems with the case," Felbin said. Although he thought the pursuit of these claims against these defendants would be a long shot, he didn't want to spoil the moment and the hope of good things to come to this man. "But I think we need to give it a shot and see what happens. Do you agree?"

"Mr. Felbin, you and Mr. Scheck and Mr. Lee and Mr. Carmine gave me my life back. I'm eternally grateful to all of you. Whatever you say is what we do. I have my freedom back, which is what really matters. I'm not counting on some pot of gold down the road. Nobody in this state is going to be looking to make me rich. I know it's up to me to figure out how I will get along in a world which has changed a lot since I've been in it," Larry said.

It was near dinner time as they approached St. Louis. Felbin asked Larry what he wanted to eat. He suggested they go to a nice restaurant to celebrate. "We need to go to a place that doesn't cost very much. I only have a hundred dollars the warden gave me when I left," Larry said.

"You're not paying for anything, Larry. I just want to know what you would like to eat."

"Well, as long as it's not prison food prepared by a prison cook, I'm in," Larry said jokingly.

Felbin decided on LoRusso's, his favorite St. Louis restaurant. He knew Rich LoRusso, the owner, would prepare something special for Larry if he didn't like what was on the menu.

After they were seated, the waiter arrived asking whether anyone wanted a cocktail. Larry didn't drink, but the others could use a drink. Felbin ordered a dry dirty gin martini and Garner and Carmine wanted beers, Bud Light.

When the waiter brought the drinks, Larry watched as his three dinner companions picked up their napkins and put them on their laps. He followed. Felbin proposed a toast to their victory and they all raised their glasses, Larry toasting with water.

After their toast, everyone looked at the menu. Larry's focus was on the cost of each item. Forty-eight dollars for a steak. The prison didn't serve steak. In fact, he couldn't remember if he'd ever had a steak. Life outside the walls was certainly expensive. Money was never a concern to him before. He didn't have any and didn't need any. Prison didn't have many benefits, but at least they provided food, clothing, medical and housing. Of course, you had to surrender your freedom in order to take advantage of these luxuries.

Felbin watched Larry's eyes widen as he scanned each item on the menu. He knew he was focusing on the cost. "What looks good to you?" Felbin asked.

"This is really expensive," was all Larry could say.

"Listen, Larry, I told you not to worry about the cost. We have it covered. I want you to order whatever you want and as much as you want. Okay?"

"These things cost so much. I wouldn't feel good about that." Larry Jenkins had been through a lot in his lifetime. He was a proud man. Although prison stripped him of everything else, they were unable to take away his pride. His family never had very much, but everyone worked and earned a living, unskilled jobs mostly. They paid their bills. Now he had less than he did before. No money, no job, no place to live. He needed other people to help him out, a concept foreign to a prison environment. He knew he needed to swallow his pride at least until he got back on his feet. But it would be a hard thing to do.

Felbin knew he needed to do something to make his client feel comfortable. He had an idea. He excused himself, claiming he had to use the restroom. Instead, he went looking for his friend, the owner of the restaurant.

"I see you've been making the news with the guy who spent a long time in the joint for a rape he didn't do," Rich LoRusso said as Felbin approached him in the bar area of the restaurant.

"That's why we are here. We are celebrating his victory," Felbin said. He went on to explain the issue and the need to make Larry feel comfortable. They developed a plan.

Shortly after Felbin returned to the table, Rich arrived. After the introductions, the owner initiated the plan. "Congratulations on your victory. You've been through quite an ordeal, Mr. Jenkins," LoRusso said. "I can't imagine what it was like to be in prison all that time. But now you are in my house and this is what I want to do for you. Put those menus away. I'm going to select the menu for all of you." When everyone denied any food allergies, Rich told the group he would be back with their dinner.

Soon the waiter brought the first course—appetizers consisting of toasted beef ravioli, a St. Louis favorite, Mama's meatballs, and a wild mushroom trio. When they finished this course, they enjoyed a Caesar salad. The entrée the owner selected was an eight-ounce filet mignon with white truffle demi glaze, with a side of roasted asparagus and complimented with a bottle of California Merlot, 2013 vintage.

Larry was having trouble believing what he was seeing. A couple weeks ago, he was sitting in a jail cell looking to spend the rest of his life there. Now, dressed in casual street clothes, he was sitting in a fancy restaurant eating very expensive steak with some sort of sauce on it. He decided to put aside the cost issue for the time being and enjoy the moment.

When everyone was nearly finished, Rich appeared at the table asking about dessert. He had no takers. Everyone was stuffed. Instead, everyone had coffee to keep them awake. It had been a long and enjoyable day.

Over coffee, they talked some more about the future for Larry Jenkins. Since he had a place to stay, the most important thing was to find a job. He decided to try United Fruit and Produce on produce row in St. Louis. He had worked there before as a laborer, primarily unloading produce from boxcars and moving it around the warehouse in preparation for delivery to the retail stores. They'd paid a decent wage then, with some medical benefits. Medical was important because during his time in prison, he'd developed some heart and blood pressure issues requiring medication.

While they were finishing their coffee, Felbin found Rich, thanked him and paid for the meal. From the restaurant they went to the office where the cars of Garner and Carmine were parked. Larry got in Garner's car and they headed for their temporary home.

Chapter Fifty

The media coverage following the release of Larry Jenkins was relentless. Cardwell and Braxton were the focus. Would Cardwell be prosecuted for perjury? Would she be removed from the bench or disbarred? What about Sneed and Rossi, would they be prosecuted?

Braxton remained silent. She was not responding to press inquiries and incredibly, no leaks were coming out of her office.

The Missouri Commission on the Retirement, Removal and Discipline of Judges, established in 1972, was an independent state agency responsible for investigating complaints against judges. Like Braxton, this agency failed to respond to press inquiries. The work of this Commission was always confidential and seldom, if ever, did they respond to the media. It was unknown whether a complaint had even been filed against Cardwell. Felbin said his client had not done so yet.

A civil rights lawsuit was filed in the United States District Court for the Eastern District of Missouri against Cardwell only. Felbin, Scheck and Garner made the decision to exclude Rossi, the police department and Snead from the suit. Rossi was excluded because she didn't write the report. She didn't testify at the trial and testified honestly at the DNA hearing. It was also felt she would be a stronger witness against Cardwell if she was not named as a defendant. The same was true for the police department itself. Additionally, the evidence against the department was weak since the incident occurred many years before and the department knew nothing about it at the time. The idea also was to have all the guns pointed at Cardwell. She was the quarterback in the game to lock up an innocent man.

Snead was certainly not honest in either her testimony at trial or again at the DNA hearing. However, she was a traumatized victim of a rape who was under the influence of

Cardwell. The collective wisdom suggested it would not be good form to sue a victim under these circumstances. Jurors would probably not wrap their arms around this tactic. Then there was the matter of collecting any judgment. She was a teacher who had no money to pay a large or even a small judgment. She was married and her assets were jointly held and untouchable to satisfy any judgment personal to her. Rossi was in the same boat. Judgment proof. Few retired police officers have any spare funds, and their pensions cannot be used to satisfy civil judgments.

The lawsuit fueled the interest in pursuing Judge Cardwell, if not for criminal charges at least her removal from the bench. Efforts to contact her both at home and the office failed. According to her secretary, Mary McMurtry, the judge was on vacation. McMurtry was either unwilling or unable to say where her boss was or when she would return.

At a press conference announcing the filing of the suit, Felbin explained why Cardwell was the only defendant. But the reporters also asked whether his client filed a complaint against her with the Judicial Commission. Once again, he told them his client had not yet filed a complaint. When pressed why, given the testimony at the hearing, he repeated what he had told them before. He was waiting to see if the St. Louis Circuit Court was going to take some action to get rid of one of their own. "Filing a complaint against a sitting judge is a serious matter," Felbin said. "Frankly, I believe the Commission would pay greater attention to a complaint coming from her fellow judges than from my client. I also believe in the first instance her fellow judges need to be given the opportunity to clean their own house. But I can assure you if her fellow judges take no action, my client and I will."

Although Braxton and the Commission remained silent, the reporting suggested there was a movement among some of Cardwell's colleagues on the court to at least suspend her. Judge Nealon was leading the effort. He had a ringside seat for her testimony and those of the other witnesses who testified during the DNA hearing. Judge Nealon declined to comment to the media. But according to sources, he was getting push back from some of the judges on several levels. Some argued the court had no jurisdiction to remove or even suspend her. These individuals claimed this was within the exclusive jurisdiction of the Commission. As far as a complaint was concerned, they believed only individuals who claimed injury had the standing to file a complaint. Finally, some questioned the sufficiency of the evidence. They suggested her alleged improper conduct, which occurred many years before, was in her capacity as a prosecutor, not a judge, and was not supported by substantial and competent evidence. Of course, as the article pointed out, this argument ignored what some considered the false testimony she provided most recently at the DNA hearing.

Chapter Fifty-One

The exoneration of Larry Jenkins and the role Cardwell played raised additional concerns about the relationship between the judge and Senator Lee. While Lee continued to deny any relationship with Cardwell, he boldly claimed his opponent was planting false stories for his own political advantage. He also continued to deny he fathered a child with his son's girlfriend, reminding reporters he'd agreed to take a paternity test. He further claimed Singer's refusal to schedule the test was because he knew the allegation was false, and it had backfired on him.

The paternity allegation was hurting the Singer campaign, despite the explanation of the unavailability of DNA from the fetus, which was necessary to do the test. Lee had successfully used the issue to his advantage. He even inferentially implied Singer knew when he made the allegation, he wouldn't have access to the necessary sample to do the test. And therefore, Lee would not be able to prove his innocence.

The Singer campaign believed both the prosecutor and the defense had tests which could resolve the issue of whether Senator Lee was the father. They asked for the release of those tests or the DNA samples of the fetus so they could do the test. They received no response from either side.

John Peterson, Singer's campaign manager, met with Lori Stamp who was running the St. Louis office. They needed a plan. Somehow, some way, they needed to do the test. It was too late to back away from the issue, and it was not going away. Since they were unable to get the information voluntarily, Peterson was exploring other legal options which would force at least the prosecutor to surrender the test results, if not the DNA samples themselves. He suggested making a formal Sunshine Law request with the circuit attorney. Since the criminal prosecution of Garner Lee for the murder of Amy Deland was concluded, the records, including any test results maintained by the office, should be available to the public.

Lori Stamp was not sure she agreed with Peterson's analysis. She questioned whether criminal records such as these would be open and subject to a Sunshine Law request. There was also the question of a legal battle. If Braxton refused to surrender the documents, the campaign would have to file suit and a long court battle would result. Despite the potential bumps in the road, in the end she concluded it was worth a try.

In addition to a Sunshine request, Lori also thought they should offer a polygraph test to Senator Lee on the question of paternity. Her idea was to offer the test and the campaign would pay for it.

Now it was Peterson's turn to question the idea. Polygraph tests could be unreliable. They were inadmissible in court. "What if he denied paternity and tested truthful?" he asked.

"What if we do a DNA test and it proves he is not the father of this fetus?" she asked. "We would be running the same risk with a polygraph. Frankly, we are relying on his son's allegation and hoping he knows what he's talking about."

"If we are going the polygraph route, we might as well ask whether he killed the woman he impregnated," Peterson added. "Certainly, he had motive and opportunity."

"I would think his wife also did," Lori said. "Her husband, looking to be the next governor, impregnates his son's girlfriend. This situation can't be good for their marriage or their political aspirations. From what I hear, she has political ambitions of her own. We also don't know whether the kid is good for the murder. He had as much motive and opportunity as the other two. Plus, do we really know the kid is innocent since there is a suggestion that a judge dismissed his case as a favor to his father who put her on the bench? As far as I'm concerned, all three are suspects. But the kid isn't running to become the next governor of this state. His parents are, and we need to focus our attention on them."

The media was quick to run with the polygraph challenges for the senator, along with his wife, and the request for any paternity test in the possession of the prosecutor's office. Braxton responded immediately with her own press release. She explained her office was not in possession of any paternity test information.

Kelvin Bellington, Lee's campaign manager, along with Carol Hudson and Max Stapleton, who ran the campaign on the east side of the state, were huddled in the St. Louis campaign office trying to plan a counter move to the polygraph requests. The candidate and his wife were not present. Any test for the senator relating to paternity would be risky. There was also the question of the reliability of a test the courts didn't recognize.

Kelvin Bellington was the first to speak. "We have a problem. Singer's people want to do a polygraph on this question of paternity. They also want to ask the senator and his wife whether they murdered the kid's girlfriend."

"Are you kidding?" Hudson asked. "They want to know if the senator murdered someone, too?"

"And his wife," Bellington added.

"Singer must be desperate," Stapleton said.

"The paternity test backfired on them when we agreed to take it and they couldn't get the markers to do the comparison. Now they're doing an end run to keep the issue alive. We need to respond. We can't just ignore it." Bellington said. "I think we need to take the position polygraph tests are scientifically unreliable and this is nothing more than desperate harassment. Then we should repeat our offer to do a paternity test to finally prove the senator is not the father of the child."

All agreed and a press release was sent out. Lee was campaigning in Rolla and didn't know about the polygraph or the position the campaign had taken until he heard it on the news. He concurred and called Bellington to thank him for handling the issue.

While Lee was making his call, Carmine was also making a call. He needed to meet with Garner who was staying at the Chase Park Plaza Hotel, across from Forest Park in the Central West End. They decided on Culpeper's Bar and Grill, which was around the corner from the hotel.

　　　Carmine arrived first and took a table in the corner of the restaurant. Culpeper's had great chicken wings, which Carmine ordered with extra celery, blue cheese and a Bud Light to wash them down.

　　　When Garner arrived, Carmine pushed the wings. "They are the best, and you won't get these in New York City when you go back," he said. Then he got down to the purpose of the meeting. Since the Jenkins case was finished, Carmine was on a mission to destroy Winston Lee and his wife. "Did you see the latest news about your father's campaign?" he asked.

　　　"No. What are they doing now?"

　　　Carmine explained the polygraph challenge and the continued pursuit of a paternity test. "Your father is pulling some bullshit with the test. He knows Singer can't get the DNA from the fetus to do the test and he is sticking it up Singer's ass, suggesting he is ready, willing and able to take the test and prove he isn't the father. We need to do something."

　　　"Actually, I was just thinking the same thing. I thought about approaching your boss again. What do you have in mind? You know how I feel about them, and you know Felbin's position."

　　　"I think another conversation with Felbin would be good," Carmine said.

　　　"Of course, the first conversation we had with him didn't go very well." Garner was referring to the time he and Carmine disrupted the fundraiser when Darius Washington was in attendance and then escaped to Key West to avoid the Felbin fallout.

　　　"Yeah. That wasn't one of our best moments. But the last conversation, when you wanted to release the lab report, was pretty good. At least he didn't say he wasn't going to discuss the topic again. Instead, he said we could revisit the issue after the decision in Larry's case. Since Larry's case is over, maybe now we can persuade him something needs to be done to derail this campaign. I know he dislikes your father as much, if not more, than I do."

　　　"Although our last conversation with Felbin was cordial, I got the impression he really doesn't want me or the firm to get involved in this political campaign. I suspect his suggestion to wait until Larry's case was decided was just a way to put off the inevitable of him telling us we can't get involved. I think we need a plan of attack if we're going to approach him again..." Garner said.

They ate their chicken wings, ordered a couple more beers and developed a plan to approach Felbin for his cooperation in bringing down a politician.

Chapter Fifty-Two

The next morning Carmine and Garner were in the office early putting the final touches on their plan. They sat at the conference room table in the corner of Felbin's office looking out at the river and the Arch.

When Felbin finally arrived and saw the pair sitting in his office, he said, "Did I have a meeting with you guys?"

"Nothing scheduled. But we need to talk to you about something," Carmine said.

"Whatever it is, when you two gang up, it can never be good for me. What is it?" Felbin asked reluctantly.

Carmine looked at Garner. He would start the discussion. Carmine knew Felbin felt guilty about how Cassandra Lee neutralized him. Carmine wanted to use this to their benefit, but he couldn't give Garner the specifics. Guilt. Play on Felbin's guilt for what he allowed to happen. Allowing Garner to do what he wanted might help ease some of the guilt. "As you know, I have been living with what my father did to Amy," he began. "Not a day goes by I don't think about it. He is now denying what he did because he wants to be the governor of this state. And he is getting away with it because his opponent can't get the marker to match his DNA. I can't continue to sit on my hands and do nothing to correct his lie. I want to get involved."

Felbin knew exactly where this was going. The day of reckoning had arrived.

Garner didn't wait for Felbin to say anything. He pressed on. "I would like to release our DNA test and back it up with releasing the markers from the fetus we used to do the test. The last time we had this conversation, you said I had to wait until after Judge Nealon decided Larry's case. Well Larry's case has been decided and now it is time for me to focus my attention on my lying, cheating father."

Felbin knew the disclosure of the test would throw a hand grenade into the campaign. But there were problems. Except for impacting Larry's case, these were the same problems which had existed the last time this issue was discussed. "Garner, we talked about the problems this would create. First, we don't have a written report. It was just verbal because we didn't want to be in a position to disclose a report to the prosecution for fear it would be used against us. The second problem is the same as the first. It can be used against you. There will be a suggestion you found out your father was involved with Amy and killed her in a fit of rage and then lied about being in her apartment. Do you really want to go back to that mountain, particularly where your life is now?"

"Please don't misunderstand. I will forever be grateful for what you and Barry and Tony and all of you have done for me. But right now, I am living my life portrayed as a murderer who got away with it thanks to a corrupt judge. Frankly, I think Larry Jenkins is going to experience the same thing. Despite the DNA, some people will always brand him a rapist. No chance of changing the minds of those people. But my only chance to eliminate some of the noise and get to Larry's level of actual innocence is to find the truth, which means finding the real killer. But I haven't been able to get there yet. I believe a search for the truth begins with my father. Despite his denial, we know my father got my girlfriend pregnant. And I can't stay silent and let him continue to lie. I'm sorry. I know I'm rambling on. But this is important to me, regardless of where it lands. If I reopen old issues and accusations, so be it."

Carmine knew Garner struck the nerve he'd targeted. He could see it in Felbin's face. And now he was faced with a dilemma. Get into the middle of a nasty political campaign and wind up in a headline. Or stay out and continue to support Garner's mistaken belief that although not an adulterer, he wore the *Scarlet Letter* as a symbol of shame for the murder of Amy. The irony didn't escape any of them. Garner's father was the adulterer, but Garner believed he was the one who wore the *Scarlet Letter*. Perhaps if Felbin and company got into the campaign, they could put that *Letter* where it belonged.

Garner and Carmine waited for Felbin's decision. It seemed like an eternity. Finally, he looked at Garner and said, "I'll contact my guy at the lab and have him prepare and send over a paternity report, if that's what you want to do. I'm not sure this is a good idea for you personally. I think you'll take some hits. I suggest we have another discussion after we get the report and before you release it."

Garner nodded. "I understand your position. But this is something I must do. The whole truth needs to come out sooner or later, and this is a start. My *father* needs to be identified for the person he really is."

"Are you sure you're not doing this for pure revenge?"

"Oh, I suspect at some level I am. And I'd be lying if I said I wouldn't enjoy watching him fail. But in the end, it's about the truth, right and wrong. He did what he did and needs to be held accountable. Not benefit from his own lies. For me it's simple."

"When I get the report and we have another discussion so I can take another shot at dissuading you from doing this, how do you want to proceed if I fail?" Felbin asked.

It was obvious neither Garner nor Carmine had considered this aspect.

When both looked confused and didn't speak, Felbin described some options. "We can give it to the Singer campaign and let them release it. Or we can release it along with them. Or I can release it either alone, with you, or with the Singer campaign. Or with all of us together."

Carmine decided to weigh in on this one. "I think Garner needs to be involved. Otherwise, it will look like he's afraid of the backlash that'll come from his parents and those who will use this as his motive for murder." Although not stated, what Carmine really wanted was to see Garner get into his father's face. Sweet revenge, pure and simple in Carmine's world.

"I think I'd like to be involved," Garner said. "I think the three of us should do a press conference and release it. I don't think it would be a good idea to involve the Singer campaign, at least not directly. I don't want people to think I'm doing this because I'm supporting Singer. *Senator* Lee already made this claim when we confronted him during the fundraiser Darius Washington attended."

"I agree," Felbin said, ignoring the reference to Darius Washington. "I think it's cleaner that way. If Singer wants a copy, we can give him one. But I suspect the press will make one available to him for his comment. I'll arrange a press conference for the day after we get the report, if your final decision is to go forward."

After Garner left, Felbin turned to Carmine and said, "I assume this additional effort to revisit the issue was all your doing. I also assume you had him push me deeper into the guilt trip I'm already on."

"Me? Not me, boss!" Carmine said, trying to suppress a smile.

"Right. Let me remind you and caution you. The information on his mother is protected and will not be disclosed either directly or indirectly by you. Once again, do I make myself clear?"

Carmine acknowledged Felbin's statement and agreed. Felbin knew those were meaningless words designed to placate him for the moment. Tony Carmine wasn't one to give up. He just needed to find a more creative way to get the job done without being discovered.

Chapter Fifty-Three

As soon as Felbin received the paternity DNA test results, he had another conversation with Garner, with the same result. Felbin then scheduled a press conference for the following day. He invited every media outlet throughout the state of Missouri. Felbin, Garner and Carmine had waited a long time for this day. For Felbin, animosity for Winston Lee began when the senator involved himself in the prosecution of Bobby Decker. It escalated after he agreed to represent his son. For Garner, the hatred of his father began when he learned he was involved with his girlfriend and later impregnated her. For Carmine, he hated all politicians who tried to put police officers in the penitentiary. But today, regardless of how each one of them got there, the three would share the sweet taste of revenge.

The conference was in Felbin's large conference room and was standing room only. Every news outlet in the state was represented. In addition, the Lee campaign sent a representative after getting a heads up from one of the reporters.

After the television cameras were positioned and the microphones were set up in front of Felbin, Garner and Carmine, Felbin gave a brief overview of Garner's case. He then introduced Garner to explain the circumstances under which Winston Lee's DNA was obtained and compared.

Nervous at first, Garner began by thanking everyone for coming, but then went directly to the heart of the matter. "We are not holding this press conference for political purposes, although I'm certain our disclosure will have a political ramification. Instead, we are sharing this information in the interest of truth and justice. From the trial, you know I'm not the father of Amy's child. During the trial, we didn't know who was. It was only after the trial we stumbled onto some evidence which led us to suspect Winston Lee was the father.

"We obtained Senator Lee's DNA sample. It was not voluntarily provided. Instead, it was obtained from a fork he used during a lunch meeting with Mr. Felbin, his iced tea glass and the napkin he used at the meal." As the reporters looked at each other, Garner continued. "We then sent his sample to a lab along with the marker we had from the fetus for examination. This is the report," he said as he held a document in the air. "Each of you will receive a copy which clearly and scientifically identifies Winston Lee as the father of Amy Deland's child."

Garner sat down, and Carmine distributed copies of the report. Once the reporters had a chance to read it, the questions began and Felbin stood to respond.

"When Senator Lee was volunteering to take a paternity test during the campaign, did you know he was the father of the child based upon this DNA analysis?"

"We knew he was the father and had known for some period of time," Felbin said.

"Why didn't you release this information when he was denying paternity?"

"Because we had a client to represent. Larry Jenkins was fighting for his freedom through a DNA test. Garner, through the Innocence Project, was involved in the case and we didn't want anything to interfere with our ability to get the DNA test for Larry. You now know Joan Cardwell was involved in Larry's prosecution and what she did there. I have never made a secret of my belief Senator Lee put Joan Cardwell on the bench. Of course, she also presided over Garner's trial and we didn't want the focus shifted to Garner's case and away from Larry's."

"After you obtained Senator Lee's DNA sample and ran the test, did you tell him the result?"

"Yes," Felbin said, barely allowing the reporter to finish the question.

"During the campaign, Singer challenged the senator to provide a DNA sample and he agreed. But Singer couldn't get the marker from the fetus to do the test. So, if I understand what you are telling us, Senator Lee already knew he was the father when he volunteered his DNA sample at Singer's request," a reporter said.

"Absolutely, he knew."

"His agreement then to be DNA tested was nothing more than a political stunt?" a reporter shouted from the back of the room.

"Look, this firm is not going to get involved in the politics of the governor's race. That's not why we wanted to talk to all of you. The truth is the truth and our former client Garner Lee wanted the truth to be told."

As Felbin spoke, Carmine turned toward Garner with a *what the fuck is he talking about* look in his eye. The answer was clearly yes. Although not wanting to be overt, both Garner and Carmine wanted to do everything they could to torpedo the campaign of Winston Lee. Felbin just missed an opportunity.

"Doesn't this development give your client a motive to murder his girlfriend?" one of the television reporters asked.

There it was. The question Felbin feared the most and the most dangerous part of releasing the DNA report. Interest in the death of Amy Deland would now be renewed with the interest and intensity like the opening of Al Capone's vault. But Garner knew what he was getting into when he pressed for the release of the report. Unfortunately, he would not be able to identify the real killer and Felbin would be of no help. Now they held their breath no one would ask whether the senator's DNA matched that found on the murder weapon. The elimination of Senator Lee as a suspect would certainly narrow the field, and they all knew it.

"Garner didn't kill Amy. Hopefully, at some time in the future the true killer will be identified. But in the meantime, he is not going to hold back on anything, including disclosing the identity of the person who impregnated the woman he loved."

As soon as the reporters ran out of questions, the Lee campaign representative bolted out of the room and out of Felbin's office to report the substance of the conference. They wanted the candidate to be prepared and didn't want him to read about it in the online edition of the newspaper which would be appearing soon.

When he got off the phone with the representative, Kelvin Bellington, Lee's campaign manager, called an emergency meeting. They had to do some damage control. The ship had been struck by a torpedo and was taking on water.

Chapter Fifty-Four

As the politicians dealt with their issues, Karen Braxton had her own problems. She had a variety of decisions to make. Joan Cardwell was in the news again. This time responsible for convicting and incarcerating an innocent man for her own political gain. Although not involved at the time, Braxton knew Cardwell's conduct was reprehensible, unethical and perhaps criminal. As the chief law enforcement officer for the City of St. Louis, she had to do something. It would be a delicate balance of protecting her own political future while satisfying the public thirst for the blood of Cardwell.

Myra Long was her public relations person and a confidant. Ordinarily, Braxton could go to Myra for some advice. But this was no ordinary case. The Larry Jenkins case also resurrected the Garner Lee prosecution. Cardwell was involved with both, and issues would be raised about each. Braxton's skirt was clean regarding Jenkins, but not the murder case. Backdoor conversations with Cardwell in Garner Lee's case would not only be embarrassing but unethical, even potentially criminal, if they came to light. She colluded with Cardwell together with Senator Lee and his wife for the benefit of Garner Lee. Obviously, she couldn't discuss these issues with Myra or with anyone else. She was on her own.

Several options were available, but none were desirable. She could just ignore the situation. Sooner or later, the media would find something else to pursue. She could only hope it would come sooner. But even if the press went away, Braxton knew Felbin, Scheck and the Innocence project wouldn't let it go. Then there was the federal civil rights suit Jenkins had filed, which would continue to fuel the fire. So, that option wouldn't work.

A second option would be to head the investigation herself or have the police department or a special investigator do it. Necessarily, Joan Cardwell would need to be interviewed, along with Senator Lee. If they cooperated, she could be dragged into the investigation. If they failed to cooperate, she could convene a grand jury and subpoena them to testify. But what would she ask? Did we all conspire to fix the Garner Lee case for past and future political favors?

Perhaps she could ignore the Garner Lee prosecution and focus entirely on Cardwell's role in the Jenkins case. But it might be a little awkward investigating an individual with whom you conspired to obstruct justice in a different case, regardless of whether the Garner Lee matter was directly addressed. Given Felbin's disdain for Cardwell, he would most likely want to pile on with the Garner Lee case, particularly since he had routinely advocated for the innocence of his client. Clearly, this plan wouldn't work either.

In the final analysis, Braxton knew there was only one viable course of action. A different prosecutor was needed to investigate the role of Joan Cardwell in the Jenkins case. One who didn't have a horse in the race and could conduct an objective investigation, which would inevitably include the Garner Lee prosecution. But Braxton also knew this course could mean trouble for her. Regardless, she had no choice. The only remaining question was where to send this mess—United States Attorney or the Attorney General for the State of Missouri or both. She decided on both. They could figure out who had jurisdiction.

Braxton knew her decision was the correct one and certainly in the interest of justice. She was also a realist and knew, potentially at least, it could mean the beginning of the end for her career. When the facts were uncovered, she would no longer be the keeper of the gate for criminal activity in the city of St. Louis.

When Ray Singer, the current Attorney General, was briefed on the Jenkins case and understood the involvement of Cardwell and possibly his opponent, he recused himself and his office. The matter was then referred to the St. Louis Circuit Court for the appointment of a special prosecutor.

Steve Marino, born and raised in Cape Cod, went to Washington University Law School and began his legal career as a prosecutor in the circuit attorney's office. He spent fourteen years there before moving to the United State Attorney's office, where he spent an additional nine years. He was now in a private civil practice. At age seventy, Marino was an experienced and aggressive litigator. He was also a friend of Felbin's. Their friendship developed when Marino was a state prosecutor and had several cases against Felbin. They learned to respect one another because neither played the litigation games many lawyers are familiar with. They didn't try to bury the other in bullshit. Instead, they advocated their respective positions honestly, directly and with integrity. Put the cards face up on the table and see where the case goes. But their mutual respect certainly didn't mean each wouldn't cut the other's throat without hesitation in front of the jury.

Jason Hawkins was appointed by President Barrack Obama to be the United States Attorney for the Eastern District of Missouri. As the U.S. Attorney, Hawkins oversaw everything, but did nothing other than delegate responsibility for cases to his assistants. The Jenkins case would be no different. Prior to his appointment, Hawkins was a corporate lawyer with a large St. Louis firm. His practice primarily involved lobbying at both the state and national level. Those lobbying efforts allowed him to rub shoulders with politicians which ultimately led to his federal appointment.

After the court appointed Marino and gave him a generous budget, Braxton and Hawkins called a press conference.

Chapter Fifty-Five

Joan Cardwell, who had been hiding out at home ever since the Jenkins decision, watched anxiously as Braxton stood at the microphone surrounded by reporters. "I've called you all together to announce the investigation into the conviction, incarceration and exoneration of Larry Jenkins," Braxton began. After introducing Hawkins and Marino, she explained what role each would be playing in the investigation independently of her. She never specifically said she would be recusing herself.

When Braxton finished, Hawkins stepped to the microphone. Being the consummate politician, he said, "Mr. Jenkins has suffered a great injustice. The legal system failed him. I intend to put the full resources of the federal government into my investigation to get to the truth."

Marino saw no need to comment. The conference ended without questions.

Cardwell didn't need a house to fall on her to understand this was trouble. Soon FBI agents and investigators hired by Marino would be knocking on her door looking for answers. If she decided to talk to the FBI, she knew her statement would conflict with the others who testified at the DNA hearing. Undoubtedly, she would not be believed.

The statute of limitations had expired on all charges except for perjury committed at the DNA hearing. This was a real problem for Cardwell. When a rape victim contradicts the testimony of a prosecutor, it's not hard to figure out who will be believed. The testimony of a former prosecutor and a retired cop would seal the deal.

Cardwell needed a lawyer, and she needed one quickly. Jim Brandstutter was a friend. He had worked in her office when she was the circuit attorney. They dated a couple times, but it went nowhere. He was a former University of Michigan football player who had a reputation as a lawyer who made deals, plea bargains. Most of those deals were

done in Cardwell's court. Very seldom did he try anything.
If he couldn't talk a client into pleading and the client wanted a trial, he would either withdraw from the case or refer
the matter to another lawyer.

Caldwell called Brandstutter's cell phone, and he
agreed to see her in his office as soon as she could get there.
Apparently, the plea bargain business was slow. When she
arrived in the office he shared with other lawyers in the
heart of Clayton, she was flushed, disheveled and incoher-
ent. At first, she spoke like she was on speed. When he finally calmed her down, she explained the situation, all of it.
This was no time to hold back. If he was going to represent
her, he needed to know the whole story.

The story began when she met Winston Lee. At the time
he was a state representative and she recognized him as
a political climber who could probably do her some good
with her own political ambitions somewhere down the road.
When she became the circuit attorney, he was a state senator. Occasionally, he would call her for favors. Usually, it
was some friend of a friend who was in criminal trouble and
needed a sweetheart deal. Cardwell always complied. After
all, she was banking political points for a rainy day.

After St. Louis Sergeant Tom Cannon was acquitted
by a Kansas City jury of assaulting a black mentally challenged young man in his own home, Cardwell was blamed
for allowing the case to be moved outside of St. Louis where
an all-white jury decided Cannon's fate. The black community was outraged.

On the heels of Cannon, a young black male was killed
by Officer Robert Decker during an arrest on a city rooftop.
The incident added fuel to an already smoldering fire. Senator Lee, who was making plans to run for governor, got
involved by publicly condemning the police and approached
Cardwell, demanding criminal charges. To ensure Decker
was prosecuted, Lee's wife Cassandra, a political opportunist with ambitions even greater than her husband's,
promised Cardwell a judicial appointment if she prosecuted Decker. Cassandra needed the prosecution to support
her various civil rights claims against the St. Louis police
department, including the one she filed on behalf of the deceased young man's family. As always, Cardwell complied,

and Decker was charged with murder and Jonathan Felbin represented him.

When a judicial vacancy occurred following the Decker and Cannon cases, Lee was a true power broker in state government. People were singing *Hail to the Chief* in the state capitol. Cardwell decided to approach him on the vacancy. It was time for her to cash in her political chips. She approached Cassandra Lee and reminded her of the promise she made. She acknowledged the promise and agreed to have her husband do what was necessary to make the appointment. After all, every politician could use both a prosecutor and a judge in his pocket. The Lees delivered, and Joan Caldwell added the title *Honorable* to her name.

The Lees' investment in Cardwell's judicial future paid off when their son, Garner, was charged with murdering his girlfriend. Somehow Cassandra Lee arranged for Cardwell to be assigned the case. As the case proceeded and Jonathan Felbin was hired to represent the accused, Cassandra Lee demanded Cardwell report to and take direction from her. When DNA testing was an issue, Senator Lee became involved. He went to Cardwell and told her he didn't want any testing done. With few exceptions, she did as the Lees, and mostly Cassandra Lee, directed, she told her lawyer. Her failure to follow their directives would have severe consequences. In addition to the Lees, she also admitted colluding with Braxton to ensure the results were consistent with the Lees' wishes.

Brandstutter expected to get the unabridged whole story. But he wasn't expecting this type of candor. He knew from the media coverage Cardwell was going to have a problem with the testimony she gave at the Jenkins hearing. When she called and said she needed to see him immediately, he thought it would be about a potential perjury charge. Due to limited defenses, it should be a plea and probation. Of course, she would have to resign from the bench. But now with the addition of the Decker and Garner Lee cases, probation would seem to be nothing more than wishful thinking.

"Do you think the Jenkins investigation will get into the Decker and Lee cases?" Brandstutter asked, attempting to measure his friend's total criminal exposure.

Cardwell didn't hesitate. "I think Felbin will smell blood. He knew what I was doing during his client's trial. And he knew why I was doing it. He also didn't have much love for Senator Lee. They battled publicly during the Decker case and privately during his kid's case. He smelled the involvement of the senator in both cases and I'm sure he would like nothing better than to see us with adjoining cells in prison. Plus, Felbin and Marino are friends, which doesn't help. I'm confident he will bring all he knows and suspects to the attention of Marino. Marino will then run with it as the aggressive prosecutor he had always been. Did I answer your question?"

"You certainly did," Brandstutter said and then hesitated before making his next statement. "You do know a perjury prosecution will be a no brainer for Marino?"

Cardwell nodded.

"You also understand you will not be able to keep your seat on the bench?" Brandstutter stated the obvious, believing in the direct approach. No sugar coating with him. He figured this was the best way to get a client to agree to a plea.

"Only if they are able to convict me," Cardwell replied.

Brandstutter needed a different approach. He didn't like what he'd just heard. "During any of your discussions with the Lees, did you use email or any type of electronic device?"

"No email. Just the telephone. Usually, the calls would come to my office, but sometimes on my cell. Why do you ask?"

"Because use of those electronic devices could establish federal jurisdiction and interest Hawkins. And he would like nothing better than to get a judge and a state senator running for governor. A plan—we need to figure out a plan and save what we can save."

Once again, Cardwell shook her head.

Chapter Fifty-Six

While Cardwell was meeting with her lawyer, Braxton was meeting with Marino. After the press conference, Marino asked to have a word with her. He wanted to know why she recused herself from the Jenkins investigation, particularly since she was involved in the DNA hearing where potential perjury was committed.

Braxton's response was vague and unresponsive. "I just didn't think it would be appropriate, since I was involved in the case where perjury might have been committed."

The response piqued an even greater interest for Marino. He knew he needed to interview the witnesses who'd testified in the hearing. He expected those interviews to be consistent with how they testified. He then would present the evidence to the grand jury and seek a perjury indictment.

Marino also needed to interview Braxton. Braxton knew perjury occurred at the hearing. After all, she lost her objection to the DNA test because Judge Nealon didn't believe Cardwell. Yet now she was talking about where perjury *might* have been committed. Maybe she was just giving Cardwell the benefit of the presumption of innocence. He needed to find out.

"Did Judge Cardwell say anything to you before the hearing you felt was potentially a problem and put you in the position of becoming a witness against her?" Marino pressed.

"No. She told me exactly what she said on the stand," Braxton said.

"Then you didn't disqualify yourself because of any conflict of interest?"

"No. I just didn't think it would be appropriate for me to do the investigation. I didn't think it would look good."

Marino didn't believe her. There was some other reason had Braxton bowed out of the case and he believed it had something to do with her relationship with Cardwell.

Harper May was a criminal defense attorney in St. Louis. May returned to St. Louis after graduating summa cum laude from Harvard Law School and completing a clerkship with the United States Supreme Court Associate Justice Elena Kagan. She rejected numerous offers of employment from national law firms favoring a return to her hometown, where she opened her own office. Since returning, May had successfully defended several high-profile defendants in the city of St. Louis. Her success didn't go unnoticed by Karen Braxton, who now needed her own lawyer.

When Braxton arrived in May's office, she was uncertain how much information she should provide. While she had no legal jeopardy for the Jenkins and Decker cases, the situation was different for Garner Lee. Braxton knew well the dangers of selectively preparing your lawyer for the fight. She was embarrassed. Her behavior, particularly as the chief law enforcement officer for the city, was an unacceptable violation of her oath of office. Braxton was a realist and understood her potential exposure. She needed May's help.

May wanted to hear Braxton's story, but she wasn't sure she wanted to get involved. With this understanding, she told Braxton to explain why the circuit attorney needed a lawyer.

Braxton started with the Jenkins case. Although the conviction and imprisonment were a complete injustice for Larry Jenkins, she had nothing to do with his conviction. Her only vulnerability, at least from a public perspective, was in refusing to agree to the DNA test. May had followed the news coverage of the case and knew the media was already interested in this issue. "Why did you not agree to the DNA test?" May asked.

"Rape victims are not anxious to relive their very personal ordeals. And this victim was no exception. This was and continues to be a very painful process for women. Obviously, we know now the DNA didn't match. But you don't know what you don't know at the outset. These guys have nothing to lose by requesting the test. The women have a lot to lose because the case will be reopened and subject to publicity, whether or not we agree to the test."

The explanation made sense, and Braxton believed what she was saying.

"Was Cardwell's testimony consistent with what she told you?"

Before she answered this question, Braxton said, "I need to add something to my last answer. After I reviewed the file, I wanted to allow the DNA test. The victim was certain in her identification and I thought the DNA would confirm her trial testimony. She wouldn't need to testify at any DNA hearing and be subjected to rigorous cross examination. I knew there would still be publicity, but all things considered, I thought this would be the better thing for the victim. When I went to Cardwell, she went nuts and told me I couldn't allow anything. At the time, I didn't know about the victim's uncertainty, the phony police report and Cardwell's total role in the case. She never told me about any of it. Her testimony at the DNA hearing was consistent with what she told me before the hearing. Obviously, I was upset and embarrassed when I learned all the facts."

"I can only imagine," May said. "Are you saying but for Cardwell, you would have agreed to the test?"

"Yes, as long as we could have worked out an agreement on the testing procedures. And I knew we could because the Innocent Project was involved, and they have done this before."

"Okay, this sounds pretty straightforward to me. So, why are you here?"

"I recused myself from the case and the newly appointed prosecutor wanted to know why," Braxton said.

"Sounds like a reasonable question. What's the answer?"

Here it comes. No sugar coating. Put it out there. And Braxton did. She explained her concern about issues which could be raised in connection with the Garner Lee prosecution and gave May the whole story, every embarrassing detail, leaving nothing out.

She explained the conversations with Cassandra Lee about her son's murder prosecution. Braxton had no choice. She had to prosecute Garner Lee. Both the detective assigned to the case and the media were pushing hard for an indictment. Although charged with murder, the Lees and most particularly Cassandra Lee, directed the prosecution. The Lees were very powerful people, and Braxton needed their support for her future political career as the elected circuit attorney. They promised to provide their support if she would help them with their son's murder prosecution. Braxton was supposed to control the prosecutor assigned to the case, and Cardwell was supposed to control the trial evidence. Everything was designed to free their son. During the trial, Braxton would coordinate with Cassandra.

When Braxton finished speaking, Harper May clearly understood the Garner Lee case was fixed and Braxton had big problems. May agreed to represent her. The question now was how she would accomplish the impossible.

Chapter Fifty-Seven

Steve Marino didn't waste any time getting the investigation underway. He hired Derrick Watson, a retired St. Louis police officer, who was also a friend of Tony Carmine, and joined forces with the FBI in the St. Louis office. A sitting state court judge might have obstructed justice and committed perjury. Until the investigation was completed, it appeared Judge Cardwell would continue with her duties. There was no indication the presiding judge for the St. Louis Circuit Court would suspend her pending an investigation.

Along with his investigator and that of the FBI, Marino began knocking on doors to conduct interviews. Ordinarily, prosecutors had the investigators do the interviewing. However, because of both the urgency and the embarrassment to the justice system in this case, Marino wanted to examine the witnesses himself. But before he did, he wanted to prepare by reviewing a transcript of the testimony of the witnesses who appeared during the DNA hearing.

After reading the transcript, he contacted his friend Felbin and arranged a meeting. He was interested in any additional information Felbin had which was not reflected in the transcript.

Felbin was able to provide background, not only on the Jenkins case but also other dealings he'd had with Cardwell as a prosecutor and a judge. Marino was generally familiar with the Decker and Garner Lee cases from the extensive news coverage. Felbin didn't hold back in supplying information—some factual and some speculative—on Cardwell and Winston Lee. He also explained what he believed was Karen Braxton's role in the Lee case. "I think Braxton was joined at the hip with both Cardwell and my client's father," he told Marino.

"Are you suggesting the prosecution of Garner Lee was fixed in favor of your client?" Marino asked.

"That's exactly what I'm telling you," Felbin said as he proceeded to outline the factual basis for his belief.

"Wow," Marino replied, a bit surprised by the admission. "Why would you tell me that? Doesn't that damage your client's reputation as a lawyer? It suggests he was guilty of murder, but he got out from under it thanks to a corrupt judge."

"Of course it does. People believed he was a member of the lucky sperm club who got away with murder. Of course, Johnny Six Pack was wrong on both counts. Garner was adopted and didn't kill anyone. I have a reason to tell you everything I know. I believe in my client and am certain he didn't kill Amy Deland. I'm hoping someday, he will truly be exonerated, and the real killer identified. In the meantime, the corruption needs to be eradicated, which may lead to the truth of who killed this young lady."

Felbin had to be careful with what he said. He could encourage a comprehensive investigation of Deland's murder to accompany the Jenkins investigation. He explained the DNA sample he took from the senator and the paternity results. Because of the recent news accounts, Marino was aware the senator was alleged to have fathered a child with his son's girlfriend. Felbin also told Marino he had eliminated the senator as the killer when his DNA wasn't found on the murder weapon.

"If his father didn't kill Deland, doesn't it put your client between the cross hairs, particularly given what Cardwell did?" Marino asked. The logic was sound, and the question was obvious.

"That's certainly one way to look at it. However, Garner's DNA is also not on the murder weapon either. If you find the DNA match, you'll find the killer. Also, the fingerprints on the murder weapon were not Garner's. We know the statue was not wiped clean because prints were found, but they haven't been identified. I realize your investigation starts with Jenkins and Cardwell, but I would encourage you to follow the corruption of Cardwell wherever it takes you, which I believe will be to the death of Amy Deland. I obviously have an interest in both cases and will help you wherever I can."

When he'd accepted the appointment, Marino never expected the investigation to involve a murder case. In fact, like everyone else, from what he read, he figured Garner Lee was good for the murder but acquitted due to a technicality which possibly involved politics. But he was prepared to go wherever the evidence took him. The rape victim would be his first interview.

Janet Snead was not pleased when Marino and company showed up on her doorstep. She had to relive a traumatic event, but this time from the perspective of her own criminal trouble. She confirmed what she told the court during the DNA hearing without any deviation or contradiction. Although she had lied during the trial of Larry Jenkins and initially at the DNA hearing, Marino believed she was telling the truth this time. She was credible. She was protected by the statute of limitations for her prior false testimony at the trial. Likewise, her initial false testimony at the DNA hearing was remedied when she recanted during the same proceeding. No criminal prosecution available there. If the evidence led to a criminal prosecution of Judge Cardwell, the jury would have to decide whether to believe Snead or Cardwell. Marino was betting on Snead.

Ellen Rossi was in Florida and available to be interviewed by phone. She was cooperative and, like Snead, didn't deviate from her DNA hearing testimony. Once again, she admitted to participating in the falsification of a police report. Like Snead, the statute of limitations prevented any criminal prosecution. Juries usually don't appreciate police officers who lie or otherwise obstruct justice. Her behavior harmed Larry Jenkins. The jury would evaluate her conduct and the weight to be given her testimony in any case brought against Cardwell.

The investigation was progressing exactly as Marino thought. Cardwell perjured herself at the DNA hearing. Even more egregiously, her behavior caused an innocent man to be imprisoned for a large portion of his life, and then lied about it to keep him there and protect herself. The evidence was clear. Cardwell needed to be prosecuted for perjury. Unclear was whether Braxton's disqualification had anything to do with her involvement with Cardwell and Winston Lee in the prosecution of Garner Lee. It was time to interview Braxton.

Chapter Fifty-Eight

To his surprise, when Marino contacted Karen Braxton to arrange a time for an interview, he was referred to her lawyer. For prosecutors, people who hire lawyers to represent them are guilty of something. In this case, Braxton just confirmed Felbin's belief. She was involved with Cardwell and Winston Lee in the prosecution of Garner Lee. The question now was the extent of her involvement.

Marino had never met Harper May, but he was aware of her reputation based upon media exposure during the short time she was in St. Louis. They decided to meet in May's office. Just the two of them. No investigators or FBI involvement. Marino agreed.

After exchanging the customary pleasantries, May got right to the point. Her client had something which would be of interest to both Marino and potentially the Feds. But she needed a deal.

Braxton and May had decided the best course would be to come clean and try to cut a deal in the event the investigation found its way to her. In most criminal investigations, the people who make early deals and tell what they know get the best deals. This case was a little different because there was uncertainty as to whether the investigation would ever get to Braxton.

They anticipated Braxton would at least be questioned further on her disqualification, given Marino's initial curiosity. If that happened, she could be evasive. But as with any conspiracy, she would be dependent on her co-conspirators, who would be facing a greater number of criminal problems. The risk then was she could be left behind if those people cut an early deal. She couldn't take the risk. Her potential criminal exposure wasn't great. At least not now, because the investigators didn't have all the facts. But the situation could change as the facts were developed, or if she lied. If she lied to the FBI, it would carry an additional criminal charge.

Braxton's professional exposure was the greatest concern to her. While she understood her role as the chief law enforcement officer of St. Louis would end, she didn't want to lose her law license. She needed to be first in to get the best deal all the way around.

May explained her client needed immunity. "My client has information about Judge Cardwell, as well as Senator Winston Lee and his wife. I will tell you what she has to offer, but I want immunity from any criminal prosecution, both state and federal. I also want assurances you will co-operate favorably in any disciplinary action taken against her law license. She understands when all is said and done, she will not be able to remain in her current position. This should give you some idea of what she has to offer.".

"I can only make the call for me. I can't make it for the U.S. Attorney. It would be up to Hawkins. Frankly, I'm not even sure there is any federal crime here. But certainly, as you well know, the kind of deal would depend on what she has to offer. So, what does she have?" Marino asked, getting to the point.

May described in detail Braxton's dealings with both Cardwell and Garner's parents prior to, during and after Garner's trial, with the understanding the information would only be shared with Hawkins. If the deal was rejected, the information provided by May would be hearsay and inadmissible in any trial. If subpoenaed to testify, Braxton would invoke the 5th amendment and refuse to testify.

Marino was interested in what Braxton had to offer. But he was also curious about something else. "Does your client have any information Garner Lee was involved with the collusion leading to the successful outcome of his trial?"

"No. In fact, it's her understanding Felbin didn't get along with Garner's father, was not happy about having Cardwell hear the case and tried to withdraw as Garner's lawyer. But Cardwell wouldn't let him out."

May's statement was consistent with what Felbin had told Marino.

May had one other issue. "What happens to the information Braxton gives you if no one is indicted or there are pleas?"

Marino was confused. "I'm not sure what you are asking. If no one is indicted or there are pleas, Braxton's information will not be used."

"I understand the information won't be used in the criminal matters. My question pertains to what you will do with the information she gives you as far as the Office of Chief Disciplinary Counsel is concerned. Obviously, she will be providing you with information which could impact her future ability to practice law. Let me be direct. Will you report what she told you to the Disciplinary Counsel's Office?"

"Let me respond this way. The information she provides will have to be analyzed in the context of all the evidence. If it turns out her information is credible, which in this case might involve a potential violation of our ethical rules, we will have no choice but to report it, regardless of whether someone is indicted or pleads. However, I can assure you, if we can work out a deal, I will do whatever I can to make her assistance known in any disciplinary proceeding. Being the first to cut a deal and accepting responsibility before you get a look at all our cards, is an obvious benefit."

"I will let her know," May said.

"And I'll let you know what Hawkins has to say. But I am pretty sure regardless of what he decides, I'm interested in a deal."

"But you understand I have to have assurances from both you and Hawkins?"

"I understand," Marino said, ending his conference with Braxton's lawyer.

When the prosecutor left, May went into another office, where Braxton was waiting to hear about the meeting.

"I made the pitch. Marino was receptive. He's going to run it by Hawkins, a true politician masquerading as a lawyer. No telling what he'll do, assuming there is even any federal law which has been broken. But there is something you need to know. After you tell your story on the record, you can expect the Disciplinary Counsel to be involved, regardless of whether there is an indictment, a trial or a plea."

Braxton looked confused and said, "I don't understand. What are you telling me?"

"What I'm saying is regardless of what happens to Cardwell or anyone else, Marino believes he will need to notify the Chief Disciplinary Counsel of your conduct if there is reason to believe an ethical violation has occurred, and let that office deal with the issue. From what you have told me and what you will tell Marino and Hawkins, I doubt there can be much argument about ethical violations," May said.

"I'm aware what I did was wrong and violated a whole bunch of ethical rules. What I did was for political gain. There is no question about it. I can't undo it. All I can do is go forward, tell the truth and hope for leniency. I know this is not going to enhance my career. I just hope it doesn't end it. I'm prepared to take what's coming to me. In fact, I'm thinking I need to be the one who reports my conduct to the Chief Disciplinary Counsel after I have given my statement to the prosecutors."

Karen Braxton was generally an honest and decent person. Unfortunately, like so many others, her sense of right and wrong was obscured by political opportunity.

"I think self-reporting and accepting responsibility would go a long way toward keeping your law license. But for the moment, let's see what Marino comes back with."

Chapter Fifty-Nine

The Lee campaign was in a state of chaos. The campaign phone lines throughout the state were flooded with donors who were calling with questions and looking for answers, rather than to make contributions. Now there was substantive evidence Senator Winston Lee had impregnated his son's girlfriend who was murdered. If that wasn't enough to deal with, there was the implication the gubernatorial candidate murdered her to protect his political career.

While the reporting was relentless, interestingly, the Singer campaign held back and didn't weigh into the controversy. But Kelvin Bellington, the Lee campaign manager, knew it would only be a matter of time before Singer commented. Meanwhile, newspapers throughout the state highlighted three points: Amy Deland was his son's young, dead girlfriend; the senator had a motive to kill her; and he ran a con during the campaign when he volunteered to take a paternity test while believing no comparison DNA could be produced.

Inside the Lee camp, as it had from the first time this surfaced, there was a lot of screaming and finger pointing. The senator blamed his wife for consenting to the paternity test and she blamed him for having the affair. But the internal bickering was not going to solve the problem or combat the suggestion of a motive for murder.

Both Lees knew the senator didn't kill Amy Deland. But their knowledge was acquired from two separate sources. Cassandra's knowledge was firsthand. She not only knew her husband was not a murderer, but she also knew who was.

The campaign manager suggested using the senator's DNA sample they already had and comparing it to the murder weapon to clear him of the murder. The suggestion was immediately rejected by both the candidate and his wife. They both did not want to lend any credibility to Felbin's paternity test. Instead, they thought it would be better to attack the test itself and simply deny its accuracy. Bellington objected to this approach. And the debate and finger pointing continued. For the moment, the Lee campaign would not make any statement and continue to take their lumps until they could figure out a way around this catastrophe.

When the meeting ended, Cassandra Lee excused Bellington. She and her husband needed to have a private conversation. They had bigger issues. They knew Marino and Hawkins would be investigating the wrongful conviction of Larry Jenkins.

"I'm concerned about how far this Jenkins investigation is going to go," Cassandra said.

"It doesn't involve us. So, why should we care?" the senator replied.

Frustrated with his cavalier response, Cassandra said, "Have you forgotten our involvement in Garner's case? Or the Decker case?"

"What do those have to do with Jenkins?"

"It has nothing to do with him and everything to do with Cardwell. I gather from the press coverage Cardwell is the target of this investigation. I would be shocked if they don't indict her for at least perjury given the testimony at the hearing where this guy was trying to get a DNA test. The statute of limitations expired on all the bullshit she pulled to get this guy convicted of a rape he didn't commit."

As Cassandra was speaking, the senator looked confused. He wasn't understanding where his wife was going with this. Clearly, she was the smarter of the two and certainly the most manipulative and cunning.

"Felbin is involved with all of these cases, Jenkins, Garner and Decker. I have to assume he will press these prosecutors to look under all of the rocks to see what Cardwell's involvement was for all three," Cassandra continued. "And God only knows what this bitch will say.

"I know this. She won't go quietly off to the penitentiary."

"And you think she is going to involve us?" Winston asked, finally getting what his wife was saying.

"Yes, you idiot. She would screw her mother if it would help her."

"Okay. But what's she going to say about us? We were concerned about our son? We wanted justice in the Decker case?"

"You really are an idiot. I'm not as worried about the Decker case as Garner's. She could explain how we controlled his case. Manipulated the case to secure an acquittal for him."

"But if she goes down that road, she would be admitting she committed criminal acts. How do those admissions help her?"

"Because she will trade those admissions for a plea deal. She gives us up and walks or at least gets probation on the perjury and whatever else they have on her."

Winston was finally getting it. "What do we do? If this comes out, it will kill the campaign."

"It will do more than kill the campaign. I don't know about you but I'm not planning to spend any time in prison," she said. She thought for a moment and then said, "Don't worry about it. I'll take care of it like I always do. Just keep your mouth shut. Don't say or do anything to fuck it up. Understand?"

Winston nodded.

Cassandra knew she had to contact both Cardwell and Braxton. However, the question was how to do it. Being seen in public with either one would be a problem. Although not perfect, phone was a better option than face-to-face, either public or private.

Because she'd had so many conversations with Cassandra Lee during Garner's trial, Cardwell had put her cell phone number in her contacts list. When the phone rang, she answered the call as soon as she saw the name of the caller. She knew why Lee was calling.

"I'll get right to the point," Cassandra Lee began the conversation. Lee had little regard for Cardwell. She had no respect for her legal ability and believed she was nothing more than a political whore who would do anything, legal or illegal, if it benefitted her. "Marino and Hawkins are investigating the Jenkins fiasco you fucked up. The statute of limitations prevents them from charging you with the crimes you committed to prosecute an innocent black man for rape."

Cardwell just listened. She didn't appreciate the way Lee was talking to her. But she knew she needed her help and accepted the abuse without comment.

"But you fucked up when you lied at the DNA hearing. As a result, you are vulnerable on a perjury charge. We can't take care of the situation up front, because Braxton withdrew from that investigation. Bad move, but it is what it is. As a result, we need to take care of it on the back end and here's how we'll do it," Cassandra said.

Cardwell continued to listen, wondering where this was going. Her perfect world was being turned upside down. Cassandra Lee was talking about a perjury charge. And she would fix it. Cardwell didn't have a good feeling. She didn't think this was going to end well for her.

"Your indictment is inevitable. You will delay the trial as long as possible. By the time you are convicted, assuming you are, Winston will be the governor and will pardon you. In the meantime, you need to keep your mouth shut. I also suspect they may get into Garner's case as well. All you need to say is you called the shots as you saw them. Deny any collusion or obstruction. And don't tell them you had any conversations with us or Braxton. Our campaign is going great and Winston will be elected. We can't have anything getting in the way. Do you understand?"

"I understand what you're saying." Cardwell knew both Cassandra and her husband were vulnerable if the investigation wandered into Garner's murder case. But there was another potential problem. "What about Braxton? We don't know what she'll do. How are you going to deal with her?" Cardwell asked.

"I plan to talk to her. She will be on board. Don't worry."

Cardwell had one more question. "I saw where a paternity test claimed Senator Lee was the father of Deland's child. Do you think this will hurt the campaign?" Cardwell was interested in this or any other issue which could jeopardize Lee's chances of winning. Obviously, the promise of a pardon was dependent on Winston Lee becoming governor.

"Those things certainly don't help a campaign," Cassandra said, stating the obvious. "But we have it under control. Today, people want to know what you'll do for them both economically and otherwise. They really don't care about what a candidate does in the bedroom. Look at Trump. He had more publicized sexual indiscretion incidents than any fifty candidates. And he became the President of the United States."

Cardwell wasn't so sure, but decided not to argue with Cassandra, which was usually a waste of time.

When Cassandra finished her conversation with Cardwell, she called Braxton. When she didn't answer, she left a voicemail message asking her to return the call.

Chapter-Sixty

When Karen Braxton didn't recognize a number on her cell phone, she generally let it go to voicemail for a message to see who was calling. This call was no exception. When she played the voicemail and heard Cassandra Lee's voice, like Cardwell, she knew why she was calling. Her instinct was not to return the call and instead, contact her lawyer for some guidance.

May's advice was immediate. "I need to get in touch with Marino and see what he wants to do. This could be a window of opportunity. If I have your permission, I will call him right now."

After Braxton permitted the call, May told Marino what she had and asked him to join them at her office. Marino agreed to come right over but said he also wanted to contact Hawkins and bring either him or an FBI agent with him.

Marino arrived with Charles Reed, an FBI agent. They had a plan.

Before proceeding with their plan, Marino told May he had spoken to Hawkins about the immunity issue and he had applied for and received approval from the Department of Justice to grant Braxton the immunity she had requested. Since Marino was also on board, they wanted to proceed with their plan without delay and before any formal statement was taken from Braxton. May asked Marino to explain their plan.

"We would like to put a recording device on Braxton's phone and have her return Cassandra Lee's call. Based upon the information you told us your client has with respect to the Lees and particularly since she hasn't heard from them since Garner's trial, we believe the purpose of this call is to solicit the cooperation of your client and ensure she doesn't do any talking to us. Obviously, given the publicity, the Lees know where this might be headed. If the call is about something else, then we get nothing. Will your client consent?" Marino asked.

May had a question. "What happens if the call is not incriminating? Will the tapes be disclosed to the Lees?"

"Depends. As you know, if there is an indictment against either or both, a decision will have to be made as to whether the conversation is exculpatory. If it is, it will be disclosed. If not, it won't be turned over," Marino said.

May knew the rule in criminal cases established years ago by the United States Supreme Court in Brady versus Maryland. There the court required the prosecution to surrender to the defendant any information acquired by the government which tended to negate the guilt of the defendant. A failure to disclose this information could jeopardize a conviction. Her concern was with the publicity which would inevitably result from the disclosure of a secret recording involving her client where no criminal charges resulted, particularly if the senator became the next governor. The situation for Karen Braxton was going to be bad enough without any additional publicity. May was satisfied with Marino's response. It was the only thing he could tell her.

After May's meeting Braxton, who was in another office, the two women returned to the conference room where Marino and Reed were waiting. May's client was willing to cooperate with the plan. Braxton knew the more cooperation, the better the chances to keep her law license.

After the recording equipment was set up, Marino told Braxton what he wanted her to do. "Simply begin the conversation by telling Cassandra Lee you were returning her call and then let her talk. Don't press. Don't spook her. Just go with the flow and ask questions where appropriate."

When Cassandra Lee answered the phone, Braxton did as she was instructed and told Lee she was returning the call. Lee began the conversation by asking about the Jenkins DNA case. "I saw where you disqualified yourself in the investigation of how this innocent man, Larry Jenkins, wound up in prison. I was wondering why you got out and special prosecutors were appointed."

At first, she thought Lee was calling her for information because she was going to get involved in the lawsuit Jenkins filed. But then she realized in that case, Lee would be working with Felbin, which would never happen. Plus, she would be suing Cardwell which also would never occur.

"I got out because the investigation will involve Judge Cardwell, at least initially. I was concerned it would not be limited to Jenkins and would get into Garner's case and the Decker prosecution. Personally, I'm not concerned about Decker. Cardwell was the main actor there. But I am concerned about Garner. Opening Garner's prosecution would involve not only Cardwell but also you and me."

Lee didn't respond immediately. Finally, she asked, "Have you been interviewed by anyone?"

"No, but I expect to be," Braxton said. Technically true, as she had not yet been formally interviewed.

"What do you plan to tell them when they do approach you? Are you even going to talk to them?"

"I have to talk to them. I'm the circuit attorney. It would look odd if I refused. I don't know what I'm going to tell them. If the FBI gets involved, a lie to them is a federal offense. Of course, if I tell them the truth and explain how we fixed Garner's case, Cardwell, you and I would be going to the penitentiary."

Lee didn't challenge Braxton's statement. She couldn't. Both Cassandra and her husband needed Braxton's cooperation. She didn't want to alienate her by suggesting they had no involvement in fixing their son's case. Instead, she needed to assure Braxton they would be working together for a common goal. The lies would be consistent. Like they had during the trial, they would act as a team.

"Listen Karen. I already talked to Cardwell. As you know, she has perjury problems unrelated to Garner's case. I suspect she will be indicted and convicted on a perjury charge. I can't help her there since you got out of the Jenkins case. However, I can help her and you in other ways."

Fearing Lee was not going to explain her statement, Braxton immediately asked what she meant.

"I told her after Winston becomes the governor, he will pardon the perjury conviction assuming she is even prosecuted and later convicted. But this is important. She can't do anything to jeopardize the election. This would include talking about Garner's case or even the Decker case. She said she understood."

"What do you want from me?" Braxton knew what was coming. She just needed Cassandra to say it for the tape.

"Basically, the same thing. We can't do anything to jeopardize this election," Lee said.

Braxton wanted more detail. "What are you telling me? You want me to lie if I'm interviewed?"

The word *lie* hung in the air ready to come crashing down like a lead balloon. "I just want you to explain Garner's case was a regular, run of the mill murder prosecution. No favors shown to anyone. You prosecuted the son of a state senator for murder, which should speak for itself."

"We both know that's not true," Braxton said, pressing the point. "What happens if I'm interviewed by the FBI and give them the same false story and am prosecuted by the U.S. Attorney? Your husband can't pardon a federal offense."

"They would need to prove you lied. Since we are all on board with the same story, how would they ever prove you lied? Our stories will be consistent. Credible, consistent denials. As you well know, the only way people get into trouble is when they start contradicting each other. And there is no chance of contradictory statements happening in this case. Agree?"

Braxton and the prosecutors got what they needed. There was no reason to continue the conversation. Lee and Braxton agreed to stay in touch.

Marino and Reed were satisfied with what they got from the conversation. Braxton was not feeling very good about herself at this moment.

With the Cassandra Lee conversation completed, they decided to take Braxton's formal statement regarding her involvement with both Cardwell as well as the Lees. She explained in specific detail the roles of everyone in the prosecution of Garner Lee. At the direction of the Lees and most particularly, Cassandra Lee, Braxton controlled the prosecutor assigned to the case and Cardwell controlled the evidence, all with a view toward having the jury acquit the son of a state senator. But when the prosecutor assigned to the case went off the reservation and the jury returned a guilty verdict, a different plan had to be developed. Braxton was not included in this plan. She learned about it after the fact, when her prosecutor was blamed for misconduct, which resulted in Garner's freedom.

Chapter Sixty-One

After listening to Braxton's statement, Marino and Reed decided to have Braxton make another recorded call. This time to Judge Cardwell.

When Cardwell saw Braxton's number come up on her phone, she answered it. She was in her office and closed the door before starting the conversation. Cardwell had been thinking about calling her after the conversation with Cassandra Lee but wasn't sure it was a good idea.

This time Braxton needed to start the conversation since she was initiating the call. As directed, Braxton said, "I got a call from Cassandra Lee today. She said she talked to you about Garner's case. I want to make sure we are all on the same page if the Jenkins investigation gets into the Garner murder case. Tell me what she told you and I'll tell you what she told me."

"No. Turn it around. You go first," Cardwell said, seemingly concerned about whether to trust Braxton.

After relating her conversation with Lee, it was Cardwell's turn. "She told me the same thing. Her husband would pardon me if I was prosecuted and convicted of perjury when he became governor. She was emphatic about keeping our mouths shut and not doing anything to screw up the election and his chances of becoming the governor. Our future will depend on him succeeding. She assured me the election was in the bag and he would be elected. She told me to say I called all the shots in Garner's murder trial and had absolutely no conversations with her, her husband or you. Deny any obstruction or collusion. Her point was if we could all stick together with the same story, they would have nothing, and we would be home free."

"Do you trust her?" Braxton asked.

"I trusted her for the entire time I was talking to her during her kid's trial. I never told you this, but she was the one who suggested acquitting him based upon prosecutorial misconduct by that little shit Perrin. Because you couldn't control him, the jury didn't take me off the hook and I had to do something on the back end. She was pissed, as was her husband, and they blamed you. I was thinking of doing a suspended imposition of sentence with probation. She went ballistic and said the press would crucify all of us for doing probation in a murder case. Of course, the press crucified us anyway when I dismissed the case because of your prosecutor's misconduct. Since I trusted her before I got in this mess, I have no choice but to trust her to get me out of it."

"Essentially, then, she is saying we need to lie our asses off and put our trust in her, hope her husband gets elected and still remembers us when we are knee deep in the shit," Braxton summarized.

"I think you have adequately condensed it."

"I suppose you do realize our legal careers may be over when all of this comes out. We won't be keeping our current positions," Braxton said, stating the obvious.

"Our careers would be over if we wound up in the penitentiary as well. My priority is to stay out of prison. Lots of people get their law licenses reinstated after being revoked for various types of misconduct. Tax fraud comes to mind. But I have decided to worry about the license issue if and when it comes up."

After they both agreed to follow the Lee plan, Braxton ended the conversation.

Two home runs for the good guys. They were feeling pretty good and very confident. Unfortunately, they knew all too well the elimination of a corrupt judge and a couple politicians, wouldn't put a dent in white collar crime. They had job security.

Chapter Sixty-Two

From the beginning, Marino knew he had enough evidence to prosecute Cardwell for perjury. While he probably had enough evidence with both the statement of Braxton and the telephone tapes to arrest Cassandra Lee, he felt he would need more for a conviction. He didn't believe he had enough even to arrest Winston Lee. Plus, arresting a candidate for governor without good, hard evidence had its own problems.

The question these prosecutors needed to answer was whether to try to make any deals with any of the target defendants; a candidate to become the next governor, his wife and a sitting circuit judge. Not exactly an easy call.

Since the perjury evidence against Cardwell was strong along with the phone conversation, there would be more to trade with her. Marino wanted a felony conviction. Jail time and probation might be something to talk about in order to get her cooperation. But because of the promise of a pardon, Cardwell would probably want a perjury prosecution taken off the table. Then she might talk.

They needed to work around the pardon and the way around it was through the FBI. Although Cardwell was spending little time in her office, the appointed agents thought they would try there first. They were in luck. She was there. Mary McMurtry was not at her desk, so they knocked on the chamber door announcing themselves as FBI agents, Charles Reed and Carolyn Kopensky. Marino was not in attendance as they just wanted this discussion to be federal in nature. They were uncertain whether Cardwell knew lying to an FBI agent was a federal crime and Braxton hadn't mentioned it during her conversation.

After displaying their identification, they told her they needed to ask a few questions about an investigation they were conducting in connection with the Jenkins case.

"How is this a federal matter?" Cardwell asked.

"Civil rights issue," Reed said. "We have read the transcript of the DNA hearing and interviewed Ms. Snead and Detective Rossi. As you know, their testimony differs from yours." After showing her a copy of the transcript, Agent Reed asked, "Do you stand by your testimony?"

"Yes," Cardwell said without any hesitation.

"We also have a few more questions in connection with the matter of Garner Lee and the murder case over which you presided. During the trial did you have any communication with Karen Braxton about any aspect of the case, no matter how innocuous or innocent you thought it was, outside the presence of the defense?"

"No." Another response without hesitation, following Cassandra's instructions.

"What about with Cassandra Lee? Did you ever have any conversation with her before, during or after Garner Lee's murder trial?"

"No."

"Did you ever have any conversation with Winston Lee before, during or after Garner Lee's murder trial?"

"Same answer, no. Where is this going?" Cardwell demanded.

"We are interested in whether there was any obstruction or collusion in connection with the trial."

Cardwell didn't wait for a question before volunteering an answer—a big mistake for anyone talking to an FBI agent. "I called the case to the best of my ability. I applied the law as I interpreted it and the evidence consistent with the rules of evidence. The prosecutor made a mistake which, in my view, was intentional and prejudicial. I had to dismiss the case based upon his misconduct. I know the press and others took issue with my decision. But they need to blame the prosecutor, not me, for the result. And if you have no other questions, I need to get back to work. I have a docket in the courtroom I need to take care of," she said as stood up.

The agents had gotten what they needed. They would now prepare their reports and submit them to the prosecutors for a decision on how to proceed.

Chapter Sixty-Three

The decision was easy. They thought they had what they needed to get around the pardon. But there was a problem. Was there really any federal jurisdiction for the involvement of the FBI? In other words, was there sufficient probable cause to believe a federal law had been violated to justify the FBI asking questions in the first place? And if there was no federal jurisdiction and the FBI shouldn't have been asking questions, how did Cardwell commit the crime of lying to an FBI agent?

Hawkins and his assistants in the U.S. Attorney's office put their heads together to figure out federal jurisdiction. Certainly, the federal government has a right to investigate civil rights violations. But the federal prosecutors were trying to figure out whose civil rights were violated. They started with the Garner Lee prosecution. The evidence they currently had suggested the case was fixed. It was a state crime which benefitted Garner, hardly a civil rights violation there. Then they moved to the Jenkins file. The evidence here supported multiple violations of Jenkins' civil rights by Cardwell in her capacity as a prosecutor before and during the trial. But the statute of limitations on that offense had long since expired.

This federal brain trust was running out of options. Clearly, Cardwell would most likely be convicted and get prison time on the state perjury charge. But the slate could be wiped clean if Lee made good on his promise of a pardon, which was why federal involvement was needed to make anything stick. Governors have no authority to pardon federal crimes. Just when they were about ready to turn out the lights and admit defeat, one of the young prosecutors had an idea. He suggested they look to Cardwell's effort to deny Jenkins the freedom she knew he deserved when she perjured herself at the DNA hearing. While they all agreed this approach might work, at least in the short run, they understood a good lawyer would be able to blow holes in it. In the end, the consensus was to give the theory a try and see how it developed.

When they presented the theory to Marino, he had concerns similar to those expressed by some of the federal prosecutors in their meeting. But also like them, he agreed to take the chance. They would approach Cardwell since she was the most vulnerable and hope to strike a deal before she retained a smart lawyer.

Unaware of whether she was represented, Marino called Cardwell and made an appointment to see her in her office. When he and Hawkins arrived, Cardwell was present, but not alone. She had a lawyer, Jim Brandstutter. Marino knew him and had little respect for his legal ability. A break for the prosecution in this case. Word was when you hired Brandstutter, you could expect to plead guilty to something.

After exchanging pleasantries, Marino took the lead and began the conversation, directing his attention to Cardwell and pretty much ignoring her lawyer. "I think you know why we are here. But in case you don't, let me briefly explain. We have completed our investigation of the Jenkins case. We will be taking the case to the grand jury tomorrow and seeking to indict you for perjury. Based upon the evidence we have, some of which you know about and some you don't, I'm confident we'll get a true bill returned and you will be arrested."

Cardwell just stared defiantly at Marino as he spoke. She had known this was coming and she was prepared. Governor Lee would save her.

"But we have a proposal," Marino continued. "You help us, and we help you. If you agree to tell us what you know about Cassandra Lee, we might be able to work something out with the amount of time you will have to do on the perjury charge."

"Fuck you, Marino," Cardwell said while still staring at him.

"Now that's not very professional or very smart, since you haven't heard all we have to tell you. So, please allow me to continue," Marino said politely.

No reaction from either Cardwell or her lawyer.

"We know you have a promise from Cassandra Lee to be pardoned by her husband in the unlikely event he becomes our next governor."

Now he had Cardwell's attention. She had no idea how they would have gotten the information about the pardon promise. Her lawyer, sitting next to her, was clueless. He had no idea what Marino was talking about.

Marino watched the expression on Cardwell's face change as he continued by introducing the United States Attorney.

"I'm here to let you know you also have federal problems," Hawkins began as Cardwell now looked confused. "It is a federal offense to lie to an FBI agent and you did that several times when they interviewed you in connection with a civil rights investigation. We will also be taking the case to the grand jury and seeking an indictment not only on the lying but also on a civil rights violation regarding Larry Jenkins. Like Mr. Marino, I, too, am confident, you will be indicted and arrested. Of course, once you are indicted in our system, we don't have as much flexibility as Mr. Marino does in the state court. But we can talk before the indictment is returned if you are so inclined," Hawkins said.

Although not mandatory, most federal courts use sentencing guidelines to determine sentences in criminal cases. Those guidelines are rules which set out a uniform policy for individuals convicted of felony offenses. A complicated point system is used to define the nature of the offense, the criminal history of the defendant, and various other factors, which will either increase or decrease the number of points. When the points are finally tallied, a chart defines the number of months of incarceration. As far as the parties are concerned, they are free to agree or disagree on the number of points assigned to each category. It is there the prosecutor has some flexibility to bargain. If the parties cannot agree, each submits his own calculation. Usually under those circumstances, the prosecutor's calculations are high and the defendant's low.

The concept of sentencing in the federal system was foreign to Cardwell because she had no experience with the system. She'd spent her entire career in the state system. Her lawyer likewise had no experience with federal sentencing guidelines. This placed both at a serious disadvantage.

Cardwell was now concerned. If they were telling the truth, Lee couldn't help her. She would go down in both venues. "How do I know you are telling me the truth?" Cardwell asked as her lawyer sat there speechless.

Marino played a portion of the conversation Braxton had with Cassandra Lee, making sure Braxton's voice wasn't heard. "I told her after Winston becomes the governor, he will pardon the perjury conviction, assuming she is even prosecuted and later convicted. But this is important, she can't do anything to jeopardize the election. This would include talking about Garner's case or even the Decker case. She said she understood."

Cardwell recognized Lee's voice. She'd certainly heard it enough during her son's trial. She now realized they had a snitch who recorded the conversation. But she didn't know who it was. The possibilities, however, were limited. Marino didn't mention he wanted any information on Winston Lee, only Cassandra. Did he flip? The only other person would be Karen Braxton. During the trial, she'd also had conversations with Cassandra. Cardwell understood either one of them could put a nail in her coffin. But then she remembered the phone call to her from Braxton calling to talk about her conversation with Cassandra. Braxton was the snitch. If she taped Cassandra's conversation, Braxton also would have recorded her, so these prosecutors now had her admissions.

"I need some time to think this through," Cardwell finally said.

"I'm taking my case to the grand jury tomorrow afternoon. I don't know about Mr. Hawkins. You have until tomorrow afternoon to make a decision on what you want to do," Marino said.

"What kind of deal is on the table?" she asked both prosecutors.

"I think I can speak for both of us when I say the deal will depend on what kind of evidence you have to give us. The stronger the evidence, the better the deal. But I will also tell you up front so there is no misunderstanding, I will insist on a felony conviction," Marino said. He was playing hard ball with this soon to be former judge. This was a public corruption case, and he needed to get her off the bench as soon as possible, since her colleagues declined to act in the public interest.

"We are not going to the grand jury until next week. I will also need to hear what you have," the U.S. Attorney added. "As I told you before, I can be more flexible prior to the time the grand jury returns an indictment. I would consider a deal which does not involve a felony conviction. We can even talk about a non-prosecution agreement. Of course, all of this assumes your information is substantive," Hawkins said, while recognizing the flaws in the government's legal theory.

Neither Cardwell nor her lawyer challenged the issue of federal jurisdiction. No surprises there. Perhaps they were in shock from what they were hearing. She would be trading her black judicial robes for an orange jumpsuit. This wardrobe change would be enough to unnerve anyone.

Chapter Sixty-Four

Time was limited. Within a span of less than twenty-four hours, Joan Cardwell went from people kissing her ring to her kissing the asses of anyone who could help her put this nightmare behind her. How quickly and how far the mighty can fall.

In addition to her criminal troubles, Cardwell had civil problems as well. She had been served with Larry Jenkins' civil rights suit. But despite what she did to him, she couldn't care less about any possible civil penalties. She knew she was protected by the doctrine of prosecutorial immunity. In 1976 the United States Supreme Court decided prosecutors were immune from civil suits for violating the constitutional rights of the accused when performing prosecutorial duties. She turned the suit over to the city attorneys to file a motion to dismiss. They would always claim she acted as a prosecutor material in the Jenkins case.

Her immediate concern was whether to take the deal. What choice did she have? One way or the other she felt she would go down. Her back was against the wall, like a rat in a Skinner box. She couldn't find any exits. But then it occurred to her. She could find the exit if there was no federal crime. Her savior, Governor Lee, would be back in play.

She had no experience with federal law and didn't have any time to do the research. She turned to her lawyer, Jim Brandstutter. He hadn't been much help during their meeting with the prosecutors, but she hoped he knew enough about federal law to be able to answer her questions. "Was Hawkins' bullshitting us, or can he indict me in federal court?" Cardwell asked her lawyer.

"I don't do much in federal court," Brandstutter began. Not a good start. "But I am aware of the offense of lying to an FBI agent. It was headline news when several of the associates of President Trump were charged with lying to the FBI. My impression is Hawkins isn't bluffing." Typical

Brandstutter. Push the client toward a plea, so you don't have to try the case.

Cardwell wasn't interested in Brandstutter's impression. She wanted to know if Hawkins had a legal basis to charge her. "If an FBI agent interviews you about an automobile accident and you lie, there would be no underlying federal offense, so how can you be charged with the crime of lying to the FBI? The interview wouldn't be relevant to anything federal."

"I thought Hawkins said the FBI was doing a civil rights investigation which I assumed was Jenkins. And I know civil rights investigations are federal," her lawyer said.

"How did I violate his civil rights? If it was when I was a prosecutor, the statute of limitations would bar that prosecution."

Brandstutter was thinking. The last thing he wanted to do was be in the middle of a couple of high-profile cases in federal and state court involving a sitting judge. That was a loser. Plus, they hadn't even talked about a fee. If he couldn't persuade Cardwell to take whatever deal the prosecutors would be offering, he needed to get out. She needed another lawyer. This loss wasn't going to be on his shoulders. "What about the perjury?" Brandstutter asked. "I suppose they could take the position any lie you told at the DNA hearing would be designed to keep an innocent man in jail. And I would think perjury under those circumstances would violate Jenkins' civil rights," Brandstutter added, proud of himself for thinking of this issue so quickly.

Cardwell didn't dismiss his point immediately. She couldn't. Her life and career were on the line and she was dealing in the world of uncertainty. She considered the variables in typical lawyer-like fashion. Lee might pardon the perjury conviction but first he had to be elected. And his election was anything but guaranteed, particularly when Marino and Hawkins put crosshairs on his head. If Lee was defeated, she would go to prison for perjury regardless of what the Feds did. If Hawkins made good on his promise, she would do both federal and state time. But even if Lee won the election and pardoned her, she would be disgraced, would lose her judicial appointment and probably her law license. She would be left with nothing. If she continued to live in St. Louis, she would be reminded of her plight everywhere she went. So, take the deal offered by the prosecutors whatever it might be, or take nothing. A true Hobson's choice.

But why should she have to take anything? She needed to explain her position to the world, starting with her lawyer. "I did nothing wrong. I was a damn good prosecutor and a good judge. As a prosecutor, my goal was to make the community safe. Take criminals off the street. And I succeeded in achieving that goal. Of course, I made mistakes along the way and people like Larry Jenkins fell through the cracks. Big fuckin' deal. In the end, the greater good was always protected. The city was safe."

And now Jenkins was suing her. "The lawsuit is frivolous, a waste of time and filed by Felbin only to embarrass me. But he will be the one who will be embarrassed after the suit is dismissed. He should know prosecutors are immune from civil liability. Maybe his client wasn't good for this rape, but he was probably good for something else, some other crime. Putting him away for all those years probably kept the community safe in the long run. People should be thanking me, not condemning me. But like everything else in this country these days, this would not be politically correct.

"As a judge, I always tried to do the right thing. My intent was always to serve the interests of justice, and I succeeded. Judges make mistakes and I was no exception. But ~~her~~ my mistakes were unintentional and harmless. I admit my appointment to the bench was political. But name one judge now or in the past who was appointed without political help. No such person exists. And yes, Senator Lee did help me achieve my judicial goals. And yes, I did pursue Robert Decker for murdering an innocent black man at his insistence. But Decker was guilty. Although I might have been wrong about Jenkins; assuming the science was correct, I wasn't wrong about Decker."

She did wind up with the Garner Lee murder case, apparently thanks to the kid's mother. She didn't know exactly how it happened. "Powerful people can get things done. However it happened doesn't matter. I got the case. And I did consult with the defendant's mother during the trial. And yes, after the jury verdict, I did follow the direction of his mother and acquit her son because of prosecutorial misconduct. What was wrong with that? Plus, that bitch, Karen Braxton, didn't fulfill her end of the bargain. She was unable to control her prosecutor. Because Braxton couldn't get the job done, ~~she~~ I had to take care of it. I had to take the heat when I acquitted the kid. And now Braxton is turning on me and the Lees, after all everyone has done for her. That's not how the game is played. Fuck Braxton."

Self-pity dominated Cardwell's every thought. "People wanted to take me down. Put me in jail. Remove me from the bench. Ruin my career. And why? What did I do to deserve this? Nothing. Yet I'm the one who has to take the fall. I know I can't fight two governments and win. The government has all the power, all the money. I have nothing. And then there is the press. All that fuckin' fake news about me. If I was going to fight, they would join forces with the government to screw me before, during and after the trial."

Her lawyer listened to her self-serving ramblings but said nothing. He was at least smart enough to understand challenging her statements would truly be a waste of time. Plus, she was heading in the right direction, a deal and a plea.

Chapter Sixty-Five

Marino was optimistic when he got the call from Cardwell's lawyer indicating she wanted to talk to them about a deal. He notified Hawkins and then set a time to meet with her. Because of uncertainty as to whether she would follow through with what they wanted, they decided to meet at the U.S. Attorney's office in the federal courthouse, a symbol of the power of the federal government.

The meeting began without the customary pleasantries. In attendance were Marino, his investigator, Hawkins, one assistant U.S. Attorney and an FBI agent. Clearly, Cardwell was not happy to be there and had no interest in even pretending to be friendly or voluntarily cooperative. But she was there and would do what she had to do to survive this.

The start of the interview was rocky. If the prosecutors asked a question, they got an answer which was not overflowing with details. This back and forth battle of wits progressed for about fifteen minutes. Finally, Marino spoke. "Look, Ms. Cardwell," he said, refusing to use the title of judge, "you are either going to cooperate or you're not. This is your future, not mine. If you are going to cooperate, then it is going to be a full cooperation and not a partial sharing of information. We are not going to play the *ask the right question, get the right answer game.* Now, I want you to take it from the top, starting with when you first met Winston and Cassandra Lee and then take us through the Decker case and finish with the Garner Lee case. If we have any questions during your narrative, we will ask. Then I want you to take us through the prosecution of Larry Jenkins. If I feel you are not being forthright, and believe me I will know, then we shut this down. You will go your way and we will go ours. Am I clear?"

With her jaw clenched, Cardwell just stared at Marino, a cold, icy stare. If she'd held a .38, Marino would be dead. Finally, she said, "It's *Judge* Cardwell, and yes, it's clear."

Marino ignored the comment and simply asked her to proceed.

Cardwell began with the case of the white police sergeant who was charged with feloniously assaulting a mentally challenged young black man in his home. Cardwell lost a motion for a change of venue and the case was transferred to Kansas City where an all-white jury acquitted the officer. The African American community in St. Louis was outraged. Then came Decker. Because it came on the heels of the acquittal in Kansas City, the unrest intensified. According to Cardwell, Winston Lee approached her, threatening to burn down the city if she didn't charge Decker with murder. Concerned about the threat, she complied.

Marino interrupted her. "Are you telling us that your desire to have this politician put you on the bench played no role in the murder charge?"

"I was concerned about what Lee could do to the city," Cardwell replied.

Unimpressed with her response, Marino said, "Yes or no. Isn't it a fact that the only reason you prosecuted Decker was to curry favor with Winston Lee because you lost that first racially charged case in Kansas City after you blew the change of venue?" Starring at her, Marino added, "I would be careful how you answer this question."

She knew that if she didn't tell him what he wanted to hear, there would be no deal. After what seemed like an eternity, Cardwell finally said, "Yes." She then looked at the floor. It was the first time she admitted on the record to having prosecuted someone for political gain.

Her spin on the Garner Lee murder case was pressure from Cassandra Lee. She described Cassandra Lee's behavior as threatening and intimidating.

Marino interrupted her again. "Stop. Garner Lee's acquittal was nothing more than a political payback. Correct?"

There it was. For the second time the truth was starring her in the face and a prosecutor was waiting for an admission. As difficult as it was, she had no choice. "Correct," she said, suppressing her desire to mitigate her involvement.

The prosecutors expected her to generally tell the story about Garner Lee's trial in a light most favorable to her. Most people do. They weren't worried about this aspect because they had the trial transcript which spoke for itself and clearly showed her bias for the defendant. They were more concerned about her position regarding the directions given by Cassandra Lee ~~and~~ which she followed during the trial.

"This political payback, I want to know the specific role Cassandra Lee played during your son's trial," Marino said.

"She gave me directions which I followed on a variety of evidentiary issues like the DNA test as well as any evidence that would damage her son."

"What role did she play in the acquittal? Whose idea was it?

The prosecutors heard what Cardwell told Braxton on the tape, but they needed to hear it from her. At first, she admitted the decision to find prosecutorial misconduct and free the defendant because of the misconduct was Cassandra's. Then she seemed to suggest it was the correct call.

"The correct call?" Marino and Hawkins said almost simultaneously. "Are you telling us you would have acquitted Garner Lee on your own had it not been for the suggestion of his mother?" Marino asked.

After some additional prodding, Cardwell eventually and reluctantly admitted she never would have set a defendant free under the same circumstances.

After finishing her narrative and answering the questions, Cardwell wanted to know what kind of a deal she was getting. She was told her deal would depend on one more thing. She needed to make a phone call to Cassandra Lee, which would be recorded. She protested, claiming a phone call was never mentioned and never part of the deal. Her protest fell on deaf ears.

Everyone in the room, including Cardwell's own lawyer knew what she was, a political opportunist and a garden variety criminal. She would do anything to advance her own interests and didn't care who was hurt in the process. Marino probably knew her better than anyone else and had no sympathy for her in her current predicament. He was going to press. No phone call, no deal. He knew this would be a very uncomfortable phone call for her to make but she couldn't refuse, and she didn't. A part of him enjoyed watching her squirm when he tightened the screws.

The prosecutors needed to rehearse what Cardwell would say to Cassandra, starting with the reason for the call. They knew Lee was smart and would either shut down the conversation or make self-serving statements and turn it back on Cardwell if she suspected any law enforcement involvement. The conversation could then become a significant part of Cassandra's defense if she were indicted.

They decided the premise of the call would be to alert Cassandra about a visit Cardwell had from the prosecutors and the FBI. She would express concern and be looking for reassurances Cassandra and her husband would protect her. After informing Cardwell that any intentional missteps by her designed to let Lee know what was happening would void any deal, an FBI agent set up the recording device.

Recognizing the number, Cassandra Lee answered the phone after two rings. Rudely, she asked "What do *you* need?"

"I'm concerned," Cardwell began, concern but not panic in her voice. So far, so good. "I had a visit from the FBI, someone from Hawkins' office and Marino, along with his investigator. An entire fuckin' army."

"What did you do?" Lee asked cautiously.

"I referred them to my lawyer. But they didn't leave. It was embarrassing, because they were in my chambers." Cardwell was playing it perfectly. "They were asking a lot of questions, but I wasn't responding. I got the impression they just wanted me to know some of the things they had." She set the hook.

"What kind of questions were they asking?" Lee asked. The hook was set.

"They wanted to know what conversations I had with you and your husband during your son's trial. They asked if we had any discussions about preventing the DNA test. Then they seemed to imply they knew you were responsible for getting me to rule the prosecutor engaged in misconduct, which caused your son to be freed. But here is the worst. When I continued to refuse to answer their questions, they threatened to involve the presiding judge for my circuit and the ethics commission." She just let the last comment sit to see how Lee would respond. Smart.

As expected, Lee said, "The best approach is to say nothing. Keep your mouth shut."

"I don't disagree under ordinary circumstances. But it would seem odd to my presiding judge if I would refuse to answer a very basic question of how I handled the trial. Then I have to be concerned about being suspended and the resulting publicity wouldn't help either of us." As the prosecutors listened to the conversation, they knew Cardwell would be good because her freedom was on the line. But they never thought she would be this good. She was successfully baiting Cassandra Lee, a smart woman who never had any respect for her, to make an incriminating comment. Despite her serious problems, there was a degree of satisfaction in this for Cardwell.

There was a long pause. Cassandra Lee was trying to decide what the next step should be. There was no indication she suspected any law enforcement involvement in this conversation. Finally, she spoke. "Why don't you just tell them it was your idea and I had nothing to do with it? Then they would hopefully back off the threat to involve your presiding judge."

"I can't say that, because it would be a lie."

"And what's the problem? Since when did you get religion? This would be the first lie you ever told?" Lee asked sarcastically.

Conspicuous by its absence was any denial from Lee.

Knowing she was on tape, Cardwell chose to ignore Lee's questions and said, instead, "I can't lie to the FBI. It's another crime and I can't afford to rack up any more crimes."

Lee didn't practice any criminal law, federal or state, and didn't know whether Cardwell's statement was true. Regardless, she had a difficult decision to make now. She didn't want to argue with Cardwell and run the risk she would cut a deal with the people knocking on her door to save herself. On the other hand, there was no good advice Lee could give her. There was only one thing Lee could do to control the situation—reassure her co-conspirator. "Look, Joan, I know you're stressed," Lee said, using her first name, something that never happened before. Cardwell just shook her head when she heard it. "But I want you to understand clearly: Winston and I are here to help and protect you as long as you keep your mouth shut, as I told you before. If we all stick together, we can get through this."

"You told me your husband would pardon me if he is elected governor. While I don't disbelieve what you told me, I want to make sure Senator Lee is on board with a pardon."

"Honey, you should know by now my husband does whatever I tell him. But aside from my direction, he knows and has certainly agreed. You just need to remember he needs to be elected and we can't let anything get in the way. This is precisely why you need to keep quiet and say nothing to anyone. Understood?"

"I understand. I'm just a bit nervous. But like I did with your son's trial, I'll put my faith in you." *Nice touch,* the agents thought when they heard what she said.

When the conversation ended, Marino congratulated Cardwell for a job well done. They now had Cassandra Lee where they wanted her. But Cardwell wasn't interested in congratulations. She wanted to know what her deal would be.

After adjourning to another office to discuss what Cardwell had given them, Marino and Hawkins returned to the conference room where Cardwell and her lawyer were anxiously waiting. Marino spoke first. "We appreciate what you have done here today, as well as the information you have given us. Thank you. On behalf of the state, I am prepared to offer you a suspended execution of sentence in exchange for your plea of guilty to perjury, assuming you are willing to continue your cooperation and testify against both Cassandra and Winston Lee." Marino knew the testimony of Cardwell alone would not be enough to convict Winston. They would need to flip Cassandra.

Cardwell just looked at Marino and said nothing. She wasn't happy with the offer. Under Missouri law a suspended execution of sentence means the court imposes a period of incarceration, but then suspends the execution of the sentence and places the defendant on probation for a defined period. If the defendant successfully completes the probation, no prison time is served. While the absence of incarceration is a benefit to the defendant, this type of sentence results in a conviction with those ramifications. For a lawyer, this could mean disbarment, which was unacceptable to Cardwell.

Hawkins was the next to speak. "If you are willing to accept the state's plea deal, we will offer you a non-prosecution agreement." He couldn't bring himself to thank Cardwell for what she did. She was a criminal who violated the public trust at two levels of government, prosecutorial and judicial. In his opinion, she should be in the penitentiary. But a deal is a deal and he had no legal basis to independently override the state's deal.

"You people claim to appreciate what I did for you, which was gift wrap Cassandra Lee. Yet you want to tag me with a felony conviction and ruin my life. Some appreciation," Cardwell said, looking directly at Marino.

"When we first met, I told you I wanted a felony conviction, regardless of what information you chose to give us. Based upon what you did provide, I am willing to recommend no prison time. As you well know, the range of punishment for this offense is seven years. As I'm sure you also know, I can charge you with felony offenses like acceding to corruption or tampering with a judicial proceeding in connection with the Garner Lee prosecution. The statute of limitations hasn't expired on those offenses. And before you get on your high horse, let me remind you of something. You ruined your own life when you got into bed with the Lees and conspired to commit crimes with them," Marino said, his voice beginning to rise.

"Let's also not forget what you did to Larry Jenkins," Marino continued. "You ruined his life. You put an innocent man in the penitentiary using manufactured evidence. Frankly, if the statute hadn't run on those crimes, I would be happy to put you in Larry's old cell. And now he is suing you and I just saw where you filed a motion to dismiss his suit claiming you have immunity. And I suspect you will win. Larry Jenkins will get nothing.

"You are nothing more than a corrupt, opportunistic criminal. You're not helping us now out of some sense of righting a wrong, but rather to save your own corrupt ass. If you don't like our deal, don't take it and I will gladly seek the maximum penalty for as many charges as I can think of. Your choice."

Cardwell didn't respond. She didn't dare as Marino was on a roll and she knew it. No one had ever spoken to her so directly and harshly. But this was not the time to start a debate. Marino just stood in front of her waiting, or perhaps hoping, she would respond so he could pull the deal off the table. Finally, he asked, "Are you in or out?"

She wanted to get in his face and scream, *I'm out, you fuckin' prick.* Instead, she looked at her lawyer and as she walked to the door said, "Tell him I have no choice. I'm in."

Chapter Sixty-Six

Winston Lee scheduled a press conference for 2pm at his campaign headquarters in Jefferson City. The location was selected because it was in the middle of the state, which would give equal access to all media outlets. The press release simply said the campaign would be addressing the paternity issue raised by their son and his lawyer. No one, including the campaign manager, knew what the candidate was going to say. But the issue involved sexual allegations and attracted reporters from all over the state. Nothing like a good political sex scandal to attract media attention.

The large conference room was filled with reporters. As usual, he kept them waiting. Finally, Cassandra Lee appeared. She was alone and stepped up to the podium and adjusted the microphone. Apparently, she was going to handle the conference. Not exactly what the reporters were led to believe.

"Thank you all for coming," she began. A young reporter from the *Kansas City Star* who apparently didn't ordinary cover the political beat, leaned over and asked the St. Louis Post Dispatch reporter, "What the hell is this?"

"This, my friend, is the Bill Clinton response when you literally get caught with your pants down. You hide and send your adoring wife out to face the music with us, to explain how the marriage is still perfect. The added beauty is no one can ask you any questions, at least not at this conference. You hope your wife can knock the story off the front page sooner rather than later, and then you can resurface and act like nothing happened."

"I want to address the malicious news conference my son and his lawyer held recently," Cassandra Lee said. "As all of you know, Garner Lee was charged with and found guilty of murdering his girlfriend. Shortly after the jury verdict, his father and I had a falling out with him. Since then he has engaged in a course of conduct designed to embarrass and hurt us.

"His latest effort is the paternity test where he claims Senator Lee is the father of his girlfriend's child. I have no idea where the purported DNA report they were waving around at the press conference came from. We have never seen it before. It never surfaced during his murder trial. You would have thought if this report was a credible and authentic piece of evidence, it would have surfaced from one party or the other during his trial. It didn't surface because the report is a phony. I checked with the circuit attorney and confirmed she hadn't seen this report either."

Lee had no idea whether Braxton had seen the DNA report, but she felt comfortable making the statement because they were all playing on the same team to get her husband elected. Or so she thought. She also knew Braxton couldn't comment on the issue, because Garner had been acquitted and the case file was closed and inaccessible to the public.

"Garner and his lawyer seem to be suggesting my husband murdered Amy Deland. This accusation is even more outrageous and hurtful than their claim my husband fathered this child. If they have my husband's DNA, they can check it against the DNA on the murder weapon. I suspect they did the comparison and there was no match. Apparently, their friend who gave them the phony paternity report was unwilling to fabricate evidence on a murder weapon," Cassandra said, pausing momentarily to let her words sink in.

"My husband and I have been happily married for thirty-two years. We have always been faithful to each other, and I have no reason to believe he was involved with Amy Deland. But I do have reason to believe Garner Lee and his lawyer want to hurt us and damage this campaign. I'll take a few questions now."

From the back of the crowded room, Marino and two other individuals, both plain-clothed St. Louis police officers, began walking toward the podium. "There won't be any questions. Cassandra Lee, you are under arrest for the offenses of tampering with a judicial proceeding and tampering with a judicial officer," Marino said, holding up the warrant for Lee's arrest. One of the officers pulled out of pair of handcuffs and began cuffing her hands behind her back, as the other officer advised her of her rights.

The reporters just watched in amazement. They'd never expected a story like this.

As the cuffs were being placed on her wrists, Lee was yelling, "Take your hands off me. I'll sue you for everything you're worth. I'll have both of your jobs." While the officers were walking her out of the room, she looked at the reporters and said, "I'll be out in five minutes and then I'll be back to talk to you about Garner and his lawyer and this latest political stunt designed to hurt us."

Anxious to find out what was going on, the reporters began shouting questions at Marino.

He responded, "The only thing I will say right now is Cassandra Lee is charged with the criminal offenses of tampering with a judicial proceeding and tampering with a judicial officer. The judicial proceeding is the Garner Lee murder trial and the judicial officer is Judge Joan Cardwell. She will be transferred to St. Louis where she will be processed by the St. Louis Police Department."

"What is she accused of doing?" a reporter asked.

"That's all I have for the moment," Marino said and then left the room.

Kelvin Bellington, the campaign manager, was in his office and came out when he heard the commotion and saw Cassandra leaving with some men he didn't recognize. She hadn't wanted him in the conference room for the press conference. She wanted to handle the sensitive issue of her husband's infidelity alone. He rushed into the conference room where the reporters were packing up their equipment. "What's going on? Where is Cassandra going?" he asked the reporters.

"She was just arrested for tampering with a judicial proceeding and tampering with a judicial officer in connection with her son's murder case. They said they're taking her to St. Louis. That's all we know," one of the reporters said. "Do you have any comment?"

"Comment? Are you kidding? How can I comment on something I know nothing about?" Bellington said as he rushed back to his office to call Senator Lee. He was at a fundraiser at a supporter's private residence in St. Louis.

"Your wife was just arrested," Bellington told Lee.

Uncertain what he just heard, Lee asked him to repeat. When Bellington did, the senator excused himself to find a private place in the donor's residence where he could have a conversation with his campaign manager. "What the fuck are you talking about? Arrested for what?" Lee finally asked after stepping into the private room.

"She was arrested for tampering with a judicial pro-ceeding and tampering with a judicial officer in connection with Garner's murder case, according to what the reporters told me."

"Reporters? The media has this?"

"She was in the middle of the press conference we de-cided to do to counter the paternity test results your son and his lawyer released. I wasn't in there at her request, but apparently the police came in and arrested her while she was having the news conference."

"Are you fucking kidding me? This whole thing is on tape and will be played on the news tonight throughout the state?"

"I'm sure it will," the campaign manager said.

"We're fucked. We're done. This campaign is over." Lee said as he paced back and forth in the room.

"Slow down," Bellington said, attempting to calm his boss. "We have no idea what kind of evidence they have. The first order of business is to get her a lawyer. What do you want me to do about that?"

"Call the law firm and tell them they need to get some lawyers on this. They have a couple hundred. Then get back to St. Louis and coordinate from there," Lee directed. He knew the campaign was in trouble and they needed to get a handle on this and quickly. The lawyers would handle the criminal aspects and he and his campaign staff would handle the political side of this catastrophic development. *Stay optimistic, we'll get through this,* he told himself.

Founded by Cassandra's grandfather, McKenzie and Carter was one of the largest law firms in the Missouri with a total of 173 lawyers occupying offices in St. Louis, Kansas City and Jefferson City as well as New York, Los Angeles and Washington, D.C. The white-collar criminal section of the firm was in D.C.

As Bellington was finishing the call with Lee, Ray Singer was beginning a call with his campaign manager. "I just received several media inquiries asking for comments on the arrest of Cassandra Lee. I'm told she was arrested for some type of criminal conduct in connection with her son's murder trial. Judge Cardwell is also involved. I get the impression she fixed the case to get her kid acquitted on the murder charge. I doubt this will come as a shock to anyone who spent any time following the kid's murder trial," John Peterson said.

"Wow," was all Singer could say while he tried to digest what Peterson was telling him. "If it's true, this could be an election with only one candidate. We need to see how this plays out. I don't want us to be in the middle of the fight at this point. Let's get some more details and then we can decide how best to proceed."

Chapter Sixty-Seven

The lawyers from McKenzie and Carter wasted no time contacting Marino to find out the details about Cassandra Lee's arrest. Alan Paul headed the defense team representing Cassandra Lee. Paul was a high-profile criminal defense attorney who led the white-collar criminal defense section of McKenzie and Carter out of the DC office. He successfully defended then President Bill Clinton in connection with the two articles of impeachment filed by the House of Representatives for lying under oath and obstruction of justice in connection with Paula Jones' lawsuit for sexual harassment. More recently, he represented Michael Cohen in connection with his multi-count indictments involving President Donald Trump.

In addition to receiving a copy of the charges, Paul was interested in reducing Lee's bond from $10,000 cash only to a personal recognizance. In other words, a simple promise to appear in court. It wasn't as though she couldn't post the cash, but Paul wanted to avoid any adverse inference which could result from requiring a member of the bar and the wife of a gubernatorial candidate to post a cash bond. He was also interested in an expeditious trial setting, given the pendency of the election.

Marino had no problem with the recognizance bond or an expedited trial setting. In response to Paul's inquiry, Marino laid out the particulars of the case, except for the recorded phone calls with Braxton and Cardwell. Because Marino did not take the case to a grand jury, a preliminary hearing would be necessary for a court to determine whether probable cause existed to believe Cassandra Lee committed the crimes with which she was charged. Preliminary hearings are open to the public. Lee could waive this hearing, in which case the matter could be placed on a trial docket with an expeditious setting. Paul had to check with his client to see what she wanted to do.

Paul was on his way to the airport to board the law firm's private Learjet in route to St. Louis when he spoke to Marino. He then dispatched two lawyers from the firm to go to the city jail to arrange the recognizance release for their client, who was on her way from Jefferson City in the custody of the St. Louis Police Department. Once everyone arrived in St. Louis, they would meet at the Lee family residence.

While Marino was in Jefferson City serving an arrest warrant on Cassandra Lee, St. Louis Police officers were arresting Joan Cardwell for perjury. Her bond was already set at a personal recognizance. She was released after the booking process including fingerprints and a photograph was completed. Because Cardwell was a key witness against Cassandra Lee, Marino took the case to the grand jury and obtained an indictment behind closed doors.

The media was in a feeding frenzy. Television, radio and print reporters were somehow alerted to Cardwell's arrest and had been waiting for her to arrive at the police department with Cassandra Lee for booking. Neither made a comment, but at least the television photographers got some footage of the *perp walk*. Meanwhile, other reporters contacted the Presiding Judge for the Circuit Court of the City of St. Louis to determine the fate of Cardwell's judicial position. They were informed Cardwell would be placed on a temporary leave of absence pending a resolution of the perjury charge.

While his wife was being booked, Senator Lee met alone with Alan Paul, who had arrived at the family residence. Lee wanted to know what kind of evidence the prosecutors had. Although he had a law degree, Winston Lee never really practiced. His role with McKenzie and Carter was purely political. "How bad is it?" he asked the lawyer.

"According to the prosecutor, they have this judge and the elected prosecutor who would testify Cassandra threatened and intimidated them to control Garner's murder trial," Paul said. Since he worked out of the DC office, he didn't know any of the players in the case.

"This guy Marino claims Cassandra was the master-mind behind the dismissal of the murder charge in Garner's case. Apparently, the trial judge was threatened and coerced into ruling the prosecutor engaged in some type of misconduct during the jury trial. From what I understand, after the jury returns a guilty verdict, Garner's lawyer files a motion for a new trial contending a statement the prosecutor made was improper, prejudicial and should have result-ed in a mistrial. At the insistence of Cassandra, the judge revisits the mistrial issue, admits she erroneously denied the mistrial request and grants a new trial. Because of the prosecutorial misconduct, she finds jeopardy attached and the case against Garner must be dismissed. Garner is then freed, never to be prosecuted for this murder again. The charges pending against Cassandra are tampering with a judicial officer and tampering with a judicial proceeding. I have to pull those statutes to see what the elements are," Paul said.

"Joan Cardwell and Karen Braxton will be testifying against us? Fuckin' ingrates. Cardwell is the judge and Braxton is the elected prosecutor for St. Louis," the senator said.

"What will be the state's theory as to how Cassan-dra would have been able to control any of Garner's case through this judge?" Paul asked.

"I put her on the bench and when Garner was charged with murder, the case wound up with her."

"The theory then would be a payback?" Paul asked. "Will this judge say you put her on the bench, and will there be some supporting evidence?"

"Yes to all of your questions. But isn't it really our word against theirs?"

"I have no idea what other evidence they have. But I can tell you this. It's never a good thing to have a sitting judge and the chief law enforcement officer of a city testify-ing against you."

Senator Lee was not satisfied with the lawyer's re-sponse. It wasn't what he wanted to hear. "Okay, but at the end of the day this will boil down to their word against ours."

"You want me to tell you everything will be okay. I'm not prepared to say that. Based on what this prosecutor told me, I would say you both have a big problem. Also, let me remind you when Garner was charged, I told you then the firm needed to handle the case. You refused and I didn't then understand why. But based on what this prosecutor is saying, it is becoming clearer why you didn't want the firm involved. You're in trouble, Cassandra is in trouble and the firm may have an issue. I'm not pleased and I'm sure the other partners won't be happy."

Winston Lee didn't respond.

After fighting her way through the wall of reporters waiting outside the jail, Cassandra Lee was placed in a waiting vehicle and whisked away. She was driven to her home to meet her husband and a platoon of lawyers and senior campaign staff. When she arrived, her first meeting was only with her husband and Alan Paul.

Winston said nothing while Paul told her what the state had. After digesting the information, she cut to the chase and asked the lawyer, "Can we successfully defend this?" After Paul repeated what he told Winston, she looked at her husband and said, "We need to figure out how we are going to deal with this in the campaign."

"Deal with it? You are charged with two crimes basically involving corruption. There is no way to deal with it which will make any difference. It looks like we are fucked," her husband said.

"This campaign was fucked when you knocked up that whore," Cassandra shot back.

Paul was confused. He had no idea what they were talking about. He wasn't interested in a political campaign. He had a client who could go to prison, and he wanted to know what her role was in her son's murder trial.

"I did talk to both Cardwell and Braxton as a concerned parent whose son was accused of murder. At no time did I ever tell them what do. I suppose we could get any number of lawyers and former judges to testify Cardwell's decision to grant a new trial and then dismiss the charge based upon prosecutorial misconduct was proper," Cassandra said, contradicting what she previously told Darius Washington after Garner blew up a fundraiser. "You know as well as I do, jeopardy always attaches when a mistrial is declared based upon prosecutorial misconduct. A prosecutor can always cause a mistrial and start over with a new jury if his case isn't going well and there is no jeopardy consequence."

Alan Paul just listened to his client. He didn't respond.

"And, so what if I talked to Cardwell during the trial as a concerned parent and suggested some things?" Cassandra continued without defining what she meant by *some things*. "I'm not an attorney of record. I don't represent anyone in the case. I'm confident judges talk to all kinds of people: lawyers, non-lawyers, their spouses, and other judges, seeking advice about cases they are trying. I'm sure we can get some people to testify along this line as well. This is all a bunch of bullshit which I'm sure was orchestrated by Felbin. He hates me and hates Cardwell even more. Seems to me this is going to boil down to their word versus mine with a bunch of witnesses who will support my position. They'll lose because there was never any criminal intent."

Paul had no questions. He excused himself to meet with the other lawyers from the firm who were at the residence to plan a defense strategy.

After the lawyer left the room, Bellington was invited in to plan the political strategy. He didn't have much to offer after the senator explained the circumstances. "Unless the case is immediately dismissed, it will haunt us through the rest of the campaign. I suppose we could deny you threatened or coerced anyone but admit you had contact with both Cardwell and Braxton. The spin could be the contact was a request for an update as a concerned parent."

"Just great," Winston Lee said sarcastically, as he gave his wife a dirty look.

"Let's hear what you have to offer," Cassandra demanded. "And while you're at it, we are still waiting to see how you plan to handle the question of how your sperm wound up inside your son's girlfriend."

Once again, Bellington considered jumping off this sinking ship. He had never experienced a candidate and campaign like this before. But he knew if he did at this late date, he would never manage another political campaign. He had to hang in there until the bitter end and find a way to deal with the problems independent of the internal hostility and chaos. There was one thing he knew for sure. Win or lose, his relationship with Winston Lee would be over when the campaign ended.

Chapter Sixty-Eight

Larry Jenkins found a room he was able to rent in the city. Nothing fancy but the rent was modest and affordable. He was able to return to his old job at United Fruit and Produce. The owner was still there and remembered Larry as a good worker. Although they paid a decent wage for manual labor plus some medical benefits, he was not able to keep the job. The problem was transportation. He had no car and the public transportation to Produce Row was lacking.

Later he got a caretaker job which paid less than minimal wage and no medical. But transportation continued to be a problem. With a minimal income, he had to budget rent, food, clothing and transportation. He had no marketable skills or experience. Seventeen years in prison will do that. Larry was beginning to understand the institution where he previously called home wasn't exactly designed to prepare you for life outside the walls, which perhaps explained why there was so much recidivism in this country. But Larry Jenkins wanted to work and appreciated the opportunity.

With eviction from his room imminent, he needed to do something; otherwise he would be homeless. He needed help. After his release, Felbin and Carmine would occasionally check on him to see how he was doing. He would always tell them he was doing just fine. Not exactly the truth. But Larry was not one to rely on anyone for a handout. Now, however, the situation was different. He had no choice. He needed to ask for some help.

He decided to approach Tony Carmine. When he explained the situation, Tony was more than anxious to help. Larry insisted it would be a loan which would be repaid after his civil rights suit against Cardwell was resolved.

When he learned about the transportation problem, Carmine told him he would approach Felbin and he was certain the firm would get him a car, at least until he got on his feet. Although he appreciated the offer, he declined. If he was going to make it, he was going to do it on his own. Larry's decision came as no surprise to Carmine. He knew his friend was a proud man. But Carmine insisted on driving him, like Garner did, to look for another job. Reluctantly, Larry accepted this offer.

Carmine told Felbin about Larry's problems. They were both concerned, but there was really nothing they could do if he refused the help. "He accepted some money, but only on the condition it was a loan which would be repaid when the civil rights suit was settled. He's a really proud guy."

"I wouldn't count on the civil suit for any repayment. As expected, her lawyers filed a motion to dismiss based upon absolute and qualified immunity," Felbin said.

"Immunity? What kind of immunity can she possibly have? Look what she did to Larry. She took his life away. She put an innocent man in prison. Now he's free. But is he really? He has no job, no skills, no money. Before Cardwell got involved, he had a job, had some money and had a home. And to make matters worse, when he sought evidence which would free him, she tried to prevent his release by lying. And you're going to tell me she doesn't have to pay for what she did?" Carmine said, emotion highlighting every word.

"Unfortunately, the law protects prosecutors. They can't face civil suits for abuses, no matter how severe. We tried to say Cardwell acted outside her role as a prosecutor and more as an investigator. In that case, she wouldn't be protected by any immunity. But as we expected, her lawyers said she didn't investigate anything. Rather, she simply was preparing a witness for trial as prosecutors do. They also said she didn't write the police reports and the guy who did is dead. We have a conservative federal judge who will be ruling on her motion and I suspect we will lose," Felbin responded apologetically.

"So, Larry, a true victim, gets nothing. The law screws him and protects this criminal. Is this the way it works?" Carmine asked.

"Pretty much," Felbin said. "But at least she was charged with perjury," he added.

"A lot of good a perjury charge does for Larry who has no money. He gets no money from this corrupt judge and he got no money from the state of Missouri. Both are responsible for the pain and damage this guy has suffered. But he has his freedom. Big fuckin' deal."

"I agree with you. I wish I could do something about it, but I can't. People like Larry Jenkins are victimized twice; once when they go to prison and once when they get out. I suppose the only good thing is Cardwell's removal from the bench with a felony conviction and hopefully, prison time."

"She hasn't been convicted yet," Carmine said sarcastically. "And the way things work around here, I'm betting she doesn't see a day in jail."

"While the walls of freedom are closing on Larry Jenkins," Felbin added.

Chapter Sixty-Nine

Later in the day, Marino would appear in court for the arraignment of Cassandra Lee. He was also waiting for the court to give him a date for Cardwell's plea of guilty to the perjury charge. In the meantime, he reviewed the Garner Lee murder file and transcript. He recalled what Felbin told him when he was appointed to investigate the wrongful conviction of his client, Larry Jenkins, "Follow the corruption of Cardwell wherever it takes you, which I believe will be through the death of Amy Deland." Felbin was right. He was now reviewing this young lady's unresolved death and wondering who was responsible.

Marino also recalled the conversation with Felbin about the DNA analysis comparisons on Winston Lee. The science established he was the father of the child but didn't kill Amy. The same science also eliminated Garner Lee as well as Amy's family and friends, as their DNA was not on the murder weapon. But the DNA of *someone* was.

Motive and opportunity are the starting point for any prosecutor or criminal investigator. Garner had a motive to kill her if he found out his father was not only in a relationship with his young girlfriend but had also impregnated her. Of course, his father, a powerful politician running for governor, also had a motive to protect his political reputation and future. But DNA seemingly eliminated both.

According to the file, the victim probably knew her attacker. Nothing was missing from the apartment and there were no signs of forced entry. The neighbors didn't report hearing any commotion or disturbances. The murder weapon was a statue apparently removed from a bookshelf situated close to where the body was discovered. Everyone involved in the investigation came to the same logical conclusion—heat of passion. Something happened to anger the killer, who grabbed the statue and hit the victim.

While this was all very interesting, Marino had to remind himself he was not investigating a murder case. Rather, he was prosecuting Cassandra Lee for tampering with a murder case. He'd spent his entire life seeking justice for the victims of crime. He knew Cassandra Lee was the mastermind in securing the freedom of her son. Of course, her behavior could be explained as a mother's love for her son. But he was fixated on the third person in the Lee family, who arguably had a motive to kill Amy Deland. Cassandra Lee benefited from her husband's political success and would benefit as the first lady of Missouri and beyond.

Marino's attention was attracted to the section of the investigative file which suggested hostility between the Lees and their son's girlfriend. He figured Winston wasn't hostile. He was involved sexually with her. Eliminating Winston left only Cassandra. Neither Garner nor his father would be hostile to Amy when visiting her in her apartment. And even if they were at some point in time for whatever reason, both were eliminated through DNA. But no DNA test was done to eliminate Cassandra. Nor was any effort made to determine the whereabouts of Cassandra at the time of the murder. The focus at the time was clearly on Garner. No one eliminated the possibility of a visit from the mother who became angry at something Amy did or said. Perhaps she either knew of her husband's involvement or suspected it and wanted to have a conversation which got out of hand. All good possibilities... no proof.

According to the trial transcript, Felbin argued the murderer was left-handed. The fatal wound was on the left side of the back of Amy's skull. Given the location of the body, Felbin concluded she was walking away from the killer toward the front door when she was struck from behind by a left-handed person. Made sense to Marino. The theory would also have eliminated Garner and his father. According to Felbin both are right-hand dominant.

It was time to go to court for the arraignment of Cassandra Lee. Marino put the file aside, at least for the time being.

A criminal arraignment is a perfunctory proceeding. The court advises the defendant of the charges by reading the indictment or information unless otherwise waived. The defendant then enters a plea of guilty or not guilty usually the latter at this stage of the case. The case is then set for trial with a deadline for the filing of any pretrial motions.

Cassandra Lee arrived in court dressed in a dark blue conservative suit offset with minimal jewelry, makeup perfectly applied and not a hair out of place. She was accompanied by three lawyers, who shielded her from the cadre of reporters. Marino had handled many arraignments during his legal career. He had never seen a defendant appear with three lawyers.

Because of the involvement of Judge Cardwell, a judge from Hannibal—the boyhood home of Samuel Langhorne Clemens, also known as Mark Twain—was appointed to preside over the case. Alfred Popkess was a soft spoken, easy going country lawyer who was born and raised in Hannibal where judges are elected. Judge Popkess, a registered Democrat, had been on the bench for twenty-three consecutive years, having been reelected several times. He didn't know and had never had any dealings with Senator Winston Lee, his wife, or their son.

After taking the bench, Judge Popkess welcomed everyone and introduced himself. "Wow, this is quite a crowd," he began as he scanned the counsel tables and the spectators. "I'm Al Popkess from Hannibal. I can tell you I have never seen this many people in our courtroom in Hannibal. In fact, now that I think about it, there may not be this many folks in all of Hannibal," he said, the crowd responding with polite laughter.

After the lawyers introduced themselves, Judge Popkess offered to read the charges, but the defendant waived the reading and entered pleas of not guilty. To expedite the process, Cassandra's lawyer also waived her right to a preliminary hearing.

"Judge Popkess, since we waived the preliminary hearing, I was wondering if we can talk about a trial schedule," Alan Paul inquired as his client stood silently at his side. "As you may know, my client's husband is in the process of campaigning to be the next governor of this fine state. This may be the reason for the number of people here today. As I'm sure you can well imagine, this is a distraction, and we would like to get the matter resolved since she has professed her innocence today."

"Yes, I'm quite sure most felony charges can ruin the entire day for a person, regardless of whether a spouse is running for governor. Gentlemen, I'm at your service. What do you have in mind? And how long do you think the trial will take?" the judge asked.

"Judge, we can try the case tomorrow if they want. I will provide a discovery package later today and the witness list. I would guess we will need a couple days. We can probably get the job done with two witnesses, but we may need to add a couple more," Marino said.

In the state court, the prosecutor is required to disclose the identity of the witnesses and share the investigative reports, statements of witnesses and any other information or documents relevant to the case. The defendant then can take the depositions of the state's witnesses and endorse his own witnesses.

Paul said, "Well obviously we can't be ready tomorrow, but we appreciate the offer. We certainly will want to depose the two main witnesses, in addition to any other witnesses the state intends to call. I can talk to Mr. Marino about making them available without the necessity of a subpoena. I suspect we can then get those depositions done next week and have the trial shortly thereafter, if the court is available."

"We move cases in the country quickly but not as quickly as you folks are looking to do. I will do my level best to accommodate you as I realize what is at stake here. Why don't we do this? After you get your deposition schedule established and have a better idea when you will be ready for trial, we can meet again and pick a trial date," the judge said.

Prior to leaving the bench, the judge asked the defendant to sign the arraignment memo. He also wanted her to sign a separate memorandum acknowledging she agreed with the speedy trial setting.

Marino noticed Cassandra Lee signed both memos using her left hand.

Chapter Seventy

As promised, Marino delivered the discovery package to Alan Paul at the offices of McKenzie and Carter. It was no surprise the witness list included Judge Joan Cardwell and Circuit Attorney Karen Braxton. Others were Jonathan Felbin, Garner Lee, Winston Lee and Mary McMurtry. Paul was aware of everyone except McMurtry. He directed one of his associates to schedule the depositions of all except Winston Lee.

He began to scan the documents, most of which were summaries of the statements of witnesses when he stopped at what appeared to be transcripts. At first, he thought they were transcripts of interviews with the various witnesses. But upon closer look, he saw they were something else. Something far more damaging than what some witness had to say to an investigator. These were transcripts of what his client had to say to a third party. Someone taped the conversations, presumably without the knowledge or consent of his client. After reading the documents, he picked up the phone and asked Cassandra to come into his office.

When she arrived, he handed her three transcripts of telephone conversations, along with three audio recordings. The transcripts were of conversations between Braxton and Cassandra, Braxton and Cardwell and Cardwell and Cassandra. "What is this?" Paul asked.

Cassandra's conversation with Braxton was on top. When she saw the heading, she quickly turned to the other two and looked at those headings. She didn't need a transcript to recall the conversations with Braxton and Cardwell. Although she didn't completely recall the specifics of those conversations, she knew they would be bad. Without reading beyond the first page of each, she laid them on the desk and looked at her lawyer. "I fucked up," was all she said.

Paul could have jumped all over her statement and launched a verbal attack, repeatedly reminding her of her stupidity along the way. Those approaches to a problem are never productive. She was feeling bad enough as it was without his help. Instead, he said, "Let's get past this. What's done is done. We need to figure out what needs to be done to counter these recorded conversations. Since I'm new to this whole mess, I need to look to you for some thoughts."

"I think we all agreed to a quick resolution of these charges if Winston stood any chance of winning the election. But now when I see these transcripts..." she stopped momentarily unable to complete her thought. These tapes would take her and the campaign down. "If we are not already dead, a public trial where these transcripts come out will definitely put the final nail in the coffin. My God. What was I thinking telling them Winston would pardon her perjury conviction if we all kept our mouths shut? How very stupid," Cassandra said as she shook her head, upset with herself.

"If the campaign and election are a material part of any decision we make, I think we need to get Winston involved in this discussion. Where is he?"

"He was at a fundraiser and he just pulled into the garage downstairs. He should be here shortly. This will be another unpleasant conversation like the last one you witnessed. I need to do what is necessary to protect him. He worked too hard for this and he deserves to be the next governor. My career as a lawyer is over. And any political aspirations I had are dead," Cassandra said as she looked out the window, feeling sorry for herself.

"Never say never. As your native son, Yogi Berra, once said, 'It ain't over till it's over.'" Just as Paul finished quoting the famous New York Yankee legend and hometown hero, Winston walked in.

"Where are we with her criminal problems?" Winston asked, looking at his wife seated in front of her lawyer's desk.

"Please sit down," Paul said pointing to the chair next to Cassandra. "We need to talk after you look at these," he said as he handed the transcripts to Winston.

Generally, Cassandra wasn't afraid of her husband and she usually controlled both the campaign and their marriage. But this was different. She waited for the explosion and wasn't disappointed. "What the fuck did you do?" he screamed. "We're dead. Everything we worked for is finished, over, done, thanks to you."

"Relax, Winston," Paul said, attempting to calm the situation. "I have no reason to doubt the accuracy of those transcripts. We need to figure out how we are going to deal with them. There are two issues. The first is the defense of your wife. The second is the protection of your campaign. I would encourage both of you to stay on topic. With this in mind, let's start by focusing on the campaign because the defense of the criminal charges will seemingly get in the way of the campaign once these transcripts are released." Looking at Winston, he asked, "How do you propose to deal with this issue, since it's your future? Obviously, if we try the criminal case, we will need to defend the suggestion you agreed to pardon a sitting judge on a perjury charge."

Although still upset, Senator calmly said, "Looks like there is no good solution. However, I can tell you this. I can honestly testify, if necessary, I never agreed to pardon anyone. But the real question is what is best for my wife. The campaign must be secondary. I want to hear your thoughts on how she is protected."

"Let me turn to Cassandra for her input. How do we explain your statements to both Cardwell and Braxton which were captured on tape? Obviously, those conversations are prejudicial and inflammatory. I presume they will be the cornerstone of the state's case."

Cassandra Lee, as a lawyer, knew she had to be careful with this response. She certainly knew any statements to her lawyer were privileged. She'd schooled Felbin on this very point. But she also knew she could not contradict any statement she made to her lawyer in any future sworn testimony. The code of professional conduct prohibits a lawyer from eliciting known false testimony. If she were to admit she committed a crime, her lawyer would be unable to put her on the stand to testify to the contrary.

After careful consideration, and mindful of those ethical standards, Cassandra finally said, "I made the statements attributed to me in those transcripts freely and voluntarily without the knowledge or approval of my husband. I believe those ill-advised conversations make this case almost impossible to defend. I'm doomed. Therefore, I think we need to turn our attention to the campaign and salvage what we can. If it means my falling on the sword, then so be it. We need to move quickly to prevent any further damage."

"Are you suggesting a plea of guilty?" Paul asked.

"Yes, unless you have another option. Of course, I would hope you could negotiate something favorable. Obviously, I wouldn't be thrilled about going to prison. I realize my law license would be in jeopardy with any plea to a felony. I would hope there would be something we could do to defend a revocation."

"If she pleads, will those telephone transcripts be made public?" Winston asked.

"No. The record would contain only Cassandra's admission she tampered with a judicial proceeding, Garner's murder trial, and a judicial officer, Judge Cardwell. If everyone wants to go down this road, I will contact the prosecutor and see what kind of a deal I can work."

"I think we are all in agreement. Please make the call and see what you can do quickly," Cassandra said as she looked at her husband who nodded concurrence.

"As long as you're here, let's see if we can get him on the phone and get the conversation started," Paul said.

When Marino answered, Paul said he wanted to talk about an amicable disposition. He proposed a plea to some misdemeanor with no jail time.

Marino wasn't surprised he was receiving a phone call from Cassandra's lawyer. He was, however, a little surprised it came so quickly. He concluded the precipitating motivators were the telephone calls. Her own words were going to be tough to defend. "I can't agree to a misdemeanor. If she wants to plead, it will have to be to both felonies," Marino replied.

"What about probation and jail time?" Paul asked.

"I would want convictions on both counts. Jail time we can talk about."

"What about an Alford plea?"

An Alford plea is based upon the United States Supreme Court decision in Alford versus North Carolina. The plea allows a defendant to take the position that the evidence is sufficient for a jury to convict. However, the defendant is not required to affirmatively admit guilt at the plea proceeding.

"No. I will need affirmative admissions of guilt on both counts and convictions on both counts. Talk to your client and let me know. We can talk then about jail time," Marino said, closing the door on further plea discussions.

When the conversation ended, Paul turned to the Lees and said, "There you have it. What do you want to do?"

"No choice, I need to plead and hopefully there will just be probation without jail time," Cassandra said. "But we need to think about what we are going to say at the plea proceeding. My thought is to take the position I acted as a concerned parent when I communicated with both Cardwell and Braxton. Out of concern for my son, I made a suggestion as to how the case should be handled."

"Did you threaten them to force them to do what you wanted?" Paul asked, anticipating it as a question the court would ask.

"I would say I can be very aggressive, particularly when the life of my son is at stake. So, I'm quite sure my tone was threatening."

"Probably a good non answer, answer," Paul quipped. "But you may be pressed on the point and have to admit you threatened in order to get the plea through. I also think you need to give some thought to accepting responsibility for your actions and seeking redemption for the sins of a mother."

"Obviously, I have never pled guilty to a crime. But I agree and can do what you suggest," Cassandra said.

"I suggest we give all of this some final thought and if we are still in agreement tomorrow, I'll call Marino and firm up a deal," Paul said.

Chapter Seventy-One

Cardwell was meeting with her lawyer at his office. She would be going to court today to plead guilty and be sentenced. Her lawyer wanted to meet to prepare for the plea.

In her career both as a prosecutor and a judge she had been involved in pleas of guilty, but none personally. She had avoided the media by staying with friends. But the coverage was still as brutal as she knew it would be. She believed everyone seemed to forget all the good things she had done as both a prosecutor and judge, and dwell only on the negative. Having spent her professional life in the public eye, she understood positive news stories don't stir the pot and sell advertising.

Because her lawyer was an expert in pleading people, he reminded her she needed to admit her crime without equivocation. He wanted to review the elements of the crime of perjury. Any hint she was not freely and voluntarily admitting all the elements would blow up the plea. This deal needed to happen.

She understood the process and the elements of perjury. The uncertainty was whether she could get through it without creating something else for the media to sensationalize. Her admission of lying to keep an innocent man in prison was going to be good sensational theatre all by itself. She didn't need a sideshow on top of it.

When this ended, she would be a convicted felon. She would lose her job, her law license and have no income. She had no idea how she would support herself. And why? Why did this happen to her? Since her arrest, she asked herself this question more times than she was able to count. And each time the answer was the same. She tried to do the right thing and put a rapist behind bars. She wasn't completely convinced Larry Jenkins wasn't good for this rape like everyone was now saying. And if he wasn't good for this crime, surely, he was good for something. This wasn't the first time he was accused of rape.

Cardwell knew you can never be one hundred percent certain a rapist is guilty, given the trauma usually inflicted on the victim. Sometimes a prosecutor needs to take a chance. She took a chance when she prosecuted Jenkins. She didn't have the benefit of DNA and had to rely on the victim. Probably more for her mental stability, she persuaded herself she didn't have any conversations with either of the detectives about changing a report. She decided Rossi lied, but everyone wanted to believe Rossi and not her now. And the victim changed her story at the DNA hearing because Felbin threatened her. She took a chance, tried to do the right thing and this was the thanks she got. She needed to put this matter behind her and find a new place to live, some place where she would be appreciated.

Cardwell's private pity party was interrupted by her lawyer. It was time to leave and begin the walk to the courthouse two blocks away. Each day of her professional life, she looked forward to entering this building. But not today.

From a distance she could see the reporters and television cameras lining the front steps of the courthouse. Judges were able to enter the building through a private door. But not today. Today, she would enter with the public. No special treatment today. Although she was still a judge, she would resign her position after the plea. She would also voluntarily surrender her law license. Having concluded the Missouri Bar would revoke it anyway, she believed a voluntary surrender would enhance her potential to be reinstated somewhere down the road.

As she approached the steps, the reporters surrounded her. She held her head high. She really had done nothing wrong. Driven by the news media, a city turned against her. She would eventually forgive everyone. But now she needed to get through the crowd of people who didn't like her and were shouting obnoxious questions. "Did you lie to keep an innocent man in jail?"

"Did you know he was innocent from the beginning?"

"Did you prosecute an innocent man just to enhance your political career?"

"Do you regret what you did to Larry?"

301

"Are you willing to compensate Larry for what you did to him?" She heard all the questions but provided no answers.

When they arrived in the courtroom, Cardwell and her lawyer sat at the counsel table looking up at the bench. The view was different. Ordinarily, she was looking down at all who came before her. She was in control. But not today. Today, she traded the judicial robe for a dark blue business suit. Marino sat alone at the other table. Neither looked at the other. They were both waiting for the judge from Hannibal who would take the plea and pronounce the sentence. The standing room only gallery was waiting for the same thing. It was a rare occurrence when a sitting judge would be pleading guilty to a felony offense.

Larry Jenkins and Felbin were seated in the front row immediately behind Cardwell. She didn't look at either one or acknowledge their presence when she arrived in the courtroom.

The bailiff called the court to order. The conversation ended with all in attendance rising. Cardwell was used to people standing when she entered the courtroom. But not today. Today, she would be standing for the man who would accept her guilty plea and brand her as a felon for the rest of her life.

When the clerk called the case, Cardwell rose slowly and approached the podium beside her lawyer. She was curious how this out-of-state judge would address her. Would he respect her and use the title she still had, at least for now? A title she earned and deserved. She didn't have to wait very long before Judge Popkess spoke. "I understand we are here today on a change of plea. Am I correct, Ms. Cardwell?" After she agreed with his statement, Judge Popkess placed the defendant under oath and proceed to question her to ensure her plea was knowingly, intelligently and voluntarily made. He wanted to satisfy himself she was not under the influence of anything which would alter her ability to understand the proceedings. And, he needed to be certain no promises were made to induce her to plead guilty.

Satisfied she knew what she was doing, Judge Popkess was ready to question her regarding the elements of the perjury statute. Ordinarily, the prosecutor would just recite the facts the state intended to prove, and the defendant would simply agree with a single affirmative word. But not today. Today, Judge Popkess would ask this soon-to-be former judge the specific questions and she would provide the answer to each embarrassing question. There would be no single word of agreement to a prosecutor's narrative. Cardwell knew this was just another effort to publicly humiliate her.

"Ms. Cardwell, a person commits the crime of perjury if he or she, with the purpose to deceive, knowingly testifies falsely regarding any material fact while under oath during any official proceeding. Did you do that?"

"Yes," Cardwell simply said.

"I'm sorry to hear that, Ms. Cardwell. And you were a sitting judge in this circuit at the time." A statement not a question from this country judge. "Please describe the proceeding in which you testified falsely."

"In a hearing where Mr. Jenkins was attempting to get a DNA test."

"And as I understand it, you were the one who prosecuted Mr. Jenkins those many years ago. Am I correct?"

"Yes."

"And what did you lie about?" the judge asked, cutting right to the heart of the matter without any fancy legal terms.

"I denied telling the detectives who were investigating Ms. Costello's rape to amend the police report to remove the equivocation of the victim in connection with her identification of Mr. Jenkins," she replied. Although she convinced herself she didn't do this, she had to lie in order to get the plea through and get her deal.

"Any other lies you told during the DNA hearing?"

"I denied preparing the victim to testify without equivocation when she identified Mr. Jenkins during the trial," she said. Another lie about lying to get her deal.

"And when you gave this false testimony, you held the position as a circuit judge and knew what you were doing was material to the DNA inquiry?"

"Yes."

"And it was your intent to deceive?"

"Yes."

"I'm really sorry to hear all of this. Why would you do it?" Judge Popkess asked with a bewildered look.

"I don't know," Cardwell said, while attempting to hide her anger. This prick was now attempting to pull her fingernails off.

Larry Jenkins and Felbin were enjoying the show. Felbin figured Judge Popkess knew Larry was sitting in the first row and thought it was the least he could do for a guy who spent most of his adult life in prison for a crime he didn't commit.

"Oh, Ms. Cardwell, you're a smart lady," the judge said as he looked around the room to watch the reactions. "People know why they do the things they do. Usually, it's for personal gain. I believe you lied to protect yourself. From what I heard here today, you knew he was innocent from the start. You didn't lie to keep an innocent man in jail, did you?"

"No."

"Well then you lied to protect your reputation. You knew you couldn't be prosecuted for what you did because the statute of limitations had run. You also couldn't admit to having committed a crime, regardless of whether some statute prohibited the ability to prosecute you. Such an admission would not only damage your reputation and embarrass you, but it would also result in your removal from the bench and disbarment. Do you agree?"

Cardwell thought about ignoring the question. She knew this was nothing but harassment. She also knew if she didn't make some response, the harassment would escalate. What she wanted to say was, "Fuck all of you ingrates." Of course, she also knew instant jail time would result. Instead, she said, "I obviously didn't think about the consequences of what I was doing."

Popkess was finished asking questions. He was satisfied her plea met the legal standard and accepted it. It was time to move on to the sentencing. He looked at the prosecutor and asked for his recommendation.

"Pursuant to a plea agreement, the state recommends a suspended execution of sentence with a term of years to be determined by the court, along with the period of supervised probation," Marino said.

Popkess looked surprised, almost disappointed; there would be no prison time. "A very generous agreement, Mr.

Marino. In the country we would not be so kind. But I realize this is the city."

"There were other considerations, judge," Marino added.

"Like what?"

"Information and an agreement to testify against a defendant in another matter." Although Marino didn't name the defendant, everyone in the courtroom knew who it was.

"Very well, you know what's best for your case." Turning to Cardwell, Popkess said, "The maximum sentence here is seven years. If I could, I would sentence you to the maximum. Unfortunately, you have negotiated yourself a sweetheart deal with the prosecutor. It pains me, but I will accept your deal. You are a disgrace to the bench and the legal profession. You violated your oath as both a prosecutor and a judge. And what is even worse, I don't get the sense you are otherwise sorry for what you did to Mr. Jenkins, either recently, or in the past."

The judge looked at the audience and Jenkins in particular, before proceeding. Felbin was shaking his head. He knew what was coming. Larry looked at the judge, uncertain as to what was going to happen.

Turning back to Cardwell, he continued with the sentencing. "Ms. Cardwell, the court having accepted your plea of guilty to the felony offense of perjury, you are hereby sentenced to a term of seven years in the Missouri Department of Corrections and a ten thousand dollar fine. The execution of this sentence is suspended, and you are placed on supervised probation for a period of five years. As a special condition of probation, you shall report to the probation officer not less than once a month until further order of this court. Do you have any questions, Ms. Cardwell?"

Hearing none, the court was adjourned.

Chapter Seventy-Two

When Marino returned to his office, he had a voicemail message from Cassandra Lee's lawyer. He wanted to talk.

Marino knew he was taking a chance by having the judge sentence Cardwell before she testified in Cassandra's case if she rejected the plea deal. Ordinarily, prosecutors would wait to have cooperating witnesses sentenced. If they declined to testify as promised, the plea bargain would be off the table and a prison sentence would be recommended and probably accepted by the court.

Marino figured the risk in Cassandra's case was minimal for several reasons. He had the tape recordings and Braxton, who had immunity and wouldn't back out. He knew those tapes couldn't come out in a public trial if Lee's husband had any chance of winning the election. He also believed Cassandra would get a substantial amount of time from a judge or a jury if found guilty. He was willing to agree to probation, no prison time with a plea. Incarceration didn't matter in her case. The admission of criminal wrongdoing was the most important thing.

"Mr. Paul, I'm returning your call," Marino said.

"Thank you. I just wanted to tell you my client will accept your offer as long as there is no prison time involved. It is my understanding you have something called a suspended execution in this state where a sentence is imposed but not executed. Instead, a period of probation is ordered. Both charges are class D felonies which carry a maximum period of seven years imprisonment. We want one year on each count to run concurrently and to be served in the city jail as opposed to the penitentiary if she violates her probation. Finally, we want unsupervised probation for a period of one year."

Marino didn't respond immediately, leading Paul to ask if he was still on the line. "I'm still here. I was just considering your demand." After another pause, he said, "Okay.

I will accept your demand, as long as we can get the plea done immediately. Judge Popkess is still in town and I want to accommodate him, so he doesn't have to come back from Hannibal. I'll check with him and see when he is available."

When the conversation with the prosecutor ended, Alan Paul was pleased he got what he wanted but wondered why it was so easy. His client wondered the same thing. "I'm thinking something happened with his star witnesses. We just learned Cardwell pled guilty and was sentenced to probation. No prison time. Since she has her deal, there is no reason to get on the witness stand and further humiliate herself by testifying against me. Maybe we should rethink a plea and take the case to trial," Cassandra said.

Winston came into the room just as his wife was suggesting a trial to replace the plea. "I thought we settled this issue," he said. After Cassandra explained why she was suggesting a trial, he said, "It's bad enough you are accused of fixing a trial but when the tapes are played and people hear the pardon discussion, we are done. I thought we already talked about this and agreed to do a plea."

"I talked about a pardon, not you. And you will deny any involvement," Cassandra responded.

"It doesn't matter. As soon as people hear the tape, it won't make any difference who made the statement. All people will hear is the word *pardon,* and I will get tagged. Singer will crucify me. I haven't been elected yet, and I'm promising to pardon criminals so they will keep their mouths shut. A trial will kill the campaign," Winston said, a departure from his previous position of doing what was best for his wife with the campaign secondary.

"If we try the case, we can drag our feet, request continuances and try it after the election. Then you will be the governor and it won't matter. If I'm convicted, you can pardon me," Cassandra said with a smile. But she wasn't joking. She didn't plan to spend a day in jail, and fully expected her husband to pardon her. Why not? The Lees controlled the state of Missouri and there would be four years until the next election. Plenty of time for memories to fade.

"Look, we need to face reality," Winston began. "I've been giving this a lot of thought since your arrest. We are in big trouble. The paternity issue is hanging out there, along with your criminal charges of fixing a murder case. The

tapes and discussions of pardons are probably just the ic-
ing on the cake. We probably should anticipate those tapes
will be leaked. The most important thing right now is to
take care of you," he said, pointing to his wife. "If you think
we should try the case then we will try the case. We can put
the entire firm on it if you want."

As the Lees were discussing the options, Paul was listening and thinking. Even without the testimony of Cardwell, it was a difficult case. "As we discuss this, I want you
to understand they still have the tapes, regardless of whether they have Cardwell. Law enforcement did the taping with
the consent of Braxton. And there is no indication Braxton
is out. I suspect they probably gave her some kind of immunity. And if they did, she isn't likely to refuse to cooperate."

"Won't a jury think it's odd if Cardwell doesn't testify?
I would think you could make something out of her absence. Independently of the tapes, they need Cardwell to
talk about what she did behind the scenes. She will need to
testify I masterminded the final outcome and threatened or
intimidated her." Cassandra said.

"That's all true. But those tapes are the poison. They
will be viewed by a jury as admissions of criminal acts. Why
else would you be offering pardons to people who need to
keep their mouths shut to protect you and your husband?"

Cassandra was considering what her lawyer was saying. They were all good points.

"If a jury finds you guilty after a trial, my guess is you
will get prison time. Now, you are being offered a great deal
of probation while backing up a year in the city jail if you
violate your probation. A lot of risk in a trial with this kind
of deal."

Cassandra Lee was a very bright lady who made her
reputation in the legal community by relying on her in-
stincts. They had never let her down. Currently, those in-
stincts were telling her to go to trial. Put the state to the
test. In the meantime, the campaign would continue. They
discussed spinning the criminal charges as a political witch
hunt designed to hurt the campaign while she professed
her innocence. Innocent until proven guilty is what the constitution says. Their political base would buy it. Look what
Trump did. In the face of the report of the special prosecutor and clear evidence he obstructed justice, he continually

denied it and people believed him. "Why wouldn't the same thing work for us? We have a loyal base," Cassandra said.

"It might work. People can be pretty stupid when it comes to politics. Look at all the bullshit we fed them so far and they believed it," the candidate pointed out.

When Cassandra made up her mind to do something, she didn't look back. She pressed forward for better or worse. It was now decision time. Trial or a plea. She knew if she pled guilty to two felonies, she would lose her law license, be disbarred. In addition to the humiliation, the campaign would suffer. It would probably kill any chance of her husband becoming the next governor. On the positive side, she would get no jail or prison time.

A public trial would be equally humiliating. But at least she would be maintaining her innocence, rather than admitting guilt. If a jury found her guilty, it was on them, not her. They got it wrong. She was innocent. In the meantime, the trial would happen after the election while the campaign continued, and she proclaimed her innocence. Her claim of a political witch hunt might even help the campaign.

The scales were tipped in favor of a trial with one final point. In the unlikely event she was convicted, her husband would pardon her after he became the governor. The irony wasn't lost on anyone. What Cassandra was telling Cardwell now applied to her. If he was not elected, she would put her fate in the hands of great lawyers. If Cardwell testified, she would be doing so as a convicted felon. A judge who was a convicted perjurer can't have much credibility.

When she told Paul to reject the plea and her reasons for doing so, he thought she was delusional. But it was her decision. He was just a lawyer who gave advice, and the clients were free to accept it or reject it.

Marino didn't seem surprised when Paul told him his client had decided against pleading guilty and wanted a trial. He was a professional, and Paul figured this was not the first defendant who rejected a sweetheart deal. Marino did, however, indicate they needed to meet with the judge as soon as possible to get a trial setting. He told Paul his client needed to be present and agree to the date.

Chapter Seventy-Three

Somehow the media was alerted to Cassandra Lee's court appearance. It was unknown who made the contact but there wasn't an empty seat in the audience. Cassandra was surprised at the turnout when she walked into the courtroom. Larry Jenkins and his lawyer were not present.

With the consent of Paul, Marino had contacted the judge to let him know they needed a date for the trial. "I understand you have now reached the point where you are looking for a date to start this trial," Judge Popkess said.

Both lawyers agreed.

"The last time you were here, Mr. Paul, you indicated you wanted a quick trial setting. I can accommodate you as long as you can both agree on a date."

"Well, Your Honor, I have had a chance to review the documents and information the state provided since our last visit. I'm afraid I may have spoken prematurely the last time. It seems a little more work will be necessary than originally anticipated. Several depositions will need to be taken and the attendance of each will need to be secured."

"Mr. Paul, during your last visit with me, I thought you were hoping Mr. Marino would produce the witnesses you needed to depose to save time and the trouble of having to issue subpoenas for them," the judge noted.

"You are correct, Your Honor. And I'm confident Mr. Marino and I can agree on a time for these witnesses without the need to issue subpoenas. After reviewing the information Mr. Marino provided, I will need to depose Joan Cardwell, Karen Braxton, Mary McMurtry, Jonathan Felbin, Tony Carmine, Garner Lee, and Paul Perrin for starters," Paul said. *This list should be enough to delay the trial several months and get past the election,* Paul thought.

"I can make the arrangements to produce all of those individuals, Your Honor. Do you want Joan Cardwell first? And if so, when do you want her?" Marino asked.

"Yes. In order to move this along, I would like her as soon as possible."

"When you said we needed a trial setting, I figured you would want to depose her. I contacted her, and she is available whenever you want. Just let me know when. The rest I will need to contact and see when they are available," Marino said.

Paul was surprised by the response. Apparently, Cassandra was wrong. Cardwell would testify. *If she appears and testifies in a deposition, Cassandra can always revisit the plea deal,* Paul thought. "How about in three days?"

"Fine. I'll let her know."

"Judge, it would seem to me we need to arrange these depositions and then get back to you for a trial date," Paul suggested.

"I'm fine with whatever you and Mr. Paul want to do," Marino said.

"I agree with Mr. Paul's suggestion. I thought this was the game plan based upon what we discussed the last time we were together. Why don't you gentlemen get back to me with some dates after your depositions and we can set a time for the trial. Are you in agreement, Ms. Lee?" the judge asked.

Cassandra agreed with the proposed schedule, the court was adjourned, and she was permitted to remain free on her recognizance bond.

The reporters immediately left the courtroom and gathered outside the door to wait for Lee to leave. During her last appearance, they rushed to her while she was still seated at the counsel table. For some reason, this time was different.

In addition to the reporters, two other individuals were also waiting for Cassandra Lee outside the courtroom. As she came through the door with her lawyer, one individual stepped forward and identified himself. "Cassandra Lee, I'm Detective Sergeant Jack Sandworth, and this is Detective Leroy Anderson," he said, displaying his badge and pointing to his partner. Lee recognized Sandworth as the lead investigator from Garner's murder trial. She had no idea why he stopped her and introduced himself. With the next sentence, his purpose and presence became clear. "Cassandra Lee, you are under arrest for the murder of Amy Deland."

Cassandra Lee was speechless, frozen in time, as Detective Anderson placed a handcuff on her left wrist.

"What the hell is this?" her lawyer demanded.

"Are you her lawyer?" Sandworth asked?

"Yes. Who the hell are you?" Paul asked.

"I'm the cop who just arrested your client for murder," Sandworth said sarcastically. "By the way, Mr. Lawyer, I have another piece of good news for you. This is a warrant to obtain your client's DNA," he said as he handed the search warrant to Paul. "Now, if you will excuse me, I need to get your client off to her new home at the city jail."

As the detectives were taking Lee away, the reporters were sticking microphones in her face. "Did you kill your son's girlfriend?" "Is that why you had Cardwell fix the case against your son? You knew he was innocent because *you* killed Amy?"

Paul figured Marino was behind this and he need to find him. Marino was still in the courtroom waiting for Paul, as he expected to have a conversation with him immediately after his client was arrested. "What the hell is going on? Cassandra is charged with murder? I assume you orchestrated this little sideshow which is why you needed Cassandra to be here. You wanted to put on a show for the media. I also understand now why you were so agreeable to a plea without prison time. You wanted my client to be a convicted felon when you proceeded with your bogus murder case."

"I think you need to understand a few basic things. First, I have been appointed as a special prosecutor for the Amy Deland murder case since people in Braxton's office may be involved as witnesses, as well as Cardwell. Second, Judge Popkess was appointed to preside for the same reasons. Third, based on evidence which has been developed, your client has been charged with murder in the second degree."

Murder in the second degree in Missouri is defined as knowingly causing the death of another person or, with the purpose of causing serious physical injury to another person, which causes the death of another person. The sentence for this offense is a term of imprisonment of not less than ten or more than thirty years, or life.

"What evidence do you claim you have which supports this reckless allegation of murder? You better have some damned good irrefutable evidence, or you're going to be answering a lot of embarrassing questions before a lot of tribunals," Paul threatened.

"Mr. Paul, I take my job very seriously. I don't accuse people of crimes unless I have damned good irrefutable evidence."

"Would you mind sharing what you claim to have?"

"Certainly, I will be happy to share some of the salient points of interest with you. Cards face up. Prior to her death, your client was never in Amy Deland's apartment. We can prove that. Yet, we found her fingerprints on the murder weapon. We are taking her DNA which we will compare to the DNA which was also found on the murder weapon. We are confident they will match. I also noticed when your client signed her name, she used her left hand. We believe the killer was left-handed and used her left hand when she struck Amy. As far as motive and opportunity, your client had plenty of both. We can show she disliked Amy. No, make that hated Amy. Of the three people who had cause to kill her, science eliminated two of the three and put your client in the crosshairs. We are confident the same science will convict her."

Paul knew they got his client's fingerprints when she was booked on the tampering charges. They didn't need a search warrant for that. Once the prints matched those on the murder weapon, it was a no-brainer to get a search warrant for her DNA sample. The prints were sufficient probable cause. If her DNA didn't match the murder weapon, she would have something to talk about. But a match presented different problems. "What is her bond?" he asked Marino.

"No bond. We believe she is a flight risk. But you are free to file a motion and ask the court for a bond. Judge Popkess is still here."

The bond hearing lasted less than ten minutes. Paul made the argument his client was a pillar of the community, albeit currently charged with murder, the judge noted. She was willing to surrender her passport, wear an ankle bracelet and be confined to her home after posting a substantial cash bond the court would set. A bond was only to insure the presence of the defendant at trial. It was not for purposes of punishing the defendant who enjoyed the presumption of innocence.

When Paul finished his argument, Judge Popkess didn't look at Marino for his response. Cassandra Lee would continue to be held without bond.

Chapter Seventy-Four

Tony Carmine came into Felbin's office, out of breath, screaming, "We got her. We got her."

Felbin was on his computer and looked at his investigator, wondering what he was talking about. "Slow down and catch your breath. Do you want to tell me who we got and for what?"

"We need to get Garner in here and do a press conference immediately. This is so fuckin' great," Carmine said, obviously either ignoring or failing to hear Felbin's question.

After Felbin repeated the question, Carmine told him Cassandra Lee had been arrested for the murder of Amy Deland. At first, Felbin was unsure whether to believe what Carmine was telling him. It was truly too good to be true. Eventually, when he was convinced Carmine was telling the truth, he had his secretary contact Garner to ask him to come to the office as soon as possible. Felbin knew the media would be all over the story and would want to talk to Garner, a truly innocent man now.

Another innocent man was waiting in one of the conference rooms. Felbin had some information for Larry Jenkins and wanted to deliver it in person. He asked Carmine to join him when he talked to Larry but didn't tell him what it was about.

When Felbin opened the door to the conference room and saw Larry sitting there, he was surprised. Although he hadn't seen Larry in a while, he didn't think it had been that long. He had lost weight and his clothes appeared to be soiled. Personal hygiene seemed to be lacking. Carmine told him about Larry's financial issues, but he didn't realize it had progressed to this point. Larry's physical appearance made what Felbin had to tell him even more difficult. He thought about withholding the information but knew it wouldn't be right. Larry had a right to know.

Ignoring his physical appearance, Felbin greeted his client with a handshake and said, "It's good to see you, Larry. How have you been?"

Figuring Carmine told Felbin about the loan, Larry said," I'm fine. I had a little setback when I was between jobs and had to borrow a couple bucks from Tony. But it was just a loan and I promised to pay Tony back when my suit settles."

Felbin hesitated. He thought again about withholding the information or even lying to his client. But he knew he couldn't. Finally, he said, "Larry, I have some bad news for you." Larry didn't react. He was at the point of saturation with bad news. "The court dismissed your lawsuit, finding Cardwell had immunity."

"What does that mean?" Larry asked.

"It means you can't sue her because she was acting as a prosecutor in her official capacity. The court rejected our argument that she was acting as an investigator outside her role as a prosecutor. Prosecutors are immune from civil lawsuits when they perform their prosecutorial duties."

"Unfuckin' believable," Carmine mumbled under his breath.

"But she lied in the DNA hearing. And she had the victim lie during my trial. And she had the police officers lie in a police report. All of those things don't count?" Larry asked.

"Apparently not. We put all those things in our lawsuit and the court rejected them."

"Is this case over now?"

"No. We will appeal the decision to the court of appeals."

"What are the chances?" Larry asked.

"We are in a very conservative state and federal circuit. For the most part, the appellate court where your case will go, is more comfortable protecting governmental bodies and corporate entities than the little guy like yourself."

Larry had no additional questions. He understood he'd lost, and Cardwell had won. He was on his own and there would be no financial recovery. As he stood to leave, Felbin wanted to say something else. "I realize you are disappointed. So am I. I want to offer you some financial help until you can get back on your feet. Recalling what Carmine had told him, he added, "It would be a loan. You would have to pay it back."

"Mr. Felbin, I very much appreciate everything all of you have done for me. But the reality is I will never be able to pay you back. I was locked up too long. I need to start my life over again. At my age and with my lack of any type of useful skills, it's an uphill battle. Thanks, but I must respectfully decline," Larry said. After shaking hands with Felbin and Carmine, he left.

As Larry Jenkins was leaving, Garner Lee was arriving. Felbin and Carmine had no time to discuss Larry's future.

Garner knew his mother was pending charges of tampering with his murder case. But he had not heard about her arrest for Amy's murder. "What evidence do they have?" he asked.

"They have her fingerprints on the statue. And they are taking her DNA to compare it to the DNA on the statue. She is also left-handed, and we know the killer was left-handed. She is being held without a bond," Felbin said.

After processing what he was just told, Garner's reaction was unexpected. "I don't know how I feel about what you just told me."

"What do you mean you don't know how you feel? This is what you wanted. You have been fully exonerated. Cleared. You didn't kill the woman you loved, like you have been saying all along. The world will now know the truth," Carmine said.

"My father had a sexual relationship with my girlfriend. She was carrying his child. My mother hated her and killed her, maybe because she found out what my father did and was concerned about his indiscretions interfering with her political goals. And my girlfriend, what does all of this say about her?"

Felbin listened to what Garner was saying. He understood.

"I've had a lot of time to think about my father and Amy. When I was finally able to separate the emotion, there was only one logical conclusion I could reach before I tried to move on with my life. I was not loved by either one. Now I need to factor one more thing into this nightmare. My mother is capable of murder. And not only is she capable of murder, but she concealed what she did and allowed me to stand trial for a murder she committed. My own mother killed someone who meant the world to me at the time and then allowed me to suffer all of the indignities from all of the people who believed I was guilty."

Carmine heard what Garner was saying, but quickly tossed it aside. He knew Garner would get over it. In the meantime, Carmine wanted to do a press conference, not only to flaunt Garner's innocence but also to torpedo Winston Lee's campaign for governor. He had known for a long time Cassandra Lee killed Amy but couldn't do anything because of some bullshit lawyer rules. Those rules didn't prevent him from doing something now. Winston and Cassandra Lee needed to pay for what they did to their son. And Carmine wanted to be part of the effort.

"I don't want to do a press conference. In fact, I don't want to say anything about this in public. Let the process play out. I know I didn't kill Amy. Apparently, we now know who did. But how does knowing who did kill her help me?" he asked rhetorically.

Carmine had an immediate answer to his friend's rhetorical question. "Goddamn it, because you're innocent, and people need to know you're innocent. And they need to know what your mother did to you. All this time she allowed you to suffer for something she did. And it was all for political greed. People also need to connect the dots with Cardwell, that corrupt piece of shit."

"You don't understand, Tony. When all of this about my father first came out, I felt the same way you do. When we crashed his fundraiser, I felt good because it was sweet revenge. Since then, I have come to realize a lot of things. My father, my girlfriend and now my mother did what they did, and I was hurt. The pain was intense. And yes, I was an innocent victim. Victimized by a system which allows politics to control our daily existence from the laws which govern us to the judges who decide our future. I have concluded this will never change. Corrupt, power hungry politicians who will cause incompetent judges to be appointed will still come after my father is long gone. As a result, more innocent victims will follow. Once you are a victim, you will always be a victim. You may heal over time, but your status will never change. You can only make it worse by revisiting the issues which made you a victim in the first place."

During his career, Felbin had numerous clients who were victimized by a racist and corrupt political and judicial system. Jenkins and Garner were just the most recent victims. Then there was Bobby Decker. Although not a victim of racism, Decker was victimized by political greed, which eventually killed him. But Garner Lee was in a special class, probably because Felbin felt partially responsible for some of Garner's pain.

For her own benefit and to the detriment of her son, Cassandra Lee had emasculated Felbin when she retained him to represent her and then confessed to the murder of Amy Deland. After the damage had been done, Felbin realized Cassandra Lee's motive was to neutralize him and prevent any investigation into who really killed Amy and the total exoneration of her son. Felbin recognized then how evil Cassandra Lee was. While anger consumed his emotions at the time, like with Garner, time had helped his mental health as far as this evil woman was concerned. But it didn't completely extinguish his memory. Of course, Cassandra Lee wasn't his mother.

"I am forever grateful to you two for all you have done for me," Garner said, looking at both Felbin and Carmine. "I hope you understand my position."

This was the second time in a matter of an hour Felbin heard a client tell him he was grateful. But he understood. Carmine didn't and never would.

Chapter Seventy-Five

Felbin and Carmine watched as Cassandra Lee's case progressed slowly through the courts. The media reported every move each of the parties made, including the twenty-six motions and legal briefs filed by the defense. Cassandra remained locked up while those pretrial motions were argued and decided.

The governor's race continued, despite the murder charge pending against the senator's wife and despite the accusations of infidelity. The campaign attempted to put as much distance between the candidate and his wife, even suggesting divorce was imminent. Fortunately for the Lee campaign, the tape-recorded phone calls hadn't been leaked. The pundits believed the senator's base was strong and forgiving. The polls gave him a slight lead over Singer and the pundits were predicting a Lee victory. Garner Lee continued his silence, despite daily requests for interviews by media outlets throughout the state and the nation.

Felbin and Carmine went on to other cases until one day when Carmine received a phone call from one of his police buddies. "I just got a call from a friend at the department who told me Larry Jenkins has been arrested. He recognized him from the news coverage and knew we represented him," Carmine told Felbin.

"What's the charge?" Felbin asked.

"Burglary. Apparently, in the middle of the night, he smashed some windows in a food market in St. Louis County. The burglar alarm went off and when the police arrived, Larry was sitting on the floor eating a sandwich he had taken from the cooler. He had a bag full of groceries sitting next to him. Apparently, he was planning to take those with him. He offered no resistance when he was arrested. In fact, he told them he was waiting for them."

Felbin didn't need a house to fall on him to figure out what Larry was doing. He couldn't make it on the outside.

He was too old, had no skills and couldn't earn a wage sufficient to pay his bills. He wanted to go back to prison. There he didn't have to worry about having skills to support himself. The payment was his freedom. But now he was still in a prison, just a different type.

Larry was being held in the St. Louis County jail and they needed to pay him a visit. But first, Felbin wanted to get a clearer picture of what was occurring with his client. On the way to the jail, he asked Carmine to repeat the previous conversation he had with Larry when he loaned him some money. "He approached me and indicated he didn't have enough money to pay his rent and he would be evicted. He wanted to borrow some money and was adamant about paying me pack with the lawsuit proceeds. He couldn't hold some jobs due to transportation issues. I told him we could arrange to get him a car, but he refused," Carmine explained.

When they arrived at the jail, Larry refused to see them. He was embarrassed. He believed he'd let them down. After Felbin had one of the guards deliver a note, he finally acquiesced.

"Let's get right to the point, Larry. I'm pissed," Felbin began. "You did this because you want to go back to prison, not because you're a criminal. You told us you were grateful for what we did for you. And this is how you thank us—by going back to the place we worked so hard to get you out of?" Since he was too proud to take any money, Felbin figured this was the way to get Larry's attention. Suggest he was ungrateful.

Larry knew Felbin was really pissed. It was no act. "Mr. Felbin, I am grateful for what everyone did for me. But because I was locked up for so long, I have no skills and am too old to develop any. If I can't pay my bills, I sleep in the street and eat out of garbage cans. At least in the joint, I get a cot and three meals a day. Those meals aren't fancy, but at least they don't come out of a garbage can. I have no family on the outside. My friends and family are on the inside. And maybe those people aren't much to you, but they're all I have."

Larry Jenkins was another victim. The outside world wasn't kind to him. A judicial system took away his freedom for something he didn't do and created a different world for him. He adjusted while he was there. He had to. Had no choice. But now he had to go back. He had no choice.

"Stop feeling sorry for yourself," Felbin screamed. "You know what else really pisses me off? Not only do you thank us like this, but you also insult us by refusing our help. You would rather return to a penitentiary and give up your freedom again rather than accept our help. That really hurts, Larry."

"I wasn't trying to hurt anyone. I just couldn't see any light at the end of the tunnel. I saw this as my only option."

"Well, Larry, here is another option for you. My driver just retired, and I need another one. We also need another investigator. Here is my proposal," Felbin began. Larry listened as he tried to recover from the guilt he was feeling after hurting the people who meant the most to him. "You will come to work for us as my driver. Tony, here, will begin training you as an investigator. When you are not driving me anywhere, you will work with Tony to earn your pay learning to become an investigator. See, I believe you do have some skills. Obviously, you know how to drive. But more importantly, you survived in prison for all those years with few blemishes on your record. You know how to get along with people, and in particular, people of all races and backgrounds who are involved in the criminal justice system. A person like you is an asset in our business."

Larry just listened to what Felbin was saying. He didn't speak or otherwise react.

Felbin continued. "Let me explain what I mean. The cases we handle involve interviews of potential witnesses. Sometimes Tony has difficulty getting those interviews. Usually, it's along racial lines. We think you would be able to accomplish what he can't and would be an asset to our firm. Frankly, we have been looking for someone like you for some time now," Felbin added even though the statement wasn't completely accurate.

Tony Carmine couldn't resist. He had to say something. "You want to go back to the cage where you came from for a cot and three meals a day? Are you fuckin' kidding? You can't be serious. You'll give up your freedom for that? By the way, the crime you did was ridiculous. No judge would ever put you in prison with your friends for that shit. So, you'll have to do something bigger and better and maybe get yourself killed in the process. And now the deal Felbin is giving you—will you pass up this opportunity for the cage? Look Larry, I haven't known you for very long. But from what I have seen, I also think you would be a big plus for us. And I would be honored to work with you."

Felbin decided not to press Larry for a decision. He said all he needed to say and wanted Larry to think about it while he experienced the luxurious amenities of the county jail. "Let me know what you want to do," he said as he stood up to leave. Larry said nothing.

On the way out, Carmine asked Felbin, "What do you think he'll do?"

"I don't know. We have given him a choice. He has an opportunity to improve his life. I doubt anyone has given him an opportunity like this before. He came from humble circumstances. Did the best he could. Stayed out of trouble. And then went to prison for a crime he didn't commit, which shaped his life. He gets out to face a world he has never experienced before. Now his choice is to take his chance on a world he doesn't know or return to the one he does know. I just hope he makes the decision which is best for him."

Epilogue

Karen Braxton was never called to testify and was never publicly identified as having any involvement with the prosecution of Joan Cardwell. Shortly after Cardwell pled guilty to the perjury charge, Braxton resigned her position as the circuit attorney. She gave no reason for the resignation. But the allegations in the tampering charges pending against Cassandra Lee fueled speculation about her complicity with the defendant in causing the favorable outcome for Garner Lee in his murder trial. Although unconfirmed, there was also the suggestion she benefited from immunity as the reason she wasn't prosecuted along with Cassandra Lee. Her life now is private. She is out of the public eye. After surrendering her law license, Braxton obtained a real estate license. She is now selling real estate and is employed by a friend who owns a real estate company in Kansas City.

After resigning her judicial position and surrendering her law license, Joan Cardwell received permission to transfer the supervision of her probation to another state. According to court records, Cardwell is living in an undisclosed location in Grand Forks, North Dakota. Her employment is unknown, but unidentified media sources indicated she is doing some type of factory work.

With less than a week remaining until the election, copies of the actual tape recordings of Cassandra Lee promising pardons were leaked to the media as well as to the Singer campaign. The source of the leak was unknown. Because the election was so close, the Lee campaign couldn't adequately respond in time to offset the damage. This information changed the landscape of the election and Ray Singer received fifty three percent of the vote. He will become the next governor of the state of Missouri.

Cassandra Lee faced charges of tampering with a judicial proceeding, tampering with a judicial officer and murder in the second degree. She was looking at five years in the penitentiary on each of the tampering charges as well as ten to thirty years or life on the murder charge.

The tampering charges were tried first. After finding her guilty on both counts, the jury recommended the maximum punishment of five years on each count. The judge accepted the recommendation and imposed five years imprisonment on each count to be served concurrently. After the motion for a new trial was denied, her lawyers appealed the verdict and sentence to the court of appeals. With few trial errors committed by Judge Popkess, there was little chance the appeal would be successful.

Facing trial on the murder charge, Cassandra Lee's lawyers negotiated a plea. The charge of murder second degree would be reduced to voluntary manslaughter, which was defined as causing the death of another person while under the influence of sudden passion arising from adequate provocation. Voluntary manslaughter carried a sentence of five to fifteen years in the penitentiary. At the plea proceeding, Lee admitted she struck Amy Deland with a statue she grabbed from a bookshelf after Deland told her she was carrying her husband's child. The court accepted her plea and pursuant to the agreement, with the prosecution sentenced her to fifteen years in the penitentiary. She withdrew her appeal on the tampering convictions and those sentences would run concurrently with her fifteen-year sentence on the voluntary manslaughter charge.

Cassandra Lee's license to practice law was revoked.

Winston Lee Winston Lee lost the election and there was no hope of a pardon from his opponent. He was asked to leave the McKenzie and Carter law firm. He couldn't return to the Missouri senate because of term limits. During his political and legal careers, he had made many friends with lobbying firms. He moved to Washington, D.C. to join one of those firms and begin a career as a lobbyist on a national scale. He divorced Cassandra.

Garner went back to New York City to receive his next assignment from the Innocence Project. He struggled with the issue of whether he should see his mother and father before he left. He decided visiting them would serve no worthwhile purpose. He needed to move on and do his best to put the past behind him. He had no family. He was on his own, at least for the moment, but confident he would eventually find someone to love.

Larry Jenkins went to work for Felbin. He drove him wherever he needed to go. In the evening he would drop his boss off at home and then take the car to his two-bedroom apartment in west St. Louis County. In the morning, he would pick Felbin up.

Larry completed his training with Carmine and had his first case. It was a fight where one of the witnesses, an African American, refused to talk to Carmine. Not only did this person talk to Larry, but he also gave him valuable information which caused the prosecutor to reevaluate the case and ultimately dismiss the charges against the firm's client. Larry would never be able to completely put aside the past, but at least now he had the opportunity to find his place in a world which made him a victim of innocence.

About the Author

For the past 45 years, Chet Pleban has spent his days in a courtroom talking to juries, trying to convince them his client was right and the opposition wrong. He is a trial lawyer. Many of his clients are police officers who find themselves on the wrong side of the law. In addition to representing people accused of criminal acts, he also represents those who suffered serious injuries and whose employment was wrongfully terminated. For the most part, he has spent his career representing the underdog and fighting big governments or large corporations. Many of his cases are high-profile. Some of those cases serve as the basis for many of his novels.

Together with Melinda, Pleban divides his time between Florida in the winter where he writes, and St. Louis in the summer where he continues in the active practice of law. In addition to his two grandchildren, Harper and Cooper, he also enjoys his three children; Mimi who lives in New York City, Jake who lives in Chicago and J.C., the oldest, who practices law with him in St. Louis. An African safari with his daughter and a golf trip to St. Andrews in Scotland with his two sons, were some of the most enjoyable and memorable times of his life.

TWITTER: https://twitter.com/ChetPleban
FACEBOOK:
https://www.facebook.com/pages/Chet-Pleban/1504559349800392